THE NEGEV PROJECT

Nonfiction books by Larry Witham

Rodzianko:
An Orthodox Journey from Revolution
to Millennium, 1917-1988

Curran vs. Catholic University:
A Study of Authority and Freedom in Conflict

THE NEGEV PROJECT

LARRY WITHAM

A NOVEL

Meridian Books
College Park, Maryland

Copyright © 1994 by Larry Witham

ISBN: 0-9640428-0-0

Library of Congress Catalog Card Number — 94-75565

MERIDIAN BOOKS
PO Box 659
College Park, MD 20740

Typesetting by Edington-Rand, Inc.

Map by Henry Christopher

Printed in the United States of America

In memory of a good father

Robert Lee Witham (1920-1972)

LEBANON

SYRIA

Mediterranean Sea

● Haifa
● Nazareth

Nablus ●

Jerash ●

Jordan River

● Tel Aviv

Jericho ●

Az Zarqa ●
◉ Amman

Jerusalem ◉
Bethlehem ●

Dead Sea

Beersheba ●

ISRAEL

Mazar ●

*Negev
Desert*

JORDAN

EGYPT
(Sinai)

● Mitzpe
Ramon

● Petra

*Arava
Valley* —

● Ma'an

● Elat
● Aqaba

miles

0   20

*Red
Sea*

"Since many have undertaken to set down an orderly account of the events that have been fulfilled among us, just as they were handed on to us by those who from the beginning were eyewitnesses and servants of the word, I too decided, after investigating everything carefully from the very first, to write an orderly account . . ."
—Gospel of Luke

PROLOGUE

The Balkans: October 1990

The roads became wider and smoother as the truck crossed the outskirts of Belgrade, the last major city on its way north to the Hungarian crossing.

"They'll be checking us at the border."

Todor, a swarthy Bulgarian, spoke in a raspy voice. Mehmet drove the truck and listened, his eyes fixed on the dark road ahead. It was a clear shot now. The atlas that had guided their way sat on the dashboard.

"It's late and cold," Todor said. "If they make trouble we'll just give them a little something. They'll wave us through."

Mehmet shifted into high gear as they gained speed on the descending highway. He gripped the steering wheel, whitening the knuckles on his thin brown hands.

In shifts, they had driven northwest from Sofia over two hundred miles, most of it in rain and mist—and Todor's cigarette smoke. Their eyes had reddened like the coming sunrise.

"They say it's a new country now," Mehmet said.

Todor laughed. "No, nothing has changed. They'll still want a bribe."

A heavy green canvas covered the back of the truck, concealing the machine parts, light metals, chemicals and the Bulgarian caviar.

Before sunset, Todor had driven and Mehmet had spent the time browsing his book of color maps. He had been to only three countries in his life, but now the number was expanding. His counterfeit Turkish passport was a big help. Mehmet understood why Todor would take risks for money. But he was driving this morning to try to change things in the world, even if his role was small.

The Yugoslavian route, picturesque by day and swift by night, had been wide open for two years, since the fall of the Communists. From Turkey or Lebanon, trucks could drive into Bulgaria or Yugoslavia and on to Vienna or Budapest. The two men aimed their route through Hungary, a door to the great Central European plain.

About 5 A.M., the truck made the Yugoslavian border crossing about ninety miles north of Belgrade, a stretch of dry fields, woods and streams. A trace of red sun began to shimmer on the horizon.

In the gray stillness, the gears made a crunching sound as the truck slowed. The two lights atop the guardhouse cut through the mist and defined the two-lane highway. Todor cracked the window and lit another cigarette as Mehmet, feeling the chill, used a free hand to button his coat at the collar. Theirs was the only vehicle on the road.

A Yugoslavian officer wearing a black hat and dull green uniform met the truck, clipboard in hand. An assistant inside the lighted booth watched the truck stop. The officer came around to the driver's window.

"The manifest, please."

Todor leaned over from his passenger's seat. "It's an odd mix," he shouted. "Caviar in cases with ice. Black Sea stuff."

"May we open the back?" the officer asked, politely enough.

"I'll do that right now." Mehmet jumped to the ground. "It's great caviar, you know. I've had some." He went to the rear and swung wide the truck's two doors. The other officer came out of the station, a machine gun slung over his shoulder and a German shepherd held by a chain leash. One of the overhead lights was angled so that it shone into the guts of the vehicle.

"This is just a formality." The officer waved his associate over, and the dog jumped the three feet up into the bed of the truck. He nosed around the boxes and heavy tarpaulins.

"He'll probably like the smell of the caviar." Mehmet grinned. "That's a pretty high-class dog."

A minute passed and then the dog barked.

The assistant pulled back the dog and the lead inspector waved to a third guard inside the station.

Agitated, Todor swore under his breath and slowly stepped out

2

of the cab. His pace quickened near the back of the truck, where he pulled a steel pistol from his jacket. He crashed the butt end down on the inspector's head. The dog turned and lunged, unleashed as its master reached for his machine gun. Todor lifted his arm to block the dog. He fired twice, hitting the second officer's neck and chest. Blood sprayed in the spotlight like red sparkles. A vise of sharp teeth cut into Todor's wrist. He fired again—a bullet ripped into the dog's belly. The shepherd twisted in mid-air and fell on the dark, cold pavement, whimpering.

Mehmet slammed the truck doors and ran to the cab. As another bank of spotlights came on, two guards with machine guns ran from the station to a point in front of the truck. Todor swung up into the cab and fired. Behind the wheel, Mehmet released the brake and slammed his foot down on the accelerator. A spray of bullets from the Kalashnikov machine guns hit the cab, shattering the windshield. Smoke billowed out the tail pipe. The engine died. Slumped over the steering wheel, Mehmet struggled with his last choked breaths of life. Beside him, Todor was arched back on the seat and covered with glass.

Mehmet's crazed mind demanded an answer from the darkness. Was this his martyrdom? He clutched the atlas, which glittered with diamonds. Would he see the angel, the one who leads to Paradise, soon? His last thought was not of Paradise, but of his family.

The border post fell silent and only the dog's whine was heard. Nearby, the inspector lay unconscious and his assistant, dead, sprawled across a pool of blood.

By sunrise the ambulances, with their stretchers and body bags, had come and gone and a new inspector had taken over. The sound of rusty nails screeched from inside the truck as two officers used crowbars to pry open a crate. It let out a fishy smell and water poured from its seams. The inspector dug his hand into the ice and jars of caviar.

"Here's something." He pulled out a brown plastic package and shook off the water. "About two pounds." He shoved his hand in again. "There's three in here. Check the others."

Amid the sound of more nails being uprooted, the inspector slit the brown plastic with a small knife. Its shiny tip showed a yellowish white powder, which he dabbed on his tongue.

"Yeah, this is it. B-grade heroin."

Another officer handed him the passports and papers found on Todor and Mehmet.

In thirty minutes the caviar cases were opened and the bags removed. Melting ice and splintered wood covered the truck bed.

"Tow the truck around back and empty it," the inspector said. "Caviar's on the house."

"What about this?" The officer kicked a dry crate. "There's nothing but these." He reached down and plucked a clay pot from the straw.

"Put it in storage." The inspector's voice showed irritation as he rubbed sleep from his eyes. He regretted the fate of the other inspector, bludgeoned to death. But he was supposed to have the week off. Cleaning up was not the end of it. Damn reports, he thought. One for Belgrade. Another for Vienna.

The officer dropped the pot back into the crate and it broke into pieces. No one noticed the other antiquities. Bronze plates and small glass vials hid in the packing straw. A shiny object in the crate caught his eye. He leaned down and pocketed a Roman coin. When he saw the shred of dark and brittle papyrus, he held it up to examine its faded, blotchy script. "Some Arab's shopping list," he muttered. Then he saw the small roll of paper. It uncoiled when he grabbed it. The strip was about a foot long and a few inches wide, ripped to a point. Its curving topographical lines showed hills, valleys and flats. The torn map was not old, but it too was marked with strange words, next to dots and Xs. "Humph. This is good for nothing."

Next to him, he noticed other officers scooping up the wet caviar jars. As he jammed on the crate's lid, he let the scraps of paper drop amid the ice, mud, and split boards. In seconds, he had an armful of the Black Sea delight.

"I hope it's fresh." He sniffed a jar. His mouth watered as he pictured himself by the fireplace at home, putting the salty black paste on fresh bread, washing it down with sweet wine. And then his young wife, after the baby slept. As he left the truck, the officer used his heavy boot to shove the crate of two-thousand-year-old artifacts—a jumble of housewares, coins and a few more shreds of papyrus—out of his way.

WINTER

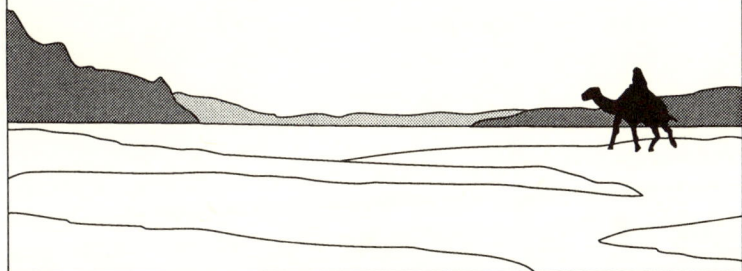

1

At the International Narcotics Control Board in Vienna, the staff member fingered the stack of drug cases, reports and weekly regional profiles. He pulled a file from the middle. Three others slid off the top and across the desk. One flew apart as it hit the floor.

Senior analyst G. Henri Bittman peered up, irritated. For deep winter the morning was warm and clear, but Bittman's bad humor cast a chilly mood over his office. The day before—17 January 1991—the United States had led the alliance in the first bombing of Baghdad. His ability to collect intelligence for the Narcotics Control Board had been hurt by the threat of war, but now it was crippled.

The staffer, a mid-level analyst, walked across the room and held out the folder. "This is the one the UN wants figured out immediately."

Bittman slipped the three-page report from the file and ran through it. "What a mess. Couldn't they have kept at least one of them alive so we could interrogate?"

"It's how they're trained. Shoot first and ask questions later. The incident is nearly three months old . . ."

"Yes, yes, don't tell me. We should have gotten to it sooner."

He scanned the report and remembered a simpler day. Now, the drug trade had become wrapped up with national economies, political parties, terrorists and organized crime. The recent opening of the Balkan route had multiplied the control board's drug cases, especially as Western capitals urged Eastern regimes to clamp down. The busts were sporadic and, like the case north of Belgrade, were a reaction, not a strategy based on patterns—the kind of patterns the Vienna board was supposed to find for drug agencies.

"A Bulgarian and a Turk," Bittman said. "That's normal. Three hundred pounds of heroin. Packed in caviar."

"We've identified the Bulgarian but the Turk . . . his papers seem forged. He doesn't look Turkish. He looks Arab, but that's not saying much."

Bittman, his face growing hot, had shed his coat, and his crisp white shirt crinkled when he reached to loosen a blue silk tie. "Where's Schmidt?" he asked, handing back the report.

Seconds later Schmidt hurried in the door with a folder in his hand.

Bittman spun in his chair. "Herr Schmidt. Shouldn't this report be further along?"

"Yes, of course. But the director sent me to Geneva to attend the International Peace Award."

"That's right. I forgot." Bittman thought of his agency's annual obligation to make a showing, and sighed. "What did he say, the winner?"

Schmidt knew the routine, so he couched his words carefully. Idealism was taboo in the hardened world of drug enforcement. "Well, he knows all the geopolitical nuts and bolts and where the bodies are buried, but he was quite optimistic." As Schmidt repeated the prognosis—a benign Soviet breakup followed by a Middle East peace—he felt the cold skepticism of his colleagues rise up around him like a flash flood.

"Very idealistic," the staffer said, doubt in his voice.

Bittman thumped the files on his desk. "He should come here and see this drug mess. Maybe he has an answer to all the government corruption."

Schmidt blushed. He would keep any further enthusiasm about the speech to himself. He would not mention what had surprised him. The statesman, who had begun his career as an archaeologist, said from the Geneva podium, "The experiences of the past are our lessons for the future." It stuck with Schmidt. Becoming a recent husband and father had driven him back to his Roman Catholic roots, where the past was everything—what his priest called the cosmic Christ of faith and the earthly Jesus of history. The old cleric had stared at him with his thick gray eyebrows furrowed, and spoken. "You'll have difficulty putting the two together. But have faith."

Schmidt was jolted back to earth by Bittman's pointed instruction. "Now tell us about this Belgrade bust."

Schmidt cleared his throat. "The load was partially refined heroin, but it was curious. Six months ago the same kind of dope and packaging was confiscated on a ship making port at Jordan on the Gulf of Aqaba."

Bittman swiveled his chair to view a large map on the wall. "What do we know about the Aqaba bust?"

"It was similar to Belgrade, but part of the payoff was guns and ammunition. The Aqaba deal is probably on the weapons trail to insurgents in Egypt, Jordan, Algeria, maybe some in Iran."

Schmidt saw Bittman's face muscles tighten with impatience, a sign that he'd better get to the point on the Belgrade-Aqaba similarity. "No guns showed up at Belgrade but they found two crates of antiquities."

"Antiquities!" the staffer said, erupting. "What on earth . . ."

Schmidt stayed cool. "You know, small oil lamps, clay and glass vials, old medallions, bronze plates. There was no heroin inside, just real antiquities. Things from a thousand, two thousand years ago."

Bittman frowned. "I still don't see the connection."

"The same kinds of antiquities were in the Aqaba shipment. The artifacts seem to come out of Jordan. Apparently they helped pay for the guns alongside the heroin."

Bittman folded his arms across his barrel chest and stared at the wall map. His eyes traced the narcotics matrix. Before the fall of Communist regimes, drugs arrived by sea or air directly from Asia, points now choked off. So heroin harvested in Afghanistan, Pakistan and Iran was being trucked from Istanbul and across Greece or Bulgaria to Yugoslavia, then on to Austria or Italy. Lebanon, with the Bekaa Valley's opium industry, was the new player. The hashish-laden Bekaa remained a stronghold of terrorists and fanatic Muslims, the ones who saw narcotics as an evangelistic tool to destroy the West.

"With the opium profits you can buy a lot of guns, can't you?"

"Lots of small arms, sure."

A knock came at the door. Bittman beckoned to his secretary.

"It's your noon appointment, sir. The Canadian journalist. Daniel LeFarbe."

"Tell him a few minutes, please." Bittman turned to the others. "He says he's writing something about Europe's black markets. I'm not sure what he's looking for."

"We could use the publicity," Schmidt said. "For the agency's good work and public service."

Bittman chuckled. "Where was I?"

The secretary walked back to the reception area and smiled at LeFarbe, who sat in a chair of chrome and polished leather. He was thinking about the contrast between the sterile Bauhaus interior of the Narcotics Control Board and the ornate Baroqueness of old Vienna outside.

"He'll be with you in a few minutes," she said.

In saying thanks, LeFarbe was all charm and politeness. "Everyone here speak English?"

"It's the tongue of the realm." Her accent was Austrian. "You need it to work here."

LeFarbe nodded and adjusted the small pad and tape recorder in his hand. He was free-lancing a cover piece on the antiquities trade for *World Interest* magazine. And he was getting back the feel for this kind of work. He had the knack years ago, when his reporting had uncovered corruption in Canadian politics. He had been hired by a major East Coast newspaper in the U.S. and then had begun to decline, spending a year on an investigative piece that had gone nowhere. Another dead-end story and yet another had followed. Above him the news management kept changing and on all sides young aggressive reporters seemed to climb over him. His drinking, his divorce and his unemployment had ensued in about two years.

LeFarbe had returned to Canada, taken a lumbering job, and whipped himself back into shape. He had failed at writing a novel, but had discovered the market for free-lance magazine pieces. An old friend, now editor of the largest newspaper in Toronto, had offered him a job but LeFarbe had had it with newspapers. That same friend had linked him with this project, for a far more prestigious journal than he was used to. LeFarbe was determined to do a good job. He had to certify his competence. To cancel his interview schedule because of the war would prove nothing, but to keep it would show backbone.

On this story, no one was shoveling him secrets or pilfered documents about the antiquities trade. It was more like being on his knees picking up pieces of a scattered puzzle. He'd gotten some background information at UNESCO, but no revelations. And he was still grappling for an angle. Government mismanagement of antiquities control? A gorged black market, fed by the chaos of war? Antiquities traded for drugs and guns? On the margin of his thought was another scenario: armed with ideas and beliefs deciphered from antiquities, archaeologists battle over the truths of religion.

This last tack always reminded him of the discoveries he'd read most about—the Gnostic cache in Egypt. If he had been around when those manuscripts had surfaced in 1945, LeFarbe mused, he could have written a hell of a magazine story.

The Gnostic texts, like the Dead Sea Scrolls, stirred controversy about the origins of Christianity. They were fifty-two Christian, Jewish and pagan tracts, most of them never seen before, bound in thirteen leather books. The language was Coptic, translated from Greek. Two peasant brothers found them in jars as they dug for fertilizer about two hundred miles south of Cairo; the Nile Valley site was known as Nag Hammadi, hence the collection's name.

The secretary's voice broke the spell. "Where do you go next?"

"Israel."

"Oh, my. You're going with the war on?"

"The only thing I'm worried about is the plane schedules." His joke didn't smooth away the furrows of concern on her face.

In Israel, LeFarbe would talk to antiquities dealers, government officials and archaeologists. Among them he would try to find the kind of source that produces a hard-hitting story, people who had lots of background but no obligations or loyalties.

Along these lines, LeFarbe planned to find an old eccentric archaeologist named Simon Rabin, an Israeli soldier-scholar who had been part of the team that had dug up ancient Jerusalem. Now, he was told, Rabin was out in the Negev Desert, which the archaeology establishment in Israel thought was insanity. What might Rabin have to tell?

Then there was an American in Israel who, like Rabin, had a reputation for independence. His name was Nicholas Hampton, an

American biblical archaeologist. LeFarbe had looked up some of his books and was struck by one in particular, the one that seemed to cut him loose from the establishment. The book had brought Hampton nominal fame about eight years earlier. Back then, he had been a young, bright and generally orthodox believer who had the wherewithal to take a risk. His book was a potboiler, even a polemic. But its careful dissection of why Bible scholarship had become irrelevant to popular religion was hard to refute, striking a nerve in the spine of academe.

Since that time, Hampton had weathered a few more academic storms, worked a bit on the Dead Sea Scrolls, and now was in Israel for archaeological digs. In fact, he had agreed to an interview, perhaps the easiest consent LeFarbe had found in the brewing atmosphere of war. Hampton surely knew the intrigues of his field, LeFarbe had decided, and that's what he would try to extract.

Inside Bittman's office, the three analysts had turned to the topic of Muslim mercenaries, trained in the holy war against the Soviets in Afghanistan but now wandering about, unemployed.

"There's thousands of these kids," the staffer said. "They're backed by Iran, the Brotherhood, whoever wants soldiers for a fundamentalist revolution. These guerrillas keep up the demand for small arms."

This was old bad news to Bittman. "My sense is that this war is not going to blow up the Middle East. Iraq will be stopped. Then there'll be attempts at a peace process. This drug and arms trade is going to hurt that process. Our job is to find where it comes from, but especially to choke it off at the point of exchange. Stop the drugs—fewer guns and less strife. More chance for peace."

Bittman stopped and chuckled. "Do I sound like a diplomat running for office or what?"

Schmidt put on a humored expression, mostly out of duty. There was, after all, a spark of optimism in his jaded, drug-fighting superior. "I have a feeling this antiquities trail is going to lead to a terminus. It stands out like a red thread."

Bittman wondered if the agents in Jordan watched these things. It would not be the first time a clue had been overlooked in the field. He stood and handed the file to Schmidt. "Write something up today."

"Right away."

"Now I've got an appointment with the press," Bittman said theatrically. He winked. "Don't worry. I won't tell him our secrets." He picked up his phone and pushed a red button. "Send him in please."

2

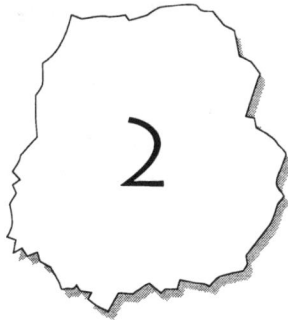

Nicholas Hampton knew it was not the end of the world. He was not going to die. No bombs would blow away the archaeological digs.

"So why this dark mood?" he asked himself. The answer, he knew, was as obvious as it was selfish. The war had wrecked his plans; he was getting nowhere.

Hampton walked a little faster through the cool Tel Aviv night. The wailing sirens seemed to drive his legs like drums pushing soldiers to march. Behind him to the east, perhaps a half-mile away, a thirty-seven-foot missile with a two-ton warhead closed in—a Scud, compliments of Iraq. Its whistle grew louder against the sirens, sounding to Hampton like giant bronze bells ringing in a tower above the city. Moments later the Scud slammed into a three-story apartment block, and a flash of orange light rose in the misty Mediterranean air. The sidewalk shook.

"God Almighty!" Hampton felt it in his knees.

The few dozen people that he could see began to scatter, dark figures running, gesturing, yelling to one another. Hampton judged that his destination was in the opposite direction of the explosion so he began to run. From behind him a group of teenagers rushed by, brushing his shoulder. Their feet slapped the concrete so hard and fast that he wondered how they kept from flying headlong off their legs. The blare of sirens pushed him to run faster, but in a moment he realized his path could lead him right into more Scuds just as easily as away from them. He stopped at the next corner and looked around, puffing to catch his breath.

In the sky above the two walls of shops that lined Dizengoff Road, he saw the glow of fire. He'd never seen a war. This seemed just an edge of it, this glow and a giant plume of smoke that a few days earlier had risen from a Tel Aviv neighborhood. The glow. It reminded him of the lab furnace used by the dig team; they would burn artifacts to carbon, dating strata by the amount of Carbon 14 radiation. Now the sirens blared louder, jogging his memory to another event, long past. It was a morning of fog and drizzle and he waited on a train platform outside Philadelphia. Down the track two freight trains collided, a flash of sparks and crumpling metal. Fire, explosion, force. They excited him and led him to the edge—a place he had rarely gone in his dull scholarly life.

He wiped his watering eyes, then pulled the gas mask from his canvas sack and squeezed it on. To his right a group of pedestrians had gathered in the overhang of a windowless shop. He jogged in that direction to join them, for a glass-free bunker seemed the safest place. He counted seven people hunkered in the cement corner. No explanation was necessary and he hunched down at the edge of the mass, next to a sobbing woman. Minutes later she was leaning against him, her fearful sounds muffled behind her gas mask. It made him long for Susan, and worry when he would see her again.

Everyone in the corner had been walking across Tel Aviv on the fifth day of the Persian Gulf War and the third day that Iraqi missiles pummeled Israel. All but a few thousand key workers in the country had been told to stay at home, seal doors and windows with tape, and have the nerve gas kits ready. Hampton presumed that a lot of them, like himself, must have felt boxed in and ventured out, apparently out of some necessity, walking the streets and sidewalks and believing no threat would fall from the skies.

Ten blocks away on the coast stood Hampton's destination, a towering black monolith sparkling with lights. Daniel LeFarbe, a Canadian journalist, had chosen the Tel Aviv Hilton as the meeting place, an alternative to a rendezvous in an obscure, noisy restaurant or Hampton's cramped apartment. The interview appointment was for 9 P.M.—still almost a half-hour off.

To be sought by the media had its allure, even intoxication. Now

15

Hampton was forced to doubt its benefits. LeFarbe had called at an opportune moment before the war looked likely. Despite Hampton's rule against easily making promises, LeFarbe had been persuasive, and now the corollary of the rule held: stick by your promises. Hampton had promised to return to Israel to assist in the Tel-Amon digs and, windswept headache that the excavations turned out to be this time, here he was, still.

On a night like this, he thought, keeping promises could have been overridden by self-preservation. But in an odd way his life didn't mean much to him—his word did. The woman clutched his arm. He stayed tense in his place, his legs beginning to ache after about ten minutes. A red gleam still hung in the sky, which he could barely glimpse through angled buildings. In a fit of imagination, he pictured himself exploding, all his tiny fragments drifting like ashes on a breeze. For the moment he could believe that he was only dust and the universe just endless, empty space. The journalist was doubtless after the big scoop. "Black market manuscripts," Hampton said to himself. "That's what he wants." What if, he mused, the story becomes that of an American archaeologist dying on a foreign street; a man too foolish to have left when the war approached?

His legs started to ache unbearably. He began to stand and the woman's clutch went tight again. She had not even looked up to see who he was. He patted her shoulder, a sign of assurance, but still had to extricate himself with a little force. He strained to see through the mask's two round eye holes, resembling an erect, green-headed insect in slacks and sport coat.

"Damn the sirens," he said out loud to bolster his resolve. "I came out here to make that appointment, and I'm going to make it."

The decision immediately became easier as the sirens changed pitch, undulating more slowly. It meant all clear.

"Enough!" He yanked the mask off his hot damp face and took a deep breath, then another. His fingers raked down his thick and tangled brown hair. Hampton appeared younger than his thirty-five years. Sharp cheekbones and an angular chin stood like outcropping granite against his soft complexion and boyish features. Years of book learning had reshaped his once athletic build, crowning it with slightly hunched shoulders.

A salt breeze swept up the street and grabbed his senses, giving him bearings on the seaside hotel. He began to walk in the dark shadows of the street. He reached the intersection and turned right, and ahead he could see the coastline. With no moon above, Tel Aviv was a painting in dark blues and browns. White stone buildings and the yellow beaches barely shone through the mist and darkness. The string of seaside hotels made that stretch the Miami Beach of the Levant, but a haunted version at night. From the dark, Hampton heard voices and imagined Phoenicians, Greeks, Romans, Arabs, Frenchmen, Englishmen and Jews pulling their boats up on the Mediterranean shore over the centuries.

It's seductive, he thought. A unique corner of the world.

Hampton liked Israel's clash of ancient and modern, for his own obsession was to fit the past with the present. Sometimes he wondered if he had lost his youth by enslaving it to ancient languages. His years of study had been like so many footsteps into a dark cavern. He had begun seeing a speck of light, an opening, as he gradually had mastered ancient Greek, Aramaic and Hebrew. Then had come the prize! As a young understudy in Jerusalem, he had translated a few tiny Dead Sea Scrolls fragments in Aramaic. Now he made a living by straddling the ancient and modern, teaching college students whose slang was more alien to him than Coptic.

At least he got his occasional escape, like now in Israel. Tonight, however, the Mediterranean worked no magic on him. It did not graft him to history and geography, to real things. Instead it was a vast emptiness in turmoil. He walked the asphalt street, smelled the salt and felt the sweat, but all was empty. The land, the sea, his knowledge, his credentials . . . even the one he loved seemed distant. Susan McQuinn seemed not to exist.

At his most intense moment during the missile blast, his mind had been a welter of confused ideas and impressions. Yet Susan seemed to be the one thought he had clung to most. He wondered if that was some kind of devotion, a test of what counts most at the time of death. "Silly stuff," he said to himself.

As he walked, Hampton tried to make Susan real by conjuring her in his mind.

"Nick, you prefer to wander among the dead," Susan had said, teasing him before he left the United States.

They always teased. She was the woman of commerce, urging people to consume to hide their emptiness. He was the academic, a pedant whose elite claim to knowledge was threatened by the

17

leveling effect of the marketplace. After years of commitment, their repartee with its kernels of truth was endearing, not harmful. They were not engaged, but something unwritten and unsigned declared their fidelity, a bond as unquestioned as it was old-fashioned.

Susan probably had summed him up as well as anyone. "You're too introspective, Nick," she would say. "Too rational. And you're too results- and task-oriented." She'd hold on to him, kiss him, and add: "Just like me." As she laughed, Nick would respond by showing just how extroverted he could be, especially with his gentle hands. Yet he wished he could be more intuitive, feel things profoundly, experience more than just brain waves and nerves.

Tonight his occasional doubt was resurfacing. Does she have somebody else? There couldn't be. But with thousands of miles dividing them, often for several months at a time, how could he really know? It was trust, he thought, and that was all.

Susan was a year younger than Hampton and now, in oblique ways, she talked of her "biological clock." Both of them, at one time, had argued the case for putting off marriage a while more. Susan was on a career path that moved like a relentless escalator.

He thought he understood how she had become like that. It was a pendulum swing. When Susan's father was dying slowly of cancer, she was the youngest, most able, of four adult children and was obligated to care for him: serving food, changing bedpans, seeing death and deterioration before her youthful eyes. For two years after high school, she delayed all her plans. She stayed home and witnessed the final days of death, then attended to her mother, who grew infirm.

When Susan finally entered the local college, she studied English literature. She wrote so well, Nick remembered, that in later years her blue pencil had helped his book get as far as it did. But her voracious appetite for fiction, mostly romance novels, finally soured her to the world of literary fancy. What did she say? "Love leads to heartache and unhappiness. I'm just tired of reading about it." That was about the time she gave up on English and went to business school. There she could avoid the passion, fitting numbers and equations together nicely with no psychic cost. That's what she had told him, all right.

Once she got this taste for independence, for learning, for crafting a career, she was driven to make up for lost time. She did very well and that was when something began to change between them. Her skill, common sense and will power pushed her up the ranks to become purchasing executive for a large department store chain, a promotion that moved her to corporate headquarters in Philadelphia.

A few years before her, Hampton had also gone east. A large university in Baltimore had noticed his academic battles and, liking professors with name recognition, hired him away from the religion department of a Baptist college. But in Baltimore the ivory tower infighting was even thicker, and Nick's tenure became uncertain. With pleasure he had taken a new offer from Northern University in Seattle. In the fall of 1987 he had moved three thousand miles west with a vague hope—that one day their careers would lead to the same city, to marriage, to the same house and to the same bed.

Here was another big promise in his life that he was trying his best to keep.

What he liked about Susan was her down-to-earth approach to life, her eschewing of the theoretical. She was healthy, loved nature, was even athletic. Her brown hair had hung short and straight as long as he could remember. To be practical, she said. Susan was small but her eyes, which were set wide apart, could be very large, so pronounced at times that she looked like a doe surprised in the woods. Her figure was lithe and round-hipped but she preferred loose baggy clothing that concealed her feminine lines. And now, after so many years, there was something new. In recent letters she spoke of growing her hair long, wearing a little more jewelry, taking an interest in fashion; apparel was a new category in her job.

Such a faithful writer of letters, he thought, a habit he had never acquired. If he barely had the patience to describe events, he balked completely at inscribing feelings on paper; to read it back aroused only ambivalence. Hampton made phone calls instead.

A street lamp illumined his watch face and he calculated Philadelphia time. It was 1:30 so she was probably nibbling lunch at her desk, he mused, and then glowered. With whom? Who was she making over her appearance for? He forced a picture of Susan alone, demure and practical. His mood rose. He could not tell whether she, the walking, or the explosion had increased his pulse; whether the rhythm he heard in his head was the sea lapping on the shore or Susan breathing.

19

A car screeched at a nearby stoplight, dispelling the intimate sound and the daydream. The car's motor revved as it turned the corner, and sped off.

On the other side of the coastal road, an uphill driveway curved in front of the Hilton. Hampton's stride forced him to catch his breath at the crest. Then he passed through automatic glass doors. A lank, ruddy man approached him from the middle of a wide lobby of plush reds, dark shadows and pink marble.

"Nicholas Hampton?" LeFarbe extended a hand.

Hampton shook it. He knew his own reason for not being scared away by the missiles, but he wondered about LeFarbe's.

"You still look like the picture on your book's dust jacket."

Hampton smiled. "That was eight years ago. Portrait of an angry young man."

"Yes, that's what I have heard," LeFarbe said with a thin smile. He had a rumpled, nonchalant look in his corduroy coat and striped button-down shirt, the studied casualness affected by many journalists. A *Jerusalem Post* was stuffed under his left arm.

Hampton speculated on what LeFarbe might already know, but he gave him credit for being there. "It's gutsy of you to be in Israel."

"Not guts, just a deadline on this article." And maybe on my career, too, LeFarbe thought.

LeFarbe suggested a dim lounge in the corner of the sprawling hotel lobby, not far from the open, circular bar. They both sank into the soft lounge chairs, and LeFarbe shifted into an alert posture appropriate for his benign inquisition.

"As I mentioned on the phone, I came here to learn about archaeological discoveries and their market. The intrigue seems to lie with ancient manuscripts."

Hampton had anticipated this opening, and expected he'd also be asked where he stood on the Dead Sea Scrolls controversy—the public charges of an unfair scholarly monopoly on unpublished materials. "My view is that when you have a discovery it should be quickly published. No scholar has the right, even if . . ."

LeFarbe listened to Hampton's logical but somewhat defensive elaboration, and then cut in.

"On the scrolls, a lot of scholars say there's no bombshells in the unpublished fragments. But what I hear . . . aren't there more scrolls out there in caves? On the black market?"

Behind a poker face, Hampton calculated. No use giving a journalist rumors, of which he'd heard plenty. He put his hands together, leaned back, and then rested his chin on his steepled fingers. "It's not like the old days."

LeFarbe felt like he was pulling teeth in this interview. "What were the old days like?"

"Well, it was less regulated. A lot more was being discovered. Look at the Gnostic stuff and the scrolls."

Hampton explained how the Gnostic books were dug up, passed through several hands, and finally purchased by the Coptic Museum in Cairo. Then the Egyptian government confiscated the artifacts only to forget them in a storage room for seven years. World scholars didn't get to them until 1956.

"That was as dramatic as the scrolls, then," LeFarbe said.

"In ways. The scrolls were found by Bedouin kids in 1947, in caves." The four main scrolls drifted into a Syrian Orthodox monastery in Jerusalem. Three others went to an Arab cobbler in Bethlehem. The Israelis got them all, one by a hair-raising trip to Bethlehem just before the Arabs closed off the city in the 1948 war. The others were bought in New York, where a Syrian monk went to sell them.

LeFarbe took occasional notes, though he used a tape recorder. "Now . . ." He paused. "I know these finds give scholars a lifetime of work, but has it really changed religion at all?"

"Aha!" Hampton began to loosen up. "That was exactly my thesis as the angry young man."

Hampton's eyes glimmered, giving LeFarbe hope. Maybe this former enfant terrible of Bible scholarship was still an iconoclast, willing to divulge a little inside information.

"Scholars have made a cottage industry out of speculation on these two major finds," Hampton said. "The scrolls tell us that medieval Old Testament texts are accurate and that Jesus' day had a lot of sectarian movements, more than we thought. That's good but it's not earthshaking." Hampton had fainter praise for scholars who spent lifetimes, who even built empires of literature, on a single goofy Gnostic tract.

"And yet," LeFarbe interrupted, "you're in that same crowd, if I understand it correctly." He put on a small, crooked smile. "Aren't

21

you also doing what the others are doing, narrow sorts of scholarship that only specialists can understand?"

From his forward perch on the lounge chair, Hampton slumped back at the onslaught of the comment. His arms gestured surrender. "You're absolutely right. Publish or perish. I quote Augustine: 'Men are in love with their own minds.' I may not be as bad as most. You start out believing in God, revelation, the Bible. Eventually you only believe in methods, theories and academic loyalties." He grinned and his hand went up with a flourish. "I'll even add belief in success and renown."

LeFarbe probed these points, asking how such scholars and archaeologists viewed their careers. As a mission? Or climbing the professional ladder? And what, he also asked, was the basis for the group loyalties—was it country or religion or politics or school of thought?

While free in his disclosure of these kinds of intricacies, Hampton held back much more than he explained. Better to keep a good face on the profession, he thought.

LeFarbe asked, "When one of you finds something, how do you determine how old it is? Or that it's not a fake?" He'd read about some ingenious antiquities scams.

"If you can date an artifact, that screens out most forgeries," Hampton said. "There are plenty of disagreements on dating, however." He returned to the Dead Sea Scrolls and Gnostic texts as an illustration. The question for those two caches, he said, was whether they were composed before, during or after the formation of primitive Christianity. Conventional scholars date the scrolls before the early church and the Gnostic writings after. On the liberal pole, scholars placed Gnostics within the diversity of early Christianity—or, more radically, argued that Gnosticism was the earliest belief of the church.

"How do you arrive at a date?"

Hampton's forehead wrinkled. "It's somewhat complicated. There are two separate aspects of the dating question." The first, he said, tries to determine when a particular manuscript was transcribed. Dating a manuscript can be done by paleography, the study of how lettering style changes, or by a Carbon 14 test. The second realm of dating is more difficult, so it naturally stirs more controversy. It tries to date the original ideas or content of a text. It's a literary and historical task, a search for clues. What contemporaneous events are in the text? Which movement had the ideas, what was that group doing, and did its viewpoint change over time?

Hampton gave LeFarbe two examples for this. Scholars would love to know exactly when Jesus' words and deeds were first written down—the original version. Another case is the Gospel of Thomas, one of the Gnostic texts. Written on pages of papyrus, Thomas is a list of one hundred fourteen sayings, all beginning with "Jesus said." The dating question, Hampton concluded, is whether the Thomas sayings come from the same time as the sayings accepted in the New Testament.

A waitress appeared from the bar's shadows, drawing their attention. She had a European accent, but was probably learning Hebrew, the language she used to address them.

"English?" Hampton asked, lulled by her brunette Jewish charm.

"Yes, yes. Pardon me."

LeFarbe ordered a beer, Hampton black coffee.

She smiled and ambled back to the bar area, both men's eyes trailing behind her.

Hampton wondered what else LeFarbe wanted to know about. There was the other side to the archaeology scene, one that was interesting but fraught with speculation. There was the Copper Scroll that seemed to be a treasure map, the former minister who battled for digging permits to find the lost Ark of the Covenant, and the alliance of fundamentalists and ultra-Orthodox Jews wanting to rebuild Solomon's Temple.

Another issue for Hampton lately, and perhaps of interest to LeFarbe, had been a Baptist missionary named Matthew Cummings. He had been in Israel for about a year, working mostly with a church school in Nazareth. But he was also the son-in-law of the famous Texas fundamentalist preacher and Bible inerrantist, the Reverend Harlan Wesley Stockwood. A number of evangelicals stood vigil in Israel, waiting for the climax of biblical prophecy. They spoke of finding secret stone inscriptions of Isaiah. They monitored Jewish immigration, an ingathering of the End Times. Stockwood, too, watched and waited. Matt Cummings, Hampton had learned, was the patri_ _h's eyes and ears.

One time, Cummings had contacted Hampton by telephone and asked what archaeologists were really doing these days in Jerusalem and elsewhere. Despite the way Stockwood had denounced Hampton as a backsliding Baptist scholar, an event now six years old, Hampton liked Cummings. The Texas missionary didn't have Stockwood's righteousness, nor his mean streak.

Hampton decided to leave all this alone, so he stayed mum and watched LeFarbe take a swallow of beer and explain what he had learned so far in Israel—facts about the black market, antiquity licensing and the volume of antiquity sales.

Then LeFarbe asked, "What do you scholars do if someone comes along with a discovery to sell?"

"We stay away from antiquities markets. Stick to our dig sites."

"Legally safe?"

"More than that. You don't get killed."

"Killed?"

"A young German archaeologist was knifed to death up in Galilee this winter. Was he dealing? I don't know for sure. He did have a few unregistered goodies. Was he robbed? The police don't know."

As they talked on for another hour, LeFarbe assessed his subject's life. Hampton was once a confident, even strident, young pedagogue. Now he was sobered by the hard knocks of experience; denied tenure at a big university and shot at from two sides, the fundamentalists and the liberals. A year earlier, Hampton's first major written work on archaeology, an overview of the unique significance of Tel-Amon, had been rejected by the prestigious *Journal of Archaeology*. The editor, Bruce Banner of Harvard, disagreed with the article's conclusions. Banner was so established, LeFarbe had heard, that many a young scholar turned chameleon just to avoid disagreeing with him. The Hampton dispute was a bloodless affair, but messy as academe goes.

"May I get back to you if I have more questions?"

Hampton pulled a business card from his wallet. "In about two months I'll be here, my Seattle office."

NORTHERN UNIVERSITY
The Gilbert Kaufman Chair
of Ancient History

"So you're leaving Israel?"

"For now. It's been a poor season."

The hex had started when the chief at Tel-Amon, Sam Thornton, suffered heat stroke and fell off a Phoenician grindstone. As chief assistant, Hampton was promoted to director. A dispute arose over who would pay the immigrant workers that fall and by then the threat of war had scared away the student volunteers for spring and summer. The digs were called off.

"I leave in March, but first I have a few more lectures and some work on the Tel-Amon progress report. It's technical but it keeps the funding coming."

They both stood up like stiff puppets, shook hands and walked toward the hotel entrance, their gaits becoming more fluid as muscles and joints limbered.

"One last thing." LeFarbe stopped at the glass doors. "Do you know the name Simon Rabin?"

"Uh, yes. Did you interview him?"

"He wasn't interested. It's a bad time, obviously. He's been described as a renegade working in the Negev Desert."

"Rabin is independent, all right. I don't know him well, but I spent a year at Oxford with his associate, Travis Marshall."

"They say Rabin's the enigma of archaeology."

Hampton shrugged. "Perhaps he is."

Outside in the salty air, they surveyed the stillness. It was 10:30. With a final thanks, LeFarbe retreated inside, back to the safety of the bar. Hampton walked along the hotel and then up a hill made black by shadows. A stone walkway, catching light, led him down the tiers of landscape and to the shoreline, which stretched on like a necklace of silver crescents.

Two months was a long time, but that was all the time Hampton had to figure things out. When he departed Israel it would be en route to San Francisco. He was invited to be an observer at a Soviet-American conference on ancient manuscript research, the first of its kind in the warming East-West relations of *glasnost*. In his most calculating moment, Hampton decided that a Soviet connection might be a career asset in the future.

The man who recommended Hampton's invitation would be there too, an old family friend and retired Bible scholar from Princeton University, Jack Winslow. But there was more. Should he invite Susan to San Francisco, mixing business with pleasure? She had always wanted to see the city.

Lately, he had even thought—it was more like a frustrated whim—of going straight home to Seattle and bowing out of everything: Tel-Amon, his last class or two, and the Soviet meeting. Yet Hampton was never good at fleeing obligations, in this case commitments to Susan, to Winslow, and even to a pack of Academy of Science Soviets he had never met. Hampton could still hear his father's exhortation: "Nick, take care of old Jack Winslow. He can see but I think his hearing is bad." This especially was a family and professional duty; plus he liked, even loved, Jack Winslow.

Hampton's pressure gauge seemed to rise with every thought. There was no safety valve for release. Even if there was one, turning it was an act of understanding, and Hampton, for now, had lost his grip; he had no way out of his disillusionment. He had always disdained people who, angry at life and its failed expectations or spurned loves, had turned their wrath against God, as if humans had no free will, not a shred of responsibility. Yet with his tangled feelings of the moment, he could see himself becoming one of those cosmic ingrates.

His chest convulsed, heavy with emotion and salt air. He opened and closed his fists like hydraulic pumps. When he was a step away from the surf, he wanted to send the blame somewhere, even if that meant screaming into the black pitch of the universe beyond the ocean.

Suddenly a giant beam of light flashed across the surf and sand, blinding him. A jeep rumbled over the beach, skidding sideways to a stop and spraying sand into the bouncing light. It disgorged running uniformed troopers in heavy gear.

A firm Israeli voice, speaking Hebrew and then English, boomed at Hampton from a dark silhouette. "Why are you here?"

Four soldiers had surrounded Hampton, two with rifles aimed and glimmering in the jeep's spotlight.

Hampton's eyes bulged and, feeling as if he'd been caught in some narcissistic act, he shrugged. "Just taking a walk."

"Are you American?"

Hampton nodded to the ferocious inquiry.

"Stay off the beach," the soldier said. "Are you crazy? This is a war."

Hampton tapped his forehead with an open hand, as if to say he had forgotten. He looked at the young Israeli soldiers, who had

26

readied for battle just like their ancestors had centuries before them. "These guys might just understand what I'm doing out here," Hampton said to himself. "The Jews have been dealing with God for almost four thousand years." Hampton waved goodbye and walked back toward the city, a military escort behind him.

It was about time, he thought, to give Susan McQuinn a phone call.

3

Simon Rabin closed his eyes and fought the dizziness.

On the television, an image of bombed housing moved about torturously as the camera jostled. The ups and downs were sharpened by klieg lights catching dust and smoke at the scene. When Rabin's head calmed, he opened his eyes. A stand-up reporter glared back at him from the screen, his damp face glistening in camera light.

Rabin had stayed inside his Jerusalem apartment since the war had begun five days earlier. He chafed under the isolation. Being dutiful, though, he acquiesced to the civil defense orders. He missed the evening walks when cool breezes cut across the Judean mountain crests on which Jerusalem sat. Walking and fresh air: these were balms for his frail health.

The television reporter, breathless and exhilarated, was talking ad lib about the damage in Tel Aviv. Occasionally he glanced back. Was another Scud zeroing in? "We can see behind us the tremendous destruction wrought on this suburb. The question American policymakers are asking is whether Israel will continue to refrain from retaliation . . ."

At age sixty-eight, Rabin had seen death before. In his early twenties he had witnessed the human wreckage across Eastern Europe. During that war, he had escaped from Austria with his parents, sister and a few relatives. They had found shelter in Denmark, fled to Sweden on a nocturnal fishing boat, and then had gone on to England. How crass and clumsy evil can be, he thought.

The Soviet-built Scud missiles were like blind bullies. Their accuracy almost always failed, ditching them in Israeli cornfields.

"Ahh," he grumbled, and cursed his headache. An artery twitched in his neck. Rabin knew his blood pressure was up again but he tried to think clearly over the physical torments. A full-scale Middle East war might begin. Would it engulf Israel and kill him along with thousands?

"Was it worth it?" Rabin asked himself. "So much work for a rumor of old papyruses."

Rabin had no family to protect. But his thoughts always wandered to his dead wife and daughter. The years of living alone had sapped his vitality. The energy to defend merely himself, a man, he thought, of no special legacy, had waned.

Even the secret, a secret that might go to the grave with him, did not stir in him the depth of life he had felt with his wife . . . . His heart jolted. His daughter had been the cruel world's sweetest joy. Rabin reminded himself constantly: this project was his last chance to do something for them, to become worthy in their eyes, as if they still lived. To succeed, he had to wash out the old painful memories with new daily challenges. When the struggle overwhelmed him, he found refuge in sleep. With the television and lamps turned off, the city lights alone softened the dark living room.

The temperature in Jerusalem began rising at noon the next day, well below the summer heat that made mirages dance on every horizon.

Rabin had thrown open two windows to survey the city and to welcome in the warm breeze. The curtains fluttered slightly. He turned to sit down in his stuffed fabric chair, his strong sculpted hands gripping the armrests. His leathery virile chest, covered with gray hair, rose and fell heavily under his pale blue cotton shirt, unbuttoned at the top. Today he had showered and shaved. And today he would decide.

The television reports from Tel Aviv had shown a quiet coastal city, the rising sun lighting up the flat shiny Mediterranean with a pinkish hue. The attacks had injured seventy-three people, the television reporter had said. Heart attacks had claimed three others.

Behind the destroyed building lay the bomb pit, surrounded by twisted wood and metal. A few small fires poured out black clouds. Rabin saw it on the television. In his mind, he smelled the acrid oil and rubber. He knew the smell of war.

His strongest impression, however, was that the building looked like a doll house. The missile explosion had ripped off the back wall of the apartments, revealing their inner workings—the way a doll house is exposed. Years ago he had given his daughter such a doll house. He had ordered it from an old friend who was a carpenter. The man had put a lot of work into it, for Rabin had helped his family find a home in Jerusalem. The doll house was painted green and blue and white and had many small details. Rabin's daughter had decorated it so splendidly, so cleverly . . . . Quickly, Rabin buried the memories before they grew. The day was serious; he had to douse the emotional flames that the toy so easily ignited.

In Israel, Rabin could talk to whoever was in power, whenever he wanted. He had spent the previous season doing that, and now it was up to them. Despite the web of personal connections that made up modern Israeli life, he was what they called his own man.

From his commando work in the fight for Israel's statehood in 1948 to his leading a tank division into the Sinai against the Egyptians in 1967, Rabin was by every measure the soldier-scholar so romanticized in his country. His work on the archaeological excavations of Jerusalem sealed his reputation, and put him in a second echelon alongside the general-poets, a type characterized by the man who was excavation leader—a onetime commander of the Haganah, the Jewish underground defense force. Israeli generals modeled themselves on Old Testament military heroes. Digging up the past was self-affirming patriotism.

Rabin's interest was not in that hill country of the north, but in the Negev of the south, a place not evocative of modern secular patriotism. In the south Abraham had dug his well and the Israelites had entered Canaan. The more Rabin had exhumed the past the more he had transcended the pride and claim of one nation. His critics cited his Negev Institute as a final leap to the fringe. For Rabin the jump was logical, even hereditary. His father had been a rabbi of both religious and cosmopolitan outlook. Rabin did not follow his father's calling, though he did study with rabbinic zeal. In the end he adopted a universal proposition, one that the great rabbis traced to the story of Noah—God gave commandments to all humanity, not just the Jews. He knew his father wouldn't mind if he learned from an Arab Muslim, for a Christian family had done more than taught them—that family had given them haven in Nazi-occupied Denmark and helped them escape. And with honesty beyond Simon Rabin's belief, the head of that Danish family had even preserved his father's savings through the war.

Rabin's wide face and deep-set eyes were placid as he considered the news reports of pending Scud attacks. He was making a decision. "Papyruses," he mumbled.

Rabin knew he could act now or wait, hoping the war would pass harmlessly. But he could not stop seeing an evil scenario of his mind's own making: missiles hailing down on Israel without mercy. He rose from his chair to sit on a couch by the telephone, which he dialed. No one answered at the Negev Institute in Beersheba, so he tried the next set of numbers. The connection to Mitzpe Ramon, a town south of Beersheba, fizzed and crackled.

"Shalom, the Negev Institute." It was a woman's voice.

Rabin was surprised. "Anne. Don't tell me Travis dragged you all the way out there. It can be a very bumpy ride."

"Simon, hello. Don't worry. I asked him to take me. The baby is about four months along and my womb feels strong."

"Wonderful." Rabin thought of his own daughter. "Anne, you know I hope that the little baby's a girl."

"Now, Simon." Anne's laugh was girlish. "We're *not* going to find out. I want a surprise! Anyway, the ride down here's done us some good. We felt a little claustrophobic this week. The desert is cool in mid-January."

"The best time of year, I agree. You're very good to Travis. For me it's always nice to hear Shalom in a Yorkshire accent."

Anne laughed. "I'll get him. He's outside working on the jeep."

After a long pause the loud voice of Travis Marshall came over the line. "Simon, did you see what happened up the coast? Bloody bad hit."

"I admit I'm a little shaken. Travis, what are the chances of reaching Habib Muhammad?"

"Well . . ." Travis calculated. "The phone is our only option now, if international calls are open. I can't make the usual trip across the Allenby."

Rabin cleared his throat. "Travis, see if you can reach him. Get across the message that I want to talk to Habib. A serious matter. Habib will understand. Ask him to contact me by phone or send one of his people to my door. I'll stay in Jerusalem."

"I'll do what I can." Marshall hung up and turned to Anne.

"You can't possibly cross the border now," she said.

"I know and Rabin knows that too. Don't worry. This war's made him eager."

Anne frowned. "I don't blame him."

Marshall's task was hit or miss. No phone lines connected Israel and Jordan. Operators in Cyprus and Europe made the link, so Marshall rigged his own channel. He called Jordan by way of England with the help of friends. They would call his message on to Az Zarqa, Habib's home and Jordan's second-largest city, just northeast of Amman. Habib initiated or responded to messages by calling the number in England.

"Will you call now?" Anne asked.

"It's too early." He surveyed Anne's bulging profile under her long and loose cotton blouse. A pregnant woman in the desert had an Old World, even biblical, romance about it. His eyes met hers. They smiled.

Anne sighed. "Would have been a nice day out on the crater. The sunset's just lovely."

"There'll be other days." Travis folded up a few maps he had spread on the small table. "I could use a coffee before the drive, but we'll stop for it. I changed the oil and even cleaned the windows."

"What service!"

Marshall would attempt the telephone call in Beersheba. And he was calculating the bigger step, one he had taken a few times before—but not in wartime. "I'm not rejecting the possibility of crossing the Allenby to Amman if it's needed, I mean, in the near future," he told Anne.

"I suppose you'd go no matter what I say."

Anne spoke in a tone of surrender, one she'd learned during their year in the Middle East. She and Travis had wanted an adventure before children came and before he settled into some British institution. Travis' obvious talents in Near East antiquity, a ken he had refined at Oxford, had earned him a few years of apprenticeship at the British Museum—and the promise of a full-time job after his field experience in the Middle East.

"We've got to help the dear old man, I guess," Anne said.

"It's not entirely sentiment. I work for the man. Until we go back to England I've got to see the project through."

That was what Rabin liked about Marshall, a young man raised in the slums of Manchester. He had not let schoolboy softness erase the grit he had learned on the streets around the textile mills. Rabin saw in him a nonconformist streak and felt he'd found a son.

Later that afternoon, Rabin paced his sun-drenched living room, stopping frequently to stare out the window. He had one more business matter to settle. Could he predict what would be happening in a week, a month, six months? Rabin grappled with a lifelong struggle of the heart. Can a man really love a nation or humanity, or can he love only a real, concrete person? He'd felt the two urges strongly and risked his life in the cause of both. His rabbi father, who had returned with Rabin's mother to die and be buried in their beloved Vienna, had explained this seeming paradox to him. The rabbi had said there was a right time under God's heaven for both loves; the heart must choose.

Rabin went to his desk in the corner and drew out enough stationery to write the letter. In the writing, he had to be absolutely clear. Later he could rescind it if he wanted. As he laid out the plan he became certain that it was right. Long ago, Rabin's lawyer, the son of old family friends, had shown him how to draft legally binding statements. When finished, he read it over three times. He addressed it to his lawyer at the firm in Vienna. The lawyer would inform the banker. Rabin decided to risk walking the two blocks to the post office. The man who ran the place lived in the back. As a notary, he could stamp the document and sign alongside Rabin's signature. Rabin was delighted when he stepped outside. The air was fresh.

At this time of his life, Rabin had few attachments to people. Besides the Marshalls, the Negev Institute's extended family included only the Arab, Habib Muhammad. Rabin's friendship with Habib was a mystery, except to them.

Like Rabin, Habib, too, could talk to power in his own country. The old imam had made his overtures a few months before the war, and slightly ahead of him Rabin had done likewise in Israel. Now all of that was out of their hands, but the small project in the desert, their quest for history, for the love of ideas, was theirs to command.

A few years earlier Rabin had set up the Negev Institute's office in Beersheba, the largest city on the northern frontier of the desert. Farther south was Mitzpe Ramon, the most developed jumping-off point into the Negev Desert. In 1950 road builders had settled the town and begun cutting byways across a desert crater that was twenty-five miles long and six hundred yards deep. The wildlife and strange geological shapes and colors had lured tourists and eventually an art colony, reviving the town. The Negev had a few farms, air bases, military training centers and a railway to the Dead Sea, but all the rest was forgotten wasteland.

Rabin knew this wedge of desert and mountains and loved its tumultuous past. Almost three millennia earlier it had been part of the kingdom of Judah. The conquering Edomites had swept down from the red sandstone mountains and, in turn, had been overrun by the Nabataeans, who had carved out trade routes to the Mediterranean and irrigated the parched sand. First-century Christian apostles had traversed the Negev, followed later by desert monks from Egypt and eventually by Byzantine soldiers. Power had shifted again in the seventh century. Arabs had expelled the Christians and the region had reverted to a backwater as history shifted its priorities.

If Rabin entertained any Jewish mysticism, it was his hunch about this land. His Negev Institute was taken to be a fool's errand. Archaeologists had long avoided the desert's twin evils of desolation and war. Faced with the same, Rabin at least had more than a vague hope—for in the sands of the Negev and south Jordan the Bedouin had found something.

4

A bove the rooftops of Mazar, a village in central Jordan, the melodious Arabic call pierced the hot noon air. Once, the *muezzin* himself had stood in the minaret atop the small mosque, practicing his trained art. Modern times had replaced him with a tape and loudspeaker, but the metallic sound still reminded good Muslims, five times a day, of their duty.

At that moment the worshipers didn't expect the crackle of automatic gunfire. It came from a neighborhood to the west and echoed off the mosque. Shots rattled off twice more. A small panic seized the faithful in the mosque's crowded courtyard.

Habib Muhammad stood amid the nervous assembly in his stocking feet. He raised his arms, palms out, a gesture of assurance. "There is nothing to fear. Nothing to fear." Then he whispered a curse on the young radicals' disrespect, their warped pride and their vanity with guns.

The peacefulness of Mazar, which lay in a wide and deep wadi surrounded by rugged cliffs, had just settled upon Habib as the gunfire had erupted. He had been admiring the steep earthen slopes of red and gray, bright here or fading there under the effects of sun, heat and atmosphere. The mosque also had its beauty, though it was poor and lacked a great dome. Tile work trimmed several interiors. Moorish-style pointed windows and doors accented the stone and stucco walls. Large colorful carpets had been rolled out in a courtyard that was swept regularly with straw brooms.

All was quiet in the village when the prayer leader finally walked to his position at the *mihrab,* a niche in the wall that, like a compass, designated southwest toward Mecca. "In the name of God, the merciful, the compassionate." The clear, opulent voice rippled over the human forms and between the buildings.

Habib listened, tired and dreamy after the four-hour bus trip from Az Zarqa, his home north of Amman. He had made the early trek to find Kalim Hasan, who was likely to attend the prayers.

Habib stood in the mosque's main quadrangle, surrounded by men and boys. The women, adorned with head scarfs, gathered in a smaller court to the side. In unison the human forms bowed, a prostration of five movements that undulated downward like the white fabric of a giant carpet under Allah's gentle foot. The prayers were always fresh for Habib. Since childhood he had seen proud men, men who never apologized for their wrongs, bowing down.

As Habib was in his mid-sixties now, his back paid a price for each bow he made, and this five times a day.

The prayer finished and the crowd began to mingle. Piety switched to social chatter. Villagers lingered in the courtyard, where the cool blue and green tiles beat back the overhead sun. Habib greeted passing friends, his voice a shadow of its former deep resonance.

Even before the gunfire, Habib had been preoccupied that day more than most. Jordan was surprisingly quiet for having its neighbors at war. But the conflict had heightened Habib's obligations. One was to Simon Rabin, who had sent Travis Marshall to see him two days earlier. Rabin was anxious. Habib wanted to help, if he could.

He also wanted to help Kalim Hasan. The young man was the other reason he had come to Mazar. Habib watched for him. Hasan often left his home in Ma'an, which was to the south, to spend time in the rustic village.

Sunni and Shi'ite Muslims worshiped together in Mazar. Elsewhere they were mortal enemies. But in Jordan and in its backwater towns such distinctions were not crucial. What mattered to young men like Hasan was membership in the Muslim Brotherhood. Habib had known Hasan since his boyhood in a troubled family in Amman. Despite Muslim prohibitions, his father had drunk too much. Kalim Hasan and his older brother had run the streets with rebellious youth. Then as teenagers the two Hasan boys had experienced conversions, religious awakenings to Islam that had evolved into political commitments. Along with other young Arabs, the two boys had joined the Brotherhood, a movement of diverse groups, leaders and cells all calling for an Islamic state and rejection of Western and secular values.

Habib loved them both. But he had lost track of Kalim Hasan's brother, who had last been heard of traveling to Syria.

The Mazar mosque was important to the more ardent wing of the Brotherhood. In this part of Jordan in 629 A.D. the first Muslim army had met in battle with the Byzantine Christians and had been repelled. The clash on the Plains of Mautah had taken the lives of three revered Muslim leaders, and now the Mazar mosque stood over their tombs. Led by Muhammad the Prophet himself, the Arabs had returned to the plains of Jordan and Syria and swept over the Byzantine armies for a hundred years of *jihad,* or holy war.

For members of the Brotherhood, the Mazar mosque represented the humiliation of defeat by Christians. That resentment had been revived in modern Arab nationalism. Now the Brotherhood was accepted in Jordan as a moderate charitable organization and arbiter of social morality, but only after its years of opposing the Hashemite Dynasty as a Western stooge. Yet, while it stopped short of imposing Koranic law, it still had a radical wing, and that drew its energy from students like Kalim Hasan.

Then Habib saw him. "Ah, Hasan."

The boy moved quietly and swiftly around the edge of the courtyard toward the entrance. Habib glanced about and walked toward the entrance as well. At one point a moving crowd blocked him, but he squeezed through. Hasan stood outside the courtyard by the wooden shoe rack, where decrepit sandals mixed with polished loafers, and began putting on his own shoes.

"My boy." Habib held out his arms. "I was hoping I would see you."

Kalim Hasan did not smile. He observed Habib from under his dark eyebrows and continued to pull on the leather shoes.

As an elder, Habib could prod the young man. Hasan's rebellious streak did not totally replace the training of Arabs to respect old men. Especially old men who had helped them in their youth.

"I'm in a hurry," Hasan said, noticing Habib's sad face. Habib stood there, his arms still open in appeal. "We can talk in the shade around the corner. But I'm supposed to meet members of my cell at noon."

Habib had a mind to give the young man several stern admonitions, but he knew that would only complicate the moment. Hasan was in an emotional transition, he sensed, and more prone to anger and impulse.

"The Brotherhood did very well in the elections, Hasan." It was the first general election in two decades, and they had taken thirty-two of eighty seats in the state parliament, including speaker. "It shows that reform can come through moderation."

Hasan looked skeptical, trying in his heart to adhere to the radicals' political line. "Moderation did not work in Egypt and there's no proof it will with the Hashemite Dynasty."

How could the boy be so blind, Habib thought. The election had been a year ago. Brotherhood influence had increased. Was this not a good reason for the radicals to abandon their vengeful plans? He spoke to Hasan in a low voice, careful with each word. "And this war, Hasan. It's not a religious war. It's secular power at its worst."

Hasan looked at Habib, quiet. He pursed his lips, a sign he was thinking through a dilemma. He knew Habib understood what was going on, how his Brotherhood group had split over vengeance, a mood that was poisoning it from within.

Hasan turned his glance away and set it on the minaret visible over the wall. "I understand your view," he said, his eyes moving back to the old man. "But my teacher says the rest of the manuscripts must be used for the glory of Islam."

Habib listened like a statue, his hand fitted gracefully around his bearded chin. Only his eyes moved, surveying the young man's determined face. The boy's heart was good, he thought. But he was young and caught up in the words of the charismatic radicals, and now the war had stirred them up like a nest of scorpions.

No matter how tense it became, however, Habib could always reach something inside Hasan, his trust in particular. A few years earlier that affinity had guided Hasan to Habib with a major surprise—an animal-skin manuscript uncovered in the Negev by Bedouin. Many other items had been found, perhaps over a decade, Hasan reported, and the Brotherhood in Ma'an was getting hold of them. They traded the clay, bronze and glass artifacts on the black market for money, weapons or other barter. But they also had rolls and shreds of parchment and papyrus, and some Brotherhood members had decided that these might be used in other ways for the cause.

Habib also understood their value, for as Simon Rabin had taught him, ancient records are priceless, and sometimes paid for in blood. In time, Hasan came back with an extraordinary rumor: some of the old texts had words from Jesus.

Habib had already used the financial lure, and now he repeated it to Hasan. "If it is money they want, we can find a buyer," he said in sheer speculation. "But you must emphasize the other reason to give us the documents. I am working quietly with scholars who can authenticate what they have found. If they insist on using these claims against Christianity, they need Western Christians to verify the material."

Habib was playing a game, and Hasan understood it, mostly. The Brotherhood was divided, and the religious faction was the one that could assist in obtaining the manuscripts. Somewhere at the core of Jesus' sayings, the teachers believed he confirmed Islam. In particular, they prayed for discovery of the original Aramaic of the Galilean's promise that the Holy Spirit would come—and thus prove the name was actually Muhammad, not the mere Greek term *Paraclete,* or Counselor.

Hasan had folded his arms, growing more self-conscious that his militant friends might walk up at any minute. He finally asked Habib a question. "Why are you doing this?"

"If they have found something important for the great religions, the world should know, Hasan." It was more complicated than that, Habib knew, especially after he and Rabin had entered the Negev scheme. But that work had been done, and now their priority was the discoveries.

Hasan was agitated. "And you would share it with the world, with Jews and with Christians, at the expense of Islam?"

"Islam has nothing to fear from the truth," Habib said. "Islam has always preserved knowledge, even science, for the world."

Habib's spirit, more than his explanation, melted the hardness in Hasan's onyxlike eyes. In his heart he could not deny Habib's appeal. Habib was wise, a man who was probably blameless.

"I will explain your reasons to them," Hasan said, "and hope they will give you something. It can't happen too quickly." He was not sure if the Brotherhood leaders would be persuaded. Then again, they might be more zealous than he understood, wanting to hurl the Jesus texts into the center of Christianity.

With a slight smile, Habib nodded and put a hand on Hasan's back. "There will be nothing to regret, Hasan. We do not know what future God has for us, but we know the future is guided by His will."

Suddenly a shout broke into their small shaded world of understanding.

"Hasan! Hasan!" It was the tallest of four young men coming his way from across the street. Habib knew by the strut that they were from the militant wing of the Brotherhood. They wore black-and-white checkered kafiya, symbol of the Palestinian cause. One of them, a dark youth in his late teens, carried a rifle with a shiny wooden stock.

"Hello, Imam Habib," the tall one said in strained formality. "How are things in the north?"

Habib, answering back in an equally stiff voice, said the parliament was every day debating Jordan's future, and when the war ended the stores would be full again.

"It will end when the West retreats," the tall one said. The other three glared at Habib but Hasan gazed downward, relieving the old man of one more stare.

"Habib, we must go now," Hasan said. "Have a safe trip home."

"You should come to Mazar more often," the tall young man said. "This is where we remember our heritage. We see the tombs of our hree great leaders, men who knew the Prophet himself and died for him. That is our pride before the arrogant West."

Habib stood, not wishing to sit below the young man and be fed his twisted view of the Prophet. "Islam is about peace, not war," Habib said. "You should remember that. Islam means surrender, surrender to God and humility before men."

The tall youth forced a smile, but the muscles around his eyes jerked. To draw confidence, he glanced at Hasan and his three cohorts. "This is true, Imam Habib. But our surrender to God also gives us the right to stand up righteously, even with a sword." The tall one's face began to contort, a mask of resentment and insecurity. When he spoke, it made Hasan cringe inside. "They killed your oldest son, Habib Muhammad. Can you forget that the Israelis killed him?"

Habib was stoic, inured to these attempts to provoke him. Yes, his son had died eight years earlier in a shower of bullets fired into a chaotic demonstration on the Temple Mount. The pilgrims had not gone to protest, but someone had instigated the mayhem. To Habib's mind, the blame could be pinned on Muslim radicals and PLO instigators just as easily as on trigger-happy Israeli soldiers and ultra-Orthodox militant Jews. The evidence, which he had scrutinized, was not clear.

"Hasan must have told you how much I loved my son," Habib said. "I work to keep his memory, but it is work that is good for our people."

In those few calm words Habib sent Hasan's militant friends into mental retreat. They knew how he could lecture them, quoting the Koran, citing history, speaking of every detail in Jordanian and Middle Eastern politics. He could lecture them on the People of the Book, the coexistence of Jews, Christians and Muslims, and how it was the Prophet who had declared it and the caliphs who practiced it.

Instead, Habib turned to the weapon-toting boy in hopes of making a lasting impression on one of them. "Why do you carry that gun?"

The young man glanced at the tall leader and then back at Habib. "We are in a war," he said.

The tall one, feeling defiant again, put his hand on the shoulder of another boy next to him. He was short and solid with deep wrinkles and large eyes, now focused up at his leader. "For three years he fought *jihad* in Afghanistan. There are many like him now. They will fight again." Then he shifted to Hasan. "And Hasan's brother is advancing our work from Syria and Lebanon. How is your brother, Hasan?"

Hasan blinked. His eyes darted around the group. "I have not heard from him for four months." He tried to sound proud, or at least confident. "But I'm sure he is well."

Rays of hot sun had invaded and dispelled the shade where they stood. All eyes squinted in its brightness and growing heat. Hasan shuddered as if a chill had burst through him. It was not a visible shudder, but a psychological one, triggered by thoughts of his brother. It was a fine vibration of the heart and soul that Habib sensed in the air between him and the young man he had known

41

for so many years. He could see that Hasan did not think like the tall young man. And that, Habib assured himself, would lead Hasan, when the crucial moment came, to make a wise decision.

Ali Basherbisi cursed the sirens and the chanting Palestinian crowds in the Amman neighborhood below. His nerves and the alcohol already disturbed his sleep. His pre-dinner nap was ruined.

The servant came out on the veranda with a wooden tray and a small mixed drink. He walked the curved path along the rail.

"Thanks, Sammy," Basherbisi said. "Look at them. They shout like children." He spat the phlegm from his throat. "They don't know how this world really works."

"Dinner in an hour, sir."

Basherbisi nodded.

Sammy disappeared into an outdoor hallway of the stucco house, which sported a red-tile roof and an abundance of palm plants and cactus on the patio.

The metal rail around his porch gave slightly as Basherbisi leaned his large fat frame into it, espying the neighborhood below.

"Shut up!" he shouted. He was a little dizzy after trying to sleep.

As sunset approached, he hoped the evening chill, the dark and the prayer or supper call would get rid of them. He loved his people, these Arabs. But since living in France and England, he sometimes viewed them as backwoods cousins.

Everyone has a right to get what they want, Basherbisi thought, leaning on the rail and sampling the drink. But there's no use in foolish spectacle. You work quietly, like a thief or a snake. That's how you succeed.

Basherbisi counted among his personal triumphs the spacious home on the Amman hillside. He had been back in Jordan for three months now, and he was glad. That was one good thing about the war. When war looked certain in the fall, he had found good reason to leave England, and quickly. The authorities in France were also a persuasive lot, so he had kept moving east. His life was good in Europe and to flee was a sacrifice, but a wise one.

The chanting below, praises for Iraq and curses for Israel, persisted.

Basherbisi growled and then finished off the spirits.

42

There are two kinds of people, he thought, those in the crowd below and those who actually get what they want in the world. Basherbisi prided himself on being the second type, and he liked his own kind. Even if they included Muslim radicals with naive utopian dreams. At least they didn't waste time chanting, raving. They got their guns and took some initiative.

"They chant for the Western media," Basherbisi said to himself, recalling what he used to see on French television. "So foolish."

Ali Basherbisi had not been born poor in Jordan. Yet his wealth, he boasted, was earned by a lifetime of work. In France, he had operated a company that had traded coffee, furniture, pirated musical recordings and textiles from Southeast Asia. The profit, however, had come in drug and arms sales. Basherbisi had friends in the Mediterranean and, more important, in Sicily. The money flow in France had backfired when the International Credit and Commerce Bank, a global mill to launder currency, was found out and collapsed.

Basherbisi had cashed in and left France before the shoe dropped. The French had nothing on him. The problem was London. His partner in crime, now a Judas, had holed away some liquid assets there. Worse still, they had not parted on good terms.

Yet Basherbisi was getting by. The war made any international inquiries, let alone extradition attempts, impossible. In December he'd even been able to arrange a few deals. That was fortunate for his antiquities collection, which he prized. In Europe the only interchangeable coins were cash and drugs and arms. But in the Middle East, well, the black market was a village bazaar with a selection of antiquities that only improved during war and social upheaval. He could already picture Iraq's museums being pilfered in the chaos of war. What those Persian treasures must be worth!

But all good things come in time. Basherbisi had learned how to wait, knowing that success in the end would calm his nerves. An occasional drug deal kept him busy, kept his mind off the mess left behind in England. Thanks to the war—and may Allah make it last—the West was too occupied to worry about Ali Basherbisi of Jordan.

"Quiet!" he shouted over his veranda one more time. He threw his glass down at the crowd. It caught a slope of rock far below and shattered.

Then he went inside. He called for another drink and headed to the corner of the living room and a small crate. He lifted out a flat slab of marble, a bas-relief of the Minotaur. Would this new acquisition go well on the mantelpiece? he wondered. He placed it there and stood back. He liked this Roman version, the body of a man and head of bull.

Sammy came in with another drink.

Basherbisi took a gulp. "That, Sammy, is the monster that was fed seven boys and seven girls by the Athenians each year." He laughed. "Those barbaric Greeks."

Basherbisi admired those who could see beauty, as he himself could. The beauty of art, a good port or the beauty of, say, a young woman. But yes, he thought, the world was also cruel, like the Minotaur. There were times when survival came first, times when one must destroy beauty, even the most fragile, innocent kind.

SPRING

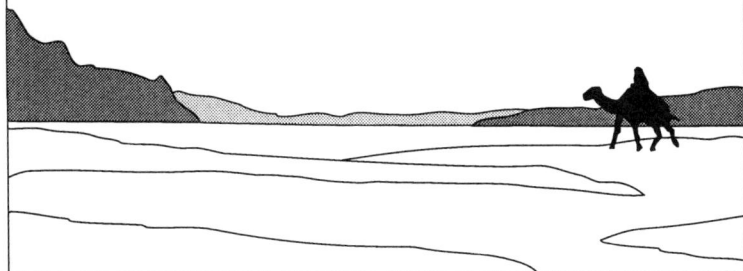

5

Irina Pleshnikov bundled herself against the icy winds that blew down the Neva River and across Nevsky Prospekt, downtown Leningrad's main street. Her dark Asian eyes peered from above a thick gray shawl. Snow on the first day of March was bad enough, but the ice! It was everywhere. She wore double socks and dreamed they had good leather shoes around them. Western shoes must hold the warmth and dryness, she thought. But eight hundred rubles! Three months pay! She would get by.

When the cold became unbearable, Irina turned to warmer thoughts—the warmest being her trip to San Francisco in two weeks.

The afternoon sun illumined the layers of an overcast sky, so heavy and metallic that it seemed about to burst with snow. Tucked under her arm was a cord bag holding bread, tangerines and tea, bound for her office at the Saltykov-Shchedrin Library.

"*Hsin min,*" she said under her breath. "*Hsin min.*" She rolled it over in her mind again and again. Is it *new people,* or *renewal of the people?* She wondered how to translate it; passive or active? The question arose frequently when conveying Chinese into Russian. More than words alone, the meaning had to carry over, too. The phrasing awaited her decision so she could transcribe the subtitle of a Chinese work on the catalogue card at her desk.

She put her hand in her pocket to check for the library pass. Her numb fingers felt the slippery surface of the worn red book. Irina didn't carry a Party card. Where she went, nobody asked anymore. She was not nomenklatura so it didn't matter. Her language skills alone had moved her into the state library jobs. The Lenin Library in Moscow was the big one. Working there, she felt, was her greatest accomplishment, even as a lowly clerk. She sorted books and documents in Chinese and even did research. Now she was at Saltykov-Shchedrin, the nation's second largest. It had opened in 1814 as the Imperial Public Library. Every book ever printed in Russian was inside, as well as twenty-five million other books and manuscripts.

A soft sleet began cutting the air as Irina hurried westward from Ostrovsky Square to the library, which stood like granite cliffs a few blocks away at the corner of Nevsky and Sadovaya Street. The icy wind blew away her worries about the translating. The weather, the food bundle and the library were *glasnost* in a nutshell, she thought. Information was liberally exchanged now but food was scarce and distrust of government plentiful. And the winter spoke for itself, hanging dagger-sharp icicles from Leningrad's ornate French- and Italian-style buildings.

The library was low and wide, with the upper half of its facade lined with giant Ionic columns. Stone statues of Greek philosophers stood in niches. Irina passed the front entrance, two large wooden doors on the street level, identified as the library only by a brass plaque, and walked around on Sadovaya to a back entrance for employees. She tugged at the heavy door.

"Umph. This door never welcomes me home."

The cold walk had sapped strength from Irina's slender legs. Inside, a second door stood between her and the alcove. She pulled off her dark wool beret and shook it free of ice. Another worker, a stout man, barged in the door with the cold wind behind him, strode past Irina, and opened the second door. She followed him in. The chill had drifted past the doors into the alcove, where others were putting down packages, taking off coats and hats, and folding umbrellas. Irina shook more sleet from her arms and shoes.

"How is my little Chinese girl?" called a heavily dressed man who sat behind a large front desk. He wore a brown inspector's cap and service uniform of the same bureaucratic color. His eyes were red and he smiled.

"I'm as Russian as you, Ivan Sergeivich." She held up her library pass, defiant. "Probably more Russian." The exchange came up occasionally, especially as familiarity grew. Irina had worked there four years. She accepted the dejected man's taunts, assuming he did not know how to be kind or make good conversation. Some people said he had worked at that desk for years and had evolved from a dutiful and erect middle-aged man to the curmudgeon before her. She pitied his loneliness. He was nice enough so she indulged him.

And he reminded her of her father, a man also worn down by a system that bred spiritual and physical illness.

Down the hall Irina could see the front lobby where the public, after passing through three doors, checked belongings and showed passes to security guards. From there they fanned out to the library's seven huge reading rooms. Before that point, she turned down another hall. It took her past the main conference room.

She heard sounds echoing from the wood-paneled room, so she edged up to the partially opened door to peek inside. There was Viktor Reznik, a Hebrew specialist for the special collection, looking on as the Americans did their work. One man was adjusting a very elaborate silver-and-black camera, aimed downward from a tripod. Below on one of the green felt-covered tables the Leningrad Codex was open and a woman, also American, was slowly turning a parchment page. An older man, the team's leader, was writing something in a large workbook. At the head of the room a giant marble bust of Lenin looked down ominously as if any mortal in his presence was an intruder.

Suddenly Irina sneezed. Reznik's gaze turned sharply toward the high-pitched sound and then his features softened into a smile. He nodded to her as the three Americans also turned to look, at least casually. Irina smiled and slid away from the door, walking softly down the hall to the stairs.

She remembered the excitement when the American archivists had come. They had brought the finest cameras and some gifts of technology for the library. Since the 1850s, the Imperial Library had held a collection of seventeen thousand Hebrew and Aramaic manuscripts. Reznik had been sending crude microfilm copies of the most prominent documents to the Americans, who operated a manuscript archive in Los Angeles. And now that *glasnost* had opened up more cultural exchange, they were the first foreigners in a century to gain access to the imperial corpus. Their priority was new photos of the Leningrad Codex, the oldest known Old Testament manuscript in Hebrew.

On the second floor Irina reached the greenish hallways and walked past glass-fronted bookcases between identical wooden doors. Cold air invaded the corridors each winter, and when Irina entered her division office she exulted in the warmth inside. The office was spacious, with a high ceiling trimmed at the wall with ornate plaster. A large window looked onto a room of book stacks. Its only other lighting came from the metal-canopy lamps on four wooden desks.

"I don't look forward to the trip home tonight, Tatyana," Irina said to her co-worker, who sat bent over a pile of index cards. She made corrections on them in pencil and kept a running list on a sheet of each book they represented.

"Neither do I," said Tatyana, her head down. "The water heater in our unit is broken again. Oh, for a hot bath! I think I could endure without it, but the neighbors who share our bathroom get so upset."

"Let's have some tea."

"Lots of sugar in mine, please."

Irina had put her bag in the corner and was taking off her heavy coat. Underneath was a bright and fine sweater. She seemed to have worn it most days since the previous summer, when she received it as a gift in Washington, D.C., as a minor staff member of a cultural exchange project. During the superpower summit, the Soviet team had opened a display of rare books at the Library of Congress. Irina had helped catalogue those seventeenth-century religious works and manuscripts by Russia's Old Believers. Her fluency in spoken English, however, had gotten her on the trip. Absorbing languages, especially Chinese, had been a source of happiness for most of her thirty-four years.

Irina brushed back her dark straight hair, which hung just above her shoulders, and straightened the woven pattern of blue, white, purple and yellow below the neck of the sweater. She took her bag into a closet-sized niche off the office and lit a small burner. The silvery kettle already held water.

"I adore this corner," she said to herself when she reached her desk. "On days like this especially." Life had not provided stability but the corner did. It gave a sense of place. Irina viewed herself as fortunate. Yes, her parents had been divided by the hard system, but not before she had grown up. Most of her neighbors worked in factories, void of personal space. It was "the people's" property. Her corner, stark as it was, was hers.

When she had returned from the trip in June 1990, reforms had been unfolding rapidly the Soviet Union. That spring the Soviet parliament took away the Communist Party's monopoly on power, Boris Yeltsin became president of Russia, and press censorship ended. As Mikhail Gorbachev survived a challenge by hardliners at the Party Congress, Yeltsin left the Party and was followed by the mayors of Leningrad and Moscow. There was serious talk of dissolving the union of republics, suggesting that nationalism might carry the future. The nation waited for the inevitable reaction, a deep convulsion of chaos, riots or tanks in the streets. The Soviet library bureaucracy had its natural alliance with the old order, and many of Irina's superiors didn't welcome change. Some said a little insecurity was tolerable, but the greater odds were still on Russia's venerable curse—suffering, done this century in Soviet style.

She had stayed apolitical, but had done what formerly had been unthinkable. She had hung the print of an icon, the Madonna and child by the painter Andrei Rublev, on her wall with two pins. It rivaled the size of the Lenin portrait on the other wall. Unlike Lenin's gaze, the icon's eyes, like the Mona Lisa's, wandered to every corner, including toward Lenin. Rublev had just been declared a saint by the Russian Orthodox Church.

A door slammed in the distance and Irina heard heavy, regular footsteps. It was Dimitry Borisov. He burst into the office and both she and Tatyana sat at attention.

"Tatyana, Tatyana." His voice was gravelly. "A whole group of books in the French B section has been left out. We'll have to amend the numbers on everything past B." Borisov was pacing, holding a wrinkled document in one hand and futilely pushing back his thin stringy hair, which fell forward easily. Irina glanced at Tatyana, who stared at the supervisor with furrows in her delicate eyebrows.

"If inventories were accurate this wouldn't happen," Tatyana said. "This is nothing new, Dimitry Ivanovich. It goes on like a long winter."

"Yes, but the director doesn't see it that way. He set a three-year plan and it's months behind schedule." Borisov frowned. He noticed Tatyana's pretty downcast eyes, set like small jewels in her round and fleshy pale face. "Tatyana, don't take my mood personally. You've done good work. We just have to go back and adjust the numbers as fast as we can."

"You mean as fast as I can. Don't worry. I can do it. I just hate working seven days a week or too late into the night. You know my situation, Dimitry Ivanovich. I'm not getting any younger and my husband complains."

"Yes, yes. We'll pace it. We'll do our best. And how are you Irina? Are things moving along in Chinese and the rare books?" He gestured his document like a pointer toward the niche. "Is that the water?"

"You're invited for tea." Irina spoke as gaily as possible under the circumstances. "Tatyana is better than I, but my materials come to me better organized. My work is going fine, on schedule, I suppose."

"Good," Borisov said with a faint smile. "And good for the tea. I could use it. Tatyana, you could use it too."

"Of course. I'm not complaining. In fact, I'll go make it." Tatyana squared her cards, list and pencils neatly on the desk and walked across the room with severe steps.

Borisov lingered for the tea. "How do you keep track of twenty-three million books with paper and pencil? It's a miracle, isn't it Irina, that we've done it at all?"

In their minds they often compared Leningrad with Moscow, as they did now. The Lenin Library in Moscow was the largest in the world with thirty-five million items. An American firm had begun to computerize its catalogues. No one in Leningrad was yet talking about computers.

"You know, Irina, my worst fear is that we may lose something. Something precious to the world. The last complete list of our rare books was drawn up in the 1870s. During the siege of Leningrad so many things were moved to safety. After they returned, why didn't this government create a library army to sort it through?" By now, Borisov was gazing out the small window onto the stacks. His voice rose during the peroration. "I don't mean to make a speech."

Tatyana stood over the three steaming teacups. "If you can't talk to us, who can you talk to?" With a cup in each hand, she carried them to Borisov and Irina. "You must say 'yes' to those above you, but here we can speak our minds. Believe me, working

52

in this dreary building is a dinner party compared to the factory. Or the Party."

"A toast to that," said Borisov. He and Irina held their blue-and-white teacups until Tatyana returned with hers.

"To humanity," Irina said, which the others repeated. The cups steamed and they all felt the warmth of hot Russian tea, and a warmth of mind. They really believed the toast.

"Ah, superb," Borisov said.

They waited to see if Borisov would give his normal speech, a sentimental discourse usually heard after schnapps. It was about the Nazi siege of Leningrad, when citizens had come to the library not to read, but to survive. They had found out how to make matches, how to make candles. They had tried to find ways to make yeast, edible wood and artificial vitamins. They had tried by looking at books in German, French and English, books that were sometimes one hundred fifty years old. This time, the speech didn't come.

Borisov pulled a little flask from his coat and spiked his tea, an offer which the women, as usual, declined. "So. Again we toast the simple things in life. That's all we have and that's what we enjoy."

They all laughed in a single emotion, part cynicism and part melancholy. This winter wasn't so bad, because the next one may be worse. Enjoy the political situation today, for where might it be in one year?

"The Americans today said many of their countrymen want to come," Borisov said. "To come here! Can you imagine?"

"There is much here," Tatyana said. "First they come to see our old manuscripts in the vault. Then they see more. Our history, our culture."

In recent days Irina had tried not to exude too much pleasure at her opportunities, at least for Tatyana's sake. And she hoped no political catastrophes would arise in the next weeks.

"Irina," Borisov said. "When do you go to San Francisco?"

She said she would finish her work before the departure in about thirteen days.

"Yes, yes, of course," Borisov said. "I am told the list of books you'll bring is not too large. And what do the Americans bring?"

"Mostly what they know. Their ancient studies exceed ours and the technology is, well, you know, quite good."

"And your English will sharpen." Irina was one of Borisov's few multilingual resources, and one available to him outside Party channels.

"She loves the topic, too," Tatyana said. "She knows the library's religious manuscripts very well. Chinese, old philosophical texts. And Buddhism, too. In Chinese, but now listed in Russian."

"Oh, Tatyana, you exaggerate. I can do the titles but I am not a scholar . . . like Mr. Borisov." She shifted her gaze from Tatyana to the older, disheveled man.

"Well, at least I am that. Somewhat, at least." Borisov's face turned pink. He finished his tea. "Now I must go. Keep working." He smiled, pushed back his hair, and left the office.

Tatyana did not peer up from her work. Irina turned to her Chinese catalogue. For the remaining hours she indexed works of the past and struggled against daydreaming of the future.

They said it was bright orange like a tangerine. She couldn't even imagine it. They also said the bridge was so tall the clouds passed below. "The golden gate," she said in English. Her mind wandered dreamlike to grasp what it would be like—the bridge, San Francisco and the Americans she would meet at the American-Soviet Ancient Manuscript Symposium.

6

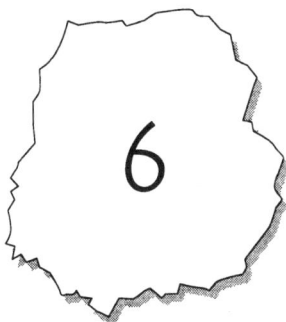

B ack from his lunch at the club, Harvard Professor Bruce Banner found the *New York Times* on his chair, folded inside out. The sun had warmed the office, which was organized around a large cluttered desk.

Banner took off his tweed coat, brushed it with three swipes of the hand, and hung it on the oak hat rack. He adjusted his cuffs, white like the collar on his blue pinstriped shirt, before walking back to the desk.

The newspaper was marked with a red circle. He lifted it to his narrowed eyes. Someone in the archaeology department must have walked it over, he thought, judging by the item.

> JERUSALEM—Archaeology in the Middle East has been set back by the Gulf War, the flight of volunteers—and the recent death of one of its leading lights.
>
> Simon Rabin, 68, a pioneer in excavating ancient Jerusalem and a proponent of unprecedented digs in the Negev Desert, died of a stroke two days before the Iraqi withdrawal. The veteran of two Middle East conflicts may have been weakened by the tension of the war, an associate said. He has no surviving family.

Banner put the paper down and thought about the immediacy of events.

"I can't possibly make a trip over there now," he said to himself. "I'm not young anymore." Not much younger, he realized, than Rabin.

The trip had occurred to Banner only because he never wanted to miss a professional opportunity. For protocol, though, he knew what to do. And he would not only send condolences, but would say a word on the man's accomplishments. Nobody asked for that, but Banner was, he believed, synonymous with Harvard. His leadership was certain, as he would show during the scholarly Jesus Colloquium in San Diego later that week.

His secretary, Carla, a former college friend of Banner's young wife, walked in for a routine check. "Anything this afternoon?"

"Let's do a letter, please."

She already had her pad in hand.

Being of the old school, Banner had never learned to type, nor was he going to be held hostage to word-processing lessons. In his esteemed academic post, he could scribble a note or dictate to a department secretary. Students often researched data for his articles and books; at times they even drafted them under his close guidance and fastidious blue pencil.

"Send this Western Union, Carla. I'll dictate."

She sat down at the corner of the heavy desk, bent over the pad. Banner paced the room, smoking a cigarette with his chin in the air, as if studying the points at which the walls met the ceiling.

"The world of archaeology mourns the loss of one of its great practitioners," Banner began. "To honor this leader in his field, my department . . . scratch that, Carla, . . . *the* Harvard school sends its condolences . . ." Banner stopped at the window to view the lawn below, crisp and trim from a mowing the night before. He stabbed his cigarette into a tray and continued. "Simon Rabin was an innovator, one who went against the grain. This spirit is his great legacy to us."

In other statements over the years, Banner had criticized Rabin. Some points of disagreement, though small, were very important. Banner believed that criticism honed scholarship and separated brilliance from mediocrity. True, there had to be mutual respect. They were all archaeologists who had struggled against the same obscure, receding past. But some, like himself, were lucky enough to have superior minds that could produce the best theories.

A few phrases later, Banner had climaxed his dictation. The secretary scribbled furiously.

"With regards, Dr. Bruce W. Banner. Got it all?"

"Yes." Her pale eyes rolled up at him as her hand still drove the pen across the pad.

"He has no family, so send it to Yosef Dan at the Israeli Antiquities Authority. The address is in the files."

As she left the room, Banner sat down at his desk and lit another cigarette.

"Oh, Carla," he said. "Just another thing."

She peeked in a few seconds later, then walked into the middle of the room.

"You've got my tickets for San Diego, don't you?"

"Yes, of course . . ."

"First class, as I requested?"

"Of course."

He nodded and she left. Banner drew on his cigarette and began to rustle through the pages of his pocket calendar.

He would stay in California longer except that he had decided not to attend the conference of Soviet and American manuscript experts in San Francisco. He had said he would go but only if he chaired the American team.

To that, the letter from the head office informed him: "I am quite sorry that such a change would be complicated as the Smithsonian director already has been given the role."

Banner had replied, "Okay, I'll co-chair the thing with him."

That, too, was "complicated." So Banner had simply said he had neither the time nor the interest. A half-week in Southern California, he had decided, would be plenty of time away.

The whole episode, and now the death of Rabin, made him think about the rivalry in his field. "I'm not so bad," his mind protested. "For God's sake, I'm not against everybody. I don't backbite and I'm not a bad loser. When I win, I win generously."

As Banner saw it, rivalry was as necessary for scholars as it was for generals and politicians. He tried to remember. As a young man, had he thought otherwise? Having foes as one matures, he mused, gives life a sort of symmetry. One side against the other. For instance, he wasn't really against the Bible scholar Jack Winslow of Princeton University. They had merely taken different sides. Banner had joined up with the Jesus Colloquium and Winslow would not. Winslow was attending the Soviet conference and Banner had demurred. Banner knew he tended to posture a bit, sometimes a lot. He presumed the same of Winslow. They were not enemies, of course. Yes, Winslow had written a good book or two. But he did not have any archae- ological discovery that Banner was jealous of. He saw Winslow as an armchair adventurer. They clashed over opposite alignments. Banner felt he was being generous; the field, he supposed, was big enough for both of them.

Banner leaned back in his chair. His thoughts flowed like so many puffs on his cigarette. "Ah!" Speaking of rivalry, one more thing crossed his mind, something he should do before leaving town. He hunched over the desk and flipped through his phone book. "Jerusalem. Nabbi. Nabbi. Nabbi. Yes." It had once been a familiar number: Nabbi, an Israeli Arab, was a sometime black marketeer. Banner pushed the phone buttons with his nicotine-stained finger.

Though well below Banner's station, the Arab trader was an old acquaintance from the American's bygone days of digs and studies. Banner missed feeling Jerusalem's pulse. On the scene one could snare the hearsay, rumors and secrets about antiquities. Banner's claim to fame was that of compiler of ancient materials, editor and builder of interpretative themes. But standing atop that peak, he lacked one thing—a discovery of his own. Any discovery. It gnawed at him. Perhaps the tumult of war had stirred the waters, dislodging some unknown quantity, now floating to the surface.

The distant ring of the phone ended in a high Arab voice.

"Hello, Nabbi. This is Dr. Banner." He smiled at the excited response. Nabbi lived with his family behind a shop, and it was past bedtime. A child's crying in the background fell silent and Nabbi came back on the line.

"Yes, Nabbi, it's been a long time, hasn't it. I'm calling to check on something. Do you know Nick Hampton, a young American down at Tel-Amon? Yes, that's him. Yes. Any word on things that Mr. Hampton might be turning up?"

He paused to listen.

"Nothing that you know, huh. Nabbi, would any of your friends know if he's looking for manuscripts, anything like that?"

Pause.

"No, huh. No, Nabbi, nothing in particular. I just have a gut feeling, like an Arab knows where to dig a well."

Banner laughed nervously as he drew on the cigarette and exhaled a genielike plume of smoke.

"Well, Nabbi, since you asked, why don't you casually check with a few friends and see if Hampton's name comes up? Won't hurt."

Years ago, the shopkeeper had done well by a group of Banner's friends. The American scholar still called him sporadically for information about the black market. Nabbi always took the calls with joy; perhaps, he thought, prosperity had come again. Hard times plagued the market now—hordes of competing sharks and dealers, even crime gangs, and then, of course, the tightening screws of Israeli authorities. A dishonor had descended on the trade, too. In the old days, one never had to cheat, threaten or harm. No one had to kill.

Nabbi's mind raced with the possibilities. Two of his good business associates—they found things and he sold them—had expanded their operation by obtaining personal transportation. The car was old, but it was registered with yellow license plates, and now even Nabbi was getting around a little more, to Bethlehem, Jericho, even Nablus and Beersheba. If Banner knew about something, Nabbi might serve a broker role and receive his fair cut. Maybe he would become a permanent agent, Mr. Banner's eyes and ears. That would be worth something, he thought. He would start asking around tomorrow. As always, he invited Banner to Jerusalem.

Banner chuckled. "Someday, Nabbi. Someday."

7

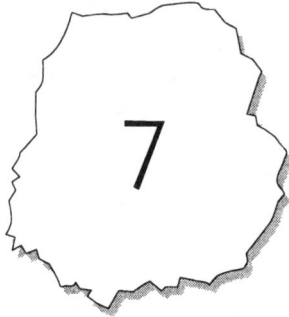

The sky was a hazy blue the day Simon Rabin was buried in a hilltop cemetery. It was covered with cypress trees and wildflowers and its slope overlooked the western Judean Hills. To dig the grave, caretakers raked aside the whitish stones that covered every inch of the highlands around Jerusalem. After friends lowered the linen-wrapped body and covered it with earth, the rocks were scattered out again to retain the natural landscape. At the cemetery entrance the white flag with a blue Star of David fluttered.

Rabin's funeral drew members of the Knesset, some in the military and a representative of the president. Most were old friends speaking in whispered tones. Travis Marshall was chatting with a French Dominican from the Ecole Biblique when Nick Hampton walked up.

"Excuse me, Pierre. We'll talk later."

The priest-scholar nodded, smiled at Nick, and walked off adjusting his beret.

"Nick, how are you?" Marshall asked.

"Not bad, considering the war."

"Well, now it's over. You've got a nice ruddy look."

The sun and wind had given them both dark rugged faces; at least compared to five years earlier, when Oxford University, with its overcast skies and dim study rooms, had made their complexions pale and soft.

Marshall, in a solemn tone, explained that Rabin had not fully recuperated after his first stroke, five months earlier. And then came the shock of war. "As I said when I called you, Simon mentioned you the week before he died. I hope we can have a good talk about the Institute."

It had not been easy for Hampton to extricate himself from Tel Aviv. He had final lectures to prepare, student papers to read, and a few more trips to make down to Tel-Amon. Attending the funeral was already required by good professional manners, but then Marshall had also called. He would not say anything on the telephone, except to trust him and make the day free.

They began to walk along the edge of the graveyard, the shade of cypress and olive trees breaking the bright dusty path.

"Why did Rabin mention me?"

"It's quite a long story," Marshall said. He began by explaining his part in the tale. He had come to work with Rabin for experience, which he got plenty of, especially since he and his wife, Anne, had stayed longer than expected. She had become pregnant at the start of winter and they hadn't wanted to risk the long plane flight. When Rabin had become ill, Anne had helped care for him as Marshall plowed ahead with the project. "So we stayed through the war. I did some more courier work to Jordan, and kept on mapping the Negev."

A small gust hit the two figures broadside. Hampton reached up to push back his hair.

"Of course, Rabin knew of your work and your independence, Nick. He knew that Americans like you can easily cross borders."

"Was he hoping I'd take over his Negev project? I know nothing about it." Hampton was thinking of all the crushing commitments he had already.

Marshall chuckled. "Not the whole project. It hasn't much of a future without Rabin. He made it bigger than life."

"Is the funding gone?"

"We never needed much money. Rabin was resourceful. He gave me a good one-time salary for the year. If the Institute expanded one day, he said don't worry, there was plenty of money."

Hampton was perplexed. "Then why me?"

"Rabin's people in Jordan know of you. They agreed that you should be brought in on an aspect of the project." Marshall glanced around furtively and then stared straight into Hampton's hazel eyes. "It's about manuscripts held by a group of Muslims."

"Hmm." Hampton suppressed a twitch of excitement. "That is interesting."

"The key man in Jordan is named Habib Muhammad. He's a Sunni Muslim, an imam and some kind of educator. I've met him a few times, briefly. He's quite old now."

Marshall explained his use of the telephone relay system, right up to the war. When the missile attacks had started, Rabin had asked him to contact Habib. It had taken three days, but then events had gone quickly. Habib had sent his courier to meet Rabin and soon afterward Marshall had been on his way to Amman.

"It was a hell of a risky trip," he said. "This was three weeks into the war and I carried some sealed papers to Habib. In Amman rumors had started that CIA agents were in the university's archaeology department. Being British sure helped, though. All my references come from blokes at the British-Jordanian digs up at Jerash."

Hampton went over the time frame again, from Marshall's trip of forty-five days ago to Rabin's death of seven days past.

"It all happened very fast," Marshall said. "Besides these rumored discoveries, Rabin has been negotiating about access to parts of the Negev along Jordan. That is politically delicate so he kept his business private."

"What about the manuscripts, then?"

"I was told they are part of the antiquities found by the Bedouin. Rabin learned all this from Habib. He has some kind of opening to the Bedouin."

Hampton did not want to suggest that Rabin was a rogue archaeologist or Marshall a bootlegger, but he had to ask the question. "Why didn't Rabin tell the authorities?"

"He talked to them, but not about this," Marshall said. "He was protecting his sources. He was following the tried-and-true methods of the scholar-generals in the old days."

Among the cornerstones of those methods was to avoid scaring off your supplier and to find a trustworthy third party, Marshall said. "Rabin and Habib decided to trust you as the one."

They reached the end of the escarpment, a cliff, and before them was a panorama of the western horizon. The Mediterranean was beyond. A cool wind blew from the north. The revelations caught Hampton off guard, but he quickly analyzed his options: get involved or back off.

"Nick, there are eyes and ears everywhere in the Middle East. I've been watched, or at least that's my strong instinct. You too, I'm sure."

"By whom?"

"Arabs or Jews or both." That reminded Marshall. "I got a call from an American Baptist fellow a week ago. Matthew Cummings. He seemed awfully interested in Rabin's work. He asked about manuscripts."

"Yeah, I know Cummings. He's inquired with me too. It's prophecy he's tying to figure out."

"That's the harmless part. Some of these people are into crime. That makes the police watch every archaeologist like he's a treasure hunter. And there are those who are always looking for a spy."

"You said 'politically delicate.' Is the Negev project dangerous?"

"No more than anything else. Simon had gotten a couple of threats. He just laughed."

Intrigues were something Hampton wanted to avoid. This appeared to be full of intrigue, but not a sinister one—if Marshall's rendering was to be believed. And Hampton felt someone was counting on his help. "Shall we drive down to the Institute and have a look?"

"That's what I had in mind," Marshall said, convinced that Hampton was almost on board. "You should see our operation before you decide."

"Let's go."

They steered their cars outside the entrance to the burial grounds, where Hampton parked his and jumped into Marshall's jeep. As they left, Hampton noticed activity in the rear-view mirror. Two Israeli police converged on a weather-beaten blue car, waving it along to leave its shady spot on the roadside. The occupants seemed to be young Arabs.

The two-lane road leaving Jerusalem switched back and forth down the Judean hills, past the ancient stone walls that terraced hillsides, past ruins of a Crusader fortress, and past the rusted remains of vehicles bombed in 1948—monuments to the war for statehood. The Ayalon Valley below was green and speckled with wildflowers and stones and a few blossoming almond trees. Several miles into the tableland, Marshall turned south on the road to Beersheba, following the coastal plain along the Judean foothills. In the next hour the landscape alternated among rocky vegetated knolls, planted fields, citrus groves, dry streambeds and grassy wastes. The fine yellow-brown earth and the reddish sand combined in a fertile corridor to Beersheba, gateway to most of Israel—the four and a half thousand square miles of desert called the Negev.

Marshall and Hampton talked little during the drive, preferring to let the hum of the motor and the warm rushing air create a backdrop for their speculations and daydreams. Hampton was saving his questions for later. For now he was thinking of Anne Marshall, whom he had met in England. She had been Travis' girlfriend then. Travis had been so smitten by her, he recalled, that his studies had suffered. Now she was his pregnant wife. A few years younger than Hampton, Travis and his bride had cavorted in the dangerous Middle East, conceived their first child, and shepherded this strange archaeological conspiracy for a Jewish eccentric.

The adventure seemed so opposite to him and Susan. From the day they met, their ideas about courtship had told them that commitment, a sober loyalty, was the main point. They never got off balance with infatuation, falling over emotional cliffs. Love was sort of businesslike, with a religious sanction above it. Each felt lucky to find a compatible and quality partner. Both had lost a parent to a fatal illness, a burden and vacuum that seemed to link them by empathy, too. And yet sometimes Hampton wondered if all these pieces meant he had never, as the poets say, fallen in love.

It was near 4 A.M. in Philadelphia, he calculated. Susan was deep asleep. Around her brick row house he saw the budding trees and early blooming gardens, visible by porch lights. Inside, her contours showed under the blanket. Perhaps she was dreaming about something. In the dirt hills of Judea he saw the orange tint of Susan's hair. A smooth limestone slope was like her pale skin.

Would she marry him, he wondered, and move to Seattle?

Then Beersheba burst on the horizon, a low skyline of square pastel buildings: a city that had grown to one hundred fifteen thousand since 1948. On the northern outskirts the road bisected Bedouin camps with their goat and sheep herds, and then older Israeli villages. Marshall began to point out Ben Gurion University, the world-famous Desert Research Center, the gray cement slab of City Hall and offices for the Dead Sea Works.

After a rumble across the rail line they emerged from the industrial sector to face open desert again.

"When you get to the desert you see how historical the Bible is," Marshall said. "Over there." He pointed to an oasis surrounded by trees. "That's the Institute."

Hampton marveled at its obscurity.

"Some of those trees are tamarisk," Marshall said. "When the settlers came here they looked in the Old Testament for what grows. They found tamarisk." So they planted two million of them for shade, for roots and fences to fight wind and water erosion, and to change the climate, to draw rain. Marshall slowed the jeep as they passed four camels and a dozen men, riding and walking. "There's real desert life out here," he said.

Chalky dust was rolling in the air by the time Marshall steered the jeep down a street and up to a stone building next to a flat-topped hill.

"We also have a little hovel in the desert, fifty miles south of here in Mitzpe Ramon," Marshall said.

From the shade of a wide portico made of black volcanic rock and white limestone, they mounted a flight of outdoor stairs to reach the top floor and entered. The air was dry inside and smelled of clay. A large topographical map of Israel and Jordan hung on the white wall, well-lit by two large windows with olive curtains drawn back. It was a stunning map, Hampton thought, portraying the actual relief of the vast geological formation.

The Negev was a tall triangle standing on its tip and the Negev Hills, which ran like a diagonal sash from the right shoulder to the waist, took up a third of its territory. Above was the Beersheba plain, and south of the hills the Paran Plateau tapered down to the tip—the Elat Hills on the Gulf of Aqaba. To the east, the plateau dropped suddenly into the Arava Valley, the hundred-mile-long rift that spanned the Israeli-Jordan border below the Dead Sea.

There was a desk with a black telephone, a few clay lamps from digs, and a tin can with pencils. Hampton scanned further, past two gray file cabinets, a door to a living area, and around a corner. His eyes widened.

"Is that what I think it is?" he asked. "A doll house?"

It was almost as large as the desk and was painted a sky blue, white and green that remained bright under the dust. The open back revealed two floors and an attic. The rooms were in chaos, filled with tiny furniture and trimmings that were soiled or broken. Some of the windows had tattered curtains.

Marshall had gone to a corner of the room to pry up a floorboard. "The doll house was his daughter's," he said, squatting with a pocket knife in his hand. "I guess I never mentioned it. He lost his family and . . ."

"Lost his family! When?"

"In 1968. They survived the 1967 war, but a year later his wife and daughter were killed in a terrorist raid on a bus. The girl was only fourteen."

"I had no idea."

"He never remarried. Since then he had been a loner." Marshall stood up to keep talking. "Simon was not one for self-pity. He didn't advertise his misfortunes. But his devotion to his family seemed to re-channel itself into this project. He liked it out here. He felt he was on the frontier. He probably felt he was with his family."

"That's why the doll house, I presume."

"He brought it out several months ago. I didn't ask why. It was obvious." Down on his knees again, Marshall jiggled two planks loose and lifted them out. In the dark hole was a metal box. "This can work as a safe." He slipped the boards back in and then turned to a file cabinet. The top drawer opened with a screech and Marshall withdrew a thick manila folder. They pulled their chairs, or in Hampton's case a stool, up to the desk.

The folder said NEGEV.

"The first thing I should give you are the phone numbers I used to reach Habib," Marshall said. From the opened file he retrieved a page with two series of digits. "You can't call Habib directly, so you'll have to do a European relay. He wants you to visit Amman so he can tell you more."

"I'm a little confused," Hampton said. "Why the office and why all the secrecy, or so it seems?"

"You know, Rabin told me once, very emphatically, the importance of screening communication. He sort of apologized for keeping me in the dark on what was probably a political side of his work with Habib. Fine with me. I was busy analyzing history and topography in the Negev."

As he retrieved another file, Marshall explained how as a Brit he had easily traveled into Jordan, visiting a mosque and home in Amman to leave messages for Habib. On the desk he unfolded a map—grid paper covered with contour lines showing mounds, wadis, gullies and flats.

"These maps cover the Negev and south Jordan in select detail," Marshall said. "We've been waiting for Habib to get more information from Bedouin in Jordan. They know this landscape and know where they've been finding things for a few generations."

During his time at Tel-Amon, Hampton had learned how the Bedouin did their collecting. They'd set up their black tents over a site they wanted to plunder, feigning a brief encampment before they moved on. Hampton said, "Now, what did Rabin think I'm supposed to do?"

"You've got to make contact with Habib. At your initiative."

"I see." Hampton wondered if Marshall had wearied of the project and if he was frustrated at the partial darkness Rabin had kept him in. Yet Hampton's instincts told him it could be the other way around. Marshall had helped Rabin, like he said, but he wasn't ambitious for control. He was young and had some years to choose his own direction.

Marshall pushed himself back in the chair and it rocked on its back legs for a moment. "There's another layer to this I should tell you about."

Hampton's eyes stayed attentive.

"There is a peace plan being talked of," Marshall said. "The idea is to create joint economic zones. Arabs and Israelis together. A decade ago, Israel offered to work with Jordan on a salt evaporation complex at the north end of the Dead Sea. But it's hard for Jordan to move. Its Palestinian population protests and other Arab states put on pressure. So on the water project Jordan refused. Well, Rabin said the idea of economic cooperation is still alive."

As Marshall painted the scenario for the Negev, it made Hampton envision something between a massive industrial expansion and a desert Disney World. A free economic zone where reconciled Jews and Arabs pursued prosperity. Rain would be captured and stored and sea water, desalinized to freshness, piped in. The nutritious soil, too fine to absorb water and washed away easily by Negev flash rains, would be tamed. They would mine minerals, grow crops, herd cattle, and make crafts. As a nature preserve, the Mitzpe Ramon crater would draw tourists to see twelve thousand plant varieties, rare animals and spectacular rock formations.

"I've never heard of it."

Neither government has talked about the proposal openly, Marshall said, noting his belief that Rabin was somewhere in the loop. "He said archaeology could prosper with joint efforts. Israelis, Arabs and us folks from the West."

"So that's his dream."

"Was his dream." Marshall creased the maps and put them in the folder. "It's all yours now. I'll give you the key for the front door. The building is paid for, so come and go as you like."

"And the maps?"

"Take them with you."

Back in the jeep, Hampton asked if there was a high view over the desert, and Marshall drove him to the top of a knoll. A warm, dustless breeze arose and blew into Hampton's face. Below he could see the twisting wadis carved so easily by heavy rains. In the distance and not visible rose the typical Negev table mounts, flint-hard on top and soft and eroded below. Hampton wondered what Rabin felt for these barren stretches. Was it that the arid winds were the voice of his family, even the voice of God? Hampton shivered. "Let's get some lunch," he said.

Marshall reversed the jeep with a jolt. "I'll drive through the old Turkish part of the city. And the outdoor Bedouin market's open today."

They rode into Beersheba raising a trail of dust. A turn east at City Hall took them around hotels and neighborhoods until the old yellow stucco and stone of the Turkish quarter began to materialize around them. At its center, where the old Turkish mosque, fort and administrative building still stood, the foot traffic grew thick. They negotiated it a few more blocks and turned toward the market, which spread over lots and parking areas.

Marshall parked on the curb a block away from a main intersection in the market, and they crossed the street to a stone cafe.

As they walked, Hampton glanced sidelong and caught sight of a car pulling into an alley. It was blue with a rusted bumper and it could have been a clone of the compact at the cemetery. The weak economy was an explanation, he thought: lots of old cars of the same make. It seemed that he'd already seen one or two like it since reaching Beersheba.

The cafe had a touch of pink neon and was cool inside. Marshall explained that it was frequented by Arabs, which to Hampton was evident. A group of four workers, their shirt collars open and sleeves rolled up past the elbows, seemed to stare at him as they ate their pita bread and paste. Hampton wondered what they were saying. Though the service was slow, he and Marshall had eaten their fill and were traversing the street again in half an hour.

Marshall turned the jeep around, picking up speed. The intersection was dead ahead.

The chaos of the open market filled Hampton's view. A nice place to stroll with Susan, he thought. The jeep kept accelerating, as if Marshall knew secretly that the intersection was only a mirage.

Then a thud rang out, and another as the brake pedal hit the jeep floor.

"Oh, shit!" Marshall shouted. "The brakes!"

He yanked on a useless manual lever, at the same time hitting the high-pitched horn. Hampton grabbed the door frame. The few cars entering the intersection moved slowly, but it was thick with pedestrians. They had begun to scatter left and right, realizing this was not the horn blare of a merely impatient driver.

"Look out!" Hampton shouted, waving his one arm wildly. "We can't stop! Look out!"

The jeep barely missed a small truck's tailgate. A bicyclist escaped by swerving, losing a stack of packages tied behind the seat. Hampton hung on as every nerve pumped signals to his chest: danger, danger, danger. A blur of dark and light figures parted like a gray fabric coming to pieces. Hampton waited to hear the heavy, bloodcurdling thump of human contact, but it never came. The crossing took only seconds, then Marshall jerked the steering wheel, diverting them out of the intersection and into the open market, a dirt lot with a back slope. Inches from his nose Hampton faced stick cages filled with chickens, their cackles and squawks a rising din. The jeep crashed through one stand and hit a cart, spinning it into a jumble. It plowed through a few more tables of bananas, baskets and cloth before it hit the dirt slope, rolled up at a precarious angle and then fell on its side.

Marshall and Hampton were thrown hard against the interior

and then a dust cloud enveloped them. A disoriented Hampton felt a hand on his shoulder and noticed its brown wrinkled skin. People and their excited voices had surrounded the jeep; the helpful hand came through the sunroof.

"I'm all right," Hampton said, patting the hand. "I'm all right."

"You really all right?" Marshall asked. He hung from a seat belt with his head and right shoulder shoved down into Hampton's midsection.

"Nothing feels wrong," Hampton said. "Thank God this glass is still in the windows. How about you?"

"The jeep's got a roll bar." Marshall groaned. "Damn. Umph. What a mess."

The two heaved and twisted until they were out. Neither of them could understand the language, but the gathering either wanted to help them or hang them. One man with a big walking stick, obviously a merchant, was yelling at them, his green eyes wide.

"I better check if anyone's injured," Hampton said. His legs shaky, he walked back over their route looking for victims. When he reached the intersection he sighed with relief. No one on the ground. Besides a larger group of spectators than usual, the intersection was filled again with cars and bicycles.

Then a police car arrived, producing two white-shirted cops in full gear. Hampton waved them over. Their presence somewhat calmed the disorder, and in Hampton's mind thwarted any merchant's thought of meting out street justice. They walked through the market, already on the repair, to the jeep.

Marshall had car insurance, but he grimaced at the thought of his savings draining off for damages. He wondered if they would lock him up for perpetrating such destruction. There'd surely be some questioning. The jeep had some scratches, but . . . He was angry now. That greasy garage in Jerusalem? He almost began swearing. "What happened to those brakes?" He limped around to check the jeep's underbelly.

Hampton and the police found him stooped down and running his finger along a narrow pipe that fed into the right front wheel.

"Nick, look at this."

Hampton leaned down to see a thin, clear fluid dripping.

Marshall looked up at the officers. "The brake line's been sliced."

8

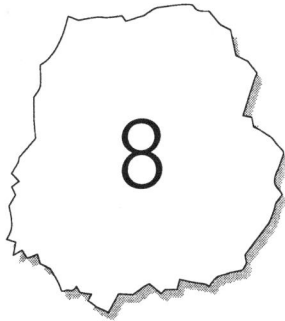

As the taxi conveyed him through Indiana's wheat fields, Jack Winslow flipped through the booklet of Russian words.

"Thank you very much." *Bolshoy speciba.*

"May I ask who you are?" *Prastiti, kak vasha imya?*

Nothing for document or manuscript. The only word about paper he could find was *tooalyetnaya boomaga.* Toilet paper.

Winslow had taken the booklet from his breast pocket just moments after the Hungarian cabdriver's heavy foot had sent them speeding away from Indianapolis International Airport.

The open fields, green from March rains, swayed in the breeze and thinned at the city outskirts like a receding lake against its shore.

"It reminds me of Danube plains." The Hungarian emigre's accent was thick. "We call it the Banat. Just the same here except no big river."

Winslow made a tight sweep with his hand. "This is what we call middle America. I'm sure that the Danube is far more picturesque . . ." He pronounced the word slowly.

"Oh, no, no. The only difference is the castles. You don't have any castles." The affable Hungarian looked like a storybook East European, with a broad open forehead and thick dark hair that stood straight up.

Years had passed since Winslow had last visited the Midwest. The vast blue and billowing white clouds with flat bottoms perfected his image of a prairie sky. In the distance, a few skyscrapers jutted up from the plain.

Since he had retired as dean of Princeton Theological Seminary, Winslow rarely traveled far from his New Jersey home. This itinerary, however, took him on a back-to-back schedule from Indianapolis to San Francisco, covering three events. The Academy of Religion had asked Winslow, a noted New Testament scholar, to be among the Americans hosting a Soviet delegation in the bay city. While there, his class of postwar graduates of Pacific Theological Union in Berkeley would attempt a reunion.

The reunion should have been the easiest of the three, but Winslow faced it with trepidation. It floated like a small cloud in front of the sun.

Would it succeed? he wondered. Or would a mere remnant show up, thinned by death and disinterest? And how would they measure what they'd become? One measure was the span of four decades and Winslow knew he'd lost touch, even with his oldest pal, David Hampton—a wartime buddy. Too ill to travel, David wouldn't be there. At the Soviet event, though, Winslow was going to see the man's son, Nicholas. Winslow was pleased at how he had engineered an invitation for Nick Hampton, but more gratified that Nick had accepted.

On the way, Winslow was stopping in Indianapolis, where he had agreed to speak at a conference on Bible illiteracy. He put the Russian booklet away and took out the program. A rather grand title, he thought: Back to the Bible—A National Quest for Literacy.

The big Hoosier cab seemed to float on its axles. The downtown streets were shaded until they reached the traffic circle at city center. The sunlight shot across Winslow's chest and he felt strangely embraced. The cab swung past the circle's monument, soldier and sailor statues around an obelisk, topped by a Columbia figure with her eagle, torch, globe and sword.

The Hungarian pulled up to the hotel across from the convention center. "Have a good stay in our middle-countryside . . . I mean middle-nation."

Winslow tipped him and got his luggage. He checked into the hotel, had a late but small lunch and then crossed the street in an enclosed walkway. This entered a vast foyer on the second floor of the convention center. Inside the Exhibit Hall rows of colorful booths ran like arcades, showing off the commercial side of the "Back to the Bible" conference. Dozens of new versions, new books about the Bible, and even computer programs to search for words, view maps and learn Greek caught his eye.

Winslow walked what seemed like a mile of hallways to reach the Benjamin Harrison—a native son—conference room. Its brown-striped walls and dark blue rug made the white ceiling seem to float. The room filled quickly and like a church started in the back rows. At the front of the hall hung a green banner, stating the conference theme in plain white letters. A wooden podium stood below on the stage. With a handshake from the emcee, Winslow was asked to sit on the stage and await his introduction.

He studied the swelling audience—church educators and Bible study teachers. There were Methodists, Presbyterians, Lutherans, Episcopalians, the heirs of Congregational and Reform traditions, Baptists and perhaps even some Roman Catholics. For centuries, he thought, they had searched the Bible for meaning. For all their different answers they had created hundreds of different churches.

A relaxed Winslow let his mind wander. Some in the audience might be Bible fundamentalists, he thought. He understood the origin of fundamentalism well, for his university had been a hand-maiden to its American version. A century earlier, Princeton had been a proponent of Common Sense philosophy, an outlook particularly suited to American optimism and pragmatism. Unlike the rationalist abstractions of much European thought, Common Sense said that what a man perceives with his senses is real. Its insights could have come from a Pennsylvania farmer whose plow struck a stone in the field. Applied to biblical interpretation, Common Sense bred a tenacious Bible literalism. Princeton dropped its old philosophy, but in 1910 a new movement, fundamentalism, rose up with similar ideas to fight modernism.

The new fundamentalist resurgence had many generals, but the Texas preacher Harlan Wesley Stockwood, architect of a crusade among Baptists, had the mightiest sword. A year earlier, Stockwood's mass rally in Houston had set the movement afire with an unequivocal message: "The Bible said it, I believe it, and that settles it." It had spread to Dallas, New Orleans, Atlanta and beyond. Battles within seminaries had ensued and reputations of Bible professors had climbed or fallen. America's biggest Protestant group, the General Baptist Convention, had become an arena for dramatic elections that finally had made the fundamentalist view official policy.

Winslow was neither fundamentalist nor modernist, and he felt fortunate for not being targeted by either. When asked, he described himself as orthodox, or conventional.

Someone waved. "How are you, Dean Winslow?" the man asked.

It took a moment, but as Winslow gestured back he recognized the former Princeton student, now an aging Midwest minister. The past was everywhere, Winslow thought. Lately, he so easily drifted into long memories, even assessments, of the bygone times.

Conference organizers had let Winslow choose his topic, and it was no easy pick. On one hand, he had thought he would talk out of his specialty. Winslow's major work had been on "the Son of Man," the Bible term that pointed to how Jesus described himself. Yet he had always found that John the Baptist was just as enigmatic. Who did John think John was? Later Christian writers, of course, created a John that was mythic and Olympian, larger than life.

Winslow had also weighed a biographical approach, a look at the life of an avid Bible student. Not his own life, of course. So he had toyed with using the story of Nick Hampton, anonymously.

He wondered about Nick. He was still on his own. What was her name? Yes. Susan McQuinn. Why don't they get together? Nick was David Hampton's second son. When he emerged as the young scholar he became Winslow's friend and academic peer, though nearly thirty years of age separated them.

Nick had turned out to be a loner, his father had told Winslow some time back. As a youth, Nicholas Peter Hampton had been the child most attentive to his father's ministry. Like "preachers' kids" everywhere, he was held to a high standard by the public. He had actually tried to fulfill the role, nearly following his dad's footsteps into the pulpit. Nick was looking around for the "truth" while his peers played sports or socialized. Of course Nick was athletic, too; he had excelled in high school track and swimming. But that had only reinforced a type of character: when the young soloist grew up he continued chasing goals and truths, leaving little time for people.

David Hampton was not surprised, then, when Nick rejected a people-oriented pastor's career, but he also felt accountable for the path his son had chosen. As a father and minister, he had led the family on its elusive quest for perfection. Nick was driven to satisfy his mother's high expectations in particular, but then saw her grow embittered with life. It had begun with a fall on the church stairs and a broken hip that wouldn't heal. Infections and complications had followed. Her last decade was full of self-absorbed illness, much of it imagined. And so, David Hampton had said, academic life suited his son Nick and Nick in turn was, for a while, the strong medicine that academia needed.

Winslow's thoughts drifted back to his speech and to where Nick was today—Nick's faith and his worldly knowledge were quarreling, something that Winslow, from experience, understood well.

If his speech were to tell a disguised Nick Hampton story, it would be about a young man who had gone the way of biblical literalism and found its ultimate contradictions. In reaction, that young man fell back on the hypercritical approach, one that dove into the texts as a relativistic sea of prejudiced editors and manipulators of the early accounts of Jesus. That, too, was a dry well. So he left it behind for archaeology, where he thought a soul could flourish. He was inspired by the Bible archaeology school of thought, an American approach that tried to support the Scriptures. That view was up against a powerful opponent, however; a secular scientific one that was sweeping the field, announcing the flaws and inaccuracies of Bible texts. Amid this torrent, as Winslow's story would go, the young man passionately wanted to find both the Christ of faith and the Jesus of history.

Winslow ultimately had swerved from the topics of Jesus and John and storytelling about a young Bible searcher. They were too complicated for middle America's Bible study at church and at home. And yet, he mused, his final title was not a great improvement: God Inspired, Human Written—Finding What is Spiritual in Ancient Literature.

It sounded dull, he thought.

Suddenly the room fell quiet.

"Our speaker today is a distinguished Bible scholar from . . . "

The mopping-up campaign in the Gulf War still dominated the news, and the radio reports made Winslow think of his own war experiences. The recollections came during a hot morning shower that could have been in the humid jungles and beachheads; he saw the Pacific War at the juncture of land and sea.

Besides catching his plane to San Francisco, Winslow had little to consider. The program with the Soviets was fairly cut-and-dried. He had no paper to deliver so he could just talk off the cuff.

Anxiety about the reunion remained, though, and that compelled him to keep thinking about old times. He had first gotten to know David Hampton when they served as chaplains in the Pacific theater. They had no special connection by creed, for he was a Presbyterian and Hampton was a Baptist. They were both seminarians upgraded to clergy by the national emergency, and then sent in behind the Marines. Their lifelong friendship was born of facing fear and death side by side. On one God-forsaken island—which was it, now?—they were pinned down for a week between the jungle's edge and the beach line.

Winslow would never forget the name of their third partner—the Roman Catholic chaplain, Joseph Sodano from Pittsburgh. Winslow visualized the tall, thin and swarthy priest, the third link in their team. They had crawled through the sand together to give soldiers last rites or solace. They had marveled at the inability of Japanese bullets to find them, at least until one smashed Sodano's shin. From a field of fire, Winslow had dragged Sodano back to a bunker. Sodano had been shipped off for treatment, pulling the trinity apart.

Winslow chuckled. It was Sodano's reading habits. In the grime of transport ships, bunkers and Quonset huts, the priest had carried three soiled books. One was in Latin. It held writings by church fathers from the second to fifth century, the time of theological ferment and battles for orthodoxy. Obsessed with the period, Sodano read them as others read novels. He tried to live in the struggling minds of those first Christian thinkers. The books were his mental playground before and after battle.

Winslow had lost track of Sodano, even though he had become bishop of a Midwest diocese in 1975. Then Sodano had made the news in 1987: "American bishop called to Rome." American know-how to fight the Vatican deficit, to inventory Vatican holdings and archives.

After the war, Winslow had remained close to Hampton. They had returned to Pacific Theological to complete degrees, be ordained, and receive calls to churches. Before long, they both had wanted to try other career paths and so had returned to school. Winslow had gone the furthest, a professorship at Princeton. While

David Hampton had not aspired to such secular erudition, his son Nick finally did.

A knock on the door ended Winslow's reminiscences. He opened it to let in the room-service man, carrying a tray of coffee and rolls and a free newspaper.

The Indiana sunshine poured in through the room's picture window, and Winslow finished his first cup of coffee on his feet. He poured another and sat back to read the newspaper, roll in hand. There was little news about the Soviet Union; all was obscured by the Gulf War aftermath. Squeezed on an inside page, next to a giant lingerie ad, he saw an article that broke the Middle East monotony.

SCHOLARS STRIP JESUS OF
WELL-KNOWN SAYINGS
Only 1 in 5 authentic, study finds

"Ah, the Jesus Colloquium." Winslow chuckled. "In the news again. I've got to hand it to them."

Since the colloquium had begun in 1985, he believed it had drawn together serious scholars. They met and voted on which sayings of Jesus were authentic.

The whole approach was not Winslow's style. It was truer to the methods of Bruce Banner, Harvard's hard-nosed biblical patrician. He was a prime mover in the colloquium. Winslow still had a soft spot for the project, though. It reminded him of a former love—the quest for the historical Jesus. In the autumn of his life, that passionate love was unrequited. He wondered if it was not going to be the same for this group. A love unreturned can hurt. And cynicism follows quickly.

In history, Winslow knew, that love had been revived, lost and found again, over and over. The quest had been given up at the turn of the century. Historians had decided there was nothing verifiable to go on; all the accounts were renditions of the early church and its theology. Then there was Jesus as autobiography—people throughout history had described Jesus in ways that reflected their time and values. In the fifth century he was a king because kings ruled. In the nineteenth century he was a rational country gentleman preaching universal love and ethics, because that was how society and its scholars viewed themselves.

Albert Schweitzer had broken that stride in 1906 when he debunked the Jesus versions to date, and then substituted his own—Jesus as an apocalyptic prophet who thought the world would end. In two decades other German scholars, led by Rudolf Bultmann, had denied the importance of the historical Jesus, saying the post-resurrection Jesus was real in faith, an existential savior who freed the personal soul from dependence and dread.

Now came the Jesus Colloquium, arguing that the effort to reconstruct Jesus historically was not futile.

But these days, as a colleague had said to Winslow, Jesus had become an egalitarian, pacifist, feminist, mystical, anti-establishment free thinker. "Jesus as a sort of 1960s American university professor," the man had said, roaring with laughter.

Winslow took a few bites of the roll and a swig of coffee before leaning back on the couch to read the article.

> SAN DIEGO—A six-year study by New Testament scholars has concluded that only 20 percent of Jesus' sayings in the Bible may have come from him.
>
> "We've come to the conclusion that Jesus spoke in parables or pithy aphorisms," said Andrew Hill, professor of New Testament at St. Louis Theological Union and former president of the Bible Literature Society.
>
> Of several hundred sayings attributed to Jesus in all four Gospels, only 31 passages were considered very likely to be from the historical Jesus.

His eyes moved over the part describing the colloquium as an effort to combat fundamentalist preachers, and then a familiar name jumped out.

> "It's been controversial, but very satisfying for us serious scholars," said Bruce Banner of Harvard.

"Banner's there all right." Winslow knew a great deal about the man. When his father had died, Banner had sought the meaning of it in an Episcopalian seminary. From there had followed years of study and scholarship. He finally had become editor of a major Bible commentary series. Banner had divorced his wife to marry a young graduate student, a whim that might have sunk less established scholars. But not Banner. Yet Winslow was not impressed by the man's character or his religious commitments, which, to his knowledge, had dried up in the hot winds of academe.

Winslow knew he was prejudiced by the way Banner had treated young Nick Hampton the year before. With the power of oversight at the *Journal of Archaeology*, Banner had forced editors to reject Nick's work. The issue was not quality, Winslow believed, but blatant disagreement. It was a great monograph, he thought. It was eminently publishable, even brilliant. All scholars speculate, and Nick had garnered evidence to do so. Hampton had used traces from Tel-Amon, signs of immigration from Egypt, to argue that the Israelites had indeed migrated into Canaan. Banner and the school behind him held that contrary to biblical "lore," the Israelites were indigenous among the Canaanites, an oppressed Semitic group that rose up against them. No migration. And no Exodus from Egypt. That view fit Banner, but not Hampton.

While he read, Winslow finished his coffee. He liked it black as sin; the way the young Hampton liked it, too.

For a lifetime, Winslow had resisted doubt about the Gospel records. Faith in its authenticity was the Bible's glue, just as theory binds together the chaotic data of science and economics. Problem was, Winslow lamented, Bible scholarship was supposed to have a spiritual life. Now it had gone. And he was evidence. His wonder and belief had slipped away.

Winslow's flight would gain him two hours and he'd be in San Francisco about noon. He glanced at the newspaper, still open on the couch, and speculated.

"What if my speech yesterday had said that only fifteen sayings of Jesus were authentic?" he asked himself. "Would they take offense?" He assumed so. But he was unsure. Sometimes, he knew, they acquiesced. Other times they resented it like hell and told you so.

In a half-hour he called down for a cab and was out the door.

*   *   *

With a thump, Bishop Joseph Sodano threw aside the latch and shoved open one of the Vatican's wood-framed windows. "Let in the spring air."

Rome's most beautiful season, in his opinion—a subject of some dispute among residents of the Eternal City.

With the papal Mass over and the pontiff's appointments completed for the day, the whole Vatican seemed to relax. And after 3 P.M. everything closed down in Rome anyway, a wonderful Italian tradition. Sodano, like other prelates who lived inside the one-hundred-eight-acre city-state on the Tiber River, could steal some rest—or get something done. He chose work, sweetened by fresh air that poured into the upstairs archive.

"The Vatican and Israel is not an easy case." When doing research alone, he often spoke to himself. "Not an easy history."

As chief archivist, Sodano knew the records on Vatican interests in the Middle East had not always favored the Jews. The Christian Arab population, the uncertain borders of Israel and Jordan, and the concern about the holy sites in the Levant had made support for a Jewish state problematic. The current pope and his foreign office were waiting for signs of movement before giving Israel full diplomatic recognition.

"It's a mixed bag on the Arabs, too." Most of the Arabs were Muslim, and for the past century the Vatican had received Christian Arab appeals for help. Sodano recalled the exact words from some very old letter in the archive: "Your Holiness, please protect us and our sacred property from the Mohammedans!"

With the end of the Gulf War, the pope wanted a reassessment of Middle East peace prospects. Sodano, as a young man, had known the joys of a war's ending. He had been sent square into the Pacific war and had come out only a few months later, returned stateside with his wounded leg. He might not have made it that far, he recalled, if it hadn't been for Jack Winslow. If it seemed as if he had forgotten the name, it was only because he was a terrible letter writer—no, he had never forgotten Winslow, though he never wrote him.

On the Mideast subject, the Vatican's secretary of state had asked for a review of old archival data. Problem is, Sodano said to himself, the church's past policies were not always so generous. Roman

Catholic interests and the privileges of its orders, especially the Franciscans, seemed paramount. Not much self-effacement here to soften Jewish and Arab mistrust.

"The Vatican could justify such a development in the Negev. But it should be consistent with our historical role." That was his creative task. If peace between Arabs and Jews was to be promoted in the desert, how should the Vatican back such an effort? On what grounds—political, historical, theological? For some Jews the Israel of Providence was defined by land. For the Holy See it was a spiritual entity, one that even Christians looked forward to in the coming of a New Jerusalem. All the United Nations wanted, as best Sodano understood it, was to get Vatican endorsement.

"It would be a precedent this pope wouldn't mind setting." He chuckled and turned away from the window, back into the darker recesses of the Vatican's vast system of stored documents.

Sodano had made his home in the upper floors of the Vatican Library for several years now, with the long-term job of taking inventory: how much was it all worth?

He loved the place, this sanctuary for a million books, a hundred thousand maps and engravings, and nearly that many manuscripts in Latin, Greek, Syriac and other ancient languages. A pope returning from exile in Avignon had created the library in the early 1400s, and by mid-century Pope Nicholas V had gathered into it all the Vatican's scattered holdings. The book stacks spread across five floors. Those printed before 1501 were locked in cages.

As he worked, Sodano said under his breath, "God bless you Cardinal Josephus Garampi." He reached across to another box of files. "Thank God that you lived in the eighteenth century."

Garampi's handiwork stood all around the bishop in the Secret Archives, a repository of private papal documents. Inside more than a hundred folio boxes, the cardinal had organized one-and-a-half million papal letters. But the good cardinal had created a monster. He had filed them in alphabetical order according to place of origin, an impossible way to build a modern cross-reference library. The re-sorting and cross-indexing of those and millions of other papal letters had centuries to go.

"Just a step at a time." Sodano picked up a yellowed paper and moved it over on the desk. It matched up with some other correspondence in which popes spoke on the status of Jerusalem.

"This is good, too." He shuffled together whatever could be found that mentioned the Negev Desert and south Jordan. "This will help . . ." But then another thought intervened.

"Jack Winslow." He sighed. He felt old. "Mary, mother of God, that was forty years ago! I wonder what Jack is doing?"

9

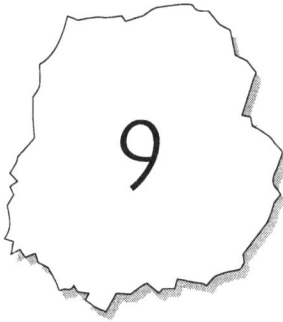

Tatyana kissed Irina on both cheeks. "Have a splendid trip," she said, giving her a third hug.

Friday had passed quickly and now they were closing the library office for the weekend. The next morning Irina would leave for the airport, bound for San Francisco.

Night had fallen by the time Irina and Tatyana said their goodbyes in the warm library space. They switched off the lamps and locked the door. With coats on, and in silence, they walked the familiar path out. Several offices were dark and the hallways dim. At the rear door they bundled into their scarfs and hats.

"Good night, Tatyana," Irina said as they stepped into the crisp air. Some clouds had been broken up by winds, revealing spots of inky dark sky like doors into an endless universe. A few stars twinkled behind the soft glare of lampposts on Nevsky Prospekt. During the White Nights of June and July, the city was out strolling. Tonight the only movements were toward shelter and home.

"Make it safely home first," Tatyana said. "And then across the world. Bring me back some sunshine, a few good pencils and some freedom."

Irina laughed behind her muffler. "Give my best to Sergei."

"He'll be home when I get there." Tatyana turned left on Nevsky Prospect to catch the bus to her home in southeast Leningrad.

Irina turned right toward Ploshchad Vosstaniya, a bustling hub of trains, buses and the subway.

"Irina."

She stopped. The call came from the dark, as if from any direction.

The footsteps came from the side. "Irina."

"Oh, Mr. Reznik." She shuddered with relief. "Are you all done tonight?"

Reznik's shock of white hair showed from under his worn cap. "Yes, yes. I wanted to say goodbye. You are very fortunate."

Irina smiled with sympathy for the old man, a real friend at the library. He had seniority in the library's special collection, which overlapped some of her work in Chinese. How many times had he tried to get permission to visit Israel, where he had grandchildren he'd never met? "And you will be fortunate someday," Irina said. "Things are changing."

"I wanted to ask if you will tell the Americans about your discovery. It's yours, you found them. Do you think that's possible?"

The materials were in Chinese, so Reznik had only learned about their content from Irina. Since early in the century, he had discovered, scholars in the West had been looking for them. Western curiosity had immense practical benefits, and that's what he wanted to teach Irina. The more the Americans want to visit the Leningrad library, the more it would prosper materially—the more freedom they would gain.

"Do you think I should?" she asked. They had decided not to approach the American photo team. Its focus was Hebrew manuscripts, of which there were plenty to draw them back.

"You should consider it." Reznik hunched his shoulders against the cold. "Don't risk getting in trouble. See what happens. Then consider it."

She agreed to be watchful and they parted, going separate ways in the dark. Irina walked past Ostrovsky Square and then the Palace of the Pioneers, once Anichkov Palace. After crossing the Fontaka River with its beautiful bridges, she hurried by the old mansion that housed local Communist Party headquarters.

Her thoughts flew to San Francisco. Already the city had become a fixation. That was where her grandfather, Giorgi Pleshnikov, had died. Walking these streets home, she felt his ghost: as a free-spirited young man, he had strutted across Leningrad when its streets still held the old Russian names.

Unlike her grandfather, Irina's father had never seen any Russian streets in freedom. He did not talk about the past and the future offered little. As a pensioner in Moscow he was now without his wife and had grown despondent. Heart trouble and arthritis, linked to winter exposure years ago, laid him up. Irina's love for him bred only melancholy, for she could no longer reach inside her father to give him happiness. To face him had become painful, one reason she had taken the job in Leningrad. Her two brothers cared for him. About six years earlier, Irina's mother had returned to Harbin, in northeast China, to live her final days devoted to the family she'd left behind. For three decades Irina's Russian father and Chinese mother had bridged two worlds which, being irreconcilable, finally had drawn them apart.

And so she reached beyond the pain of family and past her own unfathomable feelings of shame by living in her grandfather's world.

When Irina arrived at her flat, the subway ride home was like a phantom memory. It blurred into hundreds of other commutes on dreary cold nights.

She had never met Giorgi Pleshnikov, except through his diary. He had died in 1986 and the next year Irina's father had given her the memoirs, which were limited to his life as a young man. As the most literate of the three siblings, she had been asked to preserve it. Slid into its pages was an old brown photograph, a turn-of-the-century image that haunted her. The young dark Giorgi stood with other students in Moscow, their stares filled with confidence and excitement in that age of reform.

Irina's flat was on the fifth floor of a concrete high-rise. It was a single room with a separate kitchen and sink area. She shared a hallway bathroom with two other apartments.

Irina set about cooking borscht, using tomato and onion instead of beets. She peeled and cut them, placed them in a shallow pan with water and sauce, and put it on simmer. Then she went to her bookshelf and picked up the worn journal. She set aside the old photograph and turned its pages like a rare book. Irina didn't know how many times she'd read the journal, but each entry evoked the whole story once again.

Born before 1900, Giorgi Pleshnikov had spent his student years in St. Petersburg at a time of intellectual and social ferment, ending with the 1917 revolution. He had been more a thinker than actor, she surmised, as the revolutionaries and anarchists were. He had

85

married into a family of Leningrad merchants. Giorgi had passed through Marxism, then the new Russian spiritualism, and ended up with the Russophiles who wanted the soul of the East to leaven the rationalistic West. At first enthusiastic for dramatic social change, he finally had opposed the Bolshevik handiwork and in 1922 had chosen self-exile with his wife in Harbin in northeast China. Manchuria had been filling up with White Russians since 1917. As the civil war grew, it became a main sanctuary at the end of the eastern escape, the Trans-Siberian railway.

Irina's father had been born in Harbin in 1924 and at age twenty he had married a Chinese woman, possibly because of her family's nominal Christian background. The eastern sanctuary was torn open in 1945 when the Soviets occupied Manchuria after Japan's surrender. The KGB rounded up Russian nationals to send back to Moscow. Others had seen the Soviets coming in Siberia and had begun leaving China in 1938, a wave of immigration to San Francisco that included Giorgi Pleshnikov, by then a widower.

Irina's father and mother had been sent back to Russia. At first they had faced no political retribution, only the hardship of factory life near the Ural Mountains. When her parents moved to Moscow, however, they learned how long the state's memory could be when a list of political enemies was needed. As a Moscow pensioner, her father suffered the political punishment of no access to medical treatment—unless someone paid the Party thugs the right price.

Irina carefully put back the journal and stirred her bowl of soup at the small kitchen table.

Her father had given her a letter from a man who had been Giorgi Pleshnikov's friend until Pleshnikov died. That friend knew the last story and he knew the grave, which Irina wanted to visit. What was Chinese in her was moving her to remember ancestors, honor them. Her Russian side cried out to take a pilgrimage, and she had decided her grandfather's grave would be the shrine. Her inclusion on the Soviet team visiting San Francisco was a sign from God, she had decided. The last passages in Pleshnikov's diary were an allusion to the "God seekers." He had wished, his writing said, that he had truly become one of them.

The cold day had sapped her strength and the hot soup was bringing on sleep. On her way to the lamp switch, Irina stopped and gazed at the picture on her wall, an icon of Christ by Rublev.

Giorgi Pleshnikov in the old photograph and Christ in the icon—these were the two men she welcomed into her life. She knew them by written words alone, a diary and a tattered New Testament. Yet more than these, some Chinese writings about Jesus had shaped her heart and mind.

Amid the library's collection was a stack of letters, kept in two stiff leather covers tied together by a thong. They appeared to be written by a Chinese who followed Jesus. The rag paper and character styles linked them to the seventh or eighth centuries, during the T'ang emperors. For Irina, it was a puzzle. The letters spoke of others besides Jesus, people with Latin names and Greek names such as Ignatius, Peter and Clement. The Chinese writer told of what they had said, for they had heard even earlier accounts of Jesus.

Informed of her find, Victor Reznik had said they were very important. Quietly, he had tried to trace their history in the library.

During her private moments between the routine Chinese cataloguing, Irina translated parts of the letters into Russian. In laboring over the text she felt Jesus' loneliness, how he loved but was unloved. This seemed so real, so true to life.

As meditations, the sheaf of translation notes were already on her list of things to bring to San Francisco. And now she would try to follow Reznik's advice, if that was possible.

Irina undressed for bed, her soft skin rising on contact with the cold. She pulled on her gown and walked to the floor lamp. As she reached for the switch the pain returned. Sudden and sharp. It shot from her neck down the right leg. Dizzy and weak, she reached for the wall and slid to the floor. This time no numbness, like a sleeping arm or leg. A single tear trickled down her angular face, which showed not a wrinkle of pain.

As usual it came and went like lightening. Her fresh rose color returned. She stood and in the visual haze saw the icon poster. The wide-eyed Christ looked at her. She felt assured, certain that she had the strength. The room turned black and Irina went to sleep.

10

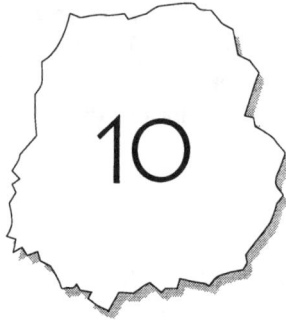

With singleness of mind, Hampton had spent the week clearing out his office and packing his belongings for shipment home. The previous night he had said farewell to Tel Aviv. Now, he departed Jerusalem on a highway that cut eastward down desolate and dusty hills. His last glimpse of Israel was to be the Judean wilderness where Jesus, the Bible said, was tempted.

"Is this my temptation?" Hampton asked himself. This intrigue in Jordan should somehow affront his professional ethics. And yet it didn't. He and Marshall were stymied by the cut brake line. They had encountered either routine mischief or a sinister plot, the latter hard to believe. During police questioning in Beersheba, Hampton had noted the old blue car as suspicious, but now that seemed extremely tenuous.

Along the road Hampton saw the medieval ruin where pilgrims believed the good Samaritan aided a beaten traveler. Maybe it was not temptation that drove him to Jordan, but a Samaritan's deed instead.

The steep road toward Jericho wriggled like a snake. Hampton put his arm up on his single suitcase to brace himself in the jostling cab. He had told the Israeli driver to step on it. The last bus from the Israeli checkpoint left for the Allenby Bridge across the Jordan River at 11 A.M. His luck had fallen in place. His visa had not expired and, through a call to the United States, he had booked a flight out of Jordan on Friday. He'd make his San Francisco appointment with the Soviets and with Susan.

Two weeks earlier Hampton had been contacted by Habib through Marshall's telephone relay system. The cryptic message had requested an appointment with Hampton at his Tel Aviv University office. Then, like clockwork, a middle-aged Arab in a business suit had arrived to present Habib's offer. Habib wished to meet Hampton in Amman and show him a manuscript fragment. The Arab answered few questions. Though he raised his eyebrows on hearing of the Beersheba incident, he had no explanation. What he had was the offer, which Hampton could decline or accept, but on the condition of secrecy. On acceptance, he would stay in Habib's confidence until "the time was right," the courier said.

"When will that be?" Hampton had asked.

"Habib Muhammad will know."

With hindsight, his colleagues would surely understand why he was bending the rules, Hampton thought. But what if a rumor mill was already turning?

Ever since his dispute with Bruce Banner over his paper on the Tel-Amon digs, Hampton had suspected the old man at Harvard was checking up on him. Only recently, though, had he heard anyone say such a thing—that Banner's old cohorts in Israel had asked about Hampton. He didn't doubt it. Like others who had worked in the Levant during the heyday of discoveries, Banner would have old friends watching the market.

If archaeologists had a Hippocratic Oath, Hampton believed, it was to avoid antiquities markets and mysterious dealers in manuscripts, and to promptly bring colleagues in on the process if the material appeared valid. Nor could he forget he had written the book that painted scholarly speculations as scurrilous. Yet proper gentlemen from Harvard or Oxford just don't stumble on antiquities in the desert. Crafty Bedouin do.

Rabin would have detected fraud, Hampton thought. Of course he would. That sinister word now entered his debate with himself. He would not fall for forgeries, that was for certain. Others had, but not him. Never.

Using the telephone relay, Hampton accepted Habib's proposal and gave Thursday, March 14, as the day of arrival in Amman. A return relay confirmed the date and added a time and place—no later than 5 P.M. at the Hotel Jordan Inter Continental.

The driver caught Hampton's eyes in the rear-view mirror.

"We're almost there. Today, not much traffic. Usually hundreds of Palestinians coming over from Jordan to visit relatives."

They were leaving the steep Judean slopes and could see the Jordan Valley and northern end of the Dead Sea already. Jericho was an Arab town, an ancient oasis that still preserved beauty and a community in its central town. Where the highway passed its outskirts on the way to Allenby, only abandoned buildings, rubbish heaps and corrugated tin shelters were seen. Long, cement-block barrackslike structures, emptied by the 1967 war, stood where a refugee camp had been. The parched land stretched from Jericho past the top of the Dead Sea to the Jordan, where river grasses finally broke the barren soil.

The compactness of the terrain between Jerusalem and Jordan fascinated Hampton. From Jericho, the Israelites had marched the twenty-three miles up the steep hills to conquer Jerusalem. When the Essene sect had fled the corruption of the Temple in Jerusalem a hundred years before Jesus was born, they had come down these same hills, turned a sharp right and a few miles away built their community. In the cliffs above they had hid their scrolls in jars.

Now the two countries, with their capitals only sixty miles apart, were linked only by the Allenby Bridge, a rickety fifty feet long, and another span farther north on the Jordan.

Israeli flags hung quietly atop the customs house, nestled at the base of steep chalky hills. Soldiers stood at two customs gates, one bustling with Arabs visiting back and forth between the West Bank and Jordan, the other for foreign travelers, mostly tourists and businessmen.

One customs officer rifled through Hampton's suitcase as the other handed back his U.S. passport. The officer, at Hampton's request, agreed to not stamp it with the Israeli seal, which might block the American's travel elsewhere in the Middle East.

"You're okay."

Hampton smiled and nodded, glad that his notes and documents—including the Negev Institute's maps—were in the mail en route to Seattle.

On the bus, the two customs lines mixed and an Israeli soldier got on board.

As the bus rattled along the quarter-mile route to the Allenby Bridge, Hampton looked back to see pyramid-shaped pillboxes of the Israeli defense line. The Jordan River was a reed-choked creek at the crossing. At a guardhouse on the Israeli side of the bridge, the bus stopped. The Israeli soldier walked off as a Jordanian soldier got on.

The Jordan Valley was hotter than Jerusalem. Sweat dripped down Hampton's back. His senses had been attuned to the melange on the first leg of the trip—the mothers, some in colorfully embroidered dresses, their fidgety children, the smell of the bread, chicken and herbs they passed around for lunch. Now he was oblivious as his mind scrolled through some reading he had done. Habib's courier had given Hampton only one piece of homework—to learn about Islam's doctrines on Jesus and about the Brotherhood, that Arab fountainhead of religious and political nationalism.

The bus, which followed a road warped by erosion, began to sway. Both the people and the bags, which hung from racks, swung like pendulums. The sun bore down, and Hampton, with a sweating brow and feeling nearly hypnotized, began to daydream in the sultry heat. Again it was Susan. He was beginning to realize that this escapade into Jordan, which could lead to open-ended entanglement, could also be a setback to their future. How could he persuade her to drop her career when he was becoming so utterly preoccupied by his own? The passion to physically unite was not the heaviest weight on their scale, at least not yet.

That morning in Philadelphia, Susan McQuinn drove up the Schuylkill River Expressway, into the thin fog of spring and the snarled traffic. At the suburban industrial park with its black glass-box offices, she parked and walked to the foyer with its four elevators, wedging her shoulder into the crowd before the mechanical door closed.

As the cocoon lifted the passengers upward, Susan meditated on the floor, a forest of pointed colored shoes and shiny black oxfords. Dark business suits hemmed her in and the scent of after-shave and perfume hung heavy in the quiet air, broken only by the electric hum of the elevator and the "ping" of the floor bells.

She hoped she wouldn't see Bill Salinger that day. He worked two floors up at Commerce Insurance, Inc. He was a nice man, handsome enough, and he'd taken to pursuing Susan—not entirely to her dislike. In fact, in recent months there had been moments when she liked nothing more.

On the fourth floor, Susan walked to her office and prepared to make two decisions. She dreaded both.

"You look nice today, Sue," said Frances, the first office worker she saw on the way in.

"Thanks, Frannie." For the past few months, Susan had felt a little self-conscious about just that. She'd grown her hair out long, done a perm on the bangs, and added a few baubles to her attire. She also had added a quarter-inch to her heels.

And she was just getting used to how the men looked at her.

"Bill already dropped by," said Frannie. "Said he'd be on the road two days and will see you Monday." Frannie's smile was as reluctant as Susan's feelings.

Susan dropped her briefcase in the small office, which had a glass wall facing the secretarial pool and a window overlooking the parking lot and a thick wood of birch and maple beyond. Then she went for a cup of coffee, her second. Back in her upholstered office chair, Susan thought more about Nick Hampton—the object of her considerations in rush-hour traffic. Both decisions centered on him. From her briefcase she pulled a handful of items.

She had just bought the plane ticket to San Francisco, a four-day junket. To mollify her industrious superiors, she had made two appointments to review textile collections in the city. It was an open-ended walk-in visit, so she could do that when Nick was occupied with the manuscript conference. And then there was her old school friend, too, a possible lunch appointment at Ghirardelli Square.

After putting aside a folder of new purchase orders, dresses from New York and Paris, Susan picked up the thick letter. She unfolded its crisp, vellum pages. The sheets were cream-colored and the letterhead, Northern Cascade—Seattle, was in elaborate black-and-gold script.

She straightened the two bends in the letter and read it again.

". . . we have been impressed by your resume and have a mid-level position open for you in purchasing. However, with your background we can almost guarantee you will be moved up to an executive level after twenty-four months."

Again Susan read the starting salary and benefits. It was only two-thirds of what she made in Philadelphia, working in the glass box by the man-made woods. This letter, however, was the only job offer she could find in the Northwest.

Of course, she thought, Seattle has a slightly lower cost of living than Philadelphia. But then her mother's health-care costs, with a move to a care unit for the elderly on the horizon, kept rising. Her mother's Social Security was only a thin buffer and the insurance claims department was beginning to contest parts of the medical coverage.

Susan sighed. She dropped the letter on her large wooden desk, which was so shiny that the reflection of the papers, the pencil holder, the gold-framed picture of her and Nick, the upright desk calendar all seemed to float an inch off the surface. She sometimes put the picture face down; she sometimes imagined it was replaced by a picture of her and Bill Salinger. Susan saw herself in the dark mirror of her desk top.

You're not getting any younger, she thought, as if addressing her reflection. But it took years to get here. Why should you leave? If Nick is patient, you may get a transfer and not lose anything.

Susan was undecided whether she would tell Nick about the Northern Cascade proposal. He might say, "So, now you can move and now we can get married."

The people at Northern Cascade said the job offer was being reserved for her, their best choice, for two months. But in summer they would broaden the search since the position needed to be filled by the fall. In a few days Susan would meet Nick in San Francisco. Would she tell him, let him help her decide, or not?

Now there was the other decision. Sex or not? She wanted to remain a virgin until they married. Her friends—most of them married now—had given it away before a wedding night. Her physical attraction to Nick was strong whenever they met, but her belief kept it in check. She was convinced that her upbringing was a kind of destiny. Traditional parents in a free-church Lutheran tradition, with its "the Bible says" morality. Three siblings, all of whom courted and married by the book. She had come to realize that she'd assumed so much about Nick that she did not even know how to date. What did men—Bill Salinger, for instance—take her to be?

She thought she understood what Nick was going through. He had always said he stayed faithful by channeling his passions into study, teaching and work—something that, he joked, Catholic priests and Sigmund Freud understand pretty well.

In San Francisco, she decided, it would be as before: commitment and then the marriage bed.

She pulled a handkerchief from her purse to absorb tears that suddenly began brimming in her eyes, and salvaged the smudging makeup. "Nick will understand," she said to herself. "He always has."

Fran tapped on the door. "I don't know why he doesn't call you on your own line." Her shoulders leaned into the office. "It's Mr. Salinger."

The Arab women on the bus began to laugh. One of them nudged Hampton, who had fallen asleep with his head drooping and bobbing down by his chest. He awoke and looked around. All the sounds and motions were the same as when he had dozed. He smiled back at the families, their dark eyes twinkling under the head scarfs and kafiyas.

The Jordanian customs house stood in a flat plain, reached by the bus after a slow, winding two-mile drive through hills carved by the Jordan River over millennia. Fortifications dotted the area and, by the inference of tank tracks, a contingent of armor hid somewhere behind the hills.

The customs guards checked baggage rigorously, but Hampton was through in fifteen minutes. At the head of the taxi line was Petra Taxi, marked yellow for private. Its driver, a bespectacled man who wore a black-and-white kafiya and smoked a cigarette, threw the head cloth over his shoulder and opened the back door in one smooth move.

As they drove out of the Jordan basin, passing the banana plantations and cultivated fields, Hampton's thoughts wandered back to his homework. Now he was in Arab lands, where ancient Christian communities had strongholds. More than in Israel, Hampton felt self-conscious that he was a Christian. The Koran viewed Muhammad as the ultimate prophet, but it esteemed "Jesus son of Mary" as a sinless prophet, even a messiah, and a restorer of true religion. But Islam taught that Christianity misinterpreted him. Muslims commonly believed, as the Koran said, that the crucifixion was an illusion or involved a substitute victim, not Jesus. And Islam rejected the idea of Jesus' divinity, just as it rejected trinitarian notions—what it called polytheism, and at worst idolatry and heresy, the unforgivable sin.

The road to Amman climbed longer and higher than the eastern ascent to Jerusalem. It curved up to the top of the massive Moab Plateau, which looked like a gigantic wall from down below. At the crest Hampton's ears popped from the altitude.

Amman stood at the plateau's highest point, and with wadis and depressions carving the land, it appeared to be spread across seven hills. After centuries of major occupations, seventy years earlier the city had devolved into a mere village. What Hampton saw now were elevations crowned with government ministries, schools, hospitals, modern gardens and villas. In the niche of one distant hill to the left of his vision, a white house with red tile roof and palm-covered veranda surveyed the city. That afternoon its owner, Ali Basherbisi, stood outside with a cool drink. He stared in the direction of the highway. Though their fates would cross, each would never know the other existed.

Amman's population was nearly a million, almost the size of Tel Aviv. It had been the stronghold of the Ammonites in 1200 B.C. and was stormed by King David, who then killed his rival, Uriah the Hittite, to take Bathsheba, his beautiful wife. With portents of its destruction, the prophets Amos, Jeremiah and Ezekiel had railed against the city's wickedness, pride and wealth.

"I can take you to the highest hill," the cab driver said. He had already noticed Hampton craning his neck for a view. "It only takes fifteen minutes and another two dinars. Then we go to the hotel."

"Sure, why not."

The cab drove up the hill and reached its oblong-shaped plateau, seventeen acres mounted by a ancient citadel fortified by Romans, Arabs and Crusaders. From here, the eye could see how the city spread across the main hilltops and as many smaller knolls and valleys between. They pulled over at the southern vista, which encompassed the old city. Directly below was the Roman amphitheater and in the middle ground, in front of the hill called Ashrafiyah, rose an extraordinary structure amid the wavering brown and gray outlines of houses and shops. The Abu Darwish Mosque, its facade in geometric patterns of white and black stone, stood crisp and stately. As a building, it impressed Hampton more than any other. He gestured and the cab moved around the high plain to the northwest side, facing Amman's affluent neighborhoods, hotels and embassies. The driver got out and Hampton followed.

"That is where we go now." The cabdriver pointed directly west.

As he peered down, Hampton suddenly realized that he had arrived and he had no strategy. He flushed with anxiety. "I shouldn't have saved this 'til last," he said to himself. "Got to think it through." He entered the cab hoping Habib would not meet him at the front door. They drove down the citadel road and along Sha'ban Street to the "third circle," site of the Jordan Inter Continental and the American Embassy. It was about 4:30 P.M. when they swung into the curved driveway of the old, eight-floor hotel.

Despite its sleek exterior, the hotel's interior had a cozy, if not threadbare, atmosphere. Habib was not in sight.

"Are you Mr. Hampton?" The hotel clerk wore a brown suit that suggested a uniform, with red epaulets, brass buttons and trim at the coat pockets. "A message came for you in mid-afternoon. An envelope."

"Yes, that's for me." He exhaled his nervousness, slowly. His worst fear was to arrive in Amman and hit a dead end, wait around helplessly and then fly out hating himself for getting sucked in. Hampton opened the envelope and withdrew a paper.

"Mr. Hampton. Welcome to Amman. Please rest and then come to the Ryabad Museum at 6 P.M. We can cover our subject in one evening. Habib Muhammad."

Hampton glanced at his watch as the clerk and cab driver fixed their eyes on him. "How far to the Ryabad Museum?"

The driver straightened up. "Half an hour."

"Can you pick me up at half past five?"

The man's head bounced up and down.

On the elevator to the fifth floor, Hampton thought up the possibilities that might face him when he met with Habib. Whatever he was going to be given, he had an hour to devise his response.

11

The Ryabad Museum specializes in artifacts excavated in Jerash, thirty miles north of Amman. Jerash was one of the ten ancient cities in the Decapolis. Once explorers began removing the rubble and sand in 1806, the ruin emerged as the world's most complete remnant of a Roman provincial city. On its south ran the Zerqa River, one of Jordan's most lush areas and the site where Jacob, on the biblical Jabbok, wrestled the angel.

The museum, a tall and slender building, was a mosaic of Turkish stonework and modern restoration. It was conspicuous in its neighborhood, squeezed between the affluent Jebel Hussein and east Nuzha, an older, poorer section of town. Hampton entered the museum by a heavy glass door with metal grating.

Now he stood in a dark narrow hallway decorated with floral tiles halfway up the wall. At the end of the corridor he saw a well-lit exhibit room. A carved limestone column, probably Roman, was in view. To his right, Hampton found a wide opening that sunk back like a dark hollow. As his eyes adapted from sunlight to darkness, he saw the pale form of someone moving against the black silhouettes of armchairs.

"You are a very reliable man, Mr. Hampton." The figure had a deep Arab voice. It reached the opening where Hampton stood. "I am Habib Muhammad." They shook hands and Habib made a slight bow.

"I was glad to receive your message at the hotel," Hampton said, also with formality. "That was when I finally felt at home in Jordan."

Habib smiled at this. Lines fanned out from his eyes as they wrinkled, like the myriad contours etched in the desert by the rains. It was a face that had been smooth and firm in youth but lined so deeply, Hampton thought, that its owner must have known great happiness and great pain. His eyebrows, like his short beard, had grayed and his kafiya was bright as snow and shone in the dim light. Habib's long cloak, broadly striped in tones of brown, fit a stout figure, slightly bent with age. In the handshake, Hampton felt a physical strength uncommon to old men.

"I hope you did not mind all the secrecy, Mr. Hampton. It may strike you as rather Byzantine compared to American ways. We have this tendency in the Middle East. But now that we are here together, how we got here does not matter."

"I reconciled myself to the process a few months ago when Travis Marshall gave me as many good reasons as I needed. Americans have their intrigues. But we don't have to deal with political and military borders and, I assume, some risk to life and limb."

Habib chuckled. "You are very understanding. I have learned that you had a small car accident, or maybe not an accident?"

"Oh, you know?"

"Word travels in our narrow circles. When we talk, you may gain some perspective. We have met here, but we will talk at another place. We can have a small supper. It's just a few blocks, if you will follow me."

"Certainly."

They walked into the museum and across the main exhibit room, which was dominated by Roman and Turkish artifacts. An exit door led into another hallway that made at least four turns, one of them past the kind of potsherd workroom Hampton knew well, and then to a back door in the museum that opened on a shaded alley. Only a few bars of light cut in and around the tall shops with balconies that lined the alley and the street ahead.

Habib lifted his hand. "This is a commercial area where many craftsmen work in their homes. The other homes are city dwellers employed at a factory or company. My friends who will host us tonight do both. The husband does maintenance work at the university and his wife and daughters make beautiful prayer rugs."

"I see." Hampton stifled the urge to ask questions. He would wait.

"I must explain a custom here. If you say how nice a particular rug is in her house, she will feel obligated to give it to you. So if you must, just compliment the entire home most generally."

"I will try to say a minimum."

They approached a door in a row of buildings, a Mideast version of row houses. When Habib knocked, a middle-aged woman with a covered head opened the door.

"*Salam aleikum.*"

After the greetings, she averted her eyes from Hampton's but directed a smile toward him as Habib motioned him forward. The smell of spices saturated the air like incense. Beyond a short hallway they passed a kitchen and entered the main room. The husband approached and he and Habib kissed each other side to side.

"We have not seen each other in several months." Habib then put his hand on Hampton's shoulder and spoke to the man, who smiled at the American and shook hands.

"Thank you for the hospitality." Hampton spoke slowly.

"We are old friends," Habib said. "His home is open to me, a home at peace with God." The man smiled when he heard Habib say *Allah*.

Ornate rugs woven in dark rich colors covered the floor and in places hung on walls. Habib and Hampton sat down in two soft chairs with wooden arms. The man left the family room and pulled the curtain closed.

"Mr. Hampton, our appointment tonight must be rather brief. But I hope it is not the last one. You have gone out of your way at some expense to yourself, so I feel I should get to the point of our meeting."

"I like a businesslike approach."

"I believe Mr. Marshall has given you some broad outlines of my work with Simon Rabin."

"General things, yes."

"And the visitor to your office, of course, mentioned the antiquity."

Hampton nodded. "He gave no details."

"The antiquity will speak for itself, Mr. Hampton, but I assume you have other questions, such as motives. Perhaps if I can explain."

"Fine." Hampton adjusted his position to listen carefully.

"I am passing this information to you, Mr. Hampton, because for my purposes a Western scholar must verify the authenticity of the materials. Simon Rabin and I wished to find someone known and competent, but also someone independent. We cannot work in the daylight yet. Too much is at stake. I am old and my powers are limited. Rabin has passed away. So we have turned to you, but with conditions. I believe I have much to offer you but in return you must offer understanding of my situation."

A small knock was heard outside the curtain. The husband brought the tea that Habib liked and some Turkish coffee for Hampton. The wife carried in a square wooden tray filled with pita bread, a pasty hummus, salad, and sliced cheese and eggs.

Habib nodded and the three exchanged brief words, a sort of *bon appetit,* Hampton assumed.

"Please, Mr. Hampton, have some while I continue."

"Thank you." Though Hampton's nerves quelled his appetite, eating was obviously the polite thing to do.

"As I was saying, we have chosen you. If you have learned about the Muslim Brotherhood as I suggested, you will understand the next part."

"Yes, I did the reading."

Habib continued as if it were not an issue. "The Muslim Brotherhood has many branches. Some are more religious than others. Many of the religious factions arose when the Israelis defeated the Arabs in 1967 and took Jerusalem. There is one today that is small but very active, especially in Jordan. It takes the name *Laylat al-Qadr,* which means 'night of power,' after the night the Koran was revealed to Muhammad. The group's motives are religious, that is, it views the triumph of Islam as essential."

Habib stopped to sip his tea and Hampton used the lull to take a bite of the pita bread he had filled with salad and hummus.

"About seven years ago al-Qadr set up an Islamic *madrasah,* a mosque school. It is in southern Jordan, in Ma'an, where there are many Bedouin."

"And Bedouin found the manuscripts?"

"Yes. We don't know how many. The members of al-Qadr are split over politics and religion and the manuscripts are caught up in this. One faction, the most religious, sees this material as a way to

100

fight Christianity. I am told some materials are about Jesus. Simon suggested they may have entered the Negev with early Christians or with desert monastics who came out of the Sinai in the fourth century. If earlier, they might have come from Jerusalem during a time of Roman siege."

Habib explained about Kalim Hasan. He was Habib's main source of information. Hasan was most closely tied to those in the Brotherhood who would use the information in a kind of holy war. "That word *jihad* is very misunderstood," Habib said. "It means the effort to live and express Islam fully, but the term was stolen by those who only preach *jihad* by the sword. I totally disagree, of course."

Habib then explained that while he and Rabin tried several means to get the materials, finally they had to convince al-Qadr that the artifacts, to be used for *jihad,* needed scholarly confirmation.

"I once had a public role in this country, but I am in the background now. Some have forgotten me. I must continue this way for the sake of the future. I cannot just intervene in Ma'an."

"You mentioned motive," Hampton said, "and that is what I don't understand. Why you and Rabin? And why, if it is an issue of a few documents, the whole Negev Institute with all its maps and the rest? I mean no offense, but one naturally asks if money or something else is involved."

"And rightly so. I can tell you one part of the motive. I want to stop the use of one religion to attack another. I believe Islam must keep its dignity. For his part, Simon Rabin was on a quest for truth. I wanted to help him." Talking about Rabin had animated every feature on Habib's face. "Perhaps I can tell you more someday about Rabin and me. Our friendship developed with unusual empathy. You see, we are both old men who lost family to war and conflict."

"I understand it was his wife and daughter."

"Yes, and for me it was my son. Neither Rabin nor I wanted revenge. But we wanted to do something, work together on a project, so the deaths would not be in vain. Now Simon is dead so I will try to complete it. This all sounds very grand, of course. But old men can think this way. The Brotherhood is divided by extremists and this is helping me obtain some of their artifacts. That is what I have for you tonight, Mr. Hampton."

Habib moved aside the tray of food and brushed the table with his sleeve. Then he reached inside his cloak and withdrew a brown envelope. From that he took a package of folded paper, put it on the table, and methodically folded back its layers. Soon the texture of old cloth appeared. He smoothed the paper flat, put the shred of cloth aside and Hampton saw two darkened papyrus fragments.

Hampton squinted. "Is there better light?"

Habib reached up and cocked the angle of the single floor lamp in the room while Hampton moved his chair closer to the table, wiping his clammy palms on his knees. Be sufficiently skeptical, he thought. And no rash judgments.

Lines of black writing crossed the papyrus scraps, yellowish-brown with age. Some scribe, maybe the writer, had produced the durable ink by mixing the black soot of burning oil with gum arabic. The fluid Hebrew script was familiar, too familiar. It appeared to be the first-century Aramaic he deciphered in his scroll work. His final redoubt, which was to reject a patent forgery, had become vulnerable. "Looks authentic." It was almost a whisper.

Habib said, "Go ahead, you may handle them."

Hampton's fingers rotated the two pieces in search of an alignment. A darkened crease at the bottom of both fragments was his first clue; next were the fiber patterns, set at the papyrus' birth in some marsh of the lower Nile or, less likely, in Lake Tiberias. They did in fact line up, a vertical rectangle and a stocking form that met in a U-shaped whole. Sentences ran from one fragment to the other. Some text had faded to nothing; some was pale gray or black. The only line Hampton could read was a phrase found in Matthew and Luke: ". . . compare the kingdom of God? It is like leaven which a woman took and hid in three measures of flour, till it was . . ."

His first wild thought was Q, the hypothetical document of Jesus sayings that informed both Luke and Matthew. Against that marvelous possibility, his mind rebelled. Discovering Q had the same odds as finding the Holy Grail. Now the language question swirled in his mind. Was this Aramaic translated from Greek, or in the original? And what was the date? He'd need a closer look and a few handbooks. Staring at the faded shapes intently, he extracted a few other words. "Very strange. One is 'Adam' and another says 'the Baptist.'"

"It's small and broken, but that is what came," Habib said. "I have been told there are larger documents."

"The script is too faded to translate. This will need infrared augmentation."

Habib shrugged, not certain what that was. "And that work you can't do here. You must take these with you to study." The ancient cloth, he noted, was found with the fragments. "I must tell you, Jordan forbids anything older than eighteenth century from leaving the country. But to avoid other problems we will draw our own guidelines. Nobody will miss these."

The fragments were easy enough to conceal, Hampton thought.

Habib folded his hands together. "Earlier I mentioned conditions and what we expected. The first is confidentiality, and second we must keep in communication. Telephone or mail is fine." He handed Hampton a piece of note paper with those details. "Take what time you need to be convinced. Then we shall talk about the next step. I must repeat, Mr. Hampton, that this cannot be publicized. We must protect certain lives. If you will simply trust me."

"I think I can relate to that." Hampton recalled chicken cages flying in a Beersheba market. Still, he requested a concession. "I'll have to approach one or two people for tests. But mainly there's a friend I want to get advice from, a Bible scholar named Jack Winslow. I know he can keep a secret."

"Do what you must. The future of this project relies on your prudence. What we have here in front of us is very little. If nothing else appears, they can be explained away. I think you understand my meaning."

As Habib folded the cloth and paper around the fragments, Hampton told him that ancient remnants can only be understood by their context. Where were the fragments found and by whom? Habib slid the thin package into an envelope and responded that the Bedouin were the context. They number forty thousand in Jordan in six main tribes, living in camps and settlements in the south, mainly east of the Desert Highway. There are more Bedouin in Israel. Before the modern states of Jordan and Israel they wandered back and forth, and some still do. From the Jordan side that means traveling down the ravines of the red hills of Edom into the flat Arava Valley, a ten- to forty-mile crossing on sand and gravel to the foothills of Israel.

"I am told that members of Jordan's al Huweitat tribe have the antiquities," Habib said, holding up the envelope. "Where this was found, which side of the border, I don't yet know."

The envelope was too large for the front pockets of Hampton's long-sleeved shirt, so he kept it in hand.

"No one will notice," Habib said. He projected his voice across the house, drawing the owner through the curtain.

"*Daimah*."

The man bowed slightly. "*Saltain aba Habib*."

Hampton followed Habib when he stood up and walked into the hallway toward the front door.

"Mr. Hampton, it is barely dark and you can catch a taxi if you turn left and go to the second corner. I will stay here for a while longer."

Hampton wasn't sure if he expected an escort back. He wondered if Habib fathomed what was transpiring. "Should I call you tomorrow morning before I leave, in case you have any more plans to outline?"

Habib chuckled. "If you were an American businessman in Jordan, Mr. Hampton, you would know we don't plan too far in the future. Some have called it the fatalistic aspect of Islamic culture. Whatever the case, the future, even tomorrow, is in God's hands and He will do the planning."

"I see. That is a reverent view of the situation."

"Perhaps. It is the way we think and I hope you can oblige it."

Hampton nodded. "We will talk again soon, I hope."

"Yes, I hope so, too." Habib put his large hand on Hampton's shoulder.

The woman scurried up the hallway and, speaking a few words, held out a necklace, a thin chain with a tiny silver object.

"The Hand of Fatima," Habib said. "She wants to give your wife a gift."

Hampton received it with a bow and smile, but did not explain the reality.

Outside the night was warm with a slight breeze. As Hampton walked by houses, he heard the lilt of Arabic voices weaving an exotic tapestry that blanketed the neighborhood. Each step across the cobblestones seemed like several minutes, as if his short walk to a taxi was time-warped into an hour's worth of thinking. A strange peace had settled upon him. On the beach the night of the missile attack, he had felt that he could forget that God existed and get on with life just as well. The God he had been taught of since he was a child, the God who had rewarded Jacob's struggle at the Jabbok, that was the God who had become a mere idea for him, an abstract symbol filtered by his intellect. No one could pray to an idea, which in fact he hadn't for perhaps years. Now the little fragments of text were changing that. He felt thrust up against a universe that held a secret, many secrets, to be disclosed. Could the scraps he held, with their wretched scribble, end up being a window on the eternal Creator of the universe? For once in his adult life he felt as if he had soared upward, had become significant in a bigger scheme.

He caught himself smiling as he had when first riding his very own bicycle as a boy. With an uncontrollable beam on his face he had pedaled that bright red object of pride and freedom down a tree-lined street in St. Louis. In the Amman alley he fought his grin.

Taxis stood at the corner just as Habib had said. "Inter Continental?" Hampton asked the first one in line.

"Ah, American?" The driver smiled and opened the door. "Please."

In fifteen minutes Hampton was back in the hotel lobby. He asked the clerk for a wake-up call at 7 A.M. Upstairs in his room, he opened the package again to examine the fragments.

Papyrus, for him at least, had always sparked reveries of wondrous places and times. Grown for centuries in the marshes of the Nile Delta, the triangular stalks with feathery tops were harvested on a scale that rivaled food production in the ancient world. Now he thought of Alan Fields, an associate in Berkeley who was tied with the university's papyrus collection. He could do the infrared photos, Hampton thought. Fields had written a chapter on papyrology in a collection Hampton had edited. The stalk's soft pith—onion-thin concentric layers—was peeled into strips and lined up vertically. Then more strips were laid across horizontally to make the paper's smooth white surface. In a press, the natural juices bonded the two layers and it dried. Ancient papyrus had been broken and smashed down through the careless centuries, but never was it found splitting apart.

Hampton looked at the fabric Habib had given him and noticed that several specks of papyrus had stuck to it. A larger one had two minute strokes of ink on it. "Great," he said under his breath. He had put aside the thought of a Carbon 14 test because that would destroy part of the two fragments, which were filled with text. One of the specks, however, was the size of a nickel and it clearly had broken off the fragment. "We've got some test material." And that test, he thought, could be finagled by Travis Marshall at Oxford's lab.

Hampton had ended his brief study at Oxford University a few years before it had set up the Radiocarbon Accelerator facility. With ten million electron volts, the machine propels carbon atoms of a burned sample through a magnetic field to separate out the radioactive Carbon 14. Everything from a human bone to a papyrus reed ingests Carbon 14 from the atmosphere. At their deaths the Carbon 14 begins a rate of decay, a clock that tells at what time in history the organic life stopped breathing.

The beauty of the accelerator technique was its scale. Less than a milligram of sample was needed to burn into carbon—postage-stamp size, just about as much as a priceless parchment or papyrus could spare. At Tel-Amon, Hampton recalled, they had to burn a half-pound to two pounds of ancient bone or wood or grain to get enough carbon for a radioactivity reading.

Hampton spent the evening wondering if the papyrus shred stuck to the fabric was enough for a test. He took a hot shower to throw off the unnatural exhilaration, and tried to get a good sleep. In an hour he was up swallowing two sleeping pills.

In the morning, the ringing wake-up call brought him straight up. Eyes closed, he recalled where he was and then caught the fading sense of a dream. Susan McQuinn was the visage but other details dropped away rapidly. She was somewhere far off. They had argued about the distance. Someone's eyes, Asian eyes, were in there. Habib's eyes? His grasp slipped so he got up, shaved, dressed, and snapped his bag together. He patted the envelope, which rested in the inside pocket of his gray sport coat.

The morning passed like a blur. Hampton found Gate 7 in the airport and took an end seat in the lounge, his view out the window, his feet on the thick carpet, and his back to the tile floor that stretched across the lobby and down hallways. The wall clock, bearing the seal of the king-pilot who had founded Royal Jordanian Airlines, said 8:30. The passengers bound for Los Angeles were mostly businessmen, Arab and Western. A few young travelers sat about and at least four families waited, one a menage of restless children, noisy and deaf to the mother's commands.

From behind him, however, the clip sound was plain. Footsteps hurrying across the gray and white squares of tile. Pilots strutting to their posts, Hampton thought, except that the rhythm converged upon him. With a glance back, he took in two airport officials escorting a man in a suit, a suit he'd seen somewhere before. The thought was chilling. "You didn't, Habib," Hampton whispered. "Why would you do it?" Hampton felt for the envelope and wondered where to hide it. He was about to saunter off when the galloping feet scuffed the rug, falling silent.

"Nicholas Hampton?" Without a smile, the suited man stared straight at him. "Are you Mr. Hampton?" Hampton turned to see six eyes fixed upon him.

"Yes. How do you know?"

"Sir, you left your wallet in the hotel room. I am glad we found you."

Hampton swung his right hand back to feel the absence. His whole body relaxed, suddenly, sending a twitch up his neck.

"Thank you very much. I obviously wasn't thinking this morning."

"We want you to leave Jordan with a good memory, especially of the Inter Continental. This is delivered at the direction of our manager, Abdul Hussein."

"Tell him I will surely stay at the hotel again."

The man bowed slightly and the stiff airport guards smiled. They turned and clattered back across the tile floor.

Hampton sank in his seat. A deep breath rose involuntarily. A little girl with large, glistening brown eyes, had climbed into the seat next to him to watch.

He whispered, "Your eyes are beautiful."

12

Irina Pleshnikov came from the Russian flatlands. Leningrad was a renovated swamp, Moscow a rising plain.

She'd never seen a view like the one she now beheld from Telegraph Hill, which rose out of the North Beach neighborhood three hundred feet above San Francisco. The morning fog rolled down the bay, clinging to the water and leaving the mountains on either side to stand out like bright green domes in the low sunlight.

Irina caught her breath when she finally saw them, the Golden Gate's two giant orange shoulders rising high above the low soupy clouds.

The Soviet delegation stayed in a small hotel, the Commodore, near the Soviet consulate. With a free hour before the day's schedule began, some of them took the consulate's offer of a short taxi drive to a morning vista. Among them were two interpreters, both KGB agents enjoying the new benign approach to chaperon duty. And then there was Boris, a big man with an ill-defined academic title, but a clear Kremlin-assigned role—to watch for possible defections.

The entire Soviet delegation would later drive to the Japan Center, a five-acre complex on the slopes of Pacific Heights. They would gather there in a conference room for a two-and-a-half day session. A third day in the middle was for sightseeing.

"Such a strange and lovely city," Irina said. With those words she looked past her compatriot, the director of preservation at the Lenin Library in Moscow. "They say many Russians live here."

His reply was low and bitter. "And they have few kind words

for our country. Did you see the Russian-language newspaper? It is so hateful toward Mikhail Sergeivich."

"They have bad memories. Can we blame them? Even Gorbachev has talked about the terrible past."

The man from the Lenin Library recalled the scene a few days earlier in Moscow. Half a million demonstrators had marched across Manezh Square and along the Kremlin wall. "Resign! Resign!" Their chants had exploded right in front of Mikhail Gorbachev and his Communist Party comrades. Protests had arisen in fourteen other cities. It was the nation's largest demonstration since 1917. The memory was distressing him still. "It is true the past is not easily forgotten, but . . ."

"Cheer up," Irina said, penetrating his gloom. "We have much to learn in the next days."

"Yes, you are right."

The shrill command of the group leader drew their attention up the hill. "Let's go back. Breakfast is waiting. We have to leave at 9 A.M."

Across town at the Lombard Hotel, Nick Hampton began his morning with black coffee. The jet lag and dreary flights from Amman to Los Angeles to San Francisco had exhausted him. Over his toast and eggs, his increasingly alert mind began to outline a plan, especially how he'd accommodate Susan. She was to arrive that night. He had settled one matter promptly by calling Travis Marshall, who would expect an Air Express package containing the cloth and papyrus samples.

Hampton would see Winslow at the conference, but he already knew they'd both use the free day, when the Soviets toured, for business in Berkeley. Could he take Susan along? Hampton wondered. She could see the campus or maybe the hilltop park, with its view of the bay. She likes Jack, he thought. Maybe she could go with him to the reunion for a while. The perfect setting to talk about their future was obviously not easy to find. "She'll understand," he said to himself.

An hour later, Hampton found Jack Winslow in the wide sunny lobby of the Intercultural Hall at the Japan Center. He was smoking his pipe and talking to two heavy men in dark ill-fitting suits.

"Jack!" Hampton waved. The attire of the two Soviets reminded Hampton of his own disheveled appearance.

"Nicholas, you're here."

They grabbed each other's hands and wrists, squeezing in manly affection. Winslow smiled wide. "You've made quite a journey."

"Where are you staying?"

"I'm at the York, about seven blocks from here. They've sure got us spread out. I rented a car at the airport."

Winslow's large forehead gave him a young and brainy countenance despite the thinning gray hair. His eyebrows were light, making the face bright and open. A blustery red hung on the old man's cheeks and his blue eyes were steady and clear.

The crowd grew and eventually flowed into a conference room, where it mingled around a table of refreshments and a long table with earphones and dials at each seat. Behind a podium hung a canvas banner with stars and stripes and hammer and sickle: American-Soviet Ancient Manuscript Symposium.

Hampton knew this was no time to break the news to Winslow, but he nudged him to leave a hint. "Jack. When you have an hour free I've got some news from Israel."

"Why don't we use lunchtime. What is it?"

"Nothing major. Let's wait for a little privacy."

They perused the schedule, printed in English and Cyrillic.

Winslow pointed at the document. "See how I managed to avoid giving a talk?"

Though invited as an observer, Hampton had anticipated the symposium with some delight. Now it seemed anticlimactic. Still, he hoped to make some fruitful connections. When he had lost his ground, and his tenure, in Baltimore, a reason had been his lack of a prestigious constituency, a plum for the university. He surveyed the gathering with all of this in mind. It was mostly men—bright but stooped older men, like he'd become one day. The Yale archivist and another female professor from Berkeley, with a demure feminine style, broke the male monopoly. Two of the Soviets were women, one older with severely tied-back hair and the other young. She had a thin face, thick reddish hair, and wore round black-rimmed glasses. The Soviet delegation had several young assistants. Then Hampton noticed her.

"She looks Asian," he said to himself. Was she with the facilities or the Soviets?

Irina Pleshnikov stood on the Soviet side of the table, a large binder in her hands and document cases on a chair behind her. She had a slight smile on her face. It was the kind that hides discomfort. She made sharp turns with her head, acute to actions all around the room. When her shiny black hair swung aside, Hampton saw her downcast eyes. They were uncertain about where to fix themselves. Then they caught his and seemed to sparkle. Penetrating. They fluttered quickly away. Then at him again.

Those are the eyes, he thought, averting his own. From the dream . . . maybe? Casually, he turned toward her and, his mouth to the coffee cup, lifted his eyes again. Her bright sweater, with blues and yellows, did not resemble Soviet apparel. She did not look Soviet herself.

Somebody tapped a water glass with a spoon and everybody moved to their chairs. The session went on for a few hours. The image of Irina's patient and sweet face, angular and silky like an Asian's but pale like a Russian's, burned into Hampton's mind. She probably thought he was staring at her, he mused. Was it his imagination that she seemed to be looking back? Then the lights dimmed. When the slide presentation ended, the room abruptly went aglow. Eyes squinted. Lunch came next. With a final glance at Irina, Hampton walked over to Winslow amid the stretching men. He espied his watch, raising an eyebrow.

"Shall we?"

Winslow nodded toward the hallway. "Let's go."

They strode down the concourse and burst through the glass doors into the cool sunny air outside. After two failed attempts with a match in the breeze, Winslow lit his pipe and they continued up the hill, their shoes striking the sidewalk evenly. At the diner, Winslow sat across from Hampton in the upholstered red booth.

"This is going to seem a little Kafkaesque," Hampton said. "I'll give it to you straight."

"Good." Winslow tapped his pipe clean.

"It's also in strict confidence, Jack. Is that acceptable?"

"It depends." Winslow grinned. "No, really. It's between you and me."

"In Jordan I was given two papyrus fragments. They're in Aramaic and appear to be first century. They seem to have Gospel sayings."

"That's great, Nick." Winslow reserved judgment and responded

111

in a paternal tone. "How on earth did . . . well, like you said, Kafkaesque."

Yes, Winslow had heard of Rabin, vaguely of Travis Marshall, but not of Habib Muhammad. The Brotherhood and Bedouin of south Jordan were alien subjects, but regarding archaeology he knew the history of other discoveries.

"I can't believe I'm carrying it with me." Hampton slipped his hand into a breast pocket and took out a stiff leather picture holder, the one that held Susan's portrait. He withdrew a paper wrapper, unfolded it, and laid the fragments in front of Winslow.

"I just hope it's not fake, Nick," Winslow said.

"That's why I came to you. I'm going to need a little wise counsel. I promised Habib I wouldn't tell anybody but you. He wants secrecy. On that condition we get more. It's not coming from a nice group in the Muslim women's auxiliary."

The waitress arrived with two plates but was thwarted by the papers spread on the table. Hampton apologized, carefully scooping them up. To the sound of plates clinking on the table, he slipped the package back into its case. He told Winslow of the cloth and papyrus samples, the hoped-for Carbon 14 test, and his plan to Air Express them to London in a day or two.

"I don't want to sound skeptical," Winslow said. "But I guess I naturally start that way." He didn't want to say he was old with experience and Nick was young. "But, yes, let's get to the bottom of it."

"Presuming it's real, this looks like Bible material," Hampton said. "It could be quite controversial."

Amid bites of lunch, Winslow gave advice. "Every find has its excitement. But it's best not to jump to the gun. Not much has shaken Christianity, as an institution at least. You know the old saw—if Jesus himself came back he'd have a hard time convincing the churches." Winslow saw in his mind the crowd he had addressed in Indianapolis. "I don't want to sound preachy, but . . ."

Hampton sat quietly, affirming in his face what Winslow said.

"There's been a lot of agitation in the United States since you left. The Jesus Colloquium and then the fundamentalists. Harlan Wesley Stockwood, the Texas preacher, has launched a crusade and it's gaining a lot of momentum."

When Hampton heard the name Stockwood he thought of the

112

man's son-in-law, Matthew Cummings, the Baptist missionary in Israel. Cummings had called Hampton again, just before he left Tel Aviv, to say he was just checking in. Just interested in archaeology.

"So you think this is worth pursuing?" Hampton asked, putting his finger on the small case holding the fragments.

"Yes, I think so."

Hampton felt relieved so he explained his next quandary. Susan would arrive at the airport that evening. Winslow had his class reunion the next day in Berkeley, and that's where Alan Fields had the infrared camera.

Simple solution, Winslow said. They'd drive over in his rental car.

"So my circle of secrecy is already widening," Hampton said. From Marshall to Winslow to Fields, and who next? "That word 'secret' bothers me."

"Me too."

Being clandestine, they both knew, was what had gotten some of the the Dead Sea Scrolls editors in trouble.

"I believe in the principle of informing peers . . ." Hampton gave his statement like a judge being sworn to the bench. Yet he was still jarred every time the rampaging jeep flashed across his mind. "But I was told lives are at risk and I made a promise."

"Well, a promise is principle, too, I suppose," Winslow said. "Don't worry. You're at an early stage so just proceed carefully."

During the afternoon symposium, Hampton's mind darted about. He had to leave early to reach the airport. About a half-hour by cab, he recalled. Irina, sitting at different locations, continued to draw his attention. By the time he stood and left, his mood had changed dramatically. For the first time in years he felt as if he were on a mission. The assurances of Winslow helped, yet that was only part of it. A personal zeal that he had thought was dead had been resuscitated. The adrenaline surge, however, was all mind and nerves, not his emotions. An hour later, as a taxi carried him to the airport, he realized that his new vigor had dulled, even nullified, his longing for Susan. They seemed to always fall into bad timing, and this was turning out no differently, thanks to him.

In their talks and letters leading up to the trip, Susan had seemed to be building some anticipation. Normal enough, Nick had thought, for he had replied with a similar promissory tone; he was on the verge, he had thought, of making a marriage proposal. Despite his curiosity, he did not expect what he saw when she arrived. Susan—he thought it was her—came up the arrival ramp with a swagger, her only piece of luggage in her hand. He had planned to say, "You haven't changed a bit." But she had, dramatically.

Her hair, long and thick, was tied in a teasing ponytail. The uncertain steps came from her high heels, black and shiny. The dress, a bright red, was pinched at her waist and the shoulders broad. The V-neck showed her creamy collarbone and the hem length revealed, in ample inches, her knees in sheer stockings. Hampton's eyes were not fast enough to take in all the details—the gold earrings, the fluffed bangs, the gold bracelets.

"Susan, you look great. You've changed."

"I told you but you just didn't believe me." Her eyes—he couldn't tell if they had extra makeup—fluttered above her sideways smile.

She still had that strong will, though, and from behind the new exterior Hampton felt it coming through already. They hugged, kissed perfunctorily, and stalled awhile longer to eye one another.

The physical contact released something in Susan's metabolism, and her memory filled with a welter of bygone passions and unrequited longings. She could get so attracted to Nick, physically. "I worried about you so much during the war," she said, repeating her lament in the letters of those days. "You're safely home."

When such long periods separated them the contact was a muted thrill. But each of them seemed to wait for the other to give in—to say, in so many words, "I'll follow you anywhere." San Francisco hadn't changed that tacit routine.

The cab seemed to take off like an airplane.

With his prompting, she brought him up to date. Her department store company's quarterly earnings had just come in from the holidays, and it had been a good year despite the slowing economy. A line of clothing and a brand of household fixtures in a country style had done well—and she been the one who had chosen them. Her reward was a bonus. That was good, she said, because her brother and two sisters were considering moving their mother into a convalescent home, one with a personal touch, of course, but rather expensive too. It had emergency care across the grounds, a complex in an arboreal section of northern St. Louis. Susan said she was stopping in St. Louis on the way back; they had to persuade her mother to leave the old house. As the baby of the family she still had a special door to her mother's heart, widened by the years she had stood by the woman's side to care for a dying father.

Hampton was a little uncomfortable. He knew the right attitude toward ailing family, but it was not coming spontaneously now. That wellspring of his emotions had dried up somewhere in the heat and dust of Tel-Amon.

The cab left Bayshore Freeway and swooped up the elevated Central Skyway. They passed dark glass buildings, mirror windows and views down streets lit in yellows, reds and blues like a carnival. The taxi came back to earth near the Opera House and Civic Center and then headed up Van Ness to the Lombard Hotel.

"Nick, you look so tired out."

"It was a long trip." He told her of his travels, and then said the wrong thing.

"Jordan?" she asked. "What took you to Jordan?"

With his promise to Habib ringing in his ears, he fabricated a story, something about Roman digs up in Jerash. It suddenly occurred to him to reach into his pocket. He had a present from Jordan, a necklace wrapped in tissue paper. "Here, this is the Hand of Fatima from Jordan. She was Muhammad's daughter."

Susan let it drape from her thumb and forefinger, looking closely at the tiny silver amulet. She kissed him. "It's pretty."

Nick said, "If you're Jewish it's the hand of Esther. If you're Christian it's the hand of Mary. It's actually from pagan times in Jericho. Either way it's good luck."

Susan drew closer and brushed back the hair falling on Nick's forehead, like a sculptor working clay. She liked to see the fullness of his face. It retained the bronze roughness and pale wrinkle lines of his Mideast adventure. The hair had been bleached at some ends, reddened at others.

Nick savored her closeness, her animal presence. He watched Susan untie her ponytail. Her soft bangs fell forward and her hair, smelling of a fresh conditioner, flowed about her shoulders. The nape of her neck was soft and pale. Her wide eyes pulled at him. Now to break the news, he thought.

"You know, Susan, I was meaning for this to be a much more relaxed time . . ."

Her thin mouth kept its modest smile. The lips were delicate

115

and perfectly symmetrical. If they frowned, he knew, her mouth would become a finely drawn wrinkled line. But it was her eyes, pulled wide by gossamer muscles that seemed attached to her emotions, that always revealed her inner condition.

She said, "We'll find time. I'm off until Tuesday. That gives us two days." Susan was not sure what this meant in detail, not if she wanted time in San Francisco for the appointments she had tentatively lined up.

Nick said, "Problem is, something happened just before I left Israel. I've got to work it out while I'm in the bay area. It just means a mixed schedule."

"Oh." Her eyes began telling a story. As if she knew that, Susan turned her gaze toward the window. "What happened?"

Hampton couldn't be sure if Susan was hurt, surprised or indifferent. So his answer was roundabout. "The Tel-Amon report is going okay, but my sabbatical ends a month before fall classes because I agreed to teach a crash course."

"Uh-huh." Her murmur sounded sympathetic. "I know you're busy. That's you in a nutshell."

Hampton plunged into his white lie. "But then in Israel I was asked to handle some translations . . . a few scraps of the Dead Sea Scrolls. They need to be photographed while I'm here. In Berkeley. Alan Fields, you helped me edit his . . ."

"The papyrus man?"

"Your memory's a gem." Nick pressed his shoulder against hers and wondered: maybe she really did have interest in his arcane work. "I'm sorry it's all coming right now, this weekend."

As a grand and generous gesture, he had thought of raising the issue of marriage. He almost told her that the Hand of Fatima was given to him for "his wife." Talk of marriage would elevate their brief time together to a new tier of meaning. No, he decided, it might go too far and dominate everything. Better to keep the mood light, he thought, but still he asked Susan about her future. "Do you see any openings for a transfer?"

"Unfortunately . . ." Susan sighed. The words Northern Cascade, the firm offering her a lower-level job in Seattle, shouted in her mind. "It's not foreseeable," she said. "The company's just not growing in the Northwest. Someday I suppose it will. Someday I may just get tired and quit. Work isn't everything, you know. Part of the reason

I go on is to support mother." Susan thought, should I tell him about Northern Cascade or not? Now? Ever? She could not take the leap. It would complicate their emotional badminton game with a new set of rules: she could go to Seattle right now, if she were willing to give up everything for him. "I've actually thought of quitting," she said. "Honestly. Just pack up and fly to Seattle."

Hampton laughed with pleasure. This was how they'd consoled each other for a few years. To trigger a real break, he would have to downright propose, draw the line in the sand and say: "Quit and be my wife." This San Francisco rendezvous was not going to be it, however. A few days earlier he had become, once again, a moving target. How could she even take aim? He might have to travel. Israel. Jordan. Who knows, even England. How things had changed since Israel.

At the Lombard Hotel, he followed Susan and carried her bag. Her stride was supple, her hips round and her waist pinched. But even this seemed businesslike. When he had missed her from across the globe, she was more than her physical presence seemed to transmit now. Neither the right words nor the right plan of seduction came to him, so he waited.

On the drive over, their glances at each other had asked and answered the question already. Again, her eyes revealed all: a sympathy for him but also a willful Susan-type declaration. He should declare his marriage intentions, seal it in the normal formality of a wedding, and then they could sleep together. Commitment and then the marriage bed. That was going to be the tone of their weekend.

As Nick stood by, Susan finished unpacking in her room and then turned to him, her arms hanging at her sides. Her entire posture seemed to say, "I'm very sorry." Nick, hands in his pockets, shrugged back. That gesture said: "I can't force you."

She was having a harder time than ever projecting her sorry look. "Nicholas, I want the same thing . . . but it's just not . . . you've been away a long time. We should enjoy our time together."

They tried that for the next hour, Nick with shoes off and feet up and Susan cushioned with pillows on the bed, her feet nestled under her thighs. They talked of family and of plans, of Jack Winslow and the city.

Then, having sorted out the flow of time, Susan decided on what she had to do. It was a long way to San Francisco. "I do have a few appointments I wanted to make in the city," she said. "One design house in particular is really on the front edge of the market."

Hampton listened, his face impassive, his mind deferential. He was doing the same thing to her, after all.

Susan also wanted to call an old business-school friend, and that might lead to a luncheon. But she would definitely have time for the trip to Berkeley.

The night grew late and Nick initiated the close, though he wished he could offer more than pleasantries. "It'll be nice weather to cross the bay tomorrow."

They stood and held each other around the waist. Susan felt her metabolism rise again, and she came the closest so far that day to throwing virginity to the wind. Hampton kissed his school-days sweetheart and mustered a smile.

She walked with him to the door. "Goodnight," she said. As Hampton reached the stairwell that led down a flight to his room, he felt as empty as the dim hallway.

The next morning was Saturday, and Alan Fields answered the door to his Berkeley apartment wearing a jeweler's magnifying glass strapped on his head.

"Excuse the hardware, Nick." Fields smirked. "I get my best work done at home. Dull, dull, dull." He let out a sardonic laugh.

Fields was examining photo reconstructions of tiny Dead Sea Scrolls fragments sent to him by a Midwest scholar who had the actual job to do. The real things were holed up in Jerusalem. Many of the scrolls, and indeed other types of old manuscripts, had faded beyond recognition. Those parts were photographed with infrared film, which picked up the carbon residue in both the seen and unseen ink. Other stains were blanched. The film negative produced a sharply contrasting black-and-white print that, when examined under a magnifying glass, revealed the smallest nuance, serif, stroke or punctuation on a letter. That small detail might be the key to translation or matching it to another fragment.

Fields was a marriageable bachelor a little older than Hampton. He kept a clean and simple house. On the wall hung a green-and-silver art deco poster of giant papyrus stalks. Elsewhere were reproductions of Egyptian paintings of papyrus boats watched by jackal-headed gods, or of reed harvesting. A scribe from a medieval illustration bent over a long papyrus scroll. Fields the papyrus man, Hampton mused. Their chemistry included trust, so Hampton gave his co-conspirator the straight facts.

Fields inspected the pitiful scraps. "I'll shoot it for you, sure. But I can't help but think it's a fake. Even with script and paper dates, it's hard to dismiss forgery. I've seen too many. Just my healthy skepticism, Nick."

Hampton shrugged. "No problem. How long to shoot and develop?"

"Tomorrow afternoon's the soonest. Well, maybe very late tonight. Or I could call the director at home and say we found the diary of Jesus Christ. He'd get out of bed to unlock the door for us."

"No thanks, Al. I'm serious about the secrecy. These Middle East intrigues are new to me and I don't want anyone getting . . ."

"Hey friend, I'm with you. I was only joking."

Hampton said he would drive back the next night, after Susan's flight left. She had gone up to Holy Hill, north of the campus, where Winslow was having lunch with the old boys of Theological Union. Under tall shade trees and on winding streets, a half-dozen theological schools had made their homes. Even for Susan, it was a nice place to sightsee. A few vistas opened up on the San Francisco Bay.

The drive back was cheerful enough. As far as Winslow could tell, Nick and Susan liked being with each other, and he tried to add something, a warm glance, a spry comment. With a certain perspective of age, he saw their relationship as a form of security, not a bad or weak kind. Rather the comfort of constancy, one that avoided passions. If he had said that out loud Nick and Susan might have agreed. They didn't have big fights and arguments, but neither did they resolve their romantic stalemate. They presumed that time would do that, with nothing to lose.

The following morning, Susan encouraged Hampton and Winslow to make the most of their conference. She had appointments beginning at lunchtime, and she'd tell them later what she saw during her morning sightseeing. "You boys don't worry about me," she said outside the Japan Center. "I've got just the tour for the single businesswoman. In fact, it only works when you're alone." She laughed.

119

In the day she'd been with him, Susan's ravishing new looks had lost some of their dramatic effect on Nick's senses. The Susan he had known for so long had come through. His confident, independent girl. He waved. "Enjoy."

"It starts right down there with a trolley car." Susan pointed with her thin graceful hand. "Bye." Her ponytail swayed in the breeze.

Winslow was making a beeline down the wide plush corridor to the men's room. "There are some things a man's got to do for himself, Jack." Hampton grinned as he headed in the other direction for an alcove with elevators.

"Mr. Hampton?" The soft accented voice came from behind. "Excuse me."

Hampton swung around and saw Irina Pleshnikov standing there with her hands held formally in front of her. She was stunning.

"Yes, hello."

"My name is Irina Pleshnikov. I think you saw me assisting with the Soviet delegation."

"Yes, I remember well. You attended all of the sessions. Was the sightseeing good yesterday?"

"It was wonderful." Irina's smile made her almond eyes turn upward at the corners. To Hampton, they transmitted a kind of wisdom absent in a round Western eye.

"I was wondering . . ."—her reluctance thundered—". . . if I can ask you a favor. I must explain."

"Uh, let's see." Hampton's watch said the morning session would begin in fifteen minutes. Down the hall he saw a gardenlike porch that turned around a corner and out of sight. "Why don't we talk over there."

"Yes, private is better."

As the sun shone through the tinted glass and dappled the tropical plants in the lounge, the Russian librarian and American archaeologist talked. Hampton was impressed at her command of English; he told her so. Irina needed to reach a Russian emigre in the city's Richmond District, according to an address she showed Hampton.

"I am here to help the delegation." Her eyes wandered down, and she seemed to repeat from memorized lines, at least for the next sentence. "Peace between our countries is important. But personally,

120

my ambition is to see my grandfather's grave. He died here. This old friend knows where it is."

"Isn't that something your superiors can help you with?"

"I haven't mentioned it to them. I am so fortunate to come. I don't want to make it seem I am taking advantage."

"I think I understand." Hampton presumed the Soviet Union was the same, despite the era of *glasnost*. He'd met Soviets before. They were cautious at best, paranoid at worst. "You'd like me to take you there?"

"That would be wonderful. If you could, I . . . if you care to you can invite me and ask my supervisor, Alexi Yensky. We can tell the truth about where we are going, of course."

"The important thing is for me to ask, though, so you don't appear as if taking advantage . . . ?"

"Oh, you understand!" Her eyes sparkled. "Thank you." For all the strain of a dozen plots coming together on the stage of his life at once, Hampton was delighted.

Yensky sized up Hampton with his eyebrows furrowed, pondering his suggestion. Irina wanted to see the Richmond District, a Russian colony. Hampton knew it well, he lied, and then he recited a hackneyed diplomatic slogan. "In the interest of peace, friendship and cultural exchange, of course."

Yensky's assistant translated. "Ah," Yensky said, raising the trademark eyebrows. He consented with little trouble. The lunch break was the best for it. As a Soviet citizen, Yensky said, Irina was a valuable librarian and was being entrusted into Hampton's hands.

"Do you know the Russian neighborhood well?" This had excited Irina, but she had saved the question for their cruise up and down the city hills in the back seat of the cab.

Seeing her joy, Hampton regretted his fib. "No. I just thought that would help get permission. A little white lie." They were mounting up this weekend, he thought. "Tell me about yourself."

Irina described her work at the library. Her interest in religion came through immediately, as did her knowledge of texts on that subject.

"And your grandfather?"

"He is Giorgi Pleshnikov." She said it with pride. "Though I am a woman, he is an example to me. His diary has inspired my life. I wanted to make his grave my pilgrimage. That's something Russians do, or used to do. It's also very Chinese, to revere grandparents. I do not know the day when my grandfather died so I must look on the grave. Then I will honor that day each year. Is this your way in America?"

"I'm afraid it's not that strong. We're individualists. We like our families, of course. But we tend not to look back. That's a difference between East and West, I suppose."

Before long they pulled up in front of 652 Newport Street, part of a hillside block of white, pink and gray stucco row houses, most of them three stories high. The Natolinsky address was an apartment house and Unit 17 was on the second floor. When they reached it, the Russian name was posted by the doorbell.

"This is it," Hampton said, giving three sharp knocks with bare knuckles.

"Da. Da." The woman's voice rang from behind the door. She opened it a crack and peered over two chain locks. Before she could cast a single doubt, Irina explained everything in Russian—who they were and why they were there. The door closed and chains rattled.

"Giorgi," the old woman said. "Da, Giorgi." She sounded happy. Hampton heard her profusion of Russian through the closed door.

"She's saying I'm the granddaughter, all the way from the Soviet Union."

The door opened wide and revealed the smiling woman. She was old but fit, the babushka Hampton had imagined. They walked in. A bluish flowered wallpaper covered the hall and living room walls. She led them across the worn rug to a kitchen area, illumined by a westward window. There a very old man sat, gray stubble on his face. A walker was beside his deep soft chair. Hampton could just watch in speculation now. The whole conversation was in Russian, sometimes happy, sometimes sad, but always animated across these two generations. The old women left to make tea and Irina told Hampton what was happening.

"They knew my father married a Chinese wife in Harbin. But they could never picture the children. He says I have my grandfather's forehead."

The husband reached for Irina and in a low weak voice began

122

to recall their trip across the Pacific, how they had worked as emigres, how things had changed. Her sense of passing time was so acute, however, that she became deaf to the tale. She'd love to hear it all, but Yensky would doubtless be watching that she was prompt. With kindness she explained this to the woman, and that they must find her grandfather's grave. The old man and woman talked back and forth as if in doubt, even forgetfulness. Irina's spirit sank.

"Oh," the woman said, holding her head with frustration. "We paid for Giorgi's grave and we don't even remember . . ." They talked back and forth again—and then agreed. Yes, they knew the place. Irina's face changed from anxiety to relief. The city had a few places known for graves of Russians, some organized plots and others just happenstance accumulation. Giorgi Pleshnikov was buried in the yard at the Church of the Savior, not far away.

As Irina translated the proceedings, Hampton wondered about the distance. "Is that still in the Richmond District?"

"Down Newport to Clement Street and right a half-mile to the church, they say." Irina turned back to their hosts and politely excused themselves. She was sad to leave them. She owed them something, she felt, because they were the last people to care for her grandfather.

The old couple, their eyes crystalline with age and red from emotion, understood. Irina and Hampton left, hearing the click of chain locks behind them.

The waiting cab took them up and down some hills, and in a few minutes they could see the onion-shaped domes of the church. High clouds had just begun to pass in front of the sun. The gilt domes lost their shine. A graveyard, darkened even more by shade, lay alongside the church. It was an odd assortment of earth-level slabs, simple tombstones and some elaborate obelisks and statues. They wandered past what seemed like two hundred graves. Hampton couldn't read Russian so he surveyed the dates.

Soon after Irina moved around the back of the church, her satisfaction echoed across the graveyard. "Here! I found it."

Giorgi Pleshnikov's tombstone was the plainest of plain, a rough, white rectangular piece of limestone, about two inches thick with smooth corners. Hampton walked over, thinking hard on the fact that here he was, strolling through a graveyard with a Russian woman he'd first talked to a few hours ago. And this while Susan was out on her own in the city. As he reached her, she was touching the stone solemnly. She lifted her hand from it as if leaving a caress.

"Here it is, Mr. Hampton." She paused. "I will say a prayer."

As she spoke in a small voice, her hands came together. She lifted them to her chin and her arms squeezed against her breasts. From the corner of his eye, Hampton saw her face. The tears spotted her plain gray coat. His throat became husky and he cleared it quietly.

He focused on the grave marker just as the sun broke from clouds and flooded the graveyard, resurrecting stark shadows against the white stones. On Giorgi Pleshnikov's slab, the inscription stood out—Died. November 27, 1986.

"That date?" Hampton skipped a breath. "Where have I seen it before?"

13

Several minutes of silence passed in the graveyard, putting Hampton on edge. He imagined his watch was ticking like Big Ben.

"You must admire your grandfather," he said.

"From afar, yes." Irina's words were calm. "I only know his thinking. When I see his remains . . . he is still young in my mind." As if swearing a pledge, Irina altered her tone. "When things get better in Russia I will earn the money and pay back the Natolinskys for the grave."

Hampton's distracted mind barely caught the bold statement. By now he was thoroughly intrigued, even enamored, by Irina. What was it about this Asian and Slavic woman? He glanced at his watch. Remarkably, all this discovery had transpired in forty-five minutes. "Miss Pleshnikov, we have nearly an hour left. I thought we might spend some time talking. Is that all right with you?"

"I didn't know we found it so fast." The surprise raised her eyebrows. "We have Russian time you know. It's very slow. Even our language comes out in long wandering sentences. I would like to talk, yes."

They decided they were not hungry and then noticed a small vacant park set off the street about half a block away. The sun had escaped the clouds. Hampton asked the cab driver to return in forty-five minutes. The park, a plaque said, had been created in 1955 to honor veterans. Its semicircular sidewalk and the bushes were swept clean of trash, and at its heart were two wooden-slat benches, painted green. They chose one.

Hampton crossed his legs, lounging back. "How do you like the conference?"

She thought a moment, sitting up straight near the edge of the bench. "The people from our two countries are very impressive. Until now, my mind was not always there. I was thinking about this, the grave site."

With all the eye contact they had shared during the conference, Hampton wondered if she had been thinking of him, too.

When standing, Irina was a half-foot shorter than Hampton. Her petite figure was long in the waist, an Oriental trait, but full in the hips and long of leg, unlike the yellow race. Slavic and Chinese genes mixing, Hampton thought. Her silky black hair had a brownish aura in sunlight.

"You were very kind to help me find it. Mr. Hampton . . ."

"You can call me Nick, or Nicholas . . . like one of your czars."

"And I am Irene, like a movie star of America."

They laughed.

"Well, tell me about your family," Hampton began awkwardly.

Irina almost frowned and averted her eyes.

"I didn't mean to pry," Hampton said.

"No, it's normal to ask about family. Normal." She stared a moment. "My father has been ill a long time and my mother returned to China."

Hampton was quiet. "Does your father get the medical treatment he needs?"

At this, her eyes watered up.

Hampton wondered how he had managed to ask just the wrong questions, then Irina faced him squarely.

"Yes, he finally got his treatment but it was too late. It only stops the pain."

Suddenly the color drained from her face and her hand went to her mouth. She wavered as if to fall. Hampton grabbed her around the shoulders and she leaned helplessly into him. He felt her shiver, but then in a moment she stiffened, sat erect, and pulled away from him.

"Irina, are you all right?" He held one of her hands.

She spoke a few words in Russian. "Oh. I'm sorry. It is the travel,

I think. And I've not been well." She had revealed her secret, by accident.

"Do you need a . . ?"

"No, it's all right. I get a little dizzy or faint . . . . It's hard to go to a doctor." She swallowed, preparing to lie. "The library is so busy."

"Can you see a doctor here?"

"We leave very soon. Please don't worry." Irina wiped her eyes and a smile lit her face. The transformation shocked Hampton.

"Nicholas, why do you like your work?"

He studied her quizzical expression and then went along with the new issue at hand. "That's not an easy question. At one time I thought of being a minister, a Baptist . . ."

"Yes, that's a sect we have in Russia."

Hampton blushed. "In the United States it's very large with many groups. But we all focus on the Bible. So I got interested in the Bible, and then history, and finally archaeology. I was in Israel recently trying to understand the Old Testament part of the Bible."

"I love history." Her disclosure was so unaffected, it was sweet. "And I love religion. We can talk about it now in the Soviet Union. But so many people don't even know what it is. I didn't learn religion in church. I learned it in the libraries. We have many old religious texts."

"You do indeed, Irina. I realized that during the conference. It may be one of the best collections of Hebrew texts in the world, and of Slavic liturgies and, well, there's more I'm sure."

"You must know many languages."

Hampton laughed. "Yes, but nobody speaks them anymore. Aramaic, archaic Greek. Well, people do speak modern Hebrew."

The bench was hard. Hampton uncrossed his legs and squirmed a bit while Irina sat like a waxwork.

"Chinese has many dialects, yes?" he asked. "How do you read them all?"

"Until the Cultural Revolution, the old characters were always used for writing, especially texts. The spoken languages are many, depending on the province. I speak Cantonese, though my mother is from the south. Her family migrated north to Manchuria. She met my Russian father in Harbin." She paused. Considering Viktor Reznik's advice, Hampton seemed a God-given opportunity. "One of my favorite texts about Jesus is in Chinese."

127

"A Chinese Bible?"

"The Bible I have is in Russian. These are Chinese letters in the library. They are seventh or eighth century from China.

"Letters about Jesus?"

"They are not the Bible but they explain about Jesus and what he said. They use Christian names like Peter, Clement, . . . I don't know how you say it in English. Ig . . . Igna . . ."

Only one name could sound like that, Hampton thought, amazed. "Ignatius? Ignatius of Antioch?"

"Yes, I think it is Ignatius of . . . excuse me, I can't say some names."

"Irina, this is remarkable! Chinese texts that mention early church fathers! What do they say about Jesus?"

"They say he is a man from God. They say he was like Adam. Pure and good . . . they say we should be like him and he would make that possible."

"They say Adam?"

"Yes, Adam. Some other part talks about three persons, but I didn't understand that."

"That's the Trinity probably."

Her eyes narrowed. "Trinity? What is this?"

"I'm surprised you haven't . . . well, it's not in the Bible. It's in church creeds and doctrines. Don't you use it in the Slavonic church texts? The Father, the Son, . . ."

"We have the Father, the Son and the Spirit." She was still puzzled. "But not a . . ."

"Well that's it, the Trinity."

"Where did it come from?"

Hampton chuckled at the childlike question, but he was perplexed. How to explain it? She'd obviously not been influenced by systematic church doctrines, just texts and readings.

"In Asian thought," Irina said, "we conceive of God as two parts, not three. There is yin and yang in the creator and there is nature that came from God, where everything is two parts. There is man and woman, heaven and earth, mind and body, and plus and minus like electricity."

"Yes, well, our concept of a triune God . . . actually it comes from the Greeks. Christians believe it is revelation. But it is sort of a Greek speculation, a pre-existing Trinity."

"Why can't God be two parts, like father and mother, and the third part be the children? Jesus was the son, one of God's children. If one part of God is the father, then the Spirit could be the mother."

Hampton faltered. He knew that the only gender reference to the Holy Spirit in Greek was masculine—one in the entire New Testament. The Hebrew tradition, and some early Christian thought, cast the Spirit as Sophia, or wisdom with a female character. "We have dualism in Christianity, but it is good and evil and is generally thought to be a heresy . . . or, that means, a mistake."

"No, no." Her hands, like small birds, became animated. "That is not the Asian concept at all. Our two parts are not good and evil, they are . . . how do you say it?" She took a deep breath, puckered her mouth, and closed her eyes. "Well, it's like dancing, two parts of God in harmony moving in the same direction. For evil there is the devil." Irina paused, and then left Hampton speechless. "Don't American believers believe in the devil, the enemy of God?"

Hampton sank into a state of perception, as if flashing back to Israel the night of the missile attack. He had heard voices from the Mediterranean Sea and had seen generations of ancestry behind the Israeli soldiers in the jeep. Beyond Irina he imagined the East, the opposite pole from Athens and the steel cage of reason. There was the Semitic and desert mind with its swaying devotion and obedience to God, but also the Asian mind: life and fate were perpetual cycles, turning in a framework of heaven above and the hierarchy of life below.

He said, "Many American Christians do believe in a devil. As you know, that's how we explain the origin of evil. God could not create evil . . ."

Hampton stopped there. Irina's delicate face filled up with earnest lines and angles, expressions of a tenacious mind. What, he thought, had launched this strange theological discussion? Her mind was theologically active, but apparently free of doctrinal convictions. He could argue Christian belief was revelation and therefore superior to Asian concepts of reality; but then he thought of the Greeks.

He asked her to talk more about the Chinese letters. By her impressionistic description, the materials seemed to be early dogmatic theology. There had been a flood of writings on Jesus back then. Letters, treatises, homilies, many debating other positions and all quoting sources supporting their case. But to mention Clement and Ignatius! That was *very* early.

"What was your feeling from these letters?

"They were like teaching letters, reminding people what to believe."

"But how, for example, was Jesus viewed?"

"The feeling was sad," she said. "Jesus had died and nobody had loved him. I don't know. From the words, that is what I felt. They used something Jesus said to show this, that nobody understood him. But they were clear that he was from God. The letters discussed this most. About what was man and what was God."

"Have you reported the texts to anyone, like Yensky?"

Irina seemed to withdraw. Religious texts, she said, had been forbidden, suppressed in the archives. For her to show personal interest could, in the not so recent past, have caused problems. She could confide in one man, a Hebrew specialist, who believed the letters were important. Otherwise, her religious search was personal and quiet.

Hampton sensed he had become the inquisitor. As he tried to shift toward a more relaxed conversation the cab pulled up—five minutes early. Irina's attention bolted in that direction, as if Yensky himself sat in the cab.

"We should go back now," she said.

Hampton wanted to continue, but the time was up.

"Are you feeling better now?" She was obviously full of life, he thought.

"I'm fine. Thank you."

As they walked to the cab he wondered how he'd keep in contact. There would be one more session the next morning, then a farewell lunch. They talked and he asked to see her one more time before the delegation said goodbye.

"Yes, please. But the morning will be so busy. When . . . ?"

Hampton frowned. "I will look for you early . . . at the session. Then we will watch for a good time. Maybe talk in the little terrace again. Is that okay?"

"Oh, yes."

Hampton felt that he was making Irina nervous, either because she was caught between him and the tight Soviet group or because his emotions were getting through to her—and she didn't know whether to welcome or fear them.

"So you haven't told anyone about the letters?" The cab pulled up at the conference center.

"No. Just my friend Tatyana . . . she catalogues in French. And Mr. Reznik. He said there is some history behind the letters. He thinks church leaders in Rome looked for them years ago."

"The Vatican?"

She nodded.

Hampton contained the ignited thought. "What you have is very important. May I try to reach you again, when you're in Leningrad? I would be excited to see the Chinese texts."

"I myself can translate them from Chinese to English for you."

"Irina, you're a miracle."

As she laughed, her hand came up to her mouth as if to stop the joy from spilling out. "I am just a worker who knows languages."

At the afternoon sessions, Hampton chafed. His mind was racing. Once again Irina sat quietly behind the delegation, her alluring image engraving on his psyche. It was the strangest experience. And tomorrow, he thought, she would fly off. Perhaps forever.

Susan McQuinn was also flying off. They had dinner together, and that evening Hampton borrowed Winslow's car and took her to the airport. She spoke with surprising eagerness about returning to work. He avoided the word marriage; she avoided the name Northern Cascade. They were being mutually stubborn, keeping up the appearance that their minds focused dutifully on other things, not on each other. As ever, Hampton had so much to say he could never say it. Where to begin? How to unravel the years of feelings and misunderstandings? Hampton took Susan's self-reliance as proof of her happiness, a state she attained, he thought, despite him. He missed the epilogue he would have written, the sight of her crying on the return flight.

He left the airport and drove north, sinking deep into melancholy. He reached the Bay Bridge and began crossing to Berkeley. On the other side his mood lifted, drifting further away as he climbed the winding city streets. Nothing changed inside. But he papered over his feelings with thoughts about the photos. This time he knocked at Fields' door in the dead of night.

The pale visage appeared in burgundy pajamas. "Come in Nick. It's on the coffee table."

Fields had photographed the two fragments separately, each now enlarged as glossy black-and-white prints. The quality had improved dramatically.

Hampton scanned the print. "Excellent."

"And it's on the house, Nick. But if this goes anywhere, it would be nice to be remembered."

"Of course. If I publish, you're in."

Hampton slid the photos into a manila envelope, checked the original fragments, and then slipped them into their protective folder.

About an hour later, Hampton drove into the underground parking garage at the York Hotel. He took the garage elevator up to the fourth floor, walked down the hall, and knocked on 418. Winslow opened the door.

"Welcome back." Winslow's eyelids were heavy and dark rims underlined his eyes. The day before Hampton had noticed his quiet mood after the reunion. Few had attended. Winslow did not look one bit revived. "It was just a gathering of old men," Winslow had said. "No zeal left in us, you know. Just old scholars wondering what our years were all about." That was Winslow's only comment.

Hampton clapped his arm around the old man's bony shoulders. "Look at these."

"Wonderful," Winslow said. He led Hampton to a table under a hanging light and they viewed it closer. "Not bad quality."

"My kingdom for a Greek-to-Aramaic New Testament."

Tiny holes in the papyrus disrupted some of the Aramaic text. Most sentences lacked beginnings or endings. Yet it was not impossible that it had come from a list of sayings by Jesus. The Gospel phrases Hampton had deciphered in Amman were clearer now, and invisible texts had revealed themselves. Hampton's pencil jotted the translation on an envelope.

"Adam . . . the temple of God . . . fell away. The Son of Man came as the temple. You shall be like . . ."

"There's nothing like that in the Gospels," Hampton said. "Jesus said he would raise the temple and Paul compares the faithful to temples. But these have never been associated with Adam."

132

Winslow produced a compact New Testament and Hampton flipped to the concordance to refresh his memory. He was right. No reference to Adam in the Gospels. Only in the letters of Saint Paul was Christ likened to Adam. Only three times.

Other fragmentary sentences seemed to match Jesus' sayings in Matthew and Luke, but one in particular was odd: this well-known text had something new in it.

". . . greater than John the Baptist, but he who . . . than he. For John the Baptist came and he did not know . . ."

"Know what?" Hampton asked.

Winslow watched, equally fluent in Aramaic. "He 'did not know' . . . . This is not part of that Bible text. Didn't know the hour, the time?" he speculated. "Didn't know Jesus?"

This was no conventional text, Hampton realized. Under normal circumstances, he said, he'd publish the translation and its history straight away. "But the situation isn't normal."

"I wish I had an idea for you, Nick, but this old mind is exhausted."

They put away the mystery for another day.

Hampton took a cab back to the Lombard Hotel. With one thought, the comfort of bed and sleep, he maneuvered through the lobby, elevator and hallways. In bed, however, his mind would not shut down. It mined the details of the day for a nugget, something to guide him. Some clue. An insight.

Why did that date stand out? he asked himself. November 27, 1986. He floated mentally in the silence of the dark night and the vacuum of his mind, half between sleep and thought.

Then the memories came flooding back, and he wondered how he could have missed it. That was the week his mother had died. That was the week he had fallen out with Susan, when his transfer to Seattle had been settled and she had refused to budge. That was the week . . . that day . . . that very day he was at the train station outside Philadelphia . . . the freight trains crashed, the commuter tracks were obstructed . . . he had missed his flight to St. Louis and been delayed in Philadelphia until the next morning. Anger and confusion had consumed him. It was a week that had tied his life in an emotional knot. The flight had not been the problem, of course, but the acute moment had revealed what his life had come to. He had sunk to bedrock cynicism. To live was to fight, he had realized.

It was full of arbitrariness, an all against all. Life made no promises and it issued no guarantees. He had only Nick Hampton to rely on, a self that had hardened like stone.

He fought the memories, for even as past events they had ordained what he continued to be. That hardened self was still inside, where he didn't want to see it, where it could lie in privacy from the world. Now it was looking at him. Hampton didn't want to deal with it, the contradiction was too great. The grave reminded him of what he had buried within. And yet that day a strange power erupted within him, and it was focused on Irina. It was wide, emotional and confusing. It felt like life and death. It was going to help him or ruin him. He withdrew from the mental struggle and drifted toward sleep.

Ten minutes later his stomach was in a knot. It was the knot of desire, with its corollary of fear—the fear of not being in control. He could rebel against his hardened self that very night. He could go to Irina, he could find out if this was love. The decision came easily, like a friend, but a careless and even reckless friend.

He turned on the bed lamp and plucked his watch from the small table. It was 11:30. She was leaving the next day. If he knocked on her door, that was his pretext. Time was passing. He knew she stayed at the Commodore, near the Soviet Consulate, and that having her own room, as she had said, overwhelmed her with luxury. But he didn't have the number. He picked up the telephone, dialed, and then put a napkin from the table over the mouthpiece.

"Commodore Hotel," a man said.

"Yes, hello." Hampton lowered his voice as a disguise. "May I reach Irina Pleshnikov? It's room 313, isn't it?" He waited a minute.

"No, Pleshnikov is 511. Shall I ring it?"

"This is long distance, ah . . . what time is it there?"

"Eleven thirty-five."

"That late? I didn't realize, uh . . . I'll call back tomorrow. Thank you."

In five minutes Hampton had hailed a cab to the Commodore. He had no idea how the Soviets used the hotel, whether it was a regular stop or not. Was it bugged or watched? That was hard for him to believe. Wasn't the Cold War over?

The street lights burned ghostly images into Hampton's vision as they drove through the dark avenues, still alive with people. At the Commodore he casually crossed the lobby, where a tired-looking man stood at the registration desk, his back turned. Hampton pushed the elevator button and a metallic "ping" echoed across the empty lounge chairs. He found room 511 and gave the door three little knocks. A minute passed.

"Yes." It was Irina.

"Irina, it's Nicholas."

With a squeak the door opened an inch, revealing Irina's eye, and then swung wide. She stood there in bare feet, a gray sweatshirt pulled over a long formless dress, like a nightgown. Her eyes were wide, showing both surprise and puzzlement.

"Nicholas!" She peeked her head out the door, glancing up and down the hall. "Come in."

"I'm really sorry, Irina, but . . . well, you're leaving tomorrow and I just enjoyed our talk so much today."

She showed him across the room to its only soft chair and she sat on the edge of the bed. Nothing in the room was mussed or disturbed.

"Is it safe to talk here?" Hampton whispered.

"I don't know. I don't think they'd use microphones."

Hampton smiled. He was trying to be calm, appear non-threatening and certain of why he was there. Yet it was part theatrical, for he did not quite know why. To engage her intellect? To befriend her? Hampton swallowed. To seduce her?

"There is one man who I know is watching us, the staff," Irina said. "He came yesterday morning to ask if I needed anything."

"KGB?"

"I guess so."

Hampton's heart raced and his stomach tightened. He was not afraid of the KGB but of what Irina had done to him, to his life, to his commitment to Susan McQuinn.

"His name is Boris," Irina said. "I think he is watching the windows of the rooms."

Hampton turned his head, seeing that Irina's curtains were closed tight but, in their translucence, permitted light to pass through.

"He has a room over there." Irina gestured toward her window, which faced across a central outdoor atrium to other hotel rooms.

"He's probably told to watch when the lights go on and off, when people come and go according to their lights."

"What's your normal schedule?"

"I go to bed between midnight and one. I keep all the lights on, then just the bed lamp before I sleep. Then I make it dark."

Hampton thought. Should he grasp her hand? "Irina, can we talk tonight?"

Her expression was serious, but not fearful. She looked down. "I suppose it's all right." She raised her eyes and smiled slightly.

"I have an idea." Hampton trembled as he whispered. "You stay here and I'll be back in ten minutes. I'll knock twice."

"What is it?"

"I'll be right back." He entered the hall, took the elevator down, and walked to the registration desk.

"I hope it's not too late, but do you have a room on the fifth floor? I'm with the Soviet conference, a professor . . ."

Hampton trailed off slightly as the man, his eyes glinting up, pecked the keys to his computer. Green light caught the downward surfaces of the man's face.

Click. Click. Click, click, click. Click.

"Yes," the man said. "Five hundred eight. Is that cash or . . ?"

"Charge." Hampton handed him the credit card and in two minutes had the key. On the fifth floor he entered the room, appraised its layout, and then went to knock on Irina's door. She opened it and he felt something sweep through him.

She had combed her hair, put on a skirt, and, he believed, applied color to her face.

"Turn your light dim now," he said. "We'll wait a few minutes and then turn off all the lights. If Boris is watching, he'll think you're asleep. If he knocks, he'll think you're asleep."

"But what do we do?" Irina set her jaw, perplexed. "Where?"

"I have a room across the hall." Hampton dangled the key.

Irina's eyes sparked with surprise and then mellowed into curiosity, a quirky and spontaneous look saying that he was a mischievous, but so far harmless, little boy. They waited a few minutes and then went to 508.

Boris, who sat with his curtains partly open, had been told he didn't need to watch past midnight. He had a flask of bourbon, a nice break from vodka, and that night was listening to American

136

radio. Easy-listening radio had taken his fancy. Combined with drink it made him sentimental. He sat in the dark and across the atrium could see the five windows, the five rooms of the staff. Their lights had gone on and off throughout the night. Only two remained lit. Then it was only one. Boris counted to the room that had just gone dim, and then dark a few minutes later.

It was Pleshnikov, he thought. Sweet girl. But so serious. As he watched her window go dark—and knowing the last one would blacken soon—he raised his glass in a toast. "One more to go." He drank it down. "Almost bedtime."

Just before dawn, Hampton dropped his room key in the desk slot at the Commodore. A woman was on duty. Neither of them was awake enough to smile. "Thank you," they exchanged.

Back at his hotel, Hampton jumped in bed for a few hours sleep. His feelings were as mixed as when he had followed his midnight urge. Joy and guilt, layered over by a sense that life had just been lived, and that seemed to justify things.

Winslow did not sleep well either, but both he and Hampton dragged themselves from bed on time. Winslow made the morning session, which concerned future cultural exchanges. Hampton arrived shortly after, intent on seeing Irina. The Soviets came in a tight group, and surrounded the table spread with coffee and Danish rolls. The Americans trickled in sporadically.

A half-hour into opening, however, Irina was still absent. Hampton began to worry. His sense of guilt deepened. When the morning session passed with no sign of her, he was nearly in panic. During the break, he languished until someone announced lunch was next door. He shuffled to the room at the front of the migration.

Hampton took a deep breath as he entered and, as he had hoped, there was Irina. Their eyes met, but as she smiled her attention returned to some duties she was fulfilling. After greeting Winslow, he looked back. She had disappeared. He took a deep breath and stood in the milling crowd.

Then he felt her touch. Irina was moving past, looking at him as she left the room. Outside, he caught up with her at the alcove and they turned into a shower of blinding sunlight.

Irina's eyes were red and puffy and Hampton thought she had

been crying, or was it no sleep? She smiled and became very businesslike. First she gave him her home and office phone numbers. Then an address for her division of the library, and Tatyana's number.

"Why Tatyana's number?"

"She is my closest friend. If there is no other way to find me, you can reach her. I will tell her about you. She barely knows English but she's fluent in French."

"I guess I'll find a translator in an emergency," Hampton said. He smiled wide and got a partial reflection on Irina's face.

"This morning I read my notes again," she said. "I wrote down these sentences in English. See."

They were written on hotel stationery in a small script, distinctive for its curling serifs. None of the sentences grabbed his attention. As he stood close to her, he could hardly read and think at the same time. She was leaving. After watching her for hours, going to the graveyard, and even spending a night together he still had not touched her inner mystery, a dark worldliness she seemed to cloak with innocence.

"Irina, you've . . ." Hampton's voice wavered and the words sounded inadequate to him. "You helped me, really. I . . ."

She was distant, impassive. Her smile was inscrutable. What was behind it?

"Nicholas," she said. "I recalled one more name from the letters. It was not in my notes, but I remembered it. Here on the last page." She turned the leaf on the hotel pad. "I translated each letter."

Hampton read the name, stated in capital letters. The writing was so sweet that the content didn't register, only that her small hands had turned the pages, brushing his as he clutched the pad.

The charged moments scattered his attention. He only felt.

At lunch he watched her and then she disappeared, vanishing into the activity commanded by Yensky, like a woman overboard in a tossing sea. The sea was the delegation, which drew together and in two hours was flying across the Pacific to Moscow.

At about the time the plane was airborne, Hampton sat in his hotel and stared at the handwritten information Irina had given him.

"N E S T O R I U S."

This was the word she had remembered. She had written it down. "He was one of their teachers." That was the last thing she had said. Only her eyes had said goodbye.

14

Matthew Cummings kicked his feet through the dusty and hilly streets of Bethlehem. Being a missionary in the Middle East was a little easier now. The war was over. It was mid-March and the region had seen a few weeks of peace.

Now what? Cummings wondered.

Besides some daily commerce and a few Israeli police jeeps, Bethlehem stood still. Foreign visitors were not expected to start flocking, even with Palm Sunday a few weeks away. The previous year had seen mostly German and Scandinavian pilgrims, but that too was a mere spurt from a dried-up faucet.

Cummings liked Bethlehem but he visited Nazareth more often. The Baptists were building a church there and already its school taught Arab children; Nazareth was also very near to the beautiful region of Galilee. Bethlehem was mostly Arab. Five miles south of Jerusalem, where he and his wife Sarah lived, and in the West Bank, the town was riven by a greater amount of political strife. For this reason, he found it had a more active Arab grapevine, especially among Christian Arabs with venerable ties to American missionaries.

He was on his way to visit just such an Arab pastor.

Cummings rode the bus to the center of Bethlehem, population seventeen thousand, and then started walking. At the northern edge of the hilltop, he peered down upon a steep, rocky valley. David had grazed sheep there and now Israelis erected settlements that displaced Arab shepherds. Across the town black and red Arabic graffiti protested on the walls of ramshackle buildings.

When faced with these issues, Cummings became confused. He knew what his father-in-law, Harlan Wesley Stockwood, believed. Humans were pawns in the fulfillment of biblical prophecy in Israel. Cummings had been sure once, but wasn't so much now.

Since awakening he had been giving some thought to the Easter holiday, not far off. This year he wouldn't visit Jerusalem's holy sites. He was repelled by the ceremonial bedlam of Latin Catholics and Orthodox, from Greeks to Copts to Armenians, vying for pride of place on the streets and in the Church of the Holy Sepulchre.

Cummings most enjoyed working at the school, but his father-in-law, Harlan Stockwood, was demanding a different priority—that he seek out signs of Bible prophecy being fulfilled in Israel. This task of intelligence gathering had been handed to Cummings a week before he had left for Israel, the same week of Stockwood's major revival meeting for the year in Houston. It was at the Central Baptist Church, a modern brick complex that occupied a block of downtown Houston, and Stockwood himself chose the title to the conference: An Inerrant Word for the Prodigal '90s. Cummings remembered the event vividly.

On that day, Stockwood had worn his three-piece light-colored suit and had preached so strenuously that sweat had rolled down his forehead and arms. He kept a white handkerchief in his right shirt cuff to stop the perspiration. There was another one in his pocket.

"We have stayed the course!" Stockwood exclaimed. He lowered his voice to create drama, drawing in thousands of listeners. "We have brought about the great corrective. It is a bold victory for the Word of God."

At the grand revival, the crowd was lit up by Stockwood's Southern-bred electricity. That year, by dint of several consecutive annual elections, the inerrantists, of whom Stockwood was a patriarch, had gained leadership control of the massive General Baptist Association.

The silver-tongued Stockwood had preached that day with a faith that was open like a book. He had revealed his personal trials, his hopes of salvation, and had applied the constant refrain, "How great Thou art." Both handkerchiefs had been required to dry his sweating brow as he moved all about the stage. "What amazing grace!" Then he had knelt, kissed his Bible with piety, and held it heavenward.

"They say that we take the Bible too literally. The Bible says Herod was like a fox. Look it up. Luke chapter thirteen, verse thirty-two. Does that mean we think Herod had red hair and a tail? Of course not!" Stockwood had evoked a tide of applause, cresting with hallelujahs.

Then he had preached Bible history as fact. "If God said seven days of creation, it must be so. If the Bible tells us that Jonah was belched out from the belly of a whale, then so be it." His foot had stomped and his arm had thrust the Bible aloft. "We believe that the original written pages, the autographs of the Bible, were true and sound as God's Word, in all matters. Those autographs, those inspired first texts written by God with the very hands of the prophets and the apostles, are not with us today"—he lifted his chin in silence to bring his listeners to wonderment—"but I tell you today, in my faith I know they did in fact exist!"

Cummings was wed to Stockwood through marriage to Sarah, the preacher's favorite daughter. So the son-in-law frequently talked with him about the General Baptists' battle over the Bible. It had been emotionally wrenching for Stockwood. Like the Civil War, it had divided families and old friends. But the cause was just, Stockwood insisted. The inerrant Bible must be defended. No close family of Stockwood's had taken the other side, though some old colleagues had, men he had once prayed with, studied with. The most tragic, he had told Cummings, were the young and bright minds coming out of the seminaries, names such as Saunders, Greene and Smithport—one of whom became Unitarian.

Then there was Nick Hampton, who had galvanized a following of young defenders of the Bible. They knew their texts, they debated, they shot holes in the modern criticism that was rife in theological school.

"And then," Stockwood had once said to Cummings, "he was tempted."

Stockwood believed Hampton had been lured down the wrong path by a beautiful siren, the secular university. Once there, he had given into her pleasures—and had given up the inerrantist cause. That had been seven years ago and Stockwood was still remembering Hampton. The old preacher's heart was embracing, but in a stern and paternalistic way.

"Alas, Nick Hampton." Cummings even recalled how Stockwood said the name, like a lament. "Where is the boy now?"

At the great revival a choir of twenty, their blue robes flowing and fluttering, had mounted the steps leading from both sides of the stage and formed four rows, their members poised at angles. They had sung with force, and then Stockwood had returned to center stage, where all was quiet.

"I want us to remember that the power of the Bible is with us in the world today." Stockwood had begun in a conversational tone, building to a shout and a final peroration. "Our work is just beginning. Your stewardship has allowed us to send fifty thousand New Testaments to the Soviet Union." Stockwood loved irony, the irony of Soviet members of parliament standing in line for Bibles when this was outlawed in American schools. Had not God said he works opposite to the world's thinking? Was not the fool his servant, while the smug and powerful were not? "You can't compromise when it comes to the Word of God." They had drunk in the words and leaned forward, like plants seeking light. "You can't mix a little here and a little there like it's some sort of cafeteria. The Bible must be taken whole!"

Applause had burst from the congregation. The preacher and his audience had become symbiotic, a theological ecosystem in which the whole was larger than the parts.

"We can make new our faith." Stockwood had planted his feet wide. "But there is nothing new under God's sun, regardless of what some so-called Bible scholars tell us." Opening his Bible, he had saved the best—the Book of Revelations—for last. He had surveyed the crowd and quoted its text: "I warn everyone who hears the words of prophecy of this book; if one adds to them, God will add to him the plagues described in this book, and if anyone takes away from the words of the book of this prophecy, God will take away his share in the tree of life and in the holy city . . ."

Cummings tingled all over as he remembered the power of the sermon and that passage, which had struck awe in the faces of the congregation—and perhaps millions who had seen the broadcast.

A day after the revival, Stockwood had given Cummings his

mission—go to Israel and watch for signs of prophecy: the Jews and the Temple Mount; the immigration; the discovery of artifacts. Several months after Cummings had arrived in the Holy Land, he heard rumors about ancient biblical texts being unearthed. Though vague and uncertain, Cummings passed the hearsay on to Stockwood, whose response was prudent, even skeptical.

"The Middle East is full of intrigues," he had told Cummings on the telephone. "Be gentle as a dove but wise as a serpent." Stockwood had advised him to monitor the rumors, but with a few presumptions. If the texts exist, he said, they are most likely three-dollar bills or of marginal relevance. And yet, Stockwood quickly added, at one time in history there had existed original impeccable autographs. Would God will the autographs' destruction? Were these not the End Times? Had not Stockwood spent his life preaching the infallible Word, and might not God be rewarding him with the chance to prove the Bible by fact? Scientific fact!

Cummings was to keep all this in mind, and watch.

Now Cummings walked in the shade. He came upon the two-story stucco building and, stepping up, knocked at the double wooden door. A minute later an olive-skinned woman with a white scarf on her head appeared and let him in. Inside was a cool room with about twenty sets of pews facing a plain wall. A simple wooden pulpit stood before the pews and behind it a plain crucifix, carved of olive wood and darkened with stain. This was the sanctuary of pastor Samir Gamal.

The Arab pastor was halfway down the stairs at the side of the room when their eyes met. "Welcome Matthew." The Arab accent had a soothing edge, honed by preaching. "This is a good day to visit."

"Thank you for the invitation," Cummings said. "In a few days we need to go back up to Nazareth and assist with the new church. It's coming along pretty well."

"Come upstairs and have some tea. Farid will be along later."

"Good." Cummings knew Farid, the owner of one of the dozen or so antiquity shops in Bethlehem, but not as he knew Gamal. "Is he well?"

"Yes, I think so. His shop is surviving."

Farid the merchant, like Gamal, was a good source of information for Cummings. They knew all the best rumors.

A cool breeze entered the upstairs apartment, home of the pastor and his small family. Gamal had been trained in mission schools on the West Bank. He had gone to Oklahoma for a year's study in a Methodist school, but for ministry he liked Baptist independence. From where they sat upstairs, Cummings could see out a window and past two other buildings. There lay the grazing valleys, growing ever greener, and beyond was the conical mountain crowned by the ruins of Herod's fort.

"Thank God the war has ended," Gamal said. "Bethlehem has quieted down. We worry though. So many Christians are leaving. It's the tough Israeli policies, but also the Muslims. Then the Communists get elected in our neighborhoods and the PLO won't let us celebrate Christmas. If the West Bank becomes Muslim we may have to convert. So they're leaving."

Cummings knew the complaint too well.

Gamal patted his own chest, over the heart. "I am not worried for myself. I will not convert and I don't foresee drastic changes. But I can't convince the others."

"You're needed here as a mediator, and to preach."

"Yes, yes." Gamal nodded, his hand clutching his tunic. "I've tried to stay unpolitical. I wish I could do more for these people, much more."

Since Cummings had arrived in the Middle East, he had been struck by the ethnic loyalties. Israel was full of them, some belligerent and narrow-minded. Others, like Gamal, loved their people but did not lord it over others. Before arriving Cummings had not understood his own racial narrowness so vividly. Not only white and middle class, he was Texan also. Life in Texas Baptist circles could be as insular as among a Druze clan in Lebanon, he thought. With his cultural skin being stripped away by the new environment, Cummings was coming to grips with who he was and what he believed.

Gamal bent forward, a gleam in his eye. "I heard United Nations people passed through a week ago. They talked to a few Israeli Arabs and perhaps the mayor. It's real quiet but someone told me they want to try a peace plan in the south. Way out in the desert!"

"I hadn't heard that. Where? At the Dead Sea?"

"The rumor is the Negev Desert." Gamal reached over and tapped Cummings. "Whatever it is, that's an out-of-the-way place all right. It's not like fighting over Jerusalem or the West Bank. And it's not really a military frontier. So those who want to do it can do it."

"I'm sorry, Gamal. Do what?"

"I guess live in peace in the Negev: the Arab, the Jew and of course the Bedouin."

Cummings was always stimulated by contact with the word-of-mouth Arab networks. Yes, he had gathered a snippet of intelligence on signs of prophecy, perhaps, but mostly he enjoyed experiencing the Arab's type of faith. It was different from the Baptist Texan's, less doctrinal but no less attached to God.

Gamal poured Cummings more tea.

"Thanks," Cummings said. "Tell me about the Negev. How can Arabs and Jews get along there?"

"Well, we can always hope they could. The Lord promises us one thing, and it is hope. The Negev is a vast place. It's desert. Its roads are the wadis, the dry riverbeds, gorges and valleys."

The two men heard a knock on the door below. Gamal's wife shuffled across the stone floor of the church sanctuary. The door creaked. They heard friendly greetings. Soon came footsteps and then Farid the merchant. Greetings were given all around and fresh rounds of tea were poured for everyone.

"We were talking about the Negev, if Jews and Arabs can get along there," Gamal said.

"The Bedouin will never agree to it," Farid insisted. "I have family who married Bedouin a generation ago. They have settled down, but the old tribes won't."

"Why not?" Cummings asked.

"They are wanderers." Gamal believed his answer was obvious. "They have old customs. Their ancestors moved into the Negev from Arabia two hundred years ago. You know, the Jews trust them more than they trust Arabs. They let Bedouin join the army but not Arabs."

Farid said, "The Israelis want them to settle down. Some of them do settle. They want towns to rise up in the desert."

Gamal's voice cut in and Farid shrank back, listening. "Let me explain." Gamal told of hard times for Bedouin, under the Egyptians in Sinai after the Israelis had withdrawn in 1982 and then under

Israelis who pushed for development—military bases, farming, nature reserves and kibbutzim—in the Negev.

"My uncle-in-law who is Bedouin became a wage laborer," Gamal said. "He could not make a living herding sheep. I know a Bedouin who is a tracker with the Israeli army. They know every corner of the desert. They survive. Some sell hashish to tourists on the Israeli and Sinai beaches of Aqaba. Some sell intelligence to Israeli officials up in Beersheba."

At this point Farid spoke over his friend, prevailed, and then added many more colorful details about things Bedouin.

Soon Gamal interrupted with his hands, flipping them back and forth between himself and Farid. "We are both Arabs, Farid and I," he said. "But the Bedouin are even more Arab. It's from their desert life. They have a special hospitality. They'll treat a visitor like a king. But they must prove they are strong to survive in the shifting desert. Revenge is their highest justice. For an offense there must be a penalty. Blood feuds are necessary for honor. That's what Arab governments can be like, too. The appearance of strength is important."

"Do you have a lot of contact with Bedouin?" Cummings asked Farid.

"We sometimes trade. I've told you about manuscripts. Well, I haven't seen them. We have a saying, 'Don't sell or buy fish in the sea.' So I have to see them to make a deal."

Manuscripts again, Cummings thought. But he hadn't seen Farid produce any.

That was because Farid, who had to play one possible source off another to stay safe and in business, was like a fox. Farid had heard something—a shopkeeper named Nabbi in Jerusalem had told him—and he needed to test it.

"Matthew, I was told that an American is trying to get some of these materials. Do you know the name Hampton?"

"In fact I do. Nick Hampton, the archaeologist."

Farid said, "In a quiet way I invite anyone with antiquities to my shop and we consider a bargain. Someone came down from Jerusalem and said he knows about something. He could not promise to provide any sample. So I could not make an offer, could I? Then he mentioned this man, Hampton. He said the Americans were trying to get these things from Bedouin when we Arabs should get them first, to sell them."

Cummings was struck by the coincidence. He had called Hampton in Tel Aviv not seven days earlier, only to learn that he was returning to the United States. It did, in fact, strike Cummings as precipitous, though Hampton had said his work schedule had been completed.

The day wore on as the three men sat and talked. They had a light lunch, said goodbyes, and Cummings took a bus back to Jerusalem. He told his wife Sarah that Hampton's name had come up. And then there was the United Nations, too.

"Should I report this to your father?" he asked her. "It's just on Farid's word that it's Hampton. He might be confusing Americans because Hampton's pretty well-known. The *Jerusalem Post* had an article on Tel-Amon, saying it was American-Israeli cooperation."

Sarah thought for a while. "Maybe you should tell Dad anyway. Nick Hampton used to be a prominent Baptist. If he's back in the United States, Dad would want to know. Why don't you just tell him?"

"Sure," said Matt, who rarely defied his wife. "I guess I should."

Harlan Wesley Stockwood took the long-distance call in his Houston church office. After a month of quiet, he was happy to hear from Matthew. As soon as he could, he'd ask to speak to Sarah.

After a few preliminaries, Cummings filled Stockwood in. "Nick Hampton's name came up two days ago, and I thought you'd want to know."

"Uh-huh. Uh-huh," Stockwood said, listening to the report. "What are these manuscripts? No idea, huh. Yes. Yes, that seems likely."

He listened to more. "United Nations, huh? Anything in the newspapers? Uh-huh. Kind of secret you think . . . okay."

Stockwood's main interest was Hampton. Hearsay about manuscripts and the United Nations was one thing. The exploits of a Baptist Bible scholar, and a former inerrantist at that, was another.

With the receiver on his shoulder, Stockwood leaned back in the upholstered chair. "Well, you just keep your ear to the ground, Matt. Nick Hampton's back in the U.S.A. Sooner or later we'll hear something. Yes, that's right. Uh-huh. Okay. I'll speak to Sarah now."

At the afternoon board meeting, Stockwood presided as usual. The church trustees fine-tuned their plan to return missionaries to the Middle East after they retreated from the war zone. Most would return to former postings. A few were reluctant and sought a different call.

"The situation seems just fine over there now," Stockwood said. "Israel, Jordan, Turkey. Even Syria. I talked to Matt Cummings in Jerusalem this morning and he agrees that stability has returned. For those of you who know Nick Hampton, he stayed over there during the war. You all know I like that boy. I wish he had that kind of dedication for our side. Seems he's chasing after ancient manuscripts, Dead Sea Scrolls type things, I suppose. If he's got something I hope he handles it wisely. The Bible has been with us for almost two thousand years, but these discoveries, which are often fake, come and go."

After the meeting, a staff member walked one flight upstairs, turned down the hall, and entered his office. It was a news bureau for the General Baptist press. By late afternoon the office was usually filled with the sound of people typing on computer keyboards.

"The story's the new arrangement for return missionaries," the man said to his editor. "Here's a list of those returning to former posts. This lists the period of time. Should I mention all the separate mission costs?"

The editor examined the data sheet. "No, just add up this column and report the entire cost. Anything else?"

"Not really, except Stockwood was talking about Nick Hampton."

"Yeah, Hampton?" the editor asked, recalling past events, mostly the war of ideas at a Baptist seminary. "What's he doing in the Middle East?"

"Archaeology and teaching. But they say he's dealing in ancient manuscripts."

"You don't say. That's mysterious."

"Do you think it's a story?"

"Don't know. Let me think about that. For now, write the missionary story for sending tonight. The state papers can use it this week if they want."

"No problem," the writer said. "I'd like to write the Hampton story if it checks out."

The editor winked. "Call around tomorrow. See what you can find."

15

N estorians! In a Russian archive!"

Jack Winslow spoke as he viewed the dark blue waters of Puget Sound, a distant vista from Nick's hillside townhouse. Winslow put his hands in his pockets and went rhetorical again.

"First an Aramaic fragment and now Nestorian documents in Chinese!"

From San Francisco, Winslow had called his wife and changed his return flight. He had followed Hampton to Seattle. The return had brought Hampton full circle, a seven-month boomerang from the Northwest to the Middle East and back to Northern University. Because it was spring term, he had no teaching until the summer's end, a crash three-week undergraduate seminar. Visions of his office as a pile of demands—phone messages, mail, course preparation, the Tel-Amon report—deterred him from the campus for now.

"She only gave me a day, Nick." Winslow paced the small dining room. He imagined his wife Edith scowling at him in New Jersey. "Edith's not used to me being gone. It's been nearly a week."

His pipe smoke drifted through bars of sunlight like a web, delicate as the intellectual cloth the two scholars were about to spin. One thread was in hand—the manuscript fragment with its anomalous references to Adam and John the Baptist. Another was Irina Pleshnikov's material from the fifth-century sect of Nestorians, who, Winslow knew, were no mean scribes. They had saved Aristotle's work from oblivion by translating it into Syriac, which through Arabic

149

had been revived in Latin for medieval Europe; so couldn't they also preserve early accounts about Jesus?

Still other threads, as puzzling as the first two, were put aside for now. The Negev Institute, Habib Muhammad, the Brotherhood—they'd face those issues later.

The reunion of three days earlier still dominated Winslow's mood. He had seen the twilight of his generation, a group of old scholars who, once daring and initiating, now surrendered to convention and skepticism. They mostly valued comfort. Not exactly the mandates of religion that had beckoned them years earlier at seminary. Winslow saw himself fitting in so well. Their collective mediocrity reflected his own self. But the Aramaic fragment was a different kind of looking glass. The tiny scrap, a mere shred of some ancient writer's thoughts, loomed over him like a storm. Was that ancient scribe a lunatic, a fake? Or was he a teller of truth?

"I never imagined I'd return to this," Winslow said. "Searching for the historical Jesus." And yet, he thought, this is just a fragment. Does it change anything? Life always has uncertainties. That's why faith is a good thing; faith in what you believe about Jesus, or about anything for that matter. From his chair by the window, Winslow watched the morning winds push a dozen sailboats across the bay. The sunshine beat on his skull, feeling warm and good.

"Okay, Nick. Let's think this out."

"You have the first hand, Dr. Holmes."

Winslow's mind, and Hampton's too, had scrolled through the basics, the details of history that they grasped more as a collage of reality than an arid time line.

The history went like this: Jesus died about 30 A.D. and those who actually heard him preach lived maybe another forty years. Perhaps there was memorization of his words, a trait found in some Jewish and Greek learning. More likely his sayings were put on lists in the manner of teaching schools; but hearsay, both accurate and blurred, was most likely of all. The disciples taught others and the stories about Jesus' deeds and predictions began to emerge—miracles, debates with Pharisees, apocalyptic sayings. Then in the 50s A.D. the first written accounts appeared. Saint Paul picked up on oral and written sources and wrote his earliest letter, First Thessalonians, the earliest with Jesus' sayings in it. Meanwhile, materials of all kinds were collected, merged or edited but not all of it ended up in the final canonical New Testament. About 70 A.D., the author of Mark wrote that book with collections and accounts he had access to. By the time Luke was written in the 80s, he said there had been many attempts to write a history of Jesus.

Winslow stated his first observation. "The anomaly here is that the text is in Aramaic. Most everything we have in New Testament or in non-canonical books is Greek, or translated from Greek. Was this thing translated from Greek? I don't know."

First-century Palestine had been such a violent milieu that it was rare for its Aramaic documents to survive. Knowing that made Hampton's mind boggle.

Winslow was pondering the significance of words, and how incredible it was that so much meaning could be packed into just one. "Adam," he said quietly. The name of the first man, and a noun meaning all men. "Adam." He thought it over. Paul was the earliest source to mention Adam. It appeared also in the Gospel of Thomas a couple of times. "Did Paul get the Adam idea from Jesus' words?" Winslow asked aloud. "Or from another source?"

This raised the issue of the Q Document, a hypothetical list that explained why the same Jesus sayings appeared in Matthew and Luke: Q was short for the German word for *source*. Convention said that Luke and Matthew wrote their gospels as they looked at the Q list and at the book of Mark, a shorter and earlier account. But no one had found such a Q list. Scholars presumed that such originals, or autographs, had perished and only later copies or hearsay accounts had survived.

Winslow leaned back and lit his pipe. A flame danced and then smoke bolted upward.

"There's no Adam in the Q list," Winslow said. "To have Jesus talking about who he is is not typical. It only comes out in Paul and the Gospel of John. Then there's a lot of self-understanding in later Gnostic works. Paul likens Christ to Adam twice in First Corinthians and once in Romans. The idea of Adam had definitely come up. Was Jesus like Adam? The supernatural Adam? The second Adam?"

With the speculation, their minds flew back in time, back against the obscurity, trying to fathom, to stand in the dusty sandals of those who followed the executed Galilean. What hope did they draw from him? What worth did he give them? And then the shock of his death. He was gone. They grasped, at first like blind men, for its meaning. How did they *finally* grasp it?

"Jack, have you ever felt like it was just between you and God . . . ?" A badly phrased question, Hampton thought, unsure of a better way. "I mean, that you could actually comprehend that relationship?"

Winslow blinked and seemed to nod. "Go on."

"That's what I felt when I got the fragments. I can't describe why, really. For a few moments I could make the connection. It was like a disciple finally comprehending who Jesus was. He was the focus, the fulcrum, of everything that was happening in the world. It looked so mundane, but behind him something supernatural was happening."

Listening to Hampton, Winslow heard a muffled voice stir in his own soul, one that seemed to protest: what and who was Jesus? Just human? God in man? What was Adam then? Winslow climbed out of his cavern of debate, sighed heavily, and spoke. "It's important to have those experiences, Nick." It came out dry, because Winslow was not sure he knew what Nick meant. He shuffled a paper in front of him and turned to history again. "Jesus spoke out of the Jewish experience. It was a messianic time and they used Son of Man one way or another. Maybe he said Adam too. It's a very Hebrew concept, like Son of Man."

Winslow bit his pipe. It had gone out. He kept thinking. Hampton held the photo of the fragment out in front of him, swaying it slightly in his finger tips.

He read the text again. "Adam . . . the temple of God . . . fell away. The Son of Man came as the temple. You shall be like . . ."

A church bell down the road struck noon. In their mental playground, the two men had escaped the real-world dilemma they were in—they harbored the fragment in secret, a scrap that might rank near the Dead Sea Scrolls for controversy. They were thinking alike now, cutting through the thicket, discarding the weeds and coming to the same stone wall.

Winslow said, "If this Adam and John the Baptist material was available, say, in Paul's or Mark's day, the big question is why it was left out of the Gospels?"

They knew the obvious. Either the writers excluded the sayings because they did not fit their belief about Jesus, or the writers never knew those sayings existed.

"After Jesus' death, his followers' understanding of him changed rapidly," Hampton said. "Paul's letters changed. At first he expects Christ's return. That did not happen so he begins to emphasize ethical norms and church order for the long haul."

Winslow saw red in those words. It sounded like the criticism he loathed—the total dismissal of divine inspiration. It said the writers, from Paul to Luke, patched together texts to make sense of their changing circumstances.

"I still hold the traditional view, Nick," Winslow said in a low voice. "Those changes of view occurred in a God-inspired process. I'm no inerrantist. I don't believe that Mark or whoever wrote the original works did it in a trance or some kind of automatic writing. The Bible's not the Koran. But you've got to have God in the process, a very fallible human process."

Hampton was deaf to Winslow's point. "As the years passed," he continued, "not only Paul but a great number of Jesus' followers tended to emphasize his divinity, his crucifixion and resurrection. But it took awhile. You don't get crosses in Christian art until the fourth century. The human Jesus was being forgotten. He was spiritualized. He becomes divine."

Winslow's mind echoed, "More than just human. More. More. More. Man *and* God. Human *and* divine." Winslow did not respond to Hampton. He changed the subject.

"The John the Baptist thing gets me more than Adam," Winslow said. After a lifetime of scrutinizing the New Testament, he knew the John the Baptist accounts were some of the most reliable. To Winslow, they were powerful. They preserved the period's mood of expectation, imminent happenings. There was baptism by water and by fire. A prophet railed and his fame rose. At the apex, he encountered Jesus at the Jordan. At the nadir, he was beheaded in an obscure dungeon. Were they close? Were Jesus and John part of the same movement? And now this strange John text: "For John the Baptist came and he did not know . . ." Winslow said, "I just don't understand it. It's hard to grasp the text the way it is positioned here."

Hampton looked on, sensing a mild struggle in the old scholar.

"Let me get you something cold to drink, Jack." Hampton got up and moved toward the small kitchen.

"Coffee's better. I can drink it when Edith's not around."

"Black, right? I was having the same." Hampton scooped coffee into the filter, poured water into the coffee maker, and flipped the switch. The steam gurgled and the scent of coffee rose.

"Now the Nestorians," Hampton said as he walked to the living room bookshelves. "Patristics . . . ah, yes." He carried a volume on early church writings and one on early Christology back to the table.

"I'm rusty on Byzantines and Christology, Jack."

"I wish an old priest I once knew was here."

"Priest, what?"

"Oh, nothing." Joseph Sodano, with his Latin books on the jungle battlefields, flashed through his mind. It was as if Sodano should have been at the reunion.

"That reminds me, Jack. Irina said the Vatican had asked Leningrad about these letters years ago. It was vague."

"Well, I'll be." Old Joe, Winslow mused, knew about Byzantines and Christology, and probably about that, too.

Hampton leafed through the book. "Let me read what's pertinent." Nestorius was a Syrian-born priest who became bishop of Constantinople in 428. His popularity as a preacher and heresy fighter grew until he met his rival—Cyril, bishop of Alexandria. Cyril's debate with Nestorius over Christ's two natures forced Emperor Theodosius II to call the Council of Ephesus in 431. By connivance, Cyril swung the imperial court to his side and Nestorius was ruled a heretic, partly for emphasizing a distinct human side to Christ. Hence, for Nestorius, Mary was not the Mother of God. She was the mother of the man Jesus. Cyril believed the opposite—and won. Nestorius' following managed to endure, however, and it moved east to Syria, Persia and beyond.

The Cyril-Nestorius clash, Winslow recalled, was one of the most complicated theological battles of the early centuries. "We still don't understand all the forces behind it. If Irina is right about these Chinese letters, the Nestorians may have had access to some early Jesus sayings with the Adam reference. And that's what went east with the sect and got written in Chinese. And then in Russia . . . it's incredible."

Hampton said he had found something on Nestorians in China.

The Nestorian sect based itself in eastern Syria on the Tigris and sent missionaries east on trade routes. They reached India and Persia and then China during the T'ang Dynasty, which ruled from 618 to 906. The T'ang emperors were tolerant of foreign creeds and the Nestorians gained the principal favor.

Hampton ended his rapid paraphrase of history, let the book flop closed, and shook his head. Scholars were stumped for lifetimes by a single source. One source is questionable. But two sources that agree, like separate police witnesses at the same crime, prove something.

"We don't know what we have, but we do know it's in two sources," Hampton said. "The fragments and the Chinese text."

Winslow banged his pipe on the ceramic ashtray. "Can't prove any of this, Nick. We're just after strong probabilities." He drew from his pipe, then pointed its stem at the fragment photo.

"Nevertheless," he said wryly, "this little scrap is going to cause a stir."

16

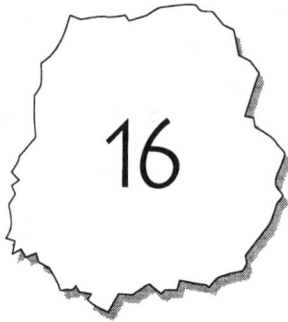

Winslow left Seattle on an overcast morning, leaving Hampton with a promise. If needed, the old Princeton professor would be the next courier into Jordan, to meet Habib and collect new materials.

Hampton, they decided, would focus on the two fragments. In the end, those might be the only things that materialized. With his standing to protect at Northern University and the Tel-Amon project to complete, Hampton could not cut loose and wander the world.

A few days later the telephone rang through the house and across the yard, a high eerie drone that broke the silence for the first time since Winslow had left. Hampton was outside squeezing caulking into wooden trim on the windows, splayed by winter ice. He ran into the house and on the fourth ring picked up the receiver, breathless.

"Nick, it's Travis Marshall."

Just what Hampton had hoped! The next stage, a new step: a Carbon 14 reading from the Oxford Radiocarbon Accelerator. Maybe.

"I've got good news and bad news," Marshall said.

"Did the samples check out?"

"Someone will do it for us, but it's going to take awhile. The soonest is late in May." Marshall said the fabric and papyrus were ample for a test on each. To get the kind of test they wanted—a confidential one—the wait was necessary. In the meantime, he had found a chemist to analyze the samples for contaminants. With a chemical treatment, he could rid the fabric and papyrus of carbon

156

impurities, such as recent carbon formation, and isolate compounds containing the ancient carbon. When burned, they'd provide pure carbon graphite.

"How much will this cost?" Hampton asked.

"Nothing so far. The electric bill goes up a little when they run the accelerator, but that's incidental. The labor is what costs, except in our case."

Hampton was awed by his co-conspirator's access and efficiency, but then Marshall unveiled its logic. The Oxford lab had wanted to do the first tests on the Dead Sea Scrolls. The Swiss Federal Institute in Zurich, however, had gotten the job. Oxford felt second best. The Shroud of Turin tests of 1988 had also muddied its reputation. The carbon accelerators at Oxford, Zurich and the University of Arizona all judged it a medieval forgery. Recriminations flew at all three but Oxford had taken it personally, as an affront. In all, it had grown sensitive about its rank and integrity.

"The man I'm working with would like to see Oxford get some major tests in the biblical field," Marshall said. "So he is sympathetic and he's confidential. I feel like we're finally . . ."

Hampton mulled the words—tests in the biblical field. That sounded like a major project, but at this point he and Marshall had no modus operandi, just seats of their pants. They had set no deadlines; they'd not established a hub for a project with pieces scattered on four continents.

". . . finally pulling it all together," Marshall said. "It's your call, of course, but maybe you should come to England. We've got everything. If the situation gets hot over there, come here."

"Not a bad idea." In fact, Hampton thought, an incredible idea! "Can a Soviet librarian get a tourist visa into England?"

"Can't imagine why not. What . . ?"

"Especially if she's invited by Oxford or the British Museum, right?"

"What Soviet librarian?" Marshall laughed. "A woman? What's up your sleeve?"

Explaining about Irina taxed Hampton's objectivity, but the significance of the Chinese texts was clear to Marshall. He said, "This is like the Dead Sea Scrolls and Nag Hammadi texts dropping out of the sky at once."

"That's too optimistic," Hampton said. "But doing it in England

. . . that has merits." Only Hampton's conscience could read his other motives; to see Irina, to obtain medical treatment for her, and to show her the world.

Impressing the librarian's boss was the issue, Marshall realized, and for doing that he had firmer roots at the museum. "The museum seems best," he said.

"Everyone knows the British Museum."

"Nick, consider a plan to come over. Then if you think it will work, just let me know."

Hampton promised to decide soon and then hung up. The next thought was about getting back to the office. A few hours later his car pulled up at the history department, a brick building with a glass-and-steel extension, landscaped with tall leafy trees. In his third-floor office, he lifted a blind and slid open a window to expel the mustiness. For a half-hour he sorted through a large stack of mail, until he came to a bulky white envelope with a logo—*World Interest.*

"LeFarbe's article." He tore open the envelope. "What did he come up with?"

The buff cover, printed in full color, showed a faded tan map of the eastern Mediterranean superimposed with images of artifacts, guns and opium poppies. "Antiquities," the bold script said. "A Doorway to the Black Market."

Hampton snickered. "He went for the sensationalism, all right."

He browsed the article, impressed at its research—how antiquities during the age of colonialism, works of art during the Second World War, and manuscript finds of the present played a role in international politics and fueled underground barter systems. It touched on the Hague Treaty's protection of cultural property and UNESCO's rules against transfer of such objects. Even the defeat of Iraq was covered; during the Persian Gulf conflict the Baghdad Museum had farmed out its great artifacts to smaller museums. When civil war followed, these sites were looted. The icons of Iraq's ancient history, going back three and a half millennia to Mesopotamia, filtered into the black market.

It took a thousand-page UNESCO catalogue to list the missing objects: cylinder seals, coins, terra cotta busts, pottery, cuneiform tablets, bronzes, silver, lapis lazuli . . .

A piece of stationery slipped from the magazine. Hampton

leaned over in the squeaking chair and retrieved it from the floor. A letter from LeFarbe.

"Dear Nick. Thought you'd like to see how it turned out. See page 95. Didn't quote you much, but background was helpful."

The letter had a personal and cheerful cast to it, but Hampton could not have known the reason. In Toronto, Daniel LeFarbe was making a comeback. Already, the article was being cited widely. A copyright logo was next to LeFarbe's byline. A UN session had quoted from the article. Talk shows, two of them with New York anchors, were requesting interviews.

What Hampton could see, however, was LeFarbe's energetic pursuit of more information. He had researched Simon Rabin further, and guess what? "Rabin is said to have a fortune holed away in Vienna, where his father died. It reportedly came from investments or business in Denmark after the war. One source estimated half a million U.S. dollars! What could it be for? More on this later."

Hampton heard an echo in his head and felt physically light, a sure sign he comprehended the trouble that might be ahead.

LeFarbe wrote, "By the way, I heard a rumor that you're dealing in manuscripts. Had a phone interview with Banner at Harvard and that's what he's heard. What's up? Didn't have time to get back to you. Give me a call if you can talk about it. Best. Dan LeFarbe."

His Toronto phone number was at the bottom of the page.

"Oh, geez," Hampton mumbled. "A rumor! How did he find out?" Hampton's stomach turned as he flipped to the jump pages of the article. Lefarbe had circled the text on the bottom of page 95 in red ink.

"International drug officials in Vienna have linked black market antiquities with a drugs-for-weapons trade that is feeding insurgent groups in Near Eastern countries, from Egypt to Syria. The antiquities are not big-value items, but they have become part of the barter system. As with types of guns and types of drug packages, the antiquities trail has helped drug-monitoring groups follow patterns of illicit trade. This is especially so in activity that appears to originate in Jordan, where some militant Muslim groups have been implicated in the trade. Jordan's population is nearly half Palestinian, making it a refuge for groups opposing Israeli and Western policies."

Hampton swallowed. He kept reading.

"Several officials involved in archaeology in the region have said that adventure-seeking archaeologists visiting the Near East may be approached by antiquities dealers. The temptation to tie into the underground antiquities flow can be strong, they said, because digs in Jordan, Syria and Egypt are limited under the regulations of the regimes. In addition to being illicit sales, the antiquities in many cases are forgeries or wrongly dated to inflate their value, officials said. 'We stay away from antiquities markets,' said Nick Hampton, an American archaeologist leading digs at Tel-Amon in southwest Israel. Professional archaeologists, he said, 'frown on people who buy from the market. So they find their objects at the dig sites.' Hampton said that serious scholars police each other through a peer system."

Hampton's stomach twisted tighter. At the bottom of the page, LeFarbe had scribbled a note.

"Do you know anyone I can talk to about this? Any scholars who've been approached? It would make a good follow-up article."

Hampton tensed with the thought: who was watching him? Who had circulated rumors? But that was just it, he realized. It's not a rumor. Someone knows and is talking.

"How in God's name did Banner find out?" he asked himself. How does LeFarbe know? Do they know about Habib? And then there was Simon Rabin's money. Was Rabin in this for profit? But how could that be, given the poverty of the Negev operation?

Hampton wasn't going to let himself fall into paranoia, so he reversed his logic. At best, Banner was getting echoes of rumors he had started himself; add a few sly Arab dealers and it wouldn't be the first time shadows had excited the international antiquities watch. If LeFarbe knew, he reasoned, why would he so casually send the article and ask questions? Wouldn't he snoop around and pin it on Hampton in some kind of exposé? No official is quoted. No precise items are mentioned. It's really the article's most speculative part, at the end, the summary.

"And he says *rumor.*" Hampton said it out loud, with assurance. "He hears lots of rumors." Journalists hear them and check them out all the time. They presume guilty until proven guilty because if someone's innocent there's no story.

He wondered if he should call LeFarbe, but decided against it. Not yet, at least.

In a short afternoon, Hampton began to feel trapped in his office. His mind pulled in three directions, toward Jordan, toward Philadelphia—and toward Leningrad. And there was no time to carefully plot a course of action. He decided to call Irina and invite her to England. Marshall would help. Surely he would. Irina would bring copies of the Nestorian letters. A mood of conspiracy seized him— why not bring the real things? His conscience struck back. "No!" it said. "Don't get Irina in trouble." As he schemed, Hampton did not sort out the personal from the professional: his longing to see Irina, his prudence about a scholarly rendezvous outside the United States. In England he could consult with Marshall, lay low from people like LeFarbe and Banner. And yes, Irina would be there with her discoveries. From his wallet Hampton pulled a folded paper with Irina's phone numbers. Midnight in Leningrad. She wouldn't mind. The British Museum was inviting her to England. Maybe she didn't even need that. Call it tourism. She just needed a week off.

Hampton crossed the cluttered office. He picked up his satchel by the door and rustled through it for more phone numbers.

"First talk to Habib," he said to himself. Ten hours difference; that made it eleven at night. He remembered Habib's words—"Call anytime, Mr. Hampton." After dialing there was static and two clicks. Then as if listening through a tunnel that opened thousands of miles away, he heard a phone begin to ring. He was back in the Middle East.

17

Kalim Hasan stood in the observation hut on the docks, sweating out the last hours of his workweek. The sun beat down on the Gulf of Aqaba, heating the southern tip of Jordan like a bar of iron in a furnace.

Caustic dust swirled about the dock as conveyors piped phosphates, dug from southern mines, into the German freighter's belly. Rusty water oozed from its portals and dried on the hull like brown tears. At sunset the ship would leave, crossing the gulf on its way to world markets. Business at Jordan's main port had picked up since the end of the Gulf War. The Allies' blockade on sea trade to Iraq was dissipating.

For hours, Hasan listened to the grinding sound of conveyors and hydraulic pumps moving the phosphate from giant mounds by the wharf. He pulled his black-and-white kafiya down over his ears to muffle the groans and creaks. In a small windowed booth, Hasan stood his post as a loading manager. It was one of several jobs he'd held in recent years. During the war, most of the port's five thousand workers had been laid off. Now labor was needed. Hasan had left his home in Ma'an, seventy miles north, and came to Aqaba for the job with Amin Kawar & Sons, the port's largest shipping firm.

Painted green, his grimy booth stood high on the dock, from where Hasan saw the sea-beaten ships, some in mid-bay, others among the twenty berths. Beyond were the azure gulf waters. The day was clear of haze. Across the water he saw Israel's resort city of

Elat, just ten miles away, and to the west the thin coastline of Egypt's Sinai.

Hasan thought about the guns. He thought of Habib. He thought about the Brotherhood. And he thought about his missing brother, a thought that inflamed his distrust for the self-anointed bosses in the Brotherhood. They would not say where his brother had gone, only that he was somewhere between Syria and Lebanon, and that he had acted heroically in the cause of *jihad*.

"Is he alive?" Hasan had asked, but he had received only a cold stare.

"You do not trust the will of Allah," one mullah had replied. "You must change your attitude."

Hasan's mind exploded with a force like the phosphate surging into the ship's belly. "They are fools! They are taking everyone down a road to death."

Under Hasan's hot eyes the phosphate stream began to thin as it belched from the pipe. He quickly turned to step outside the booth.

"Hey! Hey!" The yell sounded over the groaning machines. "Move the conveyer deeper. Into the pile," he shouted, waving his hand as if his palm was doing the task.

Three men in dusty overalls leaned into the conveyor arm and its blades cut into the dense mound. The flow at the end of the pipe expanded. Hasan waved approval. In this export phase, time was everything. The ship had to be filled. Delivery was due in Europe.

Because it was Friday, Hasan thought about the guns, about Habib, about many things. After work he would travel to Ma'an. The Brotherhood had Friday prayers at the school. Then its inner circle would hold a political meeting. Hasan would be there. And he already knew its direction. Two leaders would dominate, as they had for a year. They would demand that the cell renew its transport of guns to Syria, the West Bank and Egypt. In unison, they would curse the West and vow to send heroin to its streets. Then the two self-appointed mullahs and their factions would disagree. One took its lead from the international network, the other from the local front. After the humiliating Gulf War, their rivalry had grown.

Since joining the Brotherhood six years earlier, Hasan had tried to put his heart into this battle with the West and with Israel. At times he felt manly. He felt religious, taking revenge for Allah to one day be rewarded in Paradise. His brother, he believed, felt the same way. But unlike him, Hasan also loved learning, the Shari'a studies, the Koran, the wisdom of Islam. These had no revenge. He found in the Koran equality and justice, not the strict hierarchy some in the Brotherhood cell had erected. Mohammed had not set up mullahs, like the Shi'ite high priests in Iran and Lebanon. Yet that had happened in his Sunni Muslim cell.

Tempers had flared before, but now militant and religious cell members were trading threats of revenge, as Hasan had witnessed a week earlier.

The militant had been the strident instigator. "If you do not align yourself with our plan, you have broken the pledge. You know the Koran. Surah Nine. The Prophet said those who 'break their pledges' must be punished."

The religious brother had rebuked him. "You distort the Prophet's words. He does not invoke death, but peace."

The militant had taken an angry step toward his adversary and growled, "We will see. If you betray us, if you use the wares from the Bedouin in defiance of our plans, our crusade to wage *jihad* with arms not brittle paper, then a price must be paid."

"You have no power over us," the devout brother had said.

With a devilish squint in his eyes, the militant brother had resorted to threats. "You can test us. You go your own way and punishment will fall. At any corner of the earth, punishment will fall!"

Hasan shuddered at the recollection. It steeled his determination to stay neutral, but sly. If arguments arose over the antiquities as barter, he would have to play a delicate game: dismiss their use as money, but later present his plan privately to the religious faction. He wanted to deliver the leather package, with its curled papyrus scraps filled with Aramaic text, to the Christian West. Ma'an was a market center for the Bedouin, and here they bartered their finds from the Negev Desert. The choicest of them all, so far, were the papyri. One of the Muslim leaders in the religious faction believed that they portrayed Jesus as a man, not God. Such a revelation would vindicate Islam, that no man, even the prophet, is God. "There is no God but Allah!" With grand presumptuousness, this teacher became the force behind their belief—that the document could set Christianity reeling into confusion. Islam could march into the breach.

In his sweaty booth, Hasan considered this view, one he had

abandoned by following a wiser Habib. Now he had a promise to keep; to procure the old scripts. He'd do it by playing along.

The militant's preaching had been effective, for it had drawn many young men into the religious school. They had been trained to wage *jihad* in Afghanistan, but now had become wandering mercenaries, needing guns to build Islam. "They are fools," Hasan said, banging a metal box on the window ledge.

Aqaba was a city of about twenty thousand, growing along with the shipping port. It was a nearly twenty-mile stretch of land along the Aqaba Gulf, extended south when the Saudis gave Jordan a few more miles of coastline in exchange for desert in the east. Behind the port city rose a stadium of high mountains, steep and rugged in gray, yellow and red. The King's Highway, the overland lifeline for Red Sea shipping to Jordan, Syria, Iraq and Lebanon, wound down from the mountain passes.

Ships were loaded not only with meat, fabrics, machine parts and consumer goods. Weapons were tucked into some shipments, small arms and items as large as Soviet-made ground-to-ground missiles. Whether Arab, Persian or Turk, Muslim or Maronite, the clients fired them at each other as much as at the Jews and the West.

A steam whistle signaled the end of the workday. In two hours, the loudspeakers atop city mosques would blare with the call to the final prayer of the day. Hasan would change and take a bus to Ma'an.

When al-Qadr had founded its Islamic *madrasah* in Ma'an seven years earlier, it had begun with one school of Muslim thought. By its third year, that had been torn by two views. Internal struggle had divided the school in its approach to Shari'a, interpretation of the Prophet and Koranic law. One view was egalitarian and moderate. The other set up a priestly, even political, hierarchy and viewed militant action as the expression of holy war.

Beginning as a sincere debate over principle, the dispute had turned bitter and political. The scales had tipped when the militant faction had solicited support from the outside. A political program had crept in and begun to control the school. That power was backed by might, for the militant faction split over different loyalties and increasingly turned to symbols of power—holding and dealing in weapons. Drugs and, by chance, antiquities became part of the barter. Hasan watched as the manuscript was woven deeper into the power struggle, its fate threatened.

In Ma'an, the school continued delivering its education and social services, the benign side of the Brotherhood. Within its insulated core of leaders, however, Hasan saw the rot of corruption.

As a senior member, he knew how far he could resist and assert independence. His devotion was credible—and he knew the story behind most of the leaders. He could have broken with the group, denounced it and risked revenge. Instead, Hasan used his knowledge to bargain—to try to secure the manuscripts. His other difficult task, given with gravity by Habib, was to obtain maps, a record from the Bedouin of where they had found the artifacts.

To Hasan, the window of opportunity was closing rapidly. The Bedouin were confused by the infighting at the school; some had been offended by treatment meted out by a dominant mullah. They had started to back off, Hasan had learned. Invariably they would channel their wares to another market, of which there were many.

That night he could not halt the drugs and gunrunning, an agenda that came from the outside, the radical forces in the West Bank, Syria, Egypt. Upon this might the mullahs had built their authority. Their strength was in militant unity, for they had no money or international contacts of their own. Those came from somewhere else.

As a businessman, Ali Basherbisi usually missed Friday night prayers. He slept late and he rarely made afternoon prayers either. When he did go to the mosque, it was purely social protocol. To do business he had to at least appear observant.

At 10 A.M. he sat eating breakfast on his veranda overlooking Amman. His wife was visiting family in Kuwait and his mistress was still in bed.

"The young man is here to see you," announced the house servant, who had walked out on the patio as quietly as a drifting cloud. "He is waiting in the foyer."

"That's fine, fine," Basherbisi said in his low voice. He pushed himself up from his chair, mastering his bulky physique. It had slowed from years of rich eating and living. His nerves had relaxed since he had learned that the subpoenas in France could not touch him, and so a little more weight was hanging from his frame.

Business, he thought, makes strange partners. And this one, a young religious fanatic from Ma'an, liked power, too.

When Basherbisi entered the foyer, the young man was obeisant and charming. He was not a mullah from *Laylat al-Qadr,* but a mullah's lieutenant, a hatchet man. Basherbisi had not met him since December, when the coming war had begun to dampen business.

"So you want to get started again," Basherbisi said as they moved to the next room, where he gestured for the man to sit. He sat down as well, choosing a chair draped in sunshine. He had dyed his gray hair black but the lines in his face stood out.

"Yes, we do," the Muslim militant said. "We decided two nights ago. The brothers in Egypt, Syria, the West Bank and Lebanon have asked for supplies. The war was a blow to our cause, especially for Palestinians like me. But now we must build our strength again."

"Build it with weapons." Basherbisi's laugh was a deep cackle. "You are not so much a religion as politics and business. That's why we meet again, isn't it now. Is this right?"

The young man sat like a pillar and mustered a proud look. Basherbisi had mocked him before. He could swallow it again. He, too, could be tough. "We must find every means to our end," he said. "This is a world of reality, not hopes. We have learned this through the suffering of our people. We are clear in our consciences. The West must be faced with its own evils."

Basherbisi was ready to test the young man. "Does it not bother you that I am an Arab, a Muslim, but I have adopted the luxuries of the West? Does that put you against me too?" Such pushing and probing was a risk, but necessary. He wanted nothing to do with fanatics who were unreliable or quick to anger. He wanted a realist, agents with the ability to use means as ends. Like business.

"Islam is for Arabs, for our people. We want our people to live the Islamic way and our governments to be examples. I do not know what the future rule of Allah is. But the first step is Arabs ruling Arabs. Any ally in that is our friend."

Basherbisi laughed. "We're back in business then. How much is involved?"

Basherbisi's veneer of confidence belied insecurity. He would deal even as he was, in effect, on the run. France was not the problem; it was England. His old disgruntled partner was still unheard from. No assurances, no threats. Not even an arrest reported in the newspapers. If the man were picked up he might be a link, if not to Jordan, at least to Basherbisi's records. When the British complication crossed his mind, Basherbisi's typical thought was, "He wouldn't dare!" Or he would call the man gutless, frozen by fear for his life.

"We need small explosives, more automatic rifles and large amounts of ammunition," the young militant said. "We can provide the same as before, refined opium from the Bekaa Valley. Part of the drugs must be paid for in hard currency. As before, the rest is barter. Some of those weapons go to the Bekaa but most will be distributed."

"Yes, of course," Basherbisi said. "This time I would like to include another form of, shall we say, barter. The services of your network will count for money. You must understand that the problem for me is exposure. I'm safe enough in Jordan. But this government can put pressure on me. They do the bidding of the United Nations and others, like France and England. Jordan, you see, needs foreign aid. The Hashemites are pressured to fight the drug trade. In Vienna, the United Nations watches the Near Eastern drug flow, from Lebanon to Aqaba. If we continue, I need you to fend for me. This is not terrorism, this is security. It's self-defense. You understand?"

The man from the Brotherhood looked at him sternly. He knew he must consult with superiors, but wanted to show confidence. "We have people who are ready to act."

"Even in Europe?"

"That is more difficult but it is possible. Nothing is impossible."

"Good." Basherbisi leaned toward him. "I need that assurance. The time will come when we determine the details. For now, the currency and guns can be delivered in less than a month. Aqaba is still the best place. We still have our best cover there."

The meeting was informal, one man's word to another. It had worked before. The fewer people involved in a meeting between Basherbisi and a militant brother, the safer. They would depart and trigger their separate machinery into action. The amounts were tentatively agreed upon—fifty kilograms of Bekaa heroin refined in Syrian labs in Lebanon. On the street, Basherbisi knew, that was about one hundred pounds of pure heroin worth a few million dollars. It would cost him $700,000, a third in cash and the rest in weapons.

Basherbisi could not refrain from indulging his hobby. "I will give you good value for antiquities." He waited for a reaction, but the militant was stoic.

Basherbisi thought of how the Judas in England had stolen favorite items of his: the urns from the Umayyad Dynasty, a rare Persian amulet, a set of Roman coins and other sundry items. They'd all fetch a good black market price, even through the back door of a museum. Basherbisi was in a mood to get even.

"We have many clay items," the militant said. "We also have manuscripts, but they are . . ."

"Manuscripts! Really? What language? What period?"

The young man sat mute, realizing he had said too much. "We only have a rumor of manuscripts. The Bedouin tell many stories. What we can deliver are potteries, irons and bronzes."

Basherbisi did not know what to believe. For the moment he did not care. He was a man of ornamental tastes.

"I know that you don't drink, but let's seal our agreement with refreshments. Tea for you?"

"That is fine."

Basherbisi clapped his hands twice and the house man appeared. "Tea for my friend and I will have a brandy. Bring them to the den." Basherbisi turned to the young man. "I want to show you my collection of antiquities. It's really quite impressive."

18

In the same Amman home where Habib Muhammad had met Nick Hampton a month earlier, another guest was expected.

Habib rode the bus down from Az Zarqa and arrived about 5 P.M. As was his custom, he would conduct the meeting in the cool evening and then have a late supper.

On the ride down, Habib wondered at his plan. He had been a teacher and imam. Intrigue was new to him. He was not a plotter, a schemer. Yet he and Rabin had seen a need, and it was one they had believed they could fill.

When Habib was forced to wait, as he was this morning, he revived memories and relived events of the past. He was remembering the day of Nick Hampton's frantic phone call, about three weeks earlier. The phone line had crackled, but Habib had tried to explain as much as he could as clearly as he could.

The American's reaction had been reasonable, even predictable. "I knew these were Muslim militants," Hampton had said. "But I didn't know they dealt in guns and drugs!"

Not all of the militants dealt in drugs, Habib had said, but now it had crossed their path.

Since the day that Nick Hampton had been given the manuscript fragments, Habib had seen Hasan three times. When the illicit trading of al-Qadr came to light, the two Arabs had resolved to avoid any entanglement; they would focus on getting the artifacts and the rumored Bedouin maps.

It was a complicated political situation in Jordan, Habib had explained to Hampton, a reality that included layers of militancy and black market. But these were no reason to give up. Persuaded, Hampton had renewed his pact with Habib, making the imam more pleased than he could express. So he simply had given assurance, words that he could remember exactly: "In time many things can be understood better. Some day the desert's rich treasures will be open to you."

What Habib had not explained, however, were the details. It was too soon for Hampton to know. The rumored Bedouin maps had not been found. But the manuscripts, Hasan had last reported, were almost his.

At sunset a knock came at the door. A woman opened it and welcomed the visitor inside. He was a tall Jordanian with a thin mustache. He wore a light brown business suit and carried a small briefcase.

She led him down the hall, past the colorful carpets, and into the family room. Habib stood and extended his hand.

"Welcome Mr. Sadar. It is good to see you again."

"Thank you. Is it safe to talk here?"

"They are like family," Habib said.

No one smiled. Sadar, a United Nations agent tied with the Jordanian government, was in a serious mood.

"Habib Muhammad, I am afraid we have a problem."

"Problems do arise. What can it be?"

"A complication. It involves the Shari'a school in Ma'an and a prominent businessman in Jordan. The United Nations is very concerned not to offend the Jordanian government. But we also have reason to believe that the weapons-and-drugs route has been activated again."

Sadar was served tea and that brought a lull in the discussion.

Already, Habib had begun to count back in time. It had been more than twelve months since he and Rabin, as quiet as spirits, had sought out the leadership in their two countries. They had gone to the highest levels, to men tied to them by friendships of youth, when they all had been of no consequence. Rabin and Habib had given them a vision of the Negev as a place, a possible toehold, of cooperation. Their arguments had been convincing, Rabin to his people and Habib to his own. So persuasive, in fact, that contacts between Amman and Tel Aviv had begun, and so circumspect in execution that neither Habib nor Rabin knew the details. Neither of them was in government; they had no need to know. The important thing was that it was moving, slowly and cautiously, from idea to action. Habib mused that Sadar was coming to him for help, no doubt, with no inkling of those beginnings.

"I hear that the peace negotiation is progressing," Habib said.

"At the level of secret briefings, yes," Sadar said. "They would not say anything public yet. The immediate obstacle is the drug network. For the king to support any peace plan, he needs to know he can avoid a domestic uprising."

"And that is why you are here, Mr. Sadar?"

"You can do what government and police can't do. You can persuade them. What we need is a split in the militant faction of the southern Brotherhood. A clean split with no revenge."

"I assure you, it is splitting on its own."

"Yes, but the timetable is being stepped up. The war's end has accelerated plans to get Israelis and Arabs together, in Madrid. The United States and Soviet Union are behind it. Agreeing on land is still impossible, perhaps. But a joint economic zone in the Negev has a chance, don't you think?"

Habib reached for his tea. "As you know," he said, "my influence over the Brotherhood is only my reputation. That can be lost in a minute if I am seen in the wrong light. So I have worked quietly. I shall consider what you call the split. It is very delicate. We don't want anybody hurt."

Sadar the diplomat understood caution. Yet impatience showed in his eyes. "The complication I mentioned comes from Europe. There has been a major financial scandal. The International Credit and Commerce Bank."

"I have not heard."

Sadar folded his arms and sat back to explain. The International Narcotics Control Board in Vienna was pressing the issue. He detailed the octopus of trade, with Basherbisi as the head. The Jordanian government was caught in a political pincer, criticized by the West for not closing its port to Iraq during the war and facing an agitated Palestinian population at home. Amman needed to act on the drug and gun trafficking but could not risk a major police action. Even the

United Nations recommended against it. So the plan was to undermine. The Europeans could take Basherbisi but the militants' arms and drug trade was Jordan's problem, a delicate knot to untie.

"That is why the split is so important," Sadar concluded.

"I will encourage where I can," Habib said. This was a government concern, he thought, and had to be carefully separated from his efforts to obtain the manuscripts.

Sadar frowned. "I have to ask for a little more, this time. We want to know where the exchange of weapons and drugs is going to take place. The more precise . . ."—Sadar chopped his hand in the air—". . . the quieter it can be."

"The persons who talk about that, of course, are in danger, aren't they?" Habib asked. "You will understand if I don't make any promises now, Mr. Sadar; I must think. I must talk to my people."

"Of course." Sadar sighed. "This is not an easy step. But please, we're a little more urgent than before."

Habib's eyes feasted on a colorful wall carpet. Its rich patterns were like the complex course he would now take. "You must have some supper before you go," he said, standing to request the food from the kitchen. They ate quietly, exchanging a few more statements of concern. Then Sadar left.

Habib sat for another half-hour. Was al-Qadr on the edge as Hasan had said? It must be so, and that made the time right. He would urge Hasan to seek the manuscript aggressively. Once in hand, it would be passed to Hampton. Then they would stand ready.

Habib rose from his chair. The host heard the creaking and came to ask about the old imam's wishes. "The hospitality was fine," Habib said. "You have blessed me again with your home. Now I must go. The last bus leaves at nine."

The householder offered to walk to the bus stop with Habib, and the old teacher accepted.

Even the long day on the docks did not help Kalim Hasan sleep that night. His small ground-floor room in the rear of an Aqaba warehouse was cool enough, but the sounds outside pricked his nerves. Even as he slept, he worried over the manuscripts, bound safely in their own wooden box. Was the Brotherhood coming to get them? In the dark of night?

At work that day his boss had been angry at him for quitting his job with only two days notice. After a sharp stare the man had sighed. Hasan, after all, had done a good job. He was young and talented enough to escape a life at the docks.

Hasan had at least given a vague explanation. "I have to go to Az Zarqa. My family . . . there's a family business."

"Isn't your family in Ma'an?" The supervisor was always suspicious. "Did they move?"

"These are relatives."

The man had shown satisfaction at that, and now Hasan had but two days left of work.

A few days earlier, the Friday prayers had unfolded as he had expected, but the acrimony of the meeting afterward had caught even him unprepared. It had drawn about twenty members of the inner circle and had a major clash between the al-Qadr factions. The antiquities question had come up all right, but to his relief members of the religious faction had argued the case, the same one he would have made. Preoccupied with winning approval on the drug-and-arms deal, the two militant mullahs cared little about antiquities. Into the night, arguments over militant strategy had sharpened and fear and suspicion had cut the assembly into emotional pieces. It had voted to purchase the arms, but had left the two mullahs to fight over who would head the operation.

The next morning, Hasan had approached the religious faction leader and offered his services. First he had received the obligatory lecture.

The religious leader, surrounded by a few close disciples, had glared down at Hasan. "We must use many weapons." For being moderates in their practice, the religious cell members were still intensely committed to the power of belief. The leader had continued his sermon. "These ancient writings are powerful, for they prove Islam and they weaken Christianity. We must use this to end the idolatry of the West, which worships three Gods instead of one."

Hasan had given a confident response. "I will deliver the manuscripts to the West. A Christian scholar is waiting for them."

Already, the religious leader had decided to entrust Hasan, but two of the disciples had doubt-filled questions.

"Who is this scholar?" one of them had asked. "How does this go to him?"

Hasan had turned his face to the religious leader, answering to him, if anybody. Hasan had not been sure what to say.

"The Westerners asked for confidentiality," Hasan had said. "But I assure you they are reliable and they will spread this information to the world."

The religious leader had been stoic, impassive, but the questioning man had intervened again.

"You must have some name. We must have some proof."

Hasan had seen support for that question in the religious leader's eyes. Some information must be given, Hasan had decided. It would be of no harm.

"The American's name is Nick Hampton. He is working with an Englishman named Travis Marshall, who is from the British Museum." Hasan had made the statement reluctantly, but he had to give it weight. Even these people knew the British Museum.

"Very well," the religious leader had said. "Give them the old documents."

As Hasan recalled the episode on his sleepless bed, he also planned his trip. In two days he'd be in Az Zarqa, delivering the material to Habib—and seeking his protection.

That week, Ali Basherbisi spent many fitful nights, failing to sleep well despite the effects of his fine assortment of liquors and the comforts of his Amman home. Ever since he had talked with the young militant, Basherbisi had been haunted by England. It was far away. But one man in the country threatened him more than any other. He was an unknown, at least to the public. To the underworld, however, his name was plain. Just as plain, he had done Basherbisi's dirty work. Laundering money. Delivering drugs and other illicit items. Overseeing some of the forgery of shipping receipts, even passports.

Why, Basherbisi wondered, had the man betrayed him?

Among people like him, Basherbisi had seen the betrayal before. But he considered himself different. "Why would anyone turn on me?" he asked himself, as if blind. He had not abused this man in London. He had not humiliated him. Nor had he threatened him, or hinted that the man would be the scapegoat if anything went wrong. What Basherbisi missed, of course, was the truth. This man in London believed Basherbisi had treated him like dirt. And he'd begun to feed the authorities to get even.

"With the help of the militants," Basherbisi said under his breath, "I can nip this in the bud. I can cut off the head." England was far away, but not too far, he thought. In England the man was unknown and would die in obscurity. "May he take his secrets with him to hell." He laughed and then shuddered. Basherbisi was getting old, used to the comforts of life. To be apprehended now would dishonor his name, the name of his family. It would take away his comforts. It would make him, in fact, very uncomfortable.

The young militant had said they could handle England. And that would be the job he gave them.

19

I rina Pleshnikov!"

Dimitry Borisov's eyes opened wide as he bared the soul of a Soviet civil servant. He intoned and paced, arms behind his back. It was all show.

"You are a very privileged member of our Leningrad library staff. I hope you appreciate that. This is a highly unusual request, as you know. Yet, these are different times. I think you know what I mean."

Irina sat with hands folded in her lap. She peered up at the disheveled library supervisor. The sun of late May streamed in the high window, glancing off the shoulders of Borisov's gray suit.

"Is it acceptable, then, Dimitry Ivanovich?"

"Yensky has said yes. He was impressed at the British Museum's interest. They are paying your way. And you will bring back some things, as I understand." Borisov realized he was being too candid. He elevated the explanation. "Your knowledge in Chinese and Slavic texts, we have decided, will be a testimony to the library. That is the reason. You go as a representative of our library."

"I will always speak well of this library, and especially Comrade Yensky," Irina said, raising her voice. They had taken five weeks to decide. She couldn't believe they were allowing her to go.

She had been surprised when Hampton had called her at the library office before the invitation came. She had said she was willing. She was told it was funded by museum scholarships. Hampton had actually put up the money and Travis Marshall, taking advantage of his casual setting, had floated the invitation on British

Museum letterhead. He had gone through the Soviet Embassy in London to make it bona fide for Moscow. The Marshalls' home was listed as her host residence.

Irina thanked Borisov, stood, and began to leave the room.

"Irina, may I add another thing before you go?" Borisov said.

"Certainly." She pivoted and returned to the chair at his desk.

Borisov shed his formality. He bent close to her. "I don't like to talk about politics, you know, because we are in the library business. There are political reasons for your permission, though. We, I mean the Leningrad library, are trying to assert our independence. We don't want to be run by Moscow. Down there they call us a museum city, not a real city, with politics and those things. Well, Yensky doesn't agree." Borisov brushed back his fallen hair. "Irina, this has nothing to do with you, personally, that is. But you are a symbol. We will do what we want here. And you will go to England. I wanted to share that with you. Between just you and me, huh?"

"Of course, Dimitry Ivanovich. Between you and me. Someday all that you say will come true."

"Yes, I hope so," he said with melancholy on his face. Then he smiled. "Now get along and prepare."

Irina felt as though she floated to the door, where she looked back at Borisov warmly. Such a look always lifted his grim spirits. Outside, she rushed down the hall to her work space.

"Tatyana, I can go!" Irina hugged her friend.

"This is something you deserve, Irina."

Tatyana saw into Irina, who was transparent. How Irina had changed! Such a good change, as few Soviets can make in themselves. When Irina had arrived in Leningrad, she had been diligent but burdened somehow, as if a demon had been stalking her across the Russian steppes. It had taken a few years, but Tatyana had come to understand—for Irina had told her more dark details than she wished to know. Now Irina stood before her as if that weight had been lifted, the demon chased away; or at least as if Irina had gained the strength to hold the darkness at bay.

Tatyana said to herself, "You really do deserve this, Irina. Or the universe has no justice or mercy."

Irina carried on, speaking her every passing thought. "I have to work on the Chinese letters . . . Mr. Hampton is such a serious scholar." With Tatyana, she always referred to Hampton with formality, not wanting to appear personally involved.

"Did Viktor Reznik make you a microfilm?" Tatyana asked.

"He fit all the letters on one small roll." Irina began to lament how long the translating took, how she couldn't work in the open, how only a third of the text was converted into English.

"If I translate it into French, we'll have something for everybody." The way Tatyana said it made them both laugh, with little control.

In the two months since Irina had returned from San Francisco, the political atmosphere of the Soviet Union had thickened. For the second year, Leningrad's May Day parade had been canceled. Red flags had been swept away for the red, blue and white of Russia. In Moscow, Gorbachev and the Central Committee had watched a dull official parade and then been lambasted by slogans demanding reform. From the peasant to the Politburo, the Soviet Union awaited its first popular election on June 12.

"This," Irina said to herself, "is my door to England."

Everyone in Leningrad proffered an opinion, especially workers in the library. Many of them, intellectuals and independents who had tasted the gulags and Party discipline, wanted freedom. A March referendum had supported Gorbachev's call for keeping a Soviet Union, something reformist Leningrad would have done away with. But the referendum also allowed presidencies to be established in each republic. A Russian president could rival the leader of the Soviet Union, a revolution by voting booth that was only three weeks away.

Yes, she understood Yensky and Borisov now. In their striving for freedom, they could not deny it to her. Irina thought of Viktor Reznik when she thought of freedom. She'd talked a lot to him in the past month. He had often mentioned his grandchildren, and how he hoped he wouldn't die too soon.

"Tatyana, is there anyone who knows the library as well as Viktor Reznik? He knows so much of its history."

"He's worked here so long I'm sure he's studied everything. He's Jewish and that used to be very difficult, politically. I think that's why he's reclusive."

"He was telling me that years ago there had been inquiries by Italians in Rome about our collections. One time it came in the early 1920s when Lenin was opening to the West."

"There must have been dozens of intrigues in this old place," Tatyana said. "The Russian empire gathered up so many things, and now other countries want them back."

"And then during the Great Patriotic War there was more. The Vatican was asking about the Chinese letters and some Slavonic texts."

"Reznik usually knows what he's talking about," Tatyana said.

Irina had four days until her departure, time to visit the British consulate, pick up her Soviet visa, and catch the Sunday morning train to the Moscow airport.

At home that night, silly with excitement, she practiced packing, beginning with the blue, white and yellow sweater. She walked to her shelf and lifted up a brown folder that had her translations of the Chinese texts. The Cyrillic she had typed, but the translation into English was written by hand. She reviewed it, stopping at certain passages.

"This is what Mr. Hampton is interested in," she thought, and then began to read.

The alien names passed under her eyes like ancient bronze medallions from Christian history—Clement, bishop of Rome, Ignatius of Antioch, Nestorius . . .

Irina suddenly felt weak. She backed over to the chair and sat, bracing for the pain. A lightness filled her head. As her vision went black she saw sparkles of light, going up like fireworks and coming down like snow. Then she came back, fully conscious, to her room. Irina sat for a few minutes. She then picked up the letters she had dropped and continued to read. Her eyes moved softly across the words, for she had changed each one from Chinese to English.

> "For we have seen the early testimony of the
> apostle which some have hidden. In their report,
> the Lord says, 'For was not Adam created in
> glory, being in the Father's image. Thus the Son
> is as Adam.' The Apostle Paul follows our Lord
> on this, for he also tells us, 'Yet death reigned
> from Adam to Moses, even over those whose
> sins were not like the transgression of Adam,
> who was a type of the one who was to come.'"

The letter writer extolled teachers alongside Nestorius: Theodore; Ibas; Theodoret—and Michael of Damascus. Michael's life was lamented, as though he had faced great trials for his belief.

> "The opposition faced by Michael was foretold.
> For Michael did not speak his own word, but the
> word our Lord left with the apostles, the word
> that was hidden."

Irina hesitated. Hidden? Irina had not yet translated the part of the letter explaining what Michael of Damascus had taught. She would finish it, she decided, before she left. Browsing ahead in the Chinese, however, she saw the word bride, the word marriage, the word Logos, the word Christ. Irina had worked on the translation for more than a month. She did not understand it entirely. Nick Hampton would. He would explain it to her. She knew he would.

20

The spring shower crashed down on Harvard Yard, sending eddies cluttered with twigs and leaves along the campus paths. In the downpour, the green lawns, ivy and trees blended too well with the red brick university buildings. Only the white colonial trim etched a pattern in the gray pall.

Harvard Professor Bruce Banner stood and looked out his rain-splashed window. He wore a tweed coat and puffed a cigarette. Behind him were the massive bookshelves that symbolized his tenure, his years of presence in the department. Now it was his department.

"Hampton, what in hell are you doing?" he asked through the telephone receiver. "If this is true, you're running a cowboy operation and that's not acceptable."

Hampton sat with the telephone to his ear. The morning sunshine was coming into his office at Northern University. He listened to Banner, feeling the arrogance roll over him like hot tar. But he was not prepared for the honey pot the Harvard patriarch had brought with him, an offer that was about to dramatically tempt Hampton's soul.

"These are different times now, Nick," Banner said. "There are a lot of us who were here long before you and you just don't cut those people out of the loop."

Hampton took a heavy breath. Thank God, he thought, he wasn't a doctoral student under Banner. The pressure would be overwhelming, like betraying your father. He listened to Banner's final sentence. Hampton had a mind to charge Banner with spying on him in Israel, but contained himself.

"Professor Banner, you're launching off from some vague assumptions. You can believe what you want, I suppose, but I'm not confirming rumors. You know as well as I that people over in the Middle East get approached all the time. So, that may have happened. The natives don't like to have their business broadcast all over the place. They clam up. Frankly, the Bedouin and marketeers could care less about American scholarship, about Harvard or publication schedules." Hampton gulped. "And you've got no business telling the media some unfounded rumor . . . you know the Ten Commandments. Thou shalt not bear false witness."

"Come on, Nick," Banner cut in. "Okay. You and I disagree on a few things. Let's put aside that monograph on Tel-Amon. I just didn't think it was ready to publish. I'm calling you with good advice, as a colleague who's slogged through the trenches over there, too. Things are just different now after all this Dead Sea Scrolls stuff. The academy's closed ranks. It's a real heartache to get so much published and then have a missing piece show up that throws a wrench in the works. You know as much as I how attached these people are to their theories. If you mess them up, without even including them somehow, you're on their list."

Banner was speaking in the third person, but Hampton knew he was, in fact, referring to himself. He was a formidable scholar. His work had shaped the field. For fear of losing advancement, few bright students dissented from him. Banner wanted in on the cutting edge. He demanded it. Hampton's mind bent under the pressure. The phone call almost sounded like a threat. Banner invoked the sunshine law the Bible Literature Society had legislated. It called for open access to all finds. It gave five years to publish, but it also demanded immediate access to copies of new discoveries so that other scholars could compare them with their work. There was no enforcement agency for it, no government leverage, but the academy could assert its own pressure. It could create pariahs and close out job and publishing opportunities.

"You know what's happening now, Nick. Harry Sloan over at *Biblical Scholars Monthly* in Chicago is doing an exposé, like they did on the Dead Sea Scrolls team. They'll write editorials, run cartoons about you, demand you 'fess up."

"Yes, I know," Hampton said. "They've already called. But like I told you, these are rumors. I'm not confirming rumors."

"But people are doing the digging. They've connected you and that Negev project. Someone says you were in Jordan. Some missionary's been quoted as saying you obtained materials from West Bank Arabs."

Hampton was tasting the real world; fact and fiction flowed together. Because of fact, the suspicion about him was justified, palpable. Then fiction was spun around it, a trail of errors and speculation. That, at least, gave him plausible deniability. No one had confronted him with the right story yet.

The conversation with Banner ended with Hampton's assurance that he was not crossing anybody. Yet he had nothing to declare. His mind was on his work at Northern, where he had to finish his report on Tel-Amon and prepare for fall classes.

"Bruce, there's nothing to know about. But if there ever is, you'll be the first."

Banner backed off, half-convinced, but he was ready to try one more assault. He knew the balance of forces favored him in this, for he had a tank compared to Hampton's crossbow.

"Nick, have you ever thought of teaching at Harvard?" He paused for effect. "You're good enough."

Hampton shuddered and lost his internal balance. Harvard! They kill to get hired at Harvard. In a split second, a strange future scenario opened before his eyes. When he tried to respond, his throat was dry.

"That's quite a suggestion." Hampton knew well that Banner had the power to decide such things. "I guess everyone has thought about it." He'd clearly lost the offensive.

"Nick, I'd like to bring you on, starting as an associate. You've published enough for a quick tenure track." He paused again to let the gravitas pull on Hampton's imagination. "What I'm saying, Nick, is that you will have to do something in return."

It was crystal clear now and Hampton grew frantic. He did not know how to gauge Banner; would he be easily offended if Nick said no or maybe or "Let me think about it?" Was this phone call a choice of destinies?

"You've made a very attractive offer, Dr. Banner," Hampton said. "I don't know what to say right now. Of course, I'd love to teach at

Harvard. But something in return. I hope I would have something you're interested in, but . . ." Hampton knew what Catholics might feel in a confession booth. Should he say all that he knows? Reveal everything? "I can't say I have something in hand. I hope to have something, and I'm trying . . ."

Banner interrupted. "Nick. Take a week to consider this. It is a big decision. Does a week sound reasonable?"

Hampton thought hard, trying to be objective about the thrills coursing through him. "As I said, if something comes along then perhaps I can reply to your offer. Actually two weeks or so is better."

Banner was goaded by that. What happens in two weeks? he wondered.

"You're a hard man to turn down, Bruce."

Banner chuckled. "As you know, it's the chance of a lifetime." He pictured himself and Hampton cornering a historic discovery, a dramatic comeback for Banner. "I'm serious, Nick. Call me in two weeks, three weeks even, and let's talk again."

When they hung up, Hampton felt the kind of excitement that made him want to tell somebody. But that was the problem with being caught up in layers of secrets and intrigues. It would have been easier if Banner had not thrown the lure. Neither Banner's offer nor the publicity could have come at a worse time. When the *New York Times* and *Los Angeles Times* called, asking about new Dead Sea Scrolls he was said to have obtained, he just had said it was ridiculous. But the finger was on him and it was coming from somewhere.

Most important, he had received Habib Muhammad's assurances. Habib had called earlier in the week. It worried him to hear about the publicity, especially now: Habib had said that any day some old documents would be delivered from the grip of the Brotherhood.

Hampton immediately felt dwarfed by the vast geography. Neither he nor Winslow—partly because of the publicity—could find time or risk jetting over to Jordan.

"Could you send the materials to Travis Marshall?" Hampton had asked Habib. "I can go to England and we'll handle it there."

Habib had put his trust in the Middle East mails and agreed. They had aimed for the last week of May, a few weeks off. "We shall get it done," Habib had said, more optimistic than even Hampton.

The Banner development, his homing in, his applying pressure, was significant enough for him to apprise Travis Marshall, Hampton decided, though he'd not mention the offer.

At his suburban London home, Marshall finished his supper before beginning the test project. The technique had been invented by papyrus preservationists at the British Museum, and it was easy enough to copy—once he'd obtained the exact anti-fungal chemical. He carried the jug of distilled water over to a table in the work space and filled the small humidifier. With sheet plastic he had fashioned a square tent on a wire frame, large enough to enclose a large book page. The tent sat snug over a tray with a small four-legged stand and a petri dish under that. Now for a test. He poured anti-fungal liquid in the dish and placed a piece of rolled paper on the rack. After lowering the tent into place, he connected its hose to the humidifier and, with a click, turned it on. The fan began to circulate room-temperature moisture, picking up the liquid chemicals and bathing the paper imperceptibly. On real papyrus, twenty-four hours of the mild vapor would kill spores in its fiber and restore flexibility. To the side were the plates of glass and cotton blotter paper to flatten the papyrus.

Anne walked in, hands on her hips to ease the weight of the baby. "Will it work?"

"It should," Travis said. "A test run." He would watch to see that no humidity dripped and that the sample, a roll of heavy rag paper, did not become too damp.

When Hampton rang through on the telephone, Marshall's hands had just become free. The Banner interrogation did not surprise him.

"The reasons grow stronger to come to England," Marshall said.

Stationed in one place, it was agreed, they could better handle the unpredictable forces of the great convergence: the material from Habib, Irina and her Chinese materials, the Carbon 14 test result and the publicity on their heels.

"It may be D-Day all over again," Marshall said. "Or Dunkirk. It'll be bloody fun to find out what it all means."

Hampton couldn't laugh. "Fun, yes. But I hope not bloody."

Later in the afternoon, Banner's voice still rang in Hampton's ears. In thirteen days he would be in London. Once there, he'd have to decide a lot of things.

* * *

The copy editor at *Biblical Scholars Monthly* was working on the article about dating First Temple pottery when Harry Sloan walked up.

He had "today is the deadline" urgency on his thin, expressive face. Sloan wanted this issue off the presses in three days. "I've decided we're going to do a double truck on this Hampton thing. We've established an editorial line that we've got to stick with."

From a small office in Chicago, the magazine had led the fight to gain access to the unpublished Dead Sea Scrolls. It had taken five years, but finally the secular media had picked up the drumbeat. Scholars had divided on the issue. The topic had become part of the popular culture. Sloan's magazine had flourished. Finally, the public pressure had sprung scroll microfilms kept secretly by a few libraries, and the Israel Antiquities Authorities had buckled too—giving rights to all the unseen materials.

Sloan was feeling his oats. He had chafed at the arrogance he had seen in the scholars who controlled the closed circle of scroll materials. He was dedicated to bringing down their edifice. The magazine had taken on a crusading persona; the momentum was hard to stop.

Hampton was next.

"We add two pages and put a teaser on the magazine front. Something like, 'More scrolls in the dark?' or 'What is there to hide?' Something along those lines."

"I'll work with that and a few variants," the copy editor said. "Now, this means we'll move the secondary article on the temple dating to the back."

"Just after the editorial. And make sure the editorial's soon enough after the main piece. I'm writing it at eight hundred words. That gives space for a large headline and maybe a cartoon. Maybe a Hampton mug shot."

"We'll play it pretty straight, with his denials," the copy editor said. "But we know it's probably true. Where there's smoke there's fire. If we get it first, it's our story all the way."

"It's a great story," Sloan said, putting his hands on his hips. "We've got to be the watchdog on this kind of thing."

He turned and walked away, then snapped his fingers and swung around, giving orders.

"Set a page proof of the story and my editorial. Fax it or overnight mail it to the *Times* . . . hmm, yes. The *Times, Washington Post, L.A. Times* and the *Journal*. They've picked us up before. We'll embargo it for . . . let's see. For Thursday, before the pub date."

Clack, clack, clack-clack, cl-cl-cl, clack.

The copy editor quieted her rapid fingers. "Good idea," she said, and resumed typing.

Bishop Joseph Sodano shuffled past the windows that gave the best nighttime vista of St. Peter's dome, a block away but radiant in Vatican spotlights.

"God bless you Cardinal Garampi," Sodano said, as he often did. "You've made my job easier by not being my contemporary."

The bishop inspected the next file of papal documents.

"Letters. Letters. Oh, my. Three hundred years of work and still not in order."

That night, Bishop Joseph Sodano was working after hours on unofficial business. His authority to gain access to the Secret Archives was unquestioned. His documenting of Vatican and Israeli relations had taken up much of the winter, but now his part was done. Now the decision makers in the Curia would rule on some policy question, one that he was not privy to. A few weeks earlier he'd received the letter from Jack Winslow. He had waited for the right Friday, and now he had time to begin sniffing around.

"Leningrad, Leningrad," he whispered, casting his eyes through yet another file. "How would they file that?" He murmured and peered over the top of his bifocals.

"Ah! Soviet Union. 1940 to 1945."

The tall, solid bishop slipped the heavy carton from the shelf. He put it on the table and brushed off the lines of gray dust that striped his black cassock. He sneezed twice and then yawned. Early Mass had started his day, then meetings, inventory, a trip across Rome and then more work, another Mass.

Two years shy of retirement, and known for going out of his way, the bishop always summoned the energy to help. This time it was for a distant but singular friend. As he sorted through the files, envelopes and letters in the box, he thought of that time with Jack Winslow during the European war, when he was a young priest in the Pacific. As an American, he was two generations removed from the Italian homeland, but still his ethnic heritage had made him ill at ease as a chaplain in the U.S. Marines. The Italians had gone with Hitler—thank God, he thought, the Vatican didn't. His dark complexion, the slight Italian gestures and accents picked up from family and the immigrant neighborhood in Pittsburgh had stood out. And he was Catholic. America was still Protestant with its mainstream, and then its immigrants.

That's why his crawling in the bloodstained Pacific island sands had been so important.

"Diplomatic," he said, reading the heading on one Vatican file. He pulled it from the box and put it aside. Other files were labeled ITALIAN CITIZENS; REFUGEES; CHURCH PROPERTY. Nothing narrowed it down. "Where would they file a letter about old church letters in the Leningrad Library?" he asked himself.

Another possibility appeared. The file was labeled EXCHANGES. Another was ART TREASURES. Sodano pulled them out and dropped them atop the DIPLOMATIC file. He took the three bulky folders over to a table with a bright reading light at the edge of the archive. Out the window, beyond the basilica dome and past the black silhouettes of statues, the Roman night glowed softly.

As he sat at the table, Sodano's mind wandered again. He'd only go to this trouble for Jack Winslow. Fresh from the cloisters of seminary and shocked by military life, Sodano found that the friendly Winslow had made it bearable. There was much to remember, but clearest of all was Winslow grabbing him under the arms, dodging bullets, and dragging the priest with his bloody leg twenty yards across the sand. After they tumbled into a trench, Winslow laughed and slapped Sodano on the shoulder. "We made it, Joe. We made it."

Sodano went through each letter carefully. By 10 P.M. he had found some relevant pointers. He had plumbed files containing letters mostly from the secretary of state for the Vatican. During the war, the communiques had been sporadic, suppressed by military fronts or by caution. Spurts of activity—letters and cables between Rome and Moscow—had come late in the war, one obscure fact Sodano had learned as a Vatican archivist. What he found in the files told him even more.

189

One letter had the heading "Saltykov-Shchedrin Library."

"An appeal," he said, reading the contents. "It's a start."

It was quite good hunting for one night, he mused, glad that he might be able to answer Winslow's question.

Sodano had always wondered if he had wasted too much of his life thinking about antiquity, but now it was paying off as he found gigantic links to the wartime files. "What have you stumbled onto now, you old priest?" he asked himself. "My, how the past catches up with us, even fifteen hundred years past."

21

Travis Marshall floored his ocher-colored Volkswagen Polo and passed the lorry. His wavy hair fluttered in the wind. Ahead of him, the long straight road was bordered by flat grassland. Only sheep and low hedgerows obstructed vision on this stretch, marked by the red number 70 on the round white speed sign. It was safe to pass.

Irina Pleshnikov sat next to him. Her hands gripped either side of her seat. She was disoriented. The British drove on the wrong side of the road.

Marshall rushed to avoid the London traffic, but he was high-strung anyway. Habib had just sent new materials.

It was a Monday, May 27, and they drove out of Heathrow Airport at 3 P.M., an hour after Irina's flight had arrived.

"Nick is up at the Oxford University lab today," Marshall told her. "Oxford's where we first met about five years ago."

"You and Mr. Hampton must be very busy," Irina said.

"It's not bad. I have the time to help Nick. That's why we've met in England. He arrived two days ago. I should tell you that he arranged your trip, not the British Museum. I work at the museum, so that's how we invited you."

Irina was surprised. "Why . . . what would . . ?"

"Your Chinese letters are a remarkable find. And, honestly . . . Nick and the rest of us thought you should see the world. We try to help others starting out . . . well, you're not really starting out. Your library is . . ."

Irina laughed. "All this just because I'm a librarian."

As they drove, Marshall talked about his year and a half of work in Israel, Simon Rabin and the Negev Institute, how he had met Nick Hampton there, and about the fragments. A few days earlier a package from Jordan had arrived. The wooden case was thin, a foot wide and twenty inches long, and marked "books" on the export sticker. Slid into the backs of the two large, narrow Arabic books had been four leaves of papyrus, Habib's promise fulfilled.

"The first thing I'm doing is cleaning them, to preserve the papyrus."

Irina had an eye for the decay problem. She'd seen how extreme temperatures, mildew and humidity cannibalized books. Many had rotted in the Leningrad library's damp basements.

"We're going to take all the materials and try to put together a puzzle," Marshall said.

Irina glanced at him. "It is happening so quickly."

"I guess so. It's taken almost two months to get Carbon 14 tests on the first fragments, but we should have the result any day. The new papyri have Jesus sayings . . . but history is full of forgeries. No offense to you, but the same goes for the Chinese letters. They have to pass many tests."

"Yes, it is very complicated. In our Soviet system so many modern documents were issued. We never knew who really wrote them so it was a lot like ancient history."

The pasturelands disappeared and old suburbs, a maze of city blocks of stone houses with flower gardens, gave way to the London sprawl. Irina saw litter everywhere. Leningrad and Moscow were unkempt, too, but it was not from litter, it was because of uncompleted construction projects or buildings and sites in disrepair.

Marshall reached Osterly Park, twelve miles east of central London, and turned north. At Ealing he turned west onto highway A40 and headed into the town of Greenford, his home. He and Anne had lived in London's westernmost borough since a year before they had left for Israel. Greenford was a midsize town with dense neighborhoods of brick semidetached houses, newer freestanding homes, two low-intensity factories, a park and a commercial strip that crept out from London along the main road. To the west of Greenford, farms and pastures fanned out for twenty miles along M40 until brick towns and dark factories cropped up around Oxford.

Marshall lectured at Oxford and was an assistant curator at the British Museum, a few blocks from London University. He lived closer to London, but the trip downtown took twice the time of driving to Oxford. That drive was a thirty-minute arboreal feast, through the home counties' chalky Chiltern ridges and the pastures, cliffs and hills of the Thames Valley, guided throughout by the serpentine river. The underground to London was a trajectory through steel, cement, graffiti and grime.

Marshall pulled into the driveway alongside his brick house. It had a peak roof, slate shingles and stucco upper half that imitated a Tudor mansion. Anne opened the front door and stepped onto the porch amid a half-dozen flowerpots brimming with orange marigolds. She waved.

"She's very . . ." Irina grasped for words. "Very . . ."

"She's very pregnant," Marshall said. "Seven months."

With Irina's two suitcases in hand, they crossed the small lawn.

"Dearest, this is Irina."

"Hi!" Anne gushed. "You've come a long way. We've a bed for you upstairs."

Irina smiled, her eyes alternating from Anne's face to her smock, which billowed like a giant ship's sail.

Travis pecked Anne on the cheek. "Heard from Nick?"

"He rang a half-hour ago," she said. "He's driving back for dinner. Said you should know he's bringing the materials with him, but has to return tomorrow."

The three went inside to a carpeted hallway. Ahead were stairs that reached the second-floor bedrooms. On the hallway's left was a small work room and opposite that the living room, a tan rectangle with bay windows. Lace curtains hung across the three tall windows. One curtain draped askew on the corner of a green couch, which matched two armchairs. The brick fireplace had a gas unit with a cement log. Behind the living room was a dining area with tile floors and to its side a study, multi-windowed and furnished in wood. In the back, kitchen doors led to the garage and cellar. The dining room's French doors opened on the back yard, a narrow plot of twenty yards covered by stubby vegetable rows and bright flower patches.

Anne showed Irina upstairs. "You may want to take a nap before dinner."

"I do feel a little . . ."

"And the bath is in here."

"It's so nice!"

The enthusiasm made Anne remember her old home in Yorkshire. Coal heating and few baths. She and Nick had lived with less for stretches in the Middle East. And she could imagine Irina's living space in the Soviet Union.

At Hampton's request, Anne had arranged an appointment for Irina with her doctor at Ealing Hospital. The checkup was a few days off, so she'd tell Irina later.

"I'll knock to wake you," Anne said. "Sweet dreams."

The evening traffic around Paddington Station in central London was heavy. To deaden the noise, the man closed the front door of the shishkebab eatery, one of many north of Hyde Park. London's Arabs owned some of them but most, like himself, were service labor in restaurants, hotels and clubs.

He took his supper in the back and started home, taking the underground south across the Thames to Clapham, a low-income neighborhood. Then he walked to the lonely apartment where he had lived for three years. He had come to London as an engineering student, but was forced to work full-time instead. His parents and sister lived in Nablus, an Arab city in the West Bank. His two brothers worked in Syria.

In his kitchen, the man studied his calloused hands. They felt calm that evening; a good time to work. He heated water to brew Turkish coffee. It did not make his hands shake; it alerted his mind. Then, on a small table under a floor lamp, he moved the shiny tin lunch box to the edge, nearer to him. His thin brown fingers molded the soft brown plastic lump into the corner created by wooden dividers in the box. Every nerve in his hand and arm tingled. This part was most delicate—attaching the wire to the charge. The timer had a safety, but shorts had happened before.

In west London, nearly two years earlier, an Arab had blown himself up along with the Chatham House Hotel. The explosion had wedged his body between the third and fourth floors and started a fire on the roof. That was the year the ayatollah of Iran had issued a death sentence on the author of a blasphemous novel. For the protest, the man in the Chatham Hotel made bombs, one of which tore through Collet's Book Shop in central London. The key was Semtex, the soft plastic explosive shaped by the bomb maker's fingers. It came from Libya through the Irish Republican Army, the new masters of the explosive.

For an Arab bomb maker, there were few assignments in England. No directives came during the Gulf War. In previous active years, the terror had fallen on France and Germany. The German network of the Popular Front for the Liberation of Palestine-General Command had been uncovered in late 1988. Others had been tracked down in Paris after the 1986 wave of bombings that had killed thirteen and wounded two hundred fifty.

Compared to his restaurant wages, the pay for a job was good. He sent most of it to his parents. He also believed in the cause, the Arab cause in general and the Palestinian one in particular. He was not always sure why targets were chosen. Information was transmitted blindly, protecting one source from another. The bomb maker heard from his contact, but where that directive came from, inside or outside the country, he did not know.

Recently, he had been instructed to make one bomb. A northeast London address had been given, and the occupant's description and habits of movement. Six feet tall, slightly bald with wispy gray hair over his collar, the target was overweight and had a Germanic profile, a large sheer forehead and stout features. He stayed home by day. At night, by taxi, he went to places that satisfied his bachelor's appetite.

The bomb was to meet him at his home.

A few days later the bomb maker had received another order. An unusual development, he thought, so close behind the first. It was as if this target were connected to the first. Yet it was called a second job. There was a separate payment. It seemed almost an afterthought, for he was asked to develop a profile on the target as quickly as possible. He picked the man up near London University and followed him on foot to the Tottenham Court Road station, and from there rode the central line with him out to the westernmost stop for London, Ealing Station. The next day he followed the car home—and watched.

In his business, the bomb maker asked no questions. The first job was a death penalty; the second a punishment. The task was to be accurate and leave no trace.

It had been more than two months since Hampton had said goodbye to Irina, and now he was saying hello. Their parting moment in the sunny California hallway had stuck in his memory, and it came back to him—the mood, the smells, the light. Irina wore the same soft blue and yellow sweater. In her absence, he had transformed her into an imposing memory. At times thoughts of her could arouse passion. She could also evoke a sense of mystery that chastened his desires. Now she stood before him, flesh and blood. He realized there were two Irinas in his life, the real and the imagined.

By organizing this convergence on England, this confluence of Irina and his historic search, Hampton had set himself up for a struggle between two forces, both of them seemingly irresistible.

Something solitary and internal had been happening to him, and it was provoked by the discoveries. It was like an answer to his railing on the beach in Tel Aviv and it had begun the moment he had obtained the fragments: he felt he might be stumbling down a path to God. The doors just seemed to swing open. Grace was what the theologians called it. These were lonely moments, but elevating.

The other force was Irina, or rather what she had stirred inside him. The longing was new to Hampton; more than the discoveries, it was what made him restless and sleepless. His affection for Irina had been so immediate. His emotions were almost wild in his need for adventure and risk. And with all of this came an overwhelming need to have her love him in return, equal to his own intensity.

The two forces did not have to rival each other, but that's how he viewed them, as stark opposites—the first godly and ascetic and the second carnal. They were the peak and the valley. Such realizations were not rational for Hampton, however, for they were never settled in his mind. More than once he had told himself to forget about figuring it out. Just forget about the clash, he thought, looking at Irina.

When Hampton had arrived in London, he and Marshall had moved rapidly. Marshall had set up a large table in the well-lit corner of his den. Hampton fancied it a miniature scrollery, the dry cold room in Jerusalem where Dead Sea Scrolls fragments got sorted, translated and catalogued on long tables. Marshall operated the humidifier and flattened papyrus between glass in the work space off the hall. The risks had already begun when Marshall carried the ancient fabric and papyri shreds to Oxford for Carbon 14 dating. On their face, the samples revealed nothing, but they had divulged Marshall's possession of something more; he had said as much. As soon as possible they wanted infrared photos of Habib's new material, photos that recreated faded text and bleached away spots. Marshall was preparing just such a covert operation, again at Oxford.

But they didn't work so fast that it denied them some immediate gratification. After opening the package, their adrenaline running, they scoured the papyri for whatever could be read. Hampton found a phrase using Jesus, Adam and temple. He couldn't resist a call to Winslow.

"Well I'll be," Winslow had said, persuaded of the reliability of the Middle East source. "Work slowly and be careful with the materials." Winslow always gave good advice.

And for the first time Hampton told someone about the Harvard offer.

"That sounds like Banner," Winslow said. "Just remember, teaching at Harvard isn't everything, especially if you have to buy it . . ." Winslow didn't say "with your soul," but Hampton completed the sentence in his own mind.

That day he also revealed the Banner offer to Marshall, who said his opinion on it was neutral. He only reminded Nick—they could be frank—of his oath to Habib. To put Irina's material promptly on track, Marshall arranged to print her Leningrad microfilm at the British Museum. Then he'd find a translator to render the Chinese into English. Irina's handwritten translation was their reference in the meantime.

That day in Marshall's home, Hampton seemed to relax for the first time in a long while. When he saw Irina, the discoveries and Harvard, among other things, shrank in importance.

After dinner that night, the four drank tea in the living room. The men breached their strict Protestant upbringings when Marshall brought out the brandy and started sipping. Hampton joined him and began noticing odd things, such as the fact that he and Irina sat in matching furniture, the two green sofa chairs.

In the hallway work room, Marshall had suspended the humidifying at mid-project and put the untreated and treated papyri, one still drying, between blotter paper and identical glass panes. The cache lay stacked on a high lamp table.

"We'll get back to them in a couple days," Marshall said, pointing with the hand that held his glass. He had a few busy work days at the museum. And in case an opening with the camera popped up, he wanted all the papyri dry and in one place.

Hampton's mission was to pin down the Carbon 14 test at Oxford. As he sat pondering the ancient artifacts, all in one spot across the room, a vague uneasiness gripped him. On that table sat the figurative door to their futures, so how could he and Travis be *too* careful? "Shouldn't we find a safe place for those? Maybe a safe or a bank box?"

Marshall's response was placid. "I'll check into that tomorrow after work."

They had already chatted a lot about the old days at Oxford, renewing speculation on how Travis, four years Hampton's younger, had found affinity with the American, and vice versa. Now Travis was listening to Hampton's account of that day's visit, his first in years, to Oxford.

"I hope Freddy Cornwell was a gentleman," Marshall said. "What did he say about the carbon reading?"

"A gentleman he was," Hampton said. "And he said to come retrieve the results tomorrow."

Their rush to initiate everything had paid off, for now the expected delays were setting in. With the calm of runners who had reached first base, Travis and Nick lifted their brandy snifters in a toast. Anne and Irina listened on, happy to sip tea and repose.

When Hampton had arrived, he had told the Marshalls about Simon Rabin's money, at least according to LeFarbe's account. Anne had said she felt bad talking about other people's money. Less circumspect, her husband raised it again.

"You know, the more I think about Simon having a lot of money the more it makes sense," Travis said. "There was always this confidence, like he had money in the bank. I just thought it was him, his personality."

"It was him," Anne said. "His character was strong."

"I'm the first to agree," her husband said. "But what if? What if there's a half-million dollars in a European bank? If true, I wonder who controls the money. He has no family that I know of."

Anne wanted to change the subject. "Nick," she said. "Are you worried about what might happen in the states, with these discoveries?" She had seen some news clips Hampton had sent to her husband.

"No, not really." Hampton was lying, but continued. "Not much to lose, I guess. I think I can explain the secrecy later, if Habib consents."

Travis asked, "Or even if he doesn't?"

"That's a tough call." Hampton said it crisply and then sipped the brandy. After a pause he put his gaze on the stack of papyri between glass. It was a good time to switch topics. "We're lucky the papyrus is in such fair shape. There's a crack or two and one lacks a large chunk, but the worm holes and decay haven't taken out whole words."

"God, I've seen worse from human handling," Travis said. "You get these things cut from books with pocket knives or dealers who put Scotch tape on them . . . it's bloody awful what can happen when they're discovered. Burned for incense or to stoke a campfire." He sipped and gestured at his work. "With the right care, they'll join the great family of discoveries."

"If they're real," Hampton said.

The two men laughed, mocking what might be the end of their reputations, even their careers.

"I believe they are real," Irina said.

"So do I," Marshall said. "And I'll tell you why." Now he began to talk like the Oxford lecturer he was. "Irina, this might interest you."

Anne glanced at Irina, blushing at her husband's exhibitionism. She'd seen it before, especially over brandy.

"The first great discovery was the Nash Papyrus," Marshall said. "It contained the oldest example of the archaic Hebrew. Before the Dead Sea finds, we at least had some Aramaic texts on Egyptian papyri and clay urns. We had loads of papyri not related to the Bible, mostly from Egypt. Our earliest trace of the New Testament was just a fragment, a piece of papyrus with a few lines from the book of

John written early in the second century. The first compiled New Testament we have is on papyrus too, written as early as 200 A.D. It was found, but of course, in an Egyptian graveyard in 1931."

Hampton watched Travis and Anne and brooded over Irina, who seemed awed by the story.

"You see," said Marshall, "the oldest writings are on papyrus, in scrolls. Papyrus was least expensive but finding your place was awkward. So at the beginning of the second century they invented books, what we call codexes."

"It's pronounced codices," Anne said. "That's the Queen's English." She winked at Irina, who smiled.

Travis, a poor speller on paper too, took it in fun. He resumed his history primer: papyrus was invented in Memphis—"Egypt, not country-western"—back in 3,000 B.C. Great factories arose along the Nile and yet no trace remains. The Greeks and Romans spread its use around the world. And then it was slowly eclipsed in the West by parchment, a stretched sheepskin, and in the Arab east by the rag paper of China. Among the survivors are about five thousand ancient New Testament manuscripts. The British Museum, he reminded the group, had some of the best and earliest. He went on and on, or so it seemed to Anne.

Irina asked, "Is your papyrus unusual, then?"

Hampton was in a quiet mood so Marshall answered after a final sip of brandy. "All the Christian writings we know of are in Greek, but this seems to be in original Aramaic. We'll have to look closely and see if it's translated from Greek . . . but my hunch is that these may precede the writing of the Gospels."

"Don't forget Irina's discovery," Anne said.

"Of course not." Marshall glanced sidelong at Irina. "Irina's translation looks excellent."

"It's not my strongest language," she said. "I want to improve my English." She glanced at Hampton. "I'm amazed that I have lived to see all this happen, and to be a part. It is hard to believe."

Hampton gazed at Irina and realized how much he had missed her. It had been only a few days in San Francisco, but that time had made an indelible mark. The next week would be an adventure. It would be best if he could just bury himself in his work, but he knew that was not why he had invited Irina. Was she the cause of his quiet happiness that night? He thought of Susan and hated himself. Then

again, he rationalized, even Susan could agree that Irina was part of
the business, another doorway to historic discoveries. Sitting across
from him in the green chair, Irina was the picture of contentment,
Hampton thought, and probably unaware of the muddle that he had
created—and in which he had given her a central place.

22

Travis Marshall's reflexes failed him. The hot teakettle slipped from his hand. His bleary eyes winced at the clatter across the stove, and then at the crash on the kitchen floor. He had risen before dawn for an early shift at the museum, from seven until two. By the time he was leaving for Ealing Station, Anne was descending the dim stairs like the ghost of Lady Macbeth.

"Travis, you woke the whole house."

"Sorry, luv. Just clumsy. I'm leaving the car for Nick."

"Bye."

Everybody's morning began in a fog, a string of tiredness born of one pregnancy and two jet lags. They would get rested, though, and in two days Marshall would be off work. Then he and Nick would hunker down in the study for some undisturbed days with the manuscripts. At Anne's cheerful prompting, she and Nick and Irina stretched their late morning over a long breakfast and tea, discussing world affairs, Jews and Arabs, and the end of the Cold War.

"This means better relations between the English and Russians," Anne said. "It's a world you want to raise children in."

Irina was quiet. Her conversational English was good but she was not talkative. The sun had risen above the house now, dispelling the shadows from the back yard. Anne retreated to the garden. "It's great exercise."

The hour was 11 A.M. and Hampton needed to start driving to Oxford at noon. "Irina," he said. "Let's look over those Nestorian letters."

As they walked into the living room, Irina said, "I forgot to tell you something." It was about the Vatican. Viktor Reznik at the library, she said, had looked in old visitor logs and correspondence files and said that the Vatican had inquired about the Nestorian letters before the Revolution and in the early 1920s. It had asked again during the war, about 1944.

As they sat inches apart on the couch Hampton sensed the historic weight of Irina's translation. How big a controversy are the Chinese letters? he wondered. And who knows about them? Hampton examined the notes again and gave his opinion to Irina. The letters rang with authenticity, he said, because they exhorted in the style of the period's publicly read epistles. The writer also based his authority on revered sources—apostles' words, Gospel texts, early teachers.

"What do you find most interesting in the letters?" she asked.

"They quote Jesus. These early writers sometimes saw collections of Jesus' sayings, and quoted them. Before the Christian Bible was formed they picked out what seemed authentic. Of course, this Chinese version came much later, but it repeats the earliest accounts."

Hampton was losing his detached composure, melted by Irina's nearness and the act of shuffling through the pages of her translations. The rustling sound, like a draft, prickled his skin. In those moments when paper wrinkled softly and two minds thought together, Hampton's pulse raced. In spite of himself, he managed to find an example in the text.

"Ah, here, Irina." Hampton held out a page. "The writer says, 'In their report, the Lord says, 'For was not Adam created in glory, being in the Father's image. Thus the Son is as Adam.'"

"These are from a list of sayings, then?"

"That saying may have been. This, for example, is a saying we haven't seen anywhere. What's important here is that Jesus speaks of how he understands himself. Many historians believe these kinds of statements were invented later, by Christians. But here . . ."

"Jesus sees himself as Adam?"

Hampton loved the way she asked a question, eyes wide, innocent. "It may be read that way."

Irina easily elicited the instructor side of him. The Hebrew word *adam*, he explained, meant man created from the soil. In the Old

Testament, the name Adam appeared almost exclusively in Genesis. In the New Testament, Adam represented God's creation before the fall, before man separated from God. Adam also represented fallen man.

"What's significant here," Hampton said, "is that Jesus says he has attained what Adam lost."

As if he sat again on that bench in San Francisco, Hampton experienced the strange but wonderful intellectual dance with Irina. Her sharp inquiring mind could be, Hampton was seeing, a delicate challenge.

Irina let loose her next question. "If Jesus was like Adam, then was he to be married?"

Hampton's smile gave way to a laugh, a sort of guffaw. "A logical conclusion, I guess. But it's not what Christianity believes. It believes that Jesus' divinity canceled the need for human attachments."

Irina seemed agitated at that and responded firmly. "Then he is not really like Adam, because God created Adam and God created Eve for a Garden of Eden. He must have meant for that to succeed if he is a perfect God. Would he plan a failure?"

The simplicity of her logic! Hampton thought. Put negatively, she was asking why the world needed a Christ, part of a Trinity that existed before creation, if Adam and Eve could have lived in God's image on their own.

"Does that mean God never intended a Garden of Eden?" Irina asked.

Hampton believed his approach was far more complicated. He had studied Christology; she had not. Rather than elaborate for her, his thoughts became like a lecture to himself. The orthodox views of Christ were derived from his death and from Saint Paul's proclamation of the resurrection. Thus, the time of creation and Adam and Eve were not a measure of Christ, and only raised "what if" questions. What if, for example, Adam and Eve had never fallen? What then would be the role of Christ? What if they had used their free will to follow God, then could the fall have been predestined?

Hampton's answers, which he kept to himself, were the standard canon. But he found them fragile, even shallow, now that Irina had posed the questions. It was time to pull himself away to head for Oxford.

"We can talk about that tonight," he said. "Okay?"

She nodded.

He gathered his things, checked in with Anne, and made it to the front door with the car key in his hand before looking back at Irina. Their eyes locked onto each other with more than the mechanics of sight.

"So, you'll see the doctor?" Hampton asked.

"Anne is so good. She can do anything. I mean everything."

"Rest up. I'll see you at dinner."

She smiled and in a soft voice said, "*Do svidanya.*" It was, "Until we meet again."

"Carbon dating has gotten more precise," said Frederick Cornwell, the Oxford lab technician.

Cornwell fit the image of the young genius types Marshall knew around London and Oxford—puckish, unkempt red hair, swimming in his oversized white lab coat. He went over the process in excruciating detail, showing Hampton the room, the machines, the electric meters.

"How did it turn out?" Hampton asked.

"Both the cloth and papyrus are first century."

"That's what we hoped." The fragment was real! he thought. Progress! Now he had the patience to listen.

The Oxford facility was not like the Hollywood movies. Its interior showed age, the metal surfaces were tarnished, and the wiring was a tangle of dull, black cables.

"In effect, we utterly destroy something to give it back its life," Cornwell continued, poetic.

Each of the fourteen labs in the world with a machine for accelerator mass spectrometry handled the carbon dating a little differently. Oxford called its machine the Radiocarbon Accelerator. Over a Bunsen burner, a glass tube containing the papyrus was heated until it flared into carbon dioxide. Trapped, that gas was converted into acetylene which, in another closed module, deposited a layer of pure graphite carbon on a heated tantalum wire.

Cornwell pointed at the wire and Hampton bent for a closer look.

As pure as the graphite was, it still contained atoms such as Nitrogen 14, similar in weight to the Carbon 14 atom. To expel such "background" interference, the graphite was bombarded with electrons. This also gave the carbon atoms a charge, making them ions.

They stepped over to the cylindrical accelerator, encumbered with thick casings, wires and square gauges. Inside, Cornwell explained, a jolt of ten million electron volts sends a beam of carbon ions through a magnetic field. The beam fans wider, and the heavier and positively charged Carbon 14 stays on the outside as lighter ions curve inward. Downstream from the beam's source, other pretender ions are stripped away by magnets so that finally *each* Carbon 14 ion is counted by a detector. A count of ten thousand is sufficient, a mass that helps calculate the remaining amount of Carbon 12 and 13. When those three weights were compared, the decay rate of the radioactive Carbon 14 reveals its "clock," the time since the papyrus was cut or the flax harvested.

Cornwell held up a clipboard. The report form on it was covered with mathematical equations and atomic acronyms, and he ran a finger down its columns. "The decay rate shows a starting time between nineteen hundred and nineteen hundred sixty years ago."

"Between 30 and 90 A.D.," Hampton said.

"That's right. You must be pleased." Cornwell put his arm on Hampton's shoulder, slowly turning to go out. "Travis Marshall explained the situation here, so I've prepared this confidentially." He produced a sheet of paper topped with Oxford Radiocarbon Accelerator letterhead. In five lines it stated the test date, test parameters and test conclusions. It was notarized and signed by Cornwell. "This has been done on the side, so I hope you can tuck it away until you really need it. Maybe we'll have some more work in the future, huh?" He winked.

"Much obliged," Hampton said. He gave a single shake to Freddy Cornwell's hand and left the lab. Outside, the spring air was warm. The sinking sun cast dark and light contrasts across what could pass for a medieval landscape. Above the brick and stone buildings jutted the towers of churches and college halls, their westward sides reflecting an orange glow. As he walked the half-mile to where he had parked, his elevated mood praised the town; even the urban sprawl did not steal Oxford's pristine beauty.

He headed his Volkswagen into the gridlock of Oxford's narrow streets, seeking the breakout to the motorway home. The sun was setting behind him and the heavy traffic told him this: he would arrive home well after dark. In his rearview mirror, above the glare of headlights, he saw the orange globe become a bar of neon and then disappear along with the black spires of Oxford. He drove into a dark blue sky, which now absorbed the shapes of passing houses. He imagined a warm lighted spot pushing back the darkness, and grew eager to reach the Marshalls' cheerful home. He wanted more conversation with Irina.

Earlier that afternoon, Anne Marshall walked to the back door in her blue soiled garden smock, entered the kitchen, and dropped the handful of lettuce into the sink. In the other hand she carried a half-dozen daisies for the living room table.

When Travis got home later she was gone, up the block buying bread. On return Anne found Travis' message on the table: he had taken Irina out for an errand. Showing her the neighborhood, Anne presumed. By the time they returned, Anne was on her way upstairs to nurse her back.

"Hello, everybody," she said, and then disappeared.

Irina sat in the living room, fighting a trace of travel fatigue, and there found a world atlas in a stack of books. She opened its colorful pages to an unusual map, stretching from the Straits of Dover to northern China. In a single frame, Irina's life was laid before her. Her finger traced from Harbin to Moscow and Leningrad, across to Jerusalem and on to London. The world became so small, she thought, and she was increased by it. Under the atlas was a large picture book on England and she began leafing through it. She could hear Marshall humming in his study.

At his desk, Marshall tried to organize a few notes for the undergraduate lecture. It was four days away and he knew the subject almost by heart, but his mind wouldn't work. Instead, it fluttered with thoughts about the papyrus collection. Where to start? As he stood he let out a nervous sigh. "Maybe I should just go watch the telly and relax."

The next three days would be busy. Dinner probably would put him to sleep; he planned to excuse himself early. Upstairs, he heard Anne draining the bath. She walked more heavily now. The creak in the floorboards, supported by a great exposed beam above him, traveled from the bathroom threshold into the bedroom. He heard the door shut.

Irina had reached the pictures of Cistercian monastery ruins in Yorkshire, in north England. That's where Anne had been born, Huddersfield, she recalled. Travis was from Manchester, a little to the west. They said it was always overcast there. What little sunlight had come in through the bay windows was gone now, and Irina meditated on the pictures in the light of a table lamp by the chair. She imagined the ruins in their past splendor, great buildings where people met to feel awe and wonder about things greater than themselves.

Suddenly, the front door seemed to pop. Irina looked up. She heard a metallic tap and creaking wood. A soft scuffing sound followed. She was pleased. Hampton had returned. She waited. The door clicked a second time. Irina stood and turned to the bay window, but only saw an indigo night beyond the lace curtains. She put down the book and walked to the hall. A brown package tied in string sat on the floor.

A delivery, she thought, walking over. She picked it up, finding the package light but its weight lopsided. She set it on the hall table and took a few steps into the living room.

"You have a delivery, Travis."

"I'll be right there." Marshall had started reading a book. He finished the last paragraph on the page, turned it, and got up.

Irina took a step toward the hall and lingered, her gaze resting on the package. She leaned her hip against one of the heavy green armchairs. In a flight of thought, she wondered about the Chinese translation, the part about Jesus . . .

Then Irina saw a blinding light. A sharp pain shot everywhere. For a split second she was conscious of a deep warm sense of ultimate peace.

The neighbor across the street stood at the window, pulling the curtains closed. She saw a fireball explode out the bay window and the Marshalls' front door blow off its hinges. Broken glass flew in white lines across the yard. Flames shot up the facade and curved back on the roof, as if water was flowing uphill, and then subsided, leaving small fires on their retreat.

"Oh, my God!" She leaped backward, trembling. Tears burst from her eyes. "Call the police, call the fire . . ." She shouted to her husband, who sat in the kitchen finishing his meatloaf and potatoes.

Hampton drove into the neighborhood a half-hour later. Police cars and fire trucks jammed the block. Red and blue lights pulsated, casting bars of color across dark houses and milling crowds. Hampton's insides knotted when he saw where a spotlight flashed back and forth. He pulled over, jumped from the car, and ran.

The living room was destroyed, its square bay window now a cavernous tear clogged with smoldering furniture. The ceiling had collapsed. On the outside, the fire had turned the house into a black smoking skeleton. Three firemen searched inside with powerful flashlights.

Hampton bolted to the first uniform he saw. "I was staying here. Where is the family?" Hampton was out of breath and terror etched his face. "Is anyone alive?"

"Come this way," the policeman said. In a few steps they reached the inspector. Hampton did not wait for an introduction.

"I was staying with this family. Are they okay?"

"I'm very sorry, there's one death. A woman. A man is badly hurt . . . his wife is unharmed, just very shaken up. They were taken to Ealing Hospital about fifteen minutes ago."

Hampton had the urge to charge into the ruins as if to save what was already destroyed. With a firm arm, the constable intervened.

"No. Stop," he barked. "You're not going in there. You need to tell us who lived here. Were there more than three?"

"Only three . . . and me." Hampton's voice trailed off. "I was late."

"Then you're lucky." The officer raised his voice across the yard. "Only three. We've got them all out." He turned to Hampton. "I'm afraid you can't go in there. The lieutenant will take you to the hospital. There'll be some questions later. It's all over for now."

"What happened?" Hampton asked, his throat so tight he could barely speak. In a flash he saw Irina's face, unflinching in a sudden glow of firelight. He saw plate glass explode into crystalline shrapnel and papyrus curl into black ash. Last, he saw a furnace roar and organic life turn into carbon.

"A bomb," the constable said. "Someone brought them a bomb. The world's gone bloody mad tonight." He spat the words out like bitter seeds. "An hour before this, a bomb killed a man in northwest London."

SUMMER

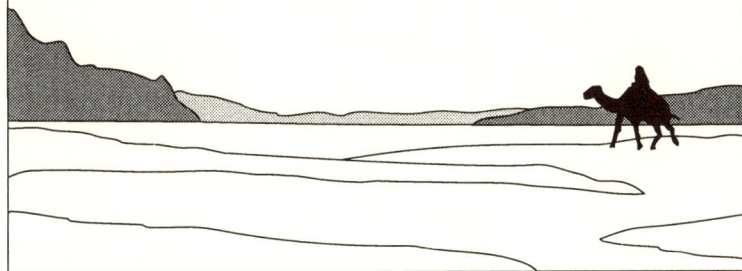

23

Two hundred protesters marched in a long oval formation. With the ease of a giant snake, the crowd moved over the curbs, sidewalks and streets in front of Northern University. The hand-painted placards danced above their heads in rhythm with the shouts.

"Jesus is Lord!" they chanted. "Defend our Lord! Jesus is . . ."

Emmanuel Bible Church and Four Square Bible Tabernacle had organized the Sunday afternoon demonstration. "Jesus is God," one sign read. "Our Lord is Almighty," read another. The largest trailed in the back, where two women held poles with a banner stretched between them.

"Down With Faithless Scholars!" it said.

The more conservative Bible-believing Christians around the country had spearheaded this protest and others. "We're fed up with modern scholars and clergy casting doubt on the Bible," a national spokesman told the network news. "They're attacking our faith."

Nick Hampton and the bombing in England had triggered the opprobrium, much of which was directed at him. Before his debacle, a volley of affronts had already landed in American religious circles: the Jesus Colloquium; a Hollywood movie that portrayed Jesus as insane; the institutional battle over Bible inerrancy; and then the Dead Sea Scrolls controversy. The tinder was dry and Hampton had provided the spark.

In Texas, Harlan Wesley Stockwood preached a series of powerful sermons. He did not fault Hampton by name, but he challenged those who would question the Bible. "No good will come of it, as certain events in England may have shown." It was Stockwood's traditional blend of both fire and compassion for the lost.

The day of the Seattle protest, Hampton sat at home and browsed through the latest *Time*. The corner teaser on the cover said, "Bible Hunters in the Black Market." He was named in the article. Then he flipped open the recent issue of *Biblical Scholars Monthly*. His photograph, which showed him grimacing, was set slightly cockeyed into the text. "Major Finds Destroyed," said the headline. "Renegade Scholar Set Back Scholarship a Century, Critics Say."

A few days after he had returned to the United States, a colleague and ally of Bruce Banner's had called from another East Coast university.

"Nick, we're asking the Bible Literature Society to strike your membership," the professor had said. "We like to be generous in this field, but we also need to send the right signals. Irresponsibility will not be tolerated by this academy."

If Banner had made the call, Hampton would have exploded, despite his glum mood; but even Banner didn't have that much gall. The offer to teach at Harvard, if it was ever true, had been incinerated along with the papyri.

Northern University's dean felt the pressure, too, and he had summoned Hampton to a meeting.

"The reason we have tenure, Nick, is to protect professors from unwanted pressures or influence from the political winds outside the university," the dean had said. "Sometimes, however, those winds are so fierce it threatens the school's reputation. It hurts everyone, which I'm sure is not your wish."

Hampton had asked what he was driving at.

"We may have to begin a review of your tenure," the dean had said. "Of course it is a lengthy process. It will involve a hearing among your academic peers. The issue will be the responsible behavior of a scholar, that it not be criminal behavior, which is the line we must draw. Then the report will go to the board of trustees."

In his living room, Hampton sat unshaven in a low-slung fabric chair. Darkness circled his eyes and lines were etched around his mouth and forehead. He felt as if he'd done only one real thing in recent days, and that had been to send a check to the Natolinskys in San Francisco. He had found their address on a crumpled paper, the one Irina had given him in the taxi, and then had scraped the bottom of his savings account for $500. He marked the check, "To pay for Giorgi Pleshnikov's grave."

He thought about Habib and his promise. He would keep it for now.

"Nick, you should get some fresh air." Susan, in stocking feet, walked into the living room. "Let's go out for a while."

Susan had flown out two days before, camped in his extra room, and become his nursemaid of sorts. Hampton had not called for her but she had come, partly on the advice of Winslow. A decision on the Northern Cascade offer had to be made soon, and she was leaning more and more that way as other options looked bleak. At work, Bill Salinger was waiting in the wings with greater frequency. Like smelling a distant tornado in the Midwestern air, Susan knew he was about to pop the big question. Then came her most painful worry: had she waited too long, allowing someone else to take Nick? He had said nothing about Irina, but the fragrance of things Russian overwhelmed her. Yes, she was jealous, but mostly mystified and depressed. She faced her inadequacies in pleasing this man she considered hers. More than her maternal instinct, she was moved to fill a vacuum she found in Hampton, a vulnerability she rarely saw—or failed to notice. "Perhaps I failed for years," she said to herself. She wore the Hand of Fatima necklace Nick had given her, and could feel its cold silver against her throat. But luck, she knew, was not going to fix things. Faith and effort just might.

Hampton assented to the beach trip and they drove out to a sunny shoreline on the bay. They walked about a mile on beaches and on sandy paths through marsh grass. Susan tried to make conversation, to draw him toward her. Hampton barely said a word. He was reliving the events of the past week.

The night of the explosion, Hampton had rushed to Ealing Hospital. The austere cement building with fluorescent lighting had presented the aura of a mortuary. A tall, thin, grim-faced doctor had told him that Irina had died almost instantly. At the morgue the next day, Hampton had identified her. The mortician had pulled the sheet back from her face only partially. Hampton had been spared the sight of gaping wounds where flesh had been torn from her left cheekbone and down along her neck and shoulder.

"Yes." Hampton had been barely audible.

Irina's soft black hair had still glistened as if rooted in warm flesh and blood. Hampton had seen her pile of clothes, the sweater of blue, yellow and white burned, tattered and bloodstained—but its colors still bright. With Hampton's identification, the authorities knew the rest. Her passport, in the upstairs bedroom, had survived the blast.

Police questioning had followed. Scotland Yard's Anti-Terrorist division had led the inquiry alongside the local police. The grilling had been sharp and suspicious, in a genteel sort of way.

"Mr. Hampton, we sense that you are a cooperative witness." The Scotland Yard inspector, an oversized man with a square ruddy face, seemed larger still in his crisp blue uniform, trimmed with buttons, leather straps, epaulets and badges. "Please tell us what brought you to England and why you think this happened. Was there any reason to expect this?"

For the inquiry, Hampton was the only source. Travis Marshall still lay in the hospital unconscious. During the explosion, a beam traversing the living and dining rooms had crashed down on him.

Hampton took the inspector's question. He explained his digs at Tel-Amon. Next was the conference in San Francisco, followed by the plan to come to England. To remain vague, he said that the manuscripts in Marshall's house had come from "dealers and Bedouin" in Jordan. Irina, he said, had been invited to England to compare these with her Chinese letters. "And for a medical appointment," Hampton said. He mentioned neither Habib nor Winslow.

"What puzzles us, Mr. Hampton, is why this terrorist attack was made against the Marshall home," the inspector said. "Was there anything in your dealings in Israel or Jordan that might hint at people of criminal intent?" This was the inspector's toughest line of questioning. "I assure you, we aren't going to take the names and ring up authorities in Jordan. We can't intervene like that. We just want to see if anyone matches our lists of terrorist organizations."

Hampton felt that the British police suspected the worst about him. He had volunteered information about the manuscripts, which were now destroyed evidence. At the police station, Hampton

216

overheard what one uniformed man thought of him: "It's a black market deal gone awry, I tell you."

The inspector continued with his questioning. "Do you know anything about this type of illicit business?"

"No. Only what I read."

"Was there any exchange of money for these manuscripts?"

"None. They were passed on to us for the sake of translation and scholarship. We could have handled them in a safer way. But we had no idea . . ."

"That someone would get killed?"

"Yes." Hampton swallowed. An image of Irina had filled his mind like a projection on a movie screen. She smiled and her dark almond eyes crinkled upward at the corners.

Two days later, British investigators had ruled there was no evidence of wrongdoing by Hampton or Marshall. The American Embassy was told, however, that the case was not entirely closed. Hampton might have faced trouble with Jordan for taking the manuscripts across its border. But that charge lacked evidence. Only Hampton and Frederick Cornwell at Oxford could testify that the various papyri manuscripts had existed.

But the police had made other links. They found traces of Semtex at both houses. They discovered that the northwest London man had been tied to Ali Basherbisi, a name emerging in investigations of the failed International Credit and Commerce Bank.

"Mr. Hampton." The man from Scotland Yard had leveled a cool stare. "Do you know what we found in the home of this other London man?"

"No, not at all."

"We found a collection of antiquities. No manuscripts. But the objects appear to be quite old and valuable. And quite illegal, I might add. At least one item has been traced to a theft from a Jordanian museum."

Hampton sat mute.

"Do you see this as having any connection to your work, or the work of Mr. Marshall?"

"Not that I know of." Hampton's eyes wandered. "I would imagine that a lot of criminals deal in antiquities, I mean illegal networks sneak them out of countries and around the world." After breathing out this statement, Hampton wished he could suck it back in.

The inspector raised his bushy right eyebrow. "Criminal, yes. This man over in London probably was a criminal blown away by other bloody criminals."

Before Hampton had left England, the British press took the story to colorful heights. Some tabloids evoked memories of the Elgin Marbles, the sculpted figures on the frieze atop the Greek Parthenon that a British envoy had absconded with in the late eighteenth century. Other newspapers speculated at a new link with the bank scandal, which already smacked of drugs, weapons and terrorists. Now the web included antiquities.

A *Sunday Times* story began, "The modern archaeologist is no longer cloaked in images of a dowdy scholar, a diplomat or even a World War II spy. This adventurer is now a black marketeer in search of dark secrets." That was tame next to the *Daily Mirror:* "Crime in Ancient Crypts" read a headline as large as its neighboring "Hanky-Panky at Royal Retreat."

Anne Marshall hadn't read the newspaper for days, spending her time between her London in-laws' house and the hospital. Travis had gained consciousness in four days.

"Good morning, luv," he had mumbled to Anne when he first opened his eyes, dark caves opening under a mountain of white bandages. Marshall's vital signs were good but his recent memory was gone. He remembered calling Hampton in Seattle about the Carbon 14 delay, but everything after that was a blank. He could not remember his lecture notes or the arrival of the papyri. He did not even remember Irina Pleshnikov—or what he did the day of the bombing.

The day before leaving England, Hampton had gone to Ealing Hospital to see Anne. During visiting hours she sat vigilantly next to Marshall's bed, her eyes wet but never narrowed to mask a grudge. "Travis can't say anything right now, but I know he'd tell you not to worry," Anne said. "We're all in this together. I know he'd say that, Nick." Her voice trailed off to a whisper. "Poor Irina."

As Hampton left the ward, the tall thin doctor who had worked over Irina the night of her death caught him in the hallway.

"Excuse me, Mr. Hampton," he called out from the end of the corridor.

Hampton stopped and the doctor approached.

"We're trying to contact the family in the Soviet Union. Her travel papers have been very helpful and the Soviet Embassy will send the information on. We don't know if they want the body or if she'll be buried here."

Hampton bobbed his head, feeling its sudden weight.

"I don't know the Soviet system," the doctor continued, "but I was told by the inspector that the government is not likely to make this death an international incident. You know, times have changed. He said it would have been used for propaganda in the past, but not now. We just want to meet the family's wishes."

"I'm sorry I haven't been of more help."

"Mr. Hampton, the main reason I approach you is . . . a medical matter. We x-rayed for bomb fragments . . . Miss Pleshnikov was a young woman, in the prime of her life. But she didn't have long to live."

"What do you mean?"

"She had a large tumor." As he spoke, the doctor touched the base of his own skull. "It wasn't cancerous yet but it had created an aneurysm which . . ."

"A blood clot?"

"A sac that could burst any time."

"Does pain . . ?"

"The aneurysm gives headaches, shots of pain. Sometimes numbness."

"My God." Hampton pressed his lips together, fighting a quiver. It was a futile attempt at control as memories rushed over him. Behind her peaceful, cheerful character had been pain.

Then the doctor, his stern face softening, said more. "The young woman had some botched surgery, maybe several years ago. It . . . it didn't help her health."

Hampton's face became a painful question mark.

"Her womb," the doctor said. "Perhaps a very careless abortion. I'm certain her death was rapid and painless. I only say this for your comfort."

Hampton had not felt comforted. He felt nothing. God had

allowed Irina to suffer and to die and even at that . . . Hampton had felt nothing.

"Look over there!" Susan McQuinn shook him from his thoughts as they walked along the beach. "Look at the way the sun reflects on the clouds and the bay, and that wisp of rainbow."

Hampton saw it, but the beauty could not sink into his senses.

"Let's walk back now," she said. "I'd love to cook you dinner."

Hampton's hair fluttered about in the soft breeze. He stared at the cloud. Sunlight flickered on the choppy water below.

"I could use a good meal." A wan smile crossed his face, like a thin line, the first tentative stroke on a sketch pad.

She kept her gaze on him. Despite his dark mood, Susan saw him as a little boy, hurt and alone. Now was not the time to talk business. That would be saved for the return to Philadelphia. She had to get back. She could handle Bill Salinger, but what about deciding to move? She did not see how she could oppose it any longer. Seattle beckoned, whatever the terms. She was weary of the battle, but no longer afraid to lose it. In the past few days she had realized that the battle was really with herself.

She walked beside him, dragging her toe in the sand now and then. They reached a widening shoreline with several ways to get back to the parking area. Nick was looking in the direction of a pebbled stretch, which passed a cove of black rocks. He had been pliant all day, so Susan had initiated most of their diversions. She was experiencing in condensed time what it was like to have complete control of him, and it didn't feel right. She was going to have to create a balance, she thought. She was going to have to grant him some power over her; better still, she thought, they had to start giving to each other. She reached for his cold hand.

"Which way should we go, Nick?"

24

The slice of moon above Aqaba annoyed the Jordanian police chief.

Total darkness, he thought, was better. A glance at his watch— 11 P.M.

The June night was hot. A small breeze stirred the waters in the port. The lapping sound rose from below the piers and every ship, even the great freighters, seemed to bob with the lightness of wood.

"The truck's leaving the warehouse," a Jordanian policeman said into his radio. From the top floor of the building, behind the window of a dark room, he spied the action a block away under the dim lighting of the loading docks. "It's turning left toward the highway."

Heavy traffic moved up and down the Desert Highway, the conduit for trade between Aqaba and northern Jordan and Iraq. A police checkpoint radioed that the truck had reached the open highway and begun the winding climb up the barren rocky hills that formed an amphitheater around the port. About fifty miles north the road crossed the high mountain pass at Ras al Naqab. From there a modern highway stretched up the center of Jordan.

"Well, we know the exchange won't be in Aqaba," said the operations chief, a wiry dark Jordanian who had moved up the ranks from a farmer-turned-soldier to a chief in anti-drug operations.

The truck's cargo of small weapons had arrived on a Scandinavian freighter two days earlier. Packed in crates marked "pipe valves" and "corner joints," they were said to be headed for Jordan's northern oil wells. Much of the time the authorities winked at the well-established smuggling routine. It helped the economy. When against it, they faced a hide-and-seek game along the sprawling docks. Hundreds of ships and thousands of crates came and went every few weeks. All hours of the day trucks pulled up at warehouses to take away cargo.

The chief pulled off his cap and wiped his forehead. On a table under a small light in the police station he studied the map. Between Aqaba and Ma'an, a seventy-mile distance, the highway had only a few turnoffs.

This was not the biggest arms and drug deal to go down in Jordan. But the government in Amman had made it a priority. In the past, the government had avoided too many crackdowns on the illicit market. Given the delicate political balance in Jordan, the Hashemite regime did not want to offend the wrong group. The regime controlled the newspapers, but the vast Brotherhood and Palestinian networks controlled public opinion. This bust, required by the peace plan, suspended government timidity.

The operations chief checked his pistol and automatic rifle. Two lieutenants did likewise. They left the light on and went outside to their jeep. The sweltering heat hung wet in the night. The three officers made radio contact and then drove after the truck. Two other police vehicles—a small commercial truck and a station wagon with a half-dozen agents—were already close behind the smuggler's truck. At major turnoffs, other agents stood watch.

An hour later, the truck bearing the crates reached the mountain pass, a sparsely populated area with scattered plateaus, a few small villages, concessions and tourist lookouts.

"I think they're going on to Ma'an," the operations chief said, speculating. "It's about a half-hour to Ma'an. Once we're over the ridge we can radio ahead."

Commercial traffic clogged the pass. Oncoming headlights blinded the agents as they tried to follow the truck. Near a fueling station the truck turned right, down a dirt road toward a small village and commercial area.

"The truck's turned off." That came over the radio from a spotter parked at the intersection.

The chief lifted the intercom to his mouth and squeezed the button. "What did it look like?"

"Two tons. Four in the rear. Commercial plates with the first digits 25. Couldn't see the . . ."

"That's it." The chief wiped sweat from his upper lip. "You and Unit Three go in behind. Tell us where it stops. All others meet at the turnoff."

In a few minutes the police truck and station wagon reached the rendezvous. Soon after the chief and a car from the north arrived. They drove slowly down the dirt road.

"We have contact"—the spotter was on the radio again. "The truck's pulled behind the warehouse next to the fueling station. The station is on the right, near the village turnoff."

The spotter and Unit Three drove past the station and then swung around, aiming their cars up the road. Truckers seeking rest spots drove by sporadically. The spotter saw a solid phalanx of headlights coming down the road, orange parking lights on the chief's jeep in front.

"Units One and Three cover the rear." The chief's dry mouth pressed against the hard intercom. "We'll spread our four cars on the approach."

The phalanx stopped and the chief counted to thirty. "Okay. Let's go in."

Wheels of the six-car pincer kicked up chalk clouds. High beams splashed across the corrugated tin walls of the warehouse, revealing two trucks; the one laden with the drugs had been waiting there. Another bank of headlights came from the rear, topped by a flashing red beacon. The two trucks jerked forward, back, and then ahead like trapped animals wanting escape. Gunshots sounded and the spotter's windshield shattered. The fleeing trucks stalled and the flash of automatic weapons spread like molten sparks in a smelter. The din rose to a deafening pitch and then quieted.

"If you surrender you will not be harmed," the chief said over a megaphone. One agent was dead and another was wounded. Then a man hollered.

"I'm coming out. Don't shoot."

Two or three shiny objects flew from behind the truck, flickered in the light, and hit the ground with little puffs.

"Their guns," the chief said. "They'll surrender."

A figure in dark clothes, a kafiya and beard emerged from behind the truck. He walked toward the four police cars slowly with his hands on his head. Suddenly his arm flung a small dark object. The man dropped to the ground, hugging it as he rolled in the dust.

He died a moment later.

The hand grenade hit the station wagon's hood, bounced once and exploded. Crouching low behind the cars, the agents escaped the shrapnel but three were cut by flying glass. Volleys of gunfire ensued for five minutes until the smugglers' bunker fell quiet.

"We stop. We stop," a voice yelled. "No more shooting."

"Don't trust them yet," the chief yelled. He grabbed the speaker phone. "Come out all at once with your hands straight up." It echoed and he gave the command again. On the second repetition a line of four men came out with their arms reaching up as if they were marionettes on strings.

In Az Zarqa three days later, Habib Muhammad read the account of the police action in the morning newspaper. After the gunfight, the authorities had tracked down the ringleaders in the Brotherhood faction. A spate of arrests had followed. Habib sighed heavily. So much had preceded this final event, he thought. Now it was over. But he knew at what price.

Kalim Hasan had moved to Az Zarqa three weeks earlier. A friend of Habib's had given him a job at a shop counter and a temporary room. Though the Brotherhood was everywhere, Hasan could start a new life in the north under Habib's protective wing.

Hasan had arrived at Habib's home in Az Zarqa late one night, dirty and tired. He had been burdened by a bag of belongings on his back and a tightly wrapped bundle under his arm. After ten minutes in Habib's presence, he had broken into tears.

Once calmed, he had been ready to tell Habib his story. But the old imam had said no. Instead, he had fed him hot tea, bread and eggs, and sent him to bed.

"You will tell me everything in the morning," Habib had said, looking at the young man's distraught face. "We are safe. You can rest."

Shortly after sunrise, Hasan had been awake and nourished by food and Turkish coffee.

"First I must show you the manuscripts," he had said. Handling the bundle carefully, he had opened the cloth sack to a heavy animal skin that contained a shabby roll of papyrus. "These are what you wanted, Imam Habib. I have done my best to fulfill your wishes."

Habib remembered how in the next two days he had obtained the large Arabic books and loosened their bindings. He had flattened the papyri, cracking only one, and slid them into the books. Then he had posted them to Marshall, an action known only to Habib. That could not have led to the bombing, Habib reasoned, but he knew what probably had. His mind went back to the morning after Hasan had arrived at his home.

"Now, Kalim, tell me your story," Habib had said to the young man. "We have not talked for several weeks."

Hasan had narrated in a somber monotone, though his voice had wavered and cracked at times. Four days after the fateful prayer meeting, Hasan had journeyed north, just as a physical clash was breaking out at the Ma'an school. Aides to the mullahs had fought over the lines of authority in the arms plan, leading to a knife fight and, before it was over, drawn guns. At least three had died. One faction had won the upper hand, taking control of the arms exchange and the decision on where to distribute the weapons.

Habib had listened intently, trying to evaluate the implications.

What Hasan had not stayed around to find out was how the spilt blood at the *madrasah* had set up calls for revenge. The fratricide had so offended the religious faction leader that he, in effect, had excommunicated the militants. They in turn had threatened him. For a period, the school had become unsafe for the weekly Shari'a study, conducted by the religious faction.

The Brotherhood, Habib thought, had been split of its own inner mistrust. The nocturnal capture of the heroin and arms north of Aqaba also had led to the arrest of key militant leaders. As the United Nations had wished, the terminus of the exchange had been crushed—at least temporarily. A window for peace talks had been opened a little wider.

But what had gone wrong in England? Habib pondered it torturously. Why the bombing at the London home and the destruction of the manuscripts? So much had been paid for these opportunities; now they were lost. The arms dealer had used an Arab terrorist network to foil his rival in England. But what about the second bombing?

"Why do you think that occurred?" Habib's questions had informed Hasan of the deaths for the first time.

An angry vicious voice had resounded in Hasan's memory, and the revengeful face also had become a clear visage. In Ma'an, a week before the assembly, Hasan had witnessed the frightening clash—the militant who had threatened the religious brother. Now the militant's words returned like a thunderclap: "If you do not ally with our plan, you have broken the pledge . . . If you betray us, if you use the wares from the Bedouin in defiance or our plans . . . then a price must be paid . . . You can test us. You go your own way and punishment will fall. At any corner of the earth, punishment will fall!"

Hasan had shuddered, then raised his eyes to Habib. "The mullahs wanted revenge. They resented the religious faction. They hated to be told that they were not of the true religion. The violent mullahs may have understood how the manuscripts could help Islam face Christianity, but it was not their interest. I think they wanted to cut down the plan of their rival. They had a bombing lined up in London, and they just added another."

"I'm afraid that they have known about Travis Marshall," Habib had speculated.

"That is my fault." Hasan's expression had turned gray and downcast.

"We don't know." Habib had hesitated, uncertain. "He was the courier between Simon Rabin and myself. He was no doubt noticed. He was no doubt linked to Rabin and perhaps to me. There were other signs. Who can know exactly? They found him and through him they tried to punish us all, I suppose, in that one evil act."

Habib had paused. A number of people, the latest being Hasan, had risked their lives for what he and Rabin had envisioned. The Negev. The peace plan. The new archaeology. Yes, those still might succeed. But the manuscripts were lost. An innocent life had been taken.

"You are safe," Habib had said to Hasan. "Now I have work to do with the government and some other men of good will. I can count on you if I need you?"

"Yes, yes, of course."

"Good." Habib had put his hand on Hasan's shoulder. "Any word of your brother?"

"No." Hasan's watery eyes had flashed suddenly and then narrowed. He had turned red and gritted his teeth. "But I think I know what happened, and I will . . ."

Later that morning, Habib again perused the newspaper. The police had confiscated fifty kilograms of heroin and hundreds of small weapons. In the small vehicle carrying the drugs, a crate of antiquities also had been found.

Habib began to think about Nick Hampton. He felt the vast distance between himself and the American scholar who, like Hasan, was another young man he had brought into the orbit of his life. A tragedy had come between. Thousands of miles of geography separated them. "How to bridge that?" Habib asked himself. Now it was safe for Hampton to tell his story, reveal the origin of the manuscripts which, ironically, were now gone, burned to ash. Habib would take a public profile in the next few weeks. No more secrets on his part were necessary.

He must transmit that to Hampton, he thought, but what was the right means? A few weeks had passed since the bombing in England. Hampton had not contacted him. Was there a chasm between them? Was trust or mistrust, friendship or hatred, growing in the confused and violent soil of the past month? Habib decided he must tell Hampton why it all had been done, why the risk had been taken.

He would tell him why he and Simon Rabin had charted this course so many years ago.

25

Hampton's mood was as dark as the room when the alarm clock rang. His hand jabbed for the clock, knocking it to the floor, silencing it. He sat up in bed, debating fiercely with himself—face the day or escape back into sleep? He stood with a grunt, crossed the room, and pulled open the curtains.

Cool light streamed inside. Outside, a northern wind rustled leaves in the small trees and bent the tall ones. Clouds scudded across the sky.

Since Susan had left for Philadelphia, Hampton had tried to get his daily life under control. At all hours his mind thrashed about. He slept poorly. After their walk on the beach, Susan had explained why.

"You need exercise, Nick." She had jogged theatrically in place, and smiled. "If the mind won't calm the body, the body must quiet the mind."

That helped but his sleep was not sound; it was always cut through with odd dreams or sudden recollections that woke him as if he had left something undone. And he could not escape memories of his night with Irina in Room 508.

Now he walked in the sand and marshes every day, straining his body, filling his lungs, and forcing the power of sleep back into his system. His mind began to work in a progression as straight and logical as his walks. At home on the dining table, his Tel-Amon report materials and his fall course work sat neatly organized.

That afternoon, winds pummeled the beach. Hampton watched

the water pick up the rhythm and cast white foamy caps across its dark green surface. Ahead of him, the ivory sand curved behind shoulders of rock that jutted into the water. The beach drew other patrons, all clad in sweaters and parkas, and Hampton recognized the faces of regulars, figures like himself who walked the sands and paths quietly. They thought about different things and different lives, united only by the same symphony of sky, earth and water. A familiar old man with a shock of thick white hair and a tan wrinkled face passed by and the two nodded, as usual.

The wind pushed the tall green and yellow reeds in the marsh at angles. Marsh finches flew about in small platoons and loner sea gulls circled higher above. A red kite, manned by three boys up the beach, soared as they pulled the string back and forth to avoid a fatal tailspin into the water.

Hampton approached a low wide outcropping of gray sandstone. It reached out twenty feet into the water, where smaller moss-covered rocks surrounded it. The blue water turned a greenish black from the interminable chilly depth that lay below the rock's farthest reach.

A family picnicked on the rocks. Their brightly colored coats fluttered in the wind and the father moved shoes, a Thermos and a cooler to anchor the blanket. The children rubbed sand from their eyes. Next to the mother a young girl sat while two fidgety boys kept standing up wanting to wander off. The family was plain, Hampton thought. Typical, middle class, suburban. Not too profound or adventurous, as in their choice of the beach on a bad day, because they wanted to conform, to picnic where everyone else did on a vacation.

Hampton veered inland, following the wavy sand behind the rock. The picnic scene had left his vision when suddenly a gust arose, followed by the sting of sand. The wind escalated, subsided slightly, and then increased. It tore into every cavity in his clothes as if they were sails on a ship. Then he heard the shout.

"Carl! Get away from there!"

Hampton turned and saw the father running across the rock.

"Get back here. Do you hear what . . ."

The boy's red jacket suddenly fluttered up around his shoulders. Hampton himself was nearly pushed over by the gust, but he saw the spot of red disappear over the rock.

"Carl!" The mother screamed. "No! Oh, God!"

The father raced to the edge, stripped off his coat and shoes, and jumped. Hampton ran to the spot. He found the man treading water, his listless son hooked under his left arm. The water was deep but its current mild. The man swam slowly to a sandy bottom thirty feet away and then trudged out of the foamy surf. His dripping face was like a pale death mask. Then Hampton saw the man as looking very ordinary, dressed in loud sports clothes. The image changed again, for as the man embraced his coughing son he became heroic, like a museum statue come to life.

Hampton walked back to the mother, who was clutching the two other children to her breast as all watched the unfolding drama. Her eyes were wide and full of fear, as if she were experiencing her son's fall into deep and cold water herself.

"Can I do anything to help?" Hampton asked.

She wiped her eyes and looked up.

"Thank you." She caught her breath. "I think he's okay. We have some blankets in the car to dry with."

Hampton was speechless, and then he thought of something to say. "Your husband saved him."

The children seemed oblivious. "Carl's going to get us all wet," his brother said.

Hampton excused himself, walked back to his car, and drove home. The warm still air of the house massaged his chilled face and muscles, relaxing his body but not his agitated mind.

Hampton awoke the next morning still bothered by images of the beach, and then he understood why. He'd had a dream of the same oceanside drama, and it was a foreboding one.

Tricks of the brain, he thought, but then he conjured a lucid memory. The winds, the hour, even the colors seemed a replay of yesterday's dramatic rescue. As he walked toward the picnicking family, the boy in the red jacket stood and ran toward the rock's edge. The boy stopped and came back, running his course again and daring the wind like a red flag before a bull. The parents watched. Finally the boy could not stop his run and the wind flung him into the treacherous water. Hampton tried to scream but couldn't. The water beyond the rock was deep and dark, a great

230

Pacific trench. In his mind's eye, he saw the boy plunging down, perhaps miles down, into the cold, green darkening water. The parents watched impassively, then returned to the picnic. Only the girl's face revealed loss and pain. The family packed and went home.

Hampton sat hunched over his breakfast. Dreams typically bring on the sensation of being out of control, he thought. The most bizarre things can happen. After pouring a cup of black coffee he cleared the dining room table, the same place where he and Winslow had speculated on the manuscript fragments. Now they were gone. The four pieces of papyrus, too, were lost to the eye but not totally to Hampton's memory, where he began to reconstruct the Aramaic.

He tried to remember groups of sentences, sayings or narratives. Whatever surfaced from his memory he jotted on a yellow legal pad. When his mind went blank, he ran an errand, did housework or walked on the beach—anything to keep shaking loose the recollections.

The morning of the fourth day he awoke emotionally empty, questioning what good the three-day exercise had done. The legal pads were filled with words, ideas, sentences, but all of them uncertainties. After checking the time, he sat down by the telephone and dialed.

"Just do your best," Winslow said on the other end of the line, responding to Hampton's frustration. Winslow viewed the project as therapy, not scholarship. By work, Hampton could grind away his self-recrimination. "Nick, my advice is for you to keep the big picture. Finish Tel-Amon. That's a way to climb back up the ladder."

Winslow had rushed to his defense publicly after London but Hampton had silenced him, warned him off. "I don't want you or Habib tainted," Hampton had said. That was stubbornness to Winslow's mind, but he had acquiesced. Still, he gave his private advice and it usually penetrated Hampton's high-strung pride.

"Jack, there's another thing," Hampton said. "I haven't contacted Habib since London. It's been two weeks and I'm not sure what's happening."

"Follow your best instincts on that, Nick. I never met the man."

"I think I'd better keep a low profile until this whole thing blows over. I'd like to wait until Travis recovers."

"I see no hurry." Winslow paused as a thought crossed his mind.

"If Habib does get back and says there's more to come, you remember my promise."

"Are you up to it? Edith won't like it."

"That's not a big worry. If you need someone to go to Jordan, I'll do it."

After Hampton hung up he mulled the advice.

That night he read through the four Gospels, searching for a sense of where to take his memory project. And that night he dreamt. Again, it was the family on the beach, the boy in the red coat, the red kite. His mood in the dream was deep frustration, as if he were unable to move or speak. Hampton sat in the sand with a Bible, searching through the book's red-letter sayings of Jesus. The red coat and red kite were telling him that the sayings were the key and he was trying to understand the previous night's dream—why the parents had not saved their drowning boy. As he turned the Bible pages the red text came off the surface. He tried to scoop the pieces up but they broke and fell on the sand. Worse still, the Bible was not his. He struggled futilely to fix the Bible before its owner arrived, but the more he tried the more the crimson mixed with the sand and changed the beach's color. Then came an ominous presence: the owner—not a figure, but two eyes. Under their gaze Hampton felt utter failure and blame. Yet he lifted his head to look. Behind the eyes, in a mind that knew him so well, he found forgiveness and the nightmare was over. He turned the Bible's pages and the red letters were restored. Beneath him, the sand, bleached clean, glistened white. He looked up and the boy in the red jacket was running carefree along the beach.

A summer fog covered the bay the next morning. Hampton awoke with a lucid mind and calm stomach. Yet as the sun burned away the pallid overcast, he also changed. He was sitting at the table pondering his work when the dream's residual joy disappeared. According to the dream, he had been forgiven. But the guilt, and its relentless interrogation, still lay just below the surface and it had returned. Who was to blame for Irina's death? Chance, fate or himself? Perhaps the emptiness came from something else. Did it come because he had truly loved her, and something had been taken away from him? Memories flooded back, some murky and stagnant, others clear and deep. He had once believed that she was naive, but now he wondered. She had talked about love as an artist examines a painting, looking for purpose, order and emotion. Once again Hampton's mind fixed on this, and once more he relived that night in San Francisco in the Commodore Hotel.

With Nick in the lead, Irina closed the door of room 511 behind her and timidly crossed the musty hallway of the Commodore to room 508. They sat the same as in her room—he in the chair and she on the bed. After a little small talk about the conference, the nice city, Hampton's voice trembled.

"I don't know what has happened, Irina, but I have fallen in love with you."

She almost laughed but kept a constant fix on his eyes. He diverted his eyes as he struggled to get his words just right, for he was speaking from a mind that was confused.

"This has never happened to me before," Hampton said. "I don't know what to do, especially since you're leaving tomorrow." Then the hardest part. "I don't know what you think of men, but our desire can be . . . and . . . that's what I feel for you. I want to hold you, be as close to you as possible."

At that point Irina took one of his hands in hers, holding it calmly. He began to rise as if to embrace her but she put out a gentle hand and pushed his chest.

"No, Nicholas. Nothing can happen this quick in life, if it's important."

He smiled sheepishly and sank back down. "I'm sorry, Irina."

"Don't you have someone you've known a long time?"

That's right, Hampton remembered. He had mentioned Susan, just in passing. He didn't remember if he had said fiancee or had just noted her visit. During the next half-hour, as they discussed friendships and affections, Hampton thought he understood what was happening. He and Susan had grown into their relationship with no fireworks at the start, and none were expected down the road. Now he was under the spell of love at first sight.

"You know, someone like me can live by his head for so many years and neglect other things. And then one day something happens. It starts small but grows big, almost overnight. It's really falling in love. Maybe infatuation's a better word." He almost told her that fatuous means foolish.

"Why is that experience so important?" Irina rested her chin on her hand and her black hair swung softly around her face. In the low light, her complexion was soft as a dream.

He couldn't answer. "All I know is that when something like this happens, it consumes everything. I had so many things to care about, and now I care only about one thing."

Irina stared ahead. "Does it last?" Her stare continued, as if she saw something that was invisible to Hampton. "I think many people get this feeling, but does it last? Does it grow? Does it change you so you become better, less selfish, more free?" She searched his expression for an answer.

Hampton resisted her dissecting this force in him, but how else could she respond? He knew that she did not reciprocate his feelings, a fact he did not want to accept. Now she was using the word commitment. And then she said a funny thing about herself.

"I am not so wise about love," Irina said. "I think it's a gift we all have, but my parents suffered for having it. Having it not in the right ways, I think . . ." Irina paused and brushed one eye. "They suffered quite a lot. They loved each other but they had to leave each other. It was a conflict of loves, for each other, for children, for their parents. Too many centers of love that were fighting each other . . ." She smiled. "So you see, I saw love, or some powerful emotion, pull my family apart. Love has a bitter side, doesn't it? If it's not returned it leads to great sadness . . . If love's not big enough, it ends up making you go against others."

They talked and did not count the hours, losing track of time and in sleepy resignation shutting out the world. As Irina spoke more and more, Hampton was struck by what seemed to be an immodesty, or experience, that was behind her thoughts. "I had to help my father," she said. "He needed medical treatment and . . . well, I had to work for someone, a terrible man who ran the hospital, who knew my family's political background. We had no money." She stared at Hampton, hoping he might understand without her saying more.

Hampton, for his part, wasn't sure; but he knew he had stumbled on deeper, darker wells of emotion than his love-tinted understanding of Irina had allowed. They moved on, if only from awkwardness.

234

Irina said, "I believe God suffers because he loves. God suffers because we don't love God back. Jesus had that same love to give. But no one returned it either. And so Jesus suffered."

Hampton wanted to embrace her, hold her as if he could hold goodness itself, but he knew his desires were too mixed up. She stayed with him until nearly dawn. They told stories from their lives, but Irina never delved into the sad recesses that Hampton sensed were there. She asked him to talk about Susan, which he did. It was for him a wonderful communion, but when it was over he came away baffled and emotionally bruised.

She did not long for him the way he desired her. And it hurt.

After that night, Hampton had looked for signs of love around him. The real kind, the love that Irina, by her hardships, seemed to understand.

Now he sat at the breakfast table alone. "I saw love at the beach," he said to himself. Hadn't the parents loved the children, loved them so much they couldn't do without them? Love became very complicated in his thoughts. Had he really loved Irina, or had he merely needed her—needed her to want only him, to need him for her happiness. Peeling away layers of illusion and self-pity, Hampton suddenly closed in on the root of his sadness. It was unrequited love, an infatuation not returned.

Emotion shook him, and in what seemed to be only an instant Hampton saw things differently. His experience of rejection shrank before a mountainous heart. His concerns were tiny in comparison to what was happening in the realm of God, a reality he was able to glimpse by his own small experience.

"God experiences unrequited love," he said to himself. "God is an unrequited lover." The understanding arrived like a revelation handed to him on Mount Sinai. "Jesus was also an unrequited lover. His love was rejected. He walked the earth feeling the same way God feels."

Hampton began to mumble, like a prayer half-spoken. When he spoke the word "sorry" it seemed so trite, but he knew no other way to talk to God. I'm so sorry! He was sorry, utterly sorry that he had never cared and never understood how God felt. The repentance plunged him to his core, to the self that God had given him. He pressed his fingers against his eyes, but it was useless. The blue ink on the yellow pads below began to smear as the tears poured down.

Eventually, Hampton rose from the table. He stretched reflexively, for his body was cramped as if it were pulled tightly together by a divine purse string. Without leaving his chair, he had taken a very far journey, both inward and outward. And God was in every place. He stood behind the chair and all the tension and mental fatigue of the past few days lifted. A new kind of tiredness came over him; it was wholesome and he succumbed easily, lying on his back on the couch to fall asleep.

When the phone rang, he opened his eyes to a twilight glow. It made his living room a fuzzy blue-gray, progressing toward darkness with every passing second.

"Hello." He sounded groggy.

"Nicholas," Susan said. "Oh, dear, did I wake you?"

Not a problem, Nick said.

"I had this urge to call you so I came home early from work. I just wanted to talk." Still, Susan was not sure if she would tell him about her job situation. But she wanted to start communicating, talking to him in more ways than her letters.

Hampton envisioned her sitting alone at home. He considered his own surroundings, dark and quiet. He saw two people in two dark houses, lonely because they stubbornly waited for each other. He reached over and turned on the lamp. As if from beyond the grave, Irina was giving him a final lesson for his life. Now he understood how so many opposites can reconcile. He did not have to condemn himself to self-absorption and selfishness, but could make his life helpful to others. And love between man and woman was not opposite to the love of God, for their love could be elevated to something godly.

"I'm really glad you called," Nick said. "It's been an unusual few days. I finally had a good sleep." He stumbled over what he was trying to say, but then recovered with straightforward language. "Sue, we really ought to get married. Will you marry me? I hope you haven't given up on me. But I don't blame you."

A high-pitched sound escaped as Susan caught her breath. "Yes, of course I will marry you." Her voice slowed to a purr. "Are you sure you can put up with me?"

"Of course I can put up with you. I can't do without you." He

236

rambled a bit more, unsuccessful at describing his past few days, and particularly that afternoon.

Susan could not believe her timing; it had never been so good. She brushed aside a tear, determined to equal Nick's frankness. She had actually called on another matter. "Nick, I may have found a way to move to Seattle."

26

The Bedouin boy saw a pillar of dust rise on the horizon. In the hazy air that covered the wide Jordanian plain, the whitish wavering column stood out against the purple cliffs. The boy ran up the sandy road, bumping into goats grazing on its brush and, breathless, reached the low black tents.

The United Nations people were coming.

From behind their black veils, Bedouin women warbled their tremulous cries, a sound that attended celebration, war, marriage or calling in the flock.

The brother-in-law of Sheik Salam al Faqir stood outside the tent looking through binoculars. He had organized the reception at the village of Umm Sayhun outside of Petra. The sheik, who represented the six tribes to Jordan's government, came out of his large goat-hair tent. Village elders surrounded him while village children were being told to stay back by the cinder-block houses. He wore a white kafiya with two black bands, a gray vest over his white robe, and a black frock with gold trim.

The hint of dust on the horizon became a two-jeep caravan, moving slowly now. It passed the reddish sandstone cliffs and slopes and penetrated the wandering herds along the road.

A blue flag with the white United Nations emblem fluttered from the front of the head jeep. The party was all Jordanian except for a French UN official, who spoke Arabic.

"*Ahlan wa Sahlan.*" The sheik gave the customary desert greeting, "Welcome, twice welcome," with aplomb, then led his visitors into the shade of the tent. They sat cross-legged or reclined on the heavy pillows cast about a large Persian rug. The sheik and the UN man sat together at the head of the group.

"We appreciate your support." The Frenchman gestured with his weather-beaten hands as he spoke. "Petra and the area along Wadi Mesa and the Jordan rift will become an international center."

The sheik nodded. "This is good for my people. It is good for the desert and the future." He gestured at a half-dozen dark-skinned children peeking at the gathering from outside the tent.

The thick sweet Turkish coffee was passed around. Bread for the meeting toasted on a fire outside the tent; its fragrance wafted into the tent on a warm breeze.

The Frenchman lifted his cup as in a toast. "For their future."

The Gulf War had been over for five months. The Middle East peace talks were scheduled for Madrid in two months. The sheik was one of the last of the Bedouin chiefs to be visited in two weeks of seeking local support.

The next day, the United Nations would announce its effort to bring peace through a joint business initiative among Jordan, Israel, Egypt and Saudi Arabia. With a military security line from Mazar to the Dead Sea to Beersheba, leaders in Jerusalem and Amman would organize an open border in the south, focusing on cities like Aqaba, Petra and Mazar in Jordan and Elat, Sedom and Dimona in Israel.

The sheik smiled throughout the talks and showed his generosity to everyone. After five generations in the mountains, his people were getting used to improved living in government-built single-room homes with amenities. The caves where they had lived in Petra's sandstone cliffs, some two thousand, had become tourist haunts. Besides their wheat harvesting and goat herding, they had taken on more contemporary roles as merchants, restaurant and hotel workers, guides and even scouts to find lost tourists.

Habib Muhammad waited until late afternoon to begin his trip to Amman. Earlier in Geneva, the joint business zone and peace plan had been announced. It was called the Abraham Pact.

Habib had heard the report from Geneva on the BBC. He wished Simon Rabin were alive. Neither of them would have attended such an official announcement, for their roles as instigators were to remain

239

unknown—a choice of their own. If Rabin were still alive, they would be continuing their symmetry, each in his own country encouraging the same peace. Now only Habib could follow through.

As a worker at the Az Zarqa mosque drove the car south, following the mountain plateau that led to Amman, Habib reviewed his speech. He reached inside his white robe for his silver-rimmed reading glasses. He would speak on Jordan Radio at 7 P.M.

Already, protests had flared. One radical sheik at Old Jerusalem's Al Aqsa Mosque, where Habib had once served, had used particularly fiery oratory. "My old rival," Habib said to himself. The sheik was his violent opposite, and yet they had come this far together.

The radical wings of the Muslim Brotherhood and the PLO were united in their sentiments: never should Arab and Jew join in settlements and business, even in the Negev and south Jordan. The right-wing parties had exploded during floor debate in Israel's Knesset, but Likud and Labor Party supporters of the plan had exploited a new weakness. The four ultra-Orthodox religious parties had waned in influence; now they were split over one party's claim that their rabbi might be the Messiah. Both Likud and Labor had other reasons to make a concession—the United States and Soviet Union had made the economic initiative a condition for financial aid and Soviet immigration. The prime minister of Israel and the king of Jordan embraced the policy by not opposing it. The Hashemites still had the historic loyalty of the Bedouin, so that southern population was a reliable backer, too.

Many of the three hundred Jewish-Arab cooperation projects, from ecology to conflict resolution and child care, supported the policy. So did private and government concerns, such as watershed farms and desert reclamation ventures. Some decried the initiative as yet another injustice to Bedouin rural life, but that was obviated by a Grazing Land Research Center plan: lease Bedouins land, form farm villages of up to eighty families, support them with roads, water and utilities, and, in summer, allow the Bedouin to graze flocks in the north.

The week of the announcement, a wealthy Jewish businessman in Florida said he would commit $10 million to a resort center and retirement community. An Egyptian financier in San Francisco tried to outdo him—he would invest in pleasure boats for recreation on the Gulf, with docking in Egypt's Sinai, Israel's Elat and Jordan's

Aqaba with its beautiful coral reefs. Corporate leaders in both Japan and South Korea announced interest in mineral export, using new, ecologically sound methods for mining. An entrepreneur in Washington state announced a plan to reforest the barren slopes below Ma'an in Jordan and to expand oases and cultivatable soil in Israel's Negev.

UNESCO heralded the new opening as a way to promote research and cultural preservation in the region. Likewise, the American Society for Oriental Research called it a new boon for archaeology, especially the ability to compare sites and finds on either side of the border.

At the Vatican, the pope supported the peace in a statement from his apartment window overlooking St. Peter's Square. Yet the next day's front-page editorial in the Vatican newspaper, *L'Osservatore Romano,* added a proviso to the papal praise, one that stirred speculation amid Vatican watchers. "With the new open territory," it said, "we must insist on the church's right of stewardship over ancient Christian treasures that surely may be found."

In a special room at the government radio station, Habib said evening prayer with other observant Muslims. He relaxed for a half-hour and then was led into the broadcast booth. He sat at a table with a large microphone. He sipped water from a glass, wetting his throat.

He too had been an imam at the great Al Aqsa Mosque in Old Jerusalem. In that vast room he had learned to project his voice, so that it bounced off the tiles that covered the domed ceiling and arched walls, like a song from heaven. His voice, he mused, was trained for this hour. A technician wearing a cumbersome headset stood on the other side of the sound room window ready to signal Habib.

A state announcer sat beside Habib and gave the introduction.

"His Excellency King Hussein has today taken a step for peace," the announcer began. "With wide consultation among the friendly nations of the world, Jordan has agreed to a joint business effort with Israel under United Nations supervision."

The king, he continued, wanted the country to reflect on the name of the pact—Abraham. To that end, the king had called on a distinguished religious leader of Jordan, who had been instrumental in the vision of the plan, to communicate its meaning.

At this, all eyes fixed on Habib. The technician swung down his forearm, his extended forefinger aimed at the imam.

"In the name of God the merciful," Habib began. "My fellow Muslims, fellow Jordanians, and Christian and Jewish friends, I speak to you tonight as one trained in the ways of Islam. That has been our ideal since the time of the prophet, who called us to submission to the will of Allah. He also called us to tolerance and peace. I am not a politician. I do not have a solution for the troubles between Arabs and Jews in the occupied territories, in our world. That is for our leaders to move forward with. They will conduct peace talks. We will trust their wisdom. What I come to support tonight is a more modest beginning, an effort to bring life to a desert shared both by Arabs and Jews."

Habib recited Islam's teachings on the heirs of Abraham, whom the Koran called People of the Book. He cited the Prophet's call for tolerance and persuasion through moral power.

"The project is an economic one. It hopes to mix Arab and Jew and improve their lives, the lives of their families. It hopes to bring the world to our doorstep. For the technicians and engineers I leave the questions about new mining projects, new cultivation of the desert, desalinization of water, reforestation of the barren hills, the harnessing of the wadis to direct water to enrichment. What I can speak of tonight is the spiritual outlook true Muslims must have toward cooperation. God is merciful, and has allowed us this chance to realize the equality of men and women before him."

As Habib spoke, he thought again of Rabin. He would not mention him, a man who had taught him something about the spirit of the speech he gave that night. He only wished Rabin could be giving the same speech in Israel. The dream of the Negev Institute was taking flesh; Habib hoped that Rabin, from whatever realm he dwelt in, could see it was so.

On the way home to Az Zarqa, Habib was at peace with his old age. The project and the future were in the hands of God, but not only God. The peace was also in the hands of the government and the people, and he could see himself spending his last years encouraging both to build that dream. In his conscience, however, one matter remained.

* * *

A day later Nick Hampton's telephone rang.

His reaction was physical. Excitement and nervousness. "Jordan," the operator said.

"Mr. Hampton." Habib's voice came through strong and clear. "Time has passed quickly. I hope you will forgive my negligence."

"That's all right." Hampton sat down. "It was easier to wait . . . wait for you to call than for me to contact you."

They shared their common and partial knowledge: the tragedy in England; the loss of the manuscripts; Marshall's recovery of health but little memory; the interdiction of the drug and arms deal; and the announcement of cooperation in the Negev.

"Mr. Hampton, you have carried a great burden on my behalf. I owe you much for that. I call to thank you for your confidentiality and to say that I release you from the promise you made to me. You may tell your story. It is tragic that the manuscripts were lost. These are the evils of our time. But there are more, I believe. The Negev has a future and that includes archaeologists like yourself."

Hampton felt relieved. Still, he did not understand all the intricacies of what stemmed from the Middle East, or from Habib, or from the Brotherhood. But he knew he could defend himself with all the facts. Days earlier, as he was hunched over his table at home, his arrogance had died. Yes, the facts were important, he felt, but not his reputation. "Thank you, Habib."

"The one thing . . ." Habib fell silent, wondering how to explain. "Hasan obtained the manuscripts for us. We also wanted to obtain maps from the Bedouin on places where they found materials. But that was not possible."

Hampton recalled the maps that Marshall had given him at the Negev Institute, land contours on a grid, the various sites marked. They were still stuffed in his suitcase, sent back from Israel but not opened since his arrival.

Hampton asked, "Rabin made his own maps, didn't he?"

"Yes, I suppose he did, but there was nothing . . . they did not include the Bedouin information."

Hampton could see the loss.

"I wish to make amends with you. Will you travel to Jordan to see me? There is more I would like to tell you."

Hampton was torn. This was no time to travel. His peers were watching him, his university was investigating his tenure. And it would separate him psychologically from Susan, who was coming to Seattle soon. With his work already behind schedule, a new development would drown him.

Then he remembered Jack Winslow's offer.

"A good friend of mine can make the trip," Hampton said. "He is older and wiser and experienced, like you. That would be best at this time."

"That is fine. I will honor you through your friend. We will talk and he can bring it back to you."

"When should the meeting take place?"

"I hope very soon. The hour is right."

Hampton said he would aim for within two weeks. He would contact Habib with the arrival time. As he hung up, he knew the task would be relatively easy.

Jack might relish the adventure.

The thin blue envelope had Italian markings on it and a brightly colored stamp that showed a prophet painted by Michelangelo on the Sistine Chapel ceiling.

Winslow opened it, knowing its likely contents.

After the reunion in San Francisco three months earlier, he had been flooded with thoughts of his past. Among those haunting images was Joseph Sodano, now a Vatican official.

Sodano began his letter with, "So nice to hear from you, Jack. The years have flown by since our youth, but it is warming to know the memories can last."

Winslow had written an equally friendly letter, not knowing if it would get through. He was not familiar with the Vatican—how its mail was delivered, how busy its officials were; whether Sodano, with his new responsibilities, would remember him, let alone respond. But he did, more than Winslow expected.

"How can a man forget the one who dragged him away from death on a sandy beach . . ." Sodano apologized that he had not remained in touch. He'd just completed an archival project on the Middle East, and now his time was free. He was eager, he said, to do an old compatriot a favor.

"Congratulations on your retirement," Sodano's letter continued. "But I see your search for truth has not retired. Good! I am intrigued by your report on the Soviet Union, especially the Nestorian letters and the Vatican inquiries of the war period. Please suggest a time for early summer and I will be happy to host you. We shut down in August to escape the heat. Mid- to late June is best."

Winslow's wife Edith would love to see Italy. They would go together.

At least that was the plan until Hampton called. On the way to Rome, Winslow would stop in Amman.

27

The two old men considered each other with empathy. Both had seen wars. Both had sought a universal truth. Both had raised families, knowing the love and heartache. And in their sixties now, both knew what was important in life. The important things were still remembered, stories that made life, with its hardships and dashed hopes, worthwhile.

"The travel must have tired you," Habib said.

"It's a strange thing about age. Sometimes the body doesn't need sleep, just a reason to go on."

"I hope I've given a good reason."

"Oh, yes, indeed."

Their laugh was mild, but deep.

Habib brought Winslow to the same house in Amman where Nick Hampton had met him. The brightly woven rugs, like timeless icons, hung on walls and covered floors. The thick scent of olive oil and herbs filled the small home.

"When Mr. Hampton said he must share the manuscript fragment with someone, I acquiesced but felt reluctant. Now I see he was wise in that."

"I've known him since he was a boy," Winslow said. "He's facing a tough time now but he'll get through. I came because I want to help him, but, frankly, these events have changed my life, too."

"And mine as well, Mr. Winslow."

"Jack."

"Yes, of course, Jack." Habib chuckled. "I keep my formalities even in old age. Tonight I want to be very candid. I trust you will pass this on to Mr. Hampton."

Winslow nodded. The woman of the house came in with tea and finger food. From outside the room her husband peeked in, honored that by serving Habib he could host the world in his small back-street home.

Habib explained how after Simon Rabin had died, Hampton had been chosen as a Western scholar to be given the manuscripts. Winslow followed much of the tale, but missing parts were filled in, such as the struggle over the manuscripts within the Brotherhood.

"Let me ask you this," Habib said. "Knowing that some Muslims wanted these materials to discredit your faith, do you resent that we were involved?"

Winslow thought, and wished he had his pipe to help him. "I do wonder how the Muslims thought such texts would be disruptive, even if heterodox. From a Christian point of view, yes, they do raise new questions. But Christianity is so far along that it cannot easily be shaken."

Habib cupped his bearded chin in his hand, his dark eyes fixed on Winslow. "I think the Muslims thought the texts could disrupt Christianity because, right or wrong, they have an impression about the Christian West. They see so much division over your sacred text."

Habib mentioned the death in London.

"Yes, I met the girl briefly in San Francisco."

Habib's face was like sadness carved in stone, its lines hardened but the eyes soft and misty. "I wish we could have avoided this violence," he said.

Winslow's eyes narrowed. "Are you safe? There's opposition to your stand on the Negev peace."

"I want others who helped me to be safe, like this young man Hasan. But for me?" He raised his hands slightly and thrust forward his bearded chin. "I don't worry. I am old. We are not fatalists in Islam, in the best of Islam. But we, I, do surrender to God's will. So the safety of my soul is what concerns me, not my physical life."

Habib fell silent and shifted in his chair, crossing his hands on his lap. "When Nick Hampton and I talked in this very room, I raised the question of motivation. Why I am doing this? Now I want to tell you everything."

Winslow sipped the tea and nodded. Absentmindedly he

reached for his pipe. Habib saw it come halfway out of his coat pocket, and then be shoved back in.

"Please," the imam said. "You may smoke. My story may go on a while so please make yourself comfortable."

Winslow took his pipe and tobacco pouch out of his coat, listening closely to Habib.

"You may know something of our history here. The Ottoman empire, the British and French occupations and the Palestine mandate after the First World War. I was born in Aleppo in Syria in that period, of Jordanian and Syrian parents."

The story paralleled Winslow's own. A search for truth. Years of study. A youthful struggle to be faithful to one's creed. Habib had studied at the leading mosque of Islam in Cairo, Al Azhar. Then, a slow rise to prominence.

"During the war I came in contact with Europeans and some Israelis," Habib said. "My young mind was broadened, and yet it drank deeply from Islam. Study helped me see the role Islam had played for the West, preserving Aristotle, medicine, science during Europe's Dark Ages. I was learning this before the resurgence in the late 1950s of what some call the anti-Western movement. I already held some view of a wider world."

In 1947, Habib said, he had been selected to teach at the Rawdah School, a building on the north side of the Temple Mount in Arab-controlled Jerusalem. On the other side of the mount was the Al Aqsa Mosque; in the middle, the Dome of the Rock.

"I think I was naive." Habib's laugh was subdued, ironic. "Rawdah was the center of Arab nationalism. When I got there I realized just how political it was. I tried to focus on teaching the Koran, leading the prayer, helping with charity."

Winslow thought of 1947. He had returned from the Pacific war, finished his degree and been ordained that year.

"When the battle for Jerusalem took place, I was twenty-eight," Habib said.

That was the year, Winslow recalled, when he had begun serving a sleepy, affluent suburban church.

Habib recounted the history. The British allowed Jews to return to Palestine under the 1917 Balfour Declaration, but reversed that during the 1939 wartime alliance with the Arabs. The mufti of Jerusalem, installed by the British in 1922, led the Palestinian Arab

248

crusade against the Jews' return. His name was Muhammad Said Haj Amin el Husseini. He had been a student at the great mosque in Cairo, the Al Azhar, before he had turned cynical about religion and turned to soldiering for the Turks. He fomented riots and killings and during the war sided with Germany, living there as a guest. After the United Nations voted in 1947 to create Jewish and Arab states and an international zone in Jerusalem, the mufti stayed in exile but his two thousand guerrillas were the main force fighting the Jews.

"He hated the British and the Jews," Habib said.

"I take it you did not respect him."

"At the time I was young, so I didn't know. It was all bigger than my comprehension. I just thought the hatred was too much, especially because the Rawdah was a religious school. Especially if he was supposed to be a mufti, a religious leader."

It was obvious to Winslow that the history narrative was leading to something, a point Habib wished to make. He listened patiently.

After the United Nations' vote, the Arabs formed a liberation army, the Jews armed themselves and small fights broke out. A month before the British Mandate ended on May 15, 1947, the Haganah captured the lands between the Mediterranean and Jerusalem. The Jews formed a provisional government in Tel Aviv. Egyptian air raids began that night, and the next day the British left as Arab armies invaded.

"The Jews tried to cut a supply line to Jerusalem," Habib said. "At least they wanted to save the Old City's Jewish quarter, which was surrounded. The Jews came to the walls of the Old City in force, so King Abdullah of Jordan sent in his Arab Legion. They kept the Old City and on May 28 the Jewish quarter surrendered."

Habib sipped his tea. He raised his hand, as if saying that everything he'd said had merely paved the way for what was to come next.

"This is the time I wanted to bring you to. The city was divided. Arabs controlled the old, the Israelis the new. There was a month-long cease-fire. No agreement was reached. When the cease-fire ended in mid-July, the Israelis began to shell East Jerusalem. To be fair, the Arabs had mercilessly shelled West Jerusalem . . . an Arab Legion commander planned to shell the Dome of the Rock and say the Jews did it . . ."

Habib grimaced. "War can be very cynical with religion, you

see." He looked vacant for a moment and then captured his train of thought. "So elsewhere, the Israelis took northern territory. In the fall they took the Negev and Beersheba. Finally the armistice talks began with the Arab states in January 1949. . . . I'm getting ahead of myself."

"We were in Jerusalem after the cease-fire," Winslow said.

"Yes, of course. After shelling the old city, the Israelis launched an attack to capture it. They had only two days because they had agreed to another UN cease-fire negotiation." Habib leaned forward and spoke in a whisper. "The history books tell what happened, but there was something more. The Israelis came up the slopes to the old city, but could not breach the wall. Only one group, the Stern Gang, who wanted to blow up the mosques on the Temple Mount, got inside the gate. The Jaffa Gate. They were held there by the Arabs. But another team got farther."

Habib told of how he and two others had been inside the Al Aqsa Mosque, replete with its rugs and tiles in reds, browns, golds and oranges, during that twenty-four-hour siege. "We sent everyone away. We could hear the artillery, the spurts of gunfire. Suddenly there was an explosion near the mount. We went into the main sanctuary of the mosque. Its doors burst open, and about a half-dozen Israeli soldiers rushed in. Three of them searched the halls and the others came toward us. They spoke Hebrew, which I understood. One of the soldiers was very angry. He aimed his machine gun right at us! 'We should kill them,' he kept saying. One of them said, 'No!'"

Habib seemed to choke. He patted his forehead with a white cloth.

"This soldier had taken off his shoes in the mosque. He was looking around, deciding on something. Then the angry soldier pulled the cock on his machine gun. That's when the one in the socks pushed him down, so the gunfire sprayed the wall beside us. They had a big argument about cowardice and Arab loving, about avenging family and blood. 'Killing is not the only answer,' the one in the socks shouted. 'They are teachers.'"

Habib's watery eyes stared at Winslow. "Do you see?"

"His respect for imams?"

"Not respect for imams who taught to kill. But for teachers of life, God, humanity."

Habib continued the story.

"Suddenly, they were radioed to retreat. The army failed to go through the wall. As the soldiers disappeared, one shouted at the soldier in the socks, 'Simon Rabin, hurry.'"

The room fell quiet. Winslow puffed on his pipe. The smoke wafted slowly to the side of the room, driven by a window draft, as he contemplated this new revelation.

For a few more years after the battle, Habib served at the mosque. He tried to be a voice of moderation. He did not last. The mosque leadership grew radical. "I was at Al Aqsa in 1951 when King Abdullah was assassinated. The suspicion became so great, at the school, the mosque. After it was all settled I asked to leave. I came to Jordan."

"When did you meet Rabin?"

"Years later. I researched who he was. We met in Geneva at a forum. He used to travel to Europe. He had a family trust to take care of. Investments, I believe. I think it was in Vienna. Simon never desired after money, but he knew it could keep him independent in his work."

Habib pulled at his beard. He had wandered off his topic.

"Well, we learned we had both lost family. Then the most uncanny thing—both our great-grandparents had come from Aleppo. A great-grandfather of his had served at the Aleppo synagogue, before it was burned. Mine were merchants. That was a time of tolerance, you see. There was Jewish and Arab interaction, cooperation. Even some intermarriage. Our ancestors had similar names."

"Were you related by blood?"

"We felt like brothers, but we didn't know. So many records were destroyed. Synagogue records, city census. Names changed."

"And you decided to work together," Winslow said.

"We had no pretense." Habib shrugged and sighed. "Two men could not alter Palestine. But we could do something, and we did. Simon would have been speaking now if he were alive. At least some of what he worked for continues today."

"The Negev Institute? The peace plan?"

"Yes." Habib grinned, and for a moment he seemed to be half his real age, young and vital. "And that I might meet people like you and Mr. Hampton and tell our story."

251

"Your family . . ."

"It's only my wife and I." Habib chuckled. "Now I must go and talk with her, make plans for the future. I must prepare. Anything might happen."

28

From the airplane, Winslow saw Rome at sunset. The Tiber wound through the city like a shiny ribbon. Orange light from the horizon caught domes, spires, arches, gardens and bridges, defining them in extreme contrasts just before the darkness fell.

The trip from Amman had driven Winslow to exhaustion. At the Columbus Hotel, a fifteenth-century building between the Vatican and the Tiber, he slept until noon. He awoke to a voice and a knock.

"Service?" an Italian maid said. "Do you need service, please?"

Winslow sat up. "No thank you." Then he said it in Latin. She laughed and trundled her cart down the hallway. His Vatican appointment was the next morning. So he decided to scout the city for places to take Edith, who had agreed to take her own flight into Rome the next evening—not their original vacation plan.

Rome's traffic lived up to its reputation. After a cab ride to the catacombs and then the Roman Forum, Winslow was ready for the Vatican on foot. The taxi dropped him at the Porta Sant' Anna, a gate and busy intersection at the northeastern corner of Vatican City. As the sky turned dark blue, he walked around the corner to St. Peter's Square and toward the obelisk at its center. Yellow light glowed in the church's upper windows and the adjacent papal apartments. A few stray clouds turned pink in the sunset. Winslow looked up at the statues on the Vatican cornice.

One of the clouds moved from behind the roof, giving a bright backdrop to the dark silhouettes. The statue of Christ, with a Latin halo, held the cross of his crucifixion in his left hand and gave the two-finger blessing. Next to Christ stood John the Baptist, dark against a passing bright cloud. A rough girdle was carved around his stone physique. His left hand held a bronze rod crowned with a cross, green from oxidation.

Winslow focused on the Baptist's second gesture, a hand raised in proclamation. In the dark face he saw a satyr, the mischievous creature of Rome, a city that mingled the pagan and Christian, the ambiguities of good and evil. The Baptist's face went dark again. Winslow's mind repeated the exercise, as he wondered at the great pride that the Baptist must have had. He saw in John the Baptist a Bruce Banner, other proud scholars and politicians, and he saw in the Baptist his own proud, puffed-up self. He saw the great John of the wilderness ensconced in a Harvard, in a Princeton. John had gained the pride of the well-born, even if he wore rags, Winslow thought; it was a spiritual pride that was not comfortable with a carpenter named Jesus.

"For John the Baptist came and he did not know . . ." The text filled Winslow's memory. Atop the Vatican, John the Baptist was at Christ's right hand. More than ever, Winslow questioned the esteemed position.

At 9:45 the next morning, Winslow waited for a green light to cross the street into Porta Sant' Anna, where he explained himself to a Swiss Guard. That got him past St. Anne's Church to a security booth. He was, after all, crossing the border of a tiny sovereign state. The guard called the Vatican Library. After a few expressive words, the guard hung up, smiled at Winslow and pointed him toward a three-story facade with an opening to the Belvedere Courtyard. The walk took Winslow past the Swiss Guard barracks, where a group lined up in blue-and-yellow-striped uniforms and berets. Workers dragged canvas mailbags out of the Vatican post office and nuns in gray habits moved about, their long shadows rippling across the cobblestone paths.

The night before, Winslow had read about the Vatican and its library; he knew he was getting privileged access. Clerical scholars and seminarians could explore the special collections, archives and the stacks—seven miles of black metal shelving. But for laity, especially non-Catholics, access was more difficult. Yet the library had come a long way, Winslow thought, from ending its Index of Forbidden Books to giving narrow access to the Secret Archives, the private realm of papal letters.

Winslow entered the Belvedere Courtyard, both a path and a parking lot for little European cars, and turned right toward the library's main entrance. Inside stood a marble statue of Hippolytus, an early canonist of scripture. Ahead was a bookstore and beside that stairs, which he climbed to the second floor. Above him now stretched a colorful expanse of curved ceilings and arches, a feast to his senses. His footsteps on the marble floor seemed to arouse the painted figures and stone statues, their eyes wide and their bodies twisted.

Winslow turned down a long hallway with brown wooden doors and reached one labeled DIRECTOR. He entered.

"I have an appointment with Bishop Sodano."

The young priest at the reception desk smiled and said, as best he could in English, "Come with me, please." He led Winslow back out the door. They walked five doors down the hall and the young man knocked.

"Come in."

Behind the door, the bright light from large windows blinded Winslow. In the glare he saw a dark silhouette, which stood and moved from behind a desk.

"Jack," Sodano said. "This is wonderful. You made it to Rome."

The priest still had his swarthy complexion, his wide grin, and still towered five inches above Winslow. In the Pacific war he had been tall and lanky, but now that impressive posture was bent. He wore a black cassock and gestured to a stuffed leather chair by the desk.

"Please sit down, Jack." Sodano seated himself. "How long has it been?"

"About forty-five years. Hard to believe."

They recounted some of that time and then Sodano brought them back to the present. "You are here to get some answers."

"I must admit, Joe, this is mostly curiosity."

Sodano chuckled. "I'm as old as you and I'm still searching. Curiosity keeps me young."

Winslow explained the events with Nick Hampton, the manuscripts, the controversy. Then he repeated what he had written

255

about: the Nestorian letters in Leningrad and the Vatican inquiry about them. "The whole thing is uncanny."

Sodano slouched comfortably behind the old wooden desk, the white collar pressing his fleshy neck. His hair had become almost entirely silver. "I investigated some of this after receiving your letter." He stood up suddenly. "Let's talk as I show you our library," he said.

Winslow saw that Sodano still limped. The two men sauntered down the hall and through an unmarked door. Chemical smells floated in the air. In a large well-lit room, book pages hung by the hundreds on clotheslines.

"This is the drying room." Sodano's arm made a sweep. "We take books apart, patch them up, put them together. We also microfilm each page. That smell is glue and film developer. It took ten years to clean and darken fifty-six faded Coptic manuscripts."

"The job looks overwhelming."

"Labor intensive." Sodano winked. "One reason the Holy See runs a deficit."

They walked up a flight of stairs, passed a door, and entered a large ornate room with windows facing north and south. The bishop was still ticking off facts about the library when he stopped at a table. They sat down in two wooden chairs with worn floral upholstery. With a sweep of his hands, Sodano said, "This is what you're interested in. Papal letters in the Secret Archives. After the Holy Father met Gorbachev we released a few letters showing Stalin had corresponded with the Vatican over the safe return of some people."

"Yes, I think I read that somewhere."

"What we didn't release was the Vatican's point of view. The church was eager to get Christian treasures out of the Soviet Union."

"The Nestorian letters among them?"

"I believe so. And I think I know the reason why."

Winslow smiled and nodded.

"The Vatican loves history, Jack. It wants to be a repository. But it also wants to protect its tradition."

"Perhaps this is none of my business, Joe, but is the Vatican trying to get the Russian materials?"

"After the Holy Father met Gorbachev, the Vatican established a diplomatic link in March 1990. And, of course, we're interested in the Kremlin's Christian holdings, for preservation. For history."

Sodano said he had found letters sent to the Kremlin about items in the Leningrad library. The bartering had been cut short by war problems and then forgotten. "I think these Nestorian texts must have been known of for some time, since before the Russian Revolution."

"What made them worth the trouble, I wonder?"

"The interest came from within the Curia. An archivist, a historian or two, the office of doctrine. It's quite a long story."

As Winslow listened, Sodano's monologue reminded him of the Pacific trenches. What was it? Then it came back. Even on the battlefield Sodano had read his books and talked about the creation of early church doctrines. Christianity was unique in its search for truth, he said, the only religion that formed creeds.

"The creeds were set down to differentiate from heresy," Sodano was saying. "The first theologians—Paul, Justin Martyr, Irenaeus—they wrote their theology to differentiate from Jewish law, from Gnostic speculation, from Stoic ethics and pantheism. That was long ago and a lot of those writings disappeared."

"Like the Nestorian texts."

"Yes, perhaps."

"Does finding them upset doctrine?"

To that, Sodano stretched his arms and rotated his huge shoulders as if to relax and clear his thoughts for a long explanation. "Christian belief was formed in a certain philosophical context," he began. "As you Bible scholars know, the disciples reported a resurrection. That was the first proclamation, the first belief. But in the next few centuries a hundred different doctrinal questions arose. The most basic fell into one category: how do you deal with the dualism of the time? How does a spiritual God relate to this physical world? They were all asking that."

"Not the simple folks, of course."

"Some of them too! I mention the dualism issue to show how a big question of the time produced an answer, a *big* Christian answer. The Stoics were pantheists and Gnostics believed in a good God and a bad God. This was competition for Christianity. Gnostics said the earth was evil, a mistake, a corruption of the spiritual. So what does Irenaeus do? He says creation is good. God created good in Adam. By sin it was corrupted but it still is retrievable. Christ comes to restore Adam."

"The doctrine of recapitulation."

"Correct," Sodano said. "The next problem was, how does God dwell in us and still be the Almighty, separate from us? The Gnostics said it happens through emanations, like radio waves from divine spirit to corrupt matter. To reject that, our theologians conceived of the Logos, the mind of God that thinks, wills and creates. The Logos, the Word, created the world in the beginning and later it came into the world to recreate fallen humanity."

"The Word made flesh. Jesus Christ."

"Yes."

Sodano continued, covering ground familiar to Winslow but helpful to the priest's logic, wherever it was taking him. The dualism clash peaked, Sodano said, at the Council of Nicea in 325, when the church debated how Jesus could be both God and man. Some leaned toward his divinity and others toward his humanity. Emperors in the East and West, with their armies, took sides for the next fifty years. Finally in 381 the Council of Constantinople settled it by adopting the Nicean Creed, a middle path tied with the work of Athanasius of Alexandria—Jesus was both God and man.

"So what comes next?" Sodano asked rhetorically. "It's the question of how God and man in Jesus interact." Sodano asked if he was taking too long, but Winslow deferred graciously.

"This is getting to Nestorius, I presume."

"You bet it is."

Usually, theologians in Antioch vied with those in Alexandria over the nature of Christ, Sodano explained, with Rome leaning toward Alexandria. This was the same battle that pitted Cyril of Alexandria against Nestorius, a bishop of Constantinople who preached Antiochian theology. Cyril said Nestorius made Jesus too human. Nestorius charged Cyril with overly divinizing the man.

"I understand that debate was not well-documented," Winslow said.

"No, it wasn't." Sodano frowned. "We have records from the Council of Chalcedon which rules Nestorius anathema on twelve points. The little that survives of Nestorius' work is mostly in Syriac, so we know him best by Cyril's damning excerpts."

Winslow's brow had wrinkled. "Cyril and Nestorius disagreed on whether Mary was Theotokos, the Mother of God, or merely the mother of man."

Sodano nodded. "And Nestorius lost, partly for political reasons.

Was that fair to Nestorius?" He shrugged. "Now we come to sources little known in history," he said, raising a finger like an instructor. "Cyril and Nestorius debated one other big thing, though we don't hear about it at all. The theologians had one more kind of dualism they needed an answer for."

"Was it . . ?" Winslow was confounded.

"It was woman."

Winslow gave out a nervous laugh. "You mean female clergy."

"More than that. They sought the female nature in the universe."

"I see. Wasn't that answered by the idea of the Virgin Mary or the church as the bride of Christ?"

"Yes, those were the answers," Sodano said. "But they came later. There was another idea, a much earlier one. It came from the Nestorian camp. Let me explain. There was a priest in the Antiochian school who argued that the Logos had both male and female sides. His name was Michael of Damascus. He used Genesis, God creating male and female in His image. More important, he used what he claimed to be sayings of Jesus. In these sayings, Jesus said he was to have a bride. Not a church, but a wife, a female incarnation. An earthly bride. Like a second Eve."

"My God! Why didn't I ever hear about this?"

"It was lost. Suppressed. Who knows? Remember the times. The Bible was being canonized to protect what seemed true, and certain texts or letters were excluded. The question of woman was explosive. Jesus had female followers. Paul gave women a role and he endorsed marriage. And many women built the early church."

"So why was the question explosive in the fifth century?" Winslow asked.

"Because they had to come to grips with Jesus' death."

"Now you've lost me."

"The early church believed in the resurrection, which came because of the death. But the cross did not become a symbol until the fourth century. Theologians said that Jesus did in fact die, but they weren't all saying he *had* to die. For a few centuries they disagreed about the death. Was it a ransom? Was it an allegory of death to life? Did it appease God? It was not crystal clear. Some said, okay, Jesus died, but did he have to? Didn't he forgive sins while he was alive?"

"If Second Adam was to have a Second Eve, then death . . ."

"Death thwarted that," Sodano replied. "That's exactly what Michael of Damascus said."

Sodano laughed and shook his head. "Oh, Michael. He said that if God meant for Jesus to die, why not make Judas a hero? Michael said that because Jesus was killed, then the Logos worked on a spiritual plane, recreating humanity in the spiritual Jesus and the Holy Spirit, his spiritual Eve, his bride. I'm not supporting it, Jack. I just find it fascinating."

"What happened to the material?"

"The male-female Logos of Michael had a following, men and women who saw marriage as the dwelling of Jesus and the Holy Spirit. They may have had communities. Probably did." Sodano rubbed his eyes for a moment. "There's one theory that this community, or part of it, moved south of Jerusalem or Syria and below the Dead Sea to an oasis, sort of a trade crossing."

That caught Winslow's attention, but he said nothing.

Sodano resumed. "Well, Paul of course endorsed marriage. But the difference in the male-female Logos was for women. They were equally part of God, so they shared spiritual authority in the family and church."

"Did that challenge the bishops' authority?"

"We don't know. Michael had a powerful opponent in the Alexandrians. Asceticism and monasticism had grown strong, and Athanasius built a monastic network that dominated the church. Naturally, the monastic way was taught as the higher way to God, a path above marriage. Well, the male-female Logos made marriage a very high path. You see the competition."

"A tension. Clergy and laity."

"In a way. Yes. So Michael of Damascus was pushed aside. Let's not say suppressed. He certainly wasn't ignored. Cyril and Nestorius may have fought over the Michael of Damascus ideas as much as any other. They were political rivals for sure, but their ideas on the nature of Christ were really not so different. There must have been some other very divisive theological point, something more than the Mother of God. You see, the Gnostics had a female element. Greek thought had psyche, a female term for mind. Syriac gave the Holy Spirit a feminine identity, but that was not the language of an empire. The church had to provide something female of its own. It produced

260

ecclesia, a female Greek word for church, and eventually elevated the Virgin Mary as an object of veneration."

"And loyalty to the church, the bride of Christ, was an important concern of the bishops."

"That is true." Sodano's olive face had reddened and it glowed next to his white hair. "Now, on to the Soviet Union."

Winslow guessed. "There's something about Michael of Damascus in Leningrad, no doubt."

"Apparently so," Sodano said. "Now just because Michael said these things doesn't mean it's true. But he claims to have these scriptural references."

"How do you know all this, Joe?"

By now, Sodano had produced a manila folder from somewhere and had thumbed it open. "I like to investigate. I don't think I ever told you what my father did. Did I?"

"Not that I recall."

"Well, he started as a police detective and then was FBI. He was Italian and he had the Italian mafia file for Pittsburgh and thereabouts. This is why my mother wanted me to be a priest; it's less dangerous."

Winslow scratched his forehead. "Fascinating."

"I didn't know what my father did, but his interest in investigating rubbed off. So I investigated history, theology. Someone noticed my taste for archives and paper trails and gave me this job. When I came here, I investigated."

Winslow was familiar with the sundry and obscure Gnostic phrases about Jesus and Mary as a couple. But they hardly formed a solid theology, especially now in contrast to Michael of Damascus. "What do you do, Joe, if you find something like this? I mean . . . for Protestants too! A Christ with an earthly bride, a Second Eve. My God! The feminists would go crazy, they'd love it."

"For us, of course, this relates to lifelong celibacy. Priestly celibacy's strongest argument is simply that Christ was single. If that goes, what's left? Now if God Almighty wanted Jesus to marry, well, I'd have to agree, wouldn't I? Then we'd need a higher definition of marriage, not just another feminist movement." Sodano leaned his elbows on the table, intent on Winslow. "Now this is no cover-up by the Holy See. It's obscure history. The Vatican doesn't open up everything it has. On this topic, well . . . maybe there is something at stake."

He lifted the manila file and handed it to Winslow. "This is everything I know about Michael of Damascus and Vatican efforts to get materials about him from Russia. I'm about to retire, so you can make it your project, Jack."

"This is extraordinary."

"I can be honest." Sodano smiled. "I'm glad to be human. I enjoy this speculation. But in the end I'll cling to reason and tradition and the leap of faith. You see, even Michael of Damascus doesn't strike at the Christ of my faith, fully God and fully man. He just adds something we didn't expect."

Sodano, his face taking a jovial cast, mumbled about years of reading and memorizing. "All this is in God's hands, Jack. If this Nestorian stuff and Michael comes out of Russia, well, God can deal with that. So can the church. Now, a question for you. What about those old manuscripts?"

Their destruction was a tragedy, Winslow said. But before that, Hampton and he had noticed recurring references to Adam and Christ. For a moment, Winslow thought about the desert, the community that had followed Michael of Damascus' teaching, and whether that teaching had come from Jesus' day. "My interest," he told Sodano, "was in an unknown statement about John the Baptist, that he 'did not know' something."

Sodano listened, his eyes slightly hooded and his head tilted back. "Did you notice the Holy See's stand on the Negev peace?" Sodano asked.

Winslow did not understand the priest's jump in logic, for he'd only known the Vatican was agreeable.

"Before the pope gave his support, the Curia ordered a several-months study of how it would affect our positions. I've heard the Holy See plans finally to give diplomatic recognition to Israel. But the pontiff still has to consider what you're talking about. What if that territory turns up all kinds of archaeological treasures, from the early Christian period in particular?"

Winslow said, "Like the Nestorian letters. Of course, that came out of Russia, but . . ."

"Yes, perhaps like the Nestorian letters." Sodano sat up, straightening his large shoulders. "Every time something is found, poor Mother Church gets in trouble."

"How so?"

"Our early bishops fought the heresies. Our archives hold the old records. When Catholic scholars get involved in the Dead Sea Scrolls, they get blamed for trying to put a spin on their meaning. When the Nag Hammadi writings of the Gnostics were discovered, the feminists said the male bishops had suppressed the helpless feminist Gnostics."

"I see."

"I don't think it's fair."

Just then a tap came at the door. Sodano lumbered up from his chair. Winslow, too, got up to stretch. A few yards away he stepped into a square of light coming in diagonally through a window. It greeted him like a warm blanket; in a flash he remembered the sun's light having the same effect on him during a taxi ride into Indianapolis. Like water beginning to boil, Winslow's brain became active. The encounter with Sodano had crystallized an unnerving image of Jesus for him: a messiah who was to fulfill the role of Second Adam, marry a Second Eve, but who was not accepted by the people because the widely influential John the Baptist had not done his job. John was proud and "he did not know . . ." Jesus condemned John, saying that the "least in the Kingdom of Heaven is greater than he." After Jesus' premature death, one early Christian movement tried to live what it believed was Jesus' mission—divine marriage. But the movement was sidelined and then suppressed by the powerful bishops who, as ascetic monks, saw marriage as second best. And maybe, Winslow thought, the records of this Michael of Damascus group, and more Jesus sayings, are still buried in the desert.

Sodano approached him and also looked out the window. "As I was saying, the real events of history often escape us."

Cafe reservations had been made, he said, gesturing for Winslow to precede him. "Let me show you some more of our small estate here. And then one of our fine Italian lunches."

263

29

Anne Marshall dug into her garden's black soil. Then, her weight on her right hip, she stretched to straighten a few more plants. The baby, due in two weeks, kicked inside her.

"How does it look?" Travis asked from the back porch.

Anne turned her head, smiling. "Still some life," she said. "Remember my green thumb."

"I can at least remember that."

She frowned. "Don't say that, dear. It was only a little bit of time. You still know everything else you ever knew."

"Except where to find a clean pair of pants."

She rolled her eyes and smiled anew for him. "They're in a box somewhere."

The garden in the back yard of the Marshalls' Greenford home had shriveled in their absence. Carpenters and masons had marched through it as well. At least, Anne thought, they had rebuilt the house quickly. She weighed that as a fair tradeoff for her dead roses, petunias, tulips, onions, squash, tomatoes and herbs.

Since her husband's release from the hospital they had lived at her family's home in south London. Life had returned to normal, except for Travis' employment.

"This looks bloody awful for the British Museum," the administrator had said, echoing the board's ruling. "You're off the staff, indefinitely." At Oxford, too, a cabal was clamoring to oust Marshall from his teaching assignment.

Marshall's one consolation, though, was a wink from a salty old member of the museum board. "Don't worry, son," he had said, his thick curving mustache dancing as he spoke. "It's happened before. When it blows over, I think they'll get you back on the ship."

Inside the Marshalls' house, fresh paint, furniture in shades of orange and new curtains had erased all memories of the explosion's burnt smell, black smoke and debris. "Cheaper to repair than to tear down and rebuild," the assessors had told Marshall in his hospital bed. Boxes and bags filled with clothes, kitchenware and Marshall's books and papers clogged the living room.

Marshall climbed the stairs, a box in his arms.

Rebuilding the house had plunged the Marshalls hopelessly into debt. Often enough, Travis and Anne said their escape from death, and the baby's, too, made their hearts thankful. The largest burdens, the finances and disruption of life, were lightened by what they felt. The daily grind was the hard part.

Marshall dropped the cardboard box of shirts on a chair by the closet and began hanging each one. Next were pants and coats. He swung a pair of brown corduroy slacks through a hanger and coins flew against the wall.

"All kinds of treasures," he said to himself. "What else did I leave in my pockets?"

One shirt had a pen still clipped in its front pocket, now soaked with a large blue inkspot. The blotch on a field of white reminded him of the blotted-out weeks since his memory had been lost. Despite assurances from the doctor, Anne and others, he was uneasy. A part of him had been cut out, some important part, he felt.

On the next trip downstairs, Marshall brought up an armful of coats. He picked off the corduroy coat and threw the others on the bed. He reached for a wooden hanger and slipped it inside the coat sleeves.

"My God. Another forgotten thing. I wonder how much money I've misplaced."

Against the coat's maroon silk lining, he glimpsed gray paper peeking from inside the coat pocket. He took it out, checked the other pockets, and hung the coat. On the corner of the gray envelope was the name of their local bank, the Ealing branch. He stuck his finger inside to flip it open and found a carbon-copied receipt. It read, "Box 477. Large. On Request."

He walked down the stairs into the kitchen, from where he saw his wife still rehabilitating the garden. On the porch he scrutinized the receipt again. "Anne? What was I doing on May 28?"

"Look on the calend . . ." Anne stopped and turned to check his expression. Was he serious? Or being macabre? Poor thing, she thought. He couldn't remember. "Dear," she said. "That was the day of . . . of the accident. It was a Tuesday and you went to work very early." She wouldn't mention Irina. Travis had only heard of her. "Then you went out in the afternoon."

Travis walked down the porch steps, leaving shade for warm sun. Anne gazed up as his shadow stretched across her plants and the soil.

He hated feeling helpless. Then he asked, "What do you think this May 28 bank receipt is for?"

Though Nick Hampton stood still, he needed to catch his breath.

"We've got to be up front from the start," he said to Marshall on the telephone. "Bring in some top people."

"I think we should put them in the hands of the museum. They'll be a little upset, at first."

"Who's in charge of antiquities?"

"Keeper of Antiquities. That's Sherwood Paley. Strictly by the book, so he'll be a little angry."

"What will Paley do?"

"It's Sir Sherwood if you ever meet him." Marshall chuckled. "I'm sure he's going to distance the museum from all the intrigues, from the bombing. That probably goes for me, too."

"What do you think, then?"

"Let's move ahead," Marshall said. He would first talk with Paley and then retrieve the papyri from the bank box. In the states, Hampton would ask Winslow to convey the news to the Bible Literature Society and request its recommendation on the academic protocol. It was all very delicate politics these days.

"We don't have to tell any governments yet," Hampton said.

"There could be an evidence problem with Scotland Yard."

Hampton thought about that, the red tape or even a possible seizure of the materials. "Well, if you think the British Museum will insulate this whole thing, that's the best move." Hampton paced in small circles by the phone desk. His palms were sweating. "What kind of shape are they in?"

"Just as we last saw them, I assume." Marshall reconstructed his probable actions. He had stacked all the papyri in a box between glass and blotter paper. He had made it snug with a few clean rags and tied down the top. It had fit into a wide bank box. The Oxford lab report also was inside.

"You were thorough, all right," Hampton said, still incredulous. "Okay, let's start the phone calls."

"A bloody strange story this is going to make."

"You mean the press?"

"Them, and explaining to Sir Sherwood. Putting away a priceless treasure, getting amnesia, and then finding it again."

"It may get stranger, Travis. To protect our reputations we've still got to explain about Rabin, Habib, the Brotherhood. Not so easy to believe."

"Well, like you say. Fact is weirder than fiction."

The massive statue of Charles Darwin stared down at the four Americans.

Under its imperious bronze gaze, Hampton couldn't help thinking about Bruce Banner. He was going to hit the Harvard ceiling when he found out, Hampton predicted.

"Quite a place," said the man next to him, a middle-aged biblical scholar from Yale Divinity School. As president of the Bible Literature Society, he was on board for the hearing. So was the curator at the Smithsonian, a tall astute woman. Winslow had persuaded them to make the trip to London on short notice.

The Society's president, clutching his briefcase, emerged from the Egyptian sculpture gallery, just off the library, after viewing the Rosetta Stone—which had broken the ancient code of hieroglyphics. In all directions, winged beasts in stone, massive friezes of lions and soldiers, giant polished urns and ancient wall paintings in reds, blacks and yellows, peered out from the maze of rooms.

"You get the feeling of Old Empire in here," the Society's president said. "Old, old empire."

From the front of the library lobby, Paley and Marshall appeared, both in gray suits and, side by side, the epitome of age and youth. For nearly an hour already, Paley had been interrogating young Marshall, alternating chastisement with sympathy. Paley's angular face and thick hair gave him a severe profile.

"Gentlemen . . ."

The voice was high and almost timid, Hampton thought, normally the tone of someone quick to forgive and slow to punish. But he could see that Marshall was on the block. This was British turf, a hard place for Hampton to plead for Marshall's amnesty.

Paley faltered as his eyes caught those of the Smithsonian curator. "And ladies," he said with a meek smile. "Follow me this way. We have the board room for the day."

They crossed the library toward the entrance, turned right and climbed the west staircase, which took them to the first floor. Right again, and they passed through the exhibit of Greek and Roman daily life. A long room extended off to the right, filled with busts and bas-reliefs of Augustus Caesar, antiquity's master of godlike sculptured propaganda. The plain hall led them to a large oak door, demarcated by a brass plaque: PRIVATE.

Inside the high-ceilinged room the walls were adorned with paintings of museum directors, etchings of exotic places and a century-old map of Africa. The group totaled seven, three British and four Americans. They sat at one end of the long table. The museum stenographer, called in to record the session, occupied the other. Paley directed his female assistant to hand out manila envelopes, each with black-and-white photos of all the papyri. They began mulling over them.

This was Paley's castle, but he had asked Winslow to preside. "My job at the outset is to clear the air on how these discoveries came about," Winslow said. "It was all very rapid, beginning in March, right after the Gulf War."

"May we ask questions in the process?" asked the Smithsonian curator.

Paley said, "Let's first get the accounts on the record, I think."

Winslow saw a consensus and so continued, asking Hampton to give an overview. Next came Marshall, who, like Hampton, prefaced his testimony with a prudent footnote—nothing yet proved that the materials were authentic. Tea arrived in an hour, as Winslow was finishing his explanation of his involvement and the meeting with Habib in Jordan.

"I pass the chair now to Sir Sherwood," Winslow said. "The manuscripts have been entrusted to the museum in the interim."

"We've got a few pieces of work here," Paley said. "This is not an official body, but we are meeting as colleagues to say something about the proper handling of discoveries, these in particular." He tapped a stack of the photos. "Of course, we recognize first rights on these unique discoveries for the finders. But I hope we can avoid the dust-up that was seen over the Dead Sea materials."

There were other objectives, Paley continued. They should suggest a few names for an informal team, preferably international, to speak for the new discoveries. This would help thwart governments, Israel and Jordan in particular, from trying to intervene. It would also discourage Scotland Yard from becoming entangled.

Hampton was surprised at what a tough politician Sir Sherwood was turning out to be.

The floor was thrown open for questions and ideas. The Yale scholar asked the question that was on all of their minds. "So Nick, you say all your actions were based on a promise to Habib Muhammad?" He raised his eyebrows. "This, of course, is important for our recommendation to the academy."

"That's correct," Hampton said as if he were a witness in court. "As best I understood it, perhaps life was at stake and breaking the promise would end access to more materials. So I acted alone."

Nobody seemed to enjoy being part of the inquisition, but it was over soon and they proceeded to the contents of the discoveries.

A man named Haydon, Paley's deputy, pushed a point about the fragments and four papyri. "Has the Aramaic script been deciphered enough to see how these might affect our views of the early church?"

Hampton and Winslow exchanged a covert glance. They had already talked about the Michael of Damascus material and had decided not to bring it into the scholarly hurricane yet.

"The material includes sayings by Jesus," Hampton said, "but our cursory review only found two new things that jump out." Hampton took a sip of water, his gulp resonating in the hardwood room. "For the first time to my knowledge, we have Jesus referring to himself as Adam. And then there's a new critical statement regarding John the Baptist."

He elaborated and Winslow cut in.

"This could be significant," he said. "At the same time, such glosses could make it suspect of not being authentic to that early period. What we know so far from carbon tests is that the fragments are first century. Discerning their content is now a historical and literary task . . ."

They all knew the range of possible public reactions. In 1898, when a non-canonical saying of Jesus was discovered on a papyrus scrap, Victorian Christianity was shaken at the novel idea of a Jesus *logia,* or sayings list. Such finds no longer stunned, unless the content was extraordinary.

The Bible Literature Society president jumped in. "We've already covered this, but in recent years I've learned to protect my rear," he said. A low rumble of amusement went around the room. "Grant the first rights to these young men, of course, but to avoid attacks for keeping these things secret someone should produce facsimiles quickly. Other scholars want to see if this is going to create big problems in their research, work they've been doing for years."

"I think we all tend to agree," Paley said, looking at Hampton.

The Smithsonian woman leaned on her elbow and faced the head of the table. "We have this immediate problem of context for these materials," she said. "We've got the many Byzantine ruins in the Negev and now they've found a sixth-century church at Petra. Yet these finds of Mr. Hampton's have been passed around, and we don't know where they came from."

"Quite true," Paley said. "You say it was Bedouin, somewhere in south Jordan or the Negev?"

"Perhaps I can help here," Marshall said. "When I worked with Rabin at the Negev Institute, we mapped Negev geography: wadis, mounds, oases, gorges, cliffs."

"Why?" The Yale man glared at Marshall.

"To know where to start digging. What Rabin did not tell me is particulars, such as this Bedouin found such and such at this mound. And I believe that was what Habib was supposed to deliver eventually—a map."

"A treasure map," the Yale man said, worried. "My God! The

press'll go crazy with that." His face sagged as if he'd been through the media thresher before.

"No, seriously," Hampton said. "I can support what Travis says. When Habib's agent got these from the Brotherhood factions, he was also talking about a map that the Bedouin either had made or were going to make, or were going to give directions on . . . that was a little unclear."

"Perhaps . . . well, this is the delicate part," Haydon of the museum said. "I don't think we want to ask the Jordanian government to go in guns blazing to find those Bedouin."

"Quite the contrary," Paley said.

Heads nodded in the affirmative.

"I think we should approach it like this." The Smithsonian curator folded her arms. "Don't make any official appeal to governments, Jordanian or Israeli, at least not yet. Set up the team, talk to people like us over in Jerusalem, Amman. If something's near the surface we will hope that it pops up. If not, well . . . we simply wait."

Paley said he'd call a press conference the next morning. No one objected.

Hampton thought of the flashy papers he'd seen in London, the *Daily Mirror,* the *Sun,* and *News of the World*—tabloids all. "I hope this whole story will get out clearly," Hampton said.

"The rascals from Fleet Street will have the first go at it," Paley said. "But eventually the serious scribes will follow." He'd seen it all before.

They talked another hour and broke for lunch. Over his private meal, Paley asked his secretary to take dictation. It would be typed and copied and circulated at the brief final session. "Our review has concluded the following," Paley began. In short, Winslow did not have complicity, except in promises kept to Hampton; Marshall and Hampton had violated academic ethics, but had acted as best they knew how under the circumstances. They were expected to have first rights to translate the materials. Any claims by foreign governments, however, also attached to those individuals, not their scholarly organizations or peers.

Apart from the review, the museum alone was to judge the Marshall case. Paley had met with Marshall that morning, a hint of the outcome. A number of foreign academies, scholarly publications and money-giving foundations were "scandalized" by the near

271

fiasco. The Soviet government linked the Pleshnikov woman's death to the British Museum invitation. These had been Fleet Street fodder so far. The museum, Paley decided discreetly, needed a scapegoat, so Marshall had to be fired.

"Could you ring me through to Scotland Yard," Paley said to his secretary. "A courtesy call."

The money transfer to England's preeminent bank, Barclays, was large enough for the bank to call in Exeter, a senior officer. Exeter was a man of exactitude and regularity. A lifelong Londoner. Whatever the weather, he carried his bowler and umbrella to the office. Once they were hung on the rack at the third-floor division entrance, he felt that order could prevail in his bank work.

Exeter had climbed to the rank of handling special cases. Dissolving estates, unpacking complex wills and closing large foreign currency transfers were his specialty.

He set his teacup on the desk, took the small reading glass from his front pocket, then untied the new case folder. Like radar, his eyes began scanning to pick out the essentials.

It began with the Bank of Vienna and a transfer of Austrian schillings to London. Now it was pounds sterling. "About five million eight in schillings to start," he murmured. "Yes. Right. Right again." The numbers fell into place nicely. "High transfer tax, of course. Some loss against the pound. Yes. Hmm." Exeter saw details, but he thought in large round numbers. That is how he gauged the people behind the money—where they came from and where they might go.

"Yes indeed," Exeter said to himself. "They'll be a happy lot. Just shy of 230,000 pounds." In American terms, he figured about $430,000.

Exeter viewed the case as exotic. On its face, it was sweetness and light. But what it lacked in betrayal, fratricide or greed, it made up in colorful quirks. An Israeli liquidated a family trust. He left a sealed testimonial letter. Some stipulations were listed but other stipulations were to remain sealed until the day of execution. The receiving party was not to know anything.

"So it's a surprise."

Usually when wills or trusts were dispersed, property auctioned

272

or long-lost fortunes found, a host of parties vied for control. In this action, there was no contest.

Exeter was pleased that the case did not enter court. For him, legal disputes meant sitting mum in long, dull hearings. Contested money, he had seen, could turn family members into monsters. He emptied his teacup before it cooled. "I must say, this one will be fun."

Exeter sat back to read the account's history. The process was governed by set dates. Spring. Summer. And then the fall. Only one more thing had to be determined. Are there any children? That was simple enough to verify, he thought. No courts and no lawyers. Just a formal meeting with a little bit of ceremony.

Exeter was not really as dull and picky as others viewed him. He was merely businesslike. Given the date restrictions, he figured he could close the Rabin case in six to eight weeks.

"Then . . ." He savored the thought. "I'll be Father Christmas."

30

"That's the whole story." Nick Hampton had been talking for nearly an hour.

The Canadian journalist, Daniel LeFarbe, jotted on his pad. "What was the date of that meeting in London?"

"About two months ago. I think June 17."

"Some of your critics have treated you well since then, haven't they?"

"Depends." Hampton grinned. "*Biblical Scholars Monthly* did a friendly piece. I used to be a pirate. Now I'm cutting-edge. My other advantage is the first rights on the texts. We still use the old Latin, *editio princeps*. First edition."

"And the university?" LeFarbe gestured out toward Seattle from Hampton's living room.

"Well, the Banner forces have grown and they're still calling for an inquiry. The Biblical Literature Society's on the fence, too."

"So the university . . ."

"I'm allowed to finish this one summer class, but otherwise the university has suspended me. And that's without pay. It may finally yank my tenure."

"Unfair?"

"I don't want to say anything in print . . ."

LeFarbe raised a hand and nodded in compliance.

"We've got fame but no fortune, Marshall and me. Travis Marshall's out of a job, too."

"That's a . . ." LeFarbe paused. "Is he really?"

"It's pure power, pure jealousy. Sure, maybe we broke some rules but we've explained why."

"And yet doesn't Banner owe you an apology?" LeFarbe paused again. He knew about Banner's offer to Hampton for a post at Harvard. LeFarbe decided not to ask; he felt he may have disrupted Hampton's life once already. "I may have aided Banner's agenda by my interview, but didn't he have people in Israel out to get you?"

"It's not entirely clear," Hampton said. "I think he started some inquiry that turned into rumors about me and the manuscripts. Ironically, his intuition was correct but wrong on everything else."

The Israeli police had put a tracer on a type of old blue car, which had turned up an Arab owner—caught with a trunk full of contraband—and a shopkeeper accomplice named Nabbi. Hearing this, Hampton still blamed everything on a ruthless black market. "It can be a crazy place," he said. "I think some zealous marketeer cut our brake line to stop us, scare us. But I'm not sure why."

There might be a story there someday, LeFarbe thought. "I have one more question, just to get it straight." He raised the can of Coca-Cola, finishing the last mouthful. "What impact is this discovery going to have? What measurable impact, once all the media dies down?"

Hampton thought he had best underestimate, at least now. "I'm not sure yet. I'll do the first translation with a commentary. Then other scholars do their translations. They may not agree with me. In the end this all builds toward a critical edition which has a consensus. So meanwhile, my edition will make theologians take a new look at the Adam concept, the role of John the Baptist."

"The Negev . . ," LeFarbe said. "Habib Muhammad looks like he's taking some risks. So outspoken."

In his imagination Hampton smelled the herbs in the Amman home, felt the heat of Jordan on his face. Memories of Habib floated about. "Yes. I hear the Negev's economic projects are moving ahead. The archaeologists had meetings. But they need an attention-getter to win funding. The Bedouin dried up after we got these manuscripts. We don't know where to look."

"The treasure map?"

"If that's what it is. No one's come forward with it."

After a short silence, LeFarbe mentioned Simon Rabin. He never did meet Rabin in Israel, he said, but he remained curious.

Hampton admitted the same and said the man was still out of focus for him. The last Hampton had heard, Rabin had money in Europe—by LeFarbe's own account, and Winslow had conveyed Habib's report of their friendship. LeFarbe said a European magazine had recently reported on the Rabin family's money. The Danish family that had hid the Rabins from the Nazis and then helped them flee had been asked by the rabbi to keep his cash savings. The Danes had invested the money wisely and some years after the war had returned it tenfold. Where an investment was profitable, Rabbi Rabin let the money work. Eventually he set up a trust in the Bank of Vienna.

"The media picked it up because of the irony," LeFarbe said. "Here were Danish Christians investing Jewish money, a reverse of the medieval role Jews played for Christians."

"What is the trust doing now?"

"Sitting there with about half a million dollars. But it's the sort of trust where you can't get public records. Nobody will say who runs it. Rabin's dead and there's no family."

Feet crunched across gravel on the front walk. The screen door opened, welcoming in a light breeze. A closet banged in the foyer and heels clicked across the kitchen.

"My wife," Hampton said.

LeFarbe's eyes widened. "I didn't know you were married."

"Almost two months now." They had flown to St. Louis for the wedding so Susan's family, including her ailing mother, and Nick's father could attend. It was a simple ceremony and only a thirty-six-hour stay in St. Louis for the bride and groom.

Susan had come in through the dining room. LeFarbe stood up, followed by Hampton.

"Sue, this is Dan LeFarbe. I told you about the story he's writing."

"Nice to meet you," she said. "You interviewed Nick in Tel Aviv?"

"You've a good memory."

Nick explained how Susan's company had transferred her to Seattle, and she followed up with enthusiasm.

"I was just about to take another job and my firm decided to open an office here. I'm supposed to keep an eye on the Pacific Rim markets."

"Soviet Union, too." Hampton looked and sounded proud.

"That's a very big maybe," she said.

"My theory is that the second Russian Revolution got Susan's boss to send her to Seattle." Hampton led a chorus of laughter.

"You'll like the Northwest," Lefarbe said.

He had a flight in two hours and a rental car to return. "When it's slated for publication I'll let you know."

The Hamptons waved at the doorstep and went back inside.

"Who's he writing for?"

"He said he could almost take his pick. Both *National Geographic* and the *New York Times Magazine* are bidding."

Susan sauntered into the kitchen and returned with a stack of mail, a blue envelope on top.

"Looks like the Soviet Union."

"My God. Irina's family?" Hampton ripped the coarse paper and extracted a handwritten letter of about a half-dozen pages. "It's in French. Irina's friend . . . uh, Tatyana. She worked at the library."

"*No hablo Francés, señor,*" Susan said. "*Hablo Español, pero un poquito.*"

Hampton's puzzled expression slackened. "I hate going down to the university, but I've got that morning seminar . . . I'll call now. Find a willing soul who speaks French."

When Exeter of Barclays arrived, he hung his umbrella and bowler on wall hooks in the hallway. He pulled up the chair and opened his briefcase. He put the documents on the coffee table.

His children had grown. So he wasn't used to working in a living room with a crying baby and the smells it produced.

"This is all so hard to believe." Anne Marshall bounced her newborn daughter at her shoulder. The burp came. A dribble of milk followed. "Simon, oh, Simon. Why would he do this?" She was near tears.

Travis Marshall was paralyzed by mild shock. He had just sat through Exeter's business presentation. So far, at least, it made little sense. Rabin had left them a fortune with no strings attached. "Not a single one," as Exeter put it.

Exeter's hands gestured symmetrically when he spoke. "When someone comes into a lot of money, I like to give them a framework," he said. The money was safe in Barclays. It could serve as a checking account. They could seek bank advice for investment, or recommendations from investors and tax advisers. They could let the money sit. But they should also know that once they signed to receive it, the state would take its share in wealth tax.

Exeter had telephoned the Marshalls the day before. Knowing they had a newborn, he had offered to come to their home. He wanted to speak to both of them. They had asked if it was about their bank loans and he had assured them it was not. As executor of the estate, he was following Rabin's exact written instructions.

"This is a sealed letter addressed to both of you," Exeter said calmly. He handed it to Travis. The Marshalls were speechless, so Exeter proceeded. "There were, of course, clear instructions for the lawyers and bankers. Mr. Rabin stipulates that you should be explained those basic details." Exeter paused.

"Before we open the letter?" Travis asked.

The baby slept now. Anne sat down next to her husband.

"Yes," the banker said. "That was his wish."

As Exeter talked, Travis and Anne learned about the Rabin family trust. The Rabin family tree was small, its branches destroyed in the European war. Three years after Simon Rabin had inherited control of the trust, his wife and daughter had been killed. He was the sole beneficiary for more than twenty years. Yet he never used the money. It just grew. He had planned eventually to inject the trust into the Negev Institute, but illness and war had come sooner. Exeter said Rabin could have rescinded the will anytime he wanted. He might have done so if his health had improved beyond the war or if the Negev Institute had found what it was looking for. Rabin's final testament, however, was this: when the Marshalls had their first child, and if Rabin was dead, the trust was to go to them.

Marshall put his arm around Anne's shoulder. The emotional aftermath of childbirth was still with her. She was trembling and nervously folding her damp handkerchief.

"And the letter?" Travis asked.

"My last instruction was to ensure that you read it, privately of course, at the time of settlement."

Marshall opened the envelope. The letter was a single sheet filled with Rabin's small precise handwriting. He held it so they both could read. Anne's eyes were too misty. She returned to the handkerchief.

Marshall read to himself. "My late father said our family should use this money with generosity. We never had a chance to use it. My father also taught me that sometimes you have to choose between love of humanity, of all the people, and love of one person or family. I could have used the money one way or the other. If you are reading this letter, you can see I have chosen the second."

Rabin had never spoken to Travis like this in Israel. Life had been rough and adventurous then and risks had been part of the business. Now, however, Rabin explained how he had worried desperately for their safety. He had felt guilty that his dream about the desert might harm even one more life. That was not all of it, though. Travis read the next lines and then repeated them for Anne to hear.

"Anne knows that I was happily awaiting the birth of your child, boy or girl. I told her, from my own experience, how wonderful a daughter is. If yours is a girl, I am asking you to do one more thing in Israel. It is not required, but for me and my daughter you will make the circle complete."

Anne had leaned over to read along. Her husband did not complete the next sentences. He was thinking about what to do, how to travel there or whom to contact. He remembered his trips south to Beersheba, and then into the Negev. He smelled the clay in that room and recalled that he had given Hampton the key.

Tears flowing, Anne burst out, "Oh Simon, you dear, dear old man."

Travis stopped reading and choked. Exeter watched, struggling to keep his composure.

At Northern University, the ten undergraduate students pulled their chairs into a rough curve. Professor Hampton leaned against the heavy desk, eventually sitting on it. Twenty eyes, all upon him, shone, some narrow, others wet and dark.

"This is a condensed course on archaeology and the Bible," Hampton said to the students. "There'll be lots of reading and one paper." The pain of obligation showed on some faces.

The class had been Hampton's assignment even before he left on sabbatical. Though the university was likely to suspend him at the least, it had asked that he complete the assignment. He didn't mind. His students' fresh inquisitive faces were worth it. His lecture, a two-hour overview broken in the middle, flowed. The responses proved it.

"I was raised in a church that said the Bible is the Word of God," a young woman said awkwardly. "And I know, well, of course, that's not how we're studying it here. But I was just wondering, how do you balance that? How do we balance that?"

"Very good question," Hampton said. "A lot of great archaeologists and Bible scholars have sought that balance." Hampton crossed his arms and looked away for a moment of thought. "Let me put it this way. This course is about history, matching the Bible accounts with what we find in Palestine, Egypt, Jordan, Syria. You'll find in your readings that many people no longer want to call this 'Bible archaeology.' That means there's skepticism. Whatever we find, take that as part of life's ambiguities. We'll find contradictions. The Bible says something and it ain't so on the ground, or at least there's no archaeological evidence. Nothing is totally provable, totally rational. Even the hardest science takes a leap of faith. So if you believe in the Word of God, keep that belief. Under a microscope, the Bible is a human record, even if those people had divine inspiration. A relationship with God is something else. That can't be measured by science, rocks or old literature."

"Did you struggle with this question?" another student asked.

"Yes, I did. But I view it this way." Hampton paused to read the students' faces. They were open. No resistance showed. "God is always there. The Bible has been between us and God, like a mediator or translator, for nearly two millennia. But I change, you change. We grow from youth to maturity and then old age. I've got to keep my sights on God, who does not change, and come to peace with this book. This is an account about God working in the world—an unchanging God trying to reach fickle human beings."

A few other students opened up. They also had been taught the Bible religiously. A couple of students said they'd never seen one in the house, but now were curious. The exchange was excited, animated, candid. The youthful egos blossomed. As the students left, a few lingered to talk. They're eager, Hampton thought, remembering vaguely how he once was, full of youthful revelations, certainties. This, he mused, is how the old stay young; run with the young, hope they will appreciate your hard-earned wisdom.

* * *

By week's end, a professor of French had finished the translation.

"Anything personal in here?" The professor was prudent, so he had asked Hampton at the outset.

"Not that I know of. She's the friend of a woman who died in England."

"Sad." The professor had recalled the much-repeated stories about Hampton's adventures. "Well, maybe by Friday. It's not long. Check with me." The professor had flipped through the pages and then back to the start. "*Cher M. Hampton*," he read aloud. "*Avant le départ d'Irina pour l'Angleterre, nous avons parlé toute une soirée. Je pense qu'elle voudrait que vous sachiez ces choses.*" He took off his spectacles. "Very good French. She opens by saying a Miss Irina would want you to know about her, about a long talk she had with the writer . . ."—he flipped to the last page—". . . a Tatyana Sovanov."

This exchange with the professor a few days earlier came back to Hampton, who was sitting in his office with the full translation, typed on a computer print-out.

As the professor had said, Tatyana was writing about Irina. They had a talk before she left for England. Tatyana spent a few pages speaking well of Irina, how she worked hard, how she always took care of the others there, how she never complained. He read on.

". . . The other day the library's giant bust of Lenin was taken outside to be carried away. As it sat on the street many people came with hammers and broke apart the marble. After that, I knew I could write this letter. Now we've had the attempted coup and everything is changing. Our city is named St. Petersburg again. Irina knew this would come. She spoke this way, not politically, but by her belief. She felt Russia was about to die and come to life again. And she said Russia could become new because so many good people had suffered, and they made Russia worthy.

"Irina suffered much, Mr. Hampton. When she was young she was forced to be the mistress of an evil man, a political boss, who ran the hospital. It was the only way she could get her father medical treatment. It was only a few months, she said, but it had scarred her soul and health for

281

a long time. After she came to Leningrad she seemed to regain them. Part of it was the love she said she felt from America, which she visited twice.

"I understood Irina best as part Chinese and part Russian. As Chinese, she was devoted to ancestors and wanted to honor at least one, her grandfather. And she wanted to be a Christian and saw Jesus as someone who suffered by loving people. You can tell Irina was very religious, much more than I. But she told me these things."

The letter continued, saying the library hoped to have more visits from Americans and others. Tatyana said she knew where Irina's Chinese texts were in the library, including the old letters that Viktor Reznik had put on microfilm for her. She said they were safe. "Viktor Reznik said he has found more letters, very old ones in Greek. He said they are Christian and talk about Jesus."

Hampton was moved by Tatyana's account. And now this, a hint of new discoveries. Too much all at once. His eyes moved to the end of the letter. "Irina said you will be married soon. She said you must have a wonderful fiancée. I hope I can meet you both someday."

Hampton had talked with Susan about Irina with almost brutal honesty. Susan knew anyway, at least by intuition, and he had thought it better to clean the slate. That night he shared the letter with her. Susan had been surprisingly noble about the revelations, Hampton thought, not jealous or vengeful. For her part, she never said a word about Bill Salinger, but that's because he was never more than a ghost, she believed. Both were guilty of letting their hearts wander off; this made it easy for Susan to be grateful for what Irina had done. She told Nick that Irina had saved his life—saved it for her.

"Do you think you can fall in love again at your age, Nick?" she asked that night. She opened her eyes wide and leaned into him. Susan liked to talk about life as seasons: the closed-off winter, the hopeful and stirring spring, summer as a steadiness, a depth. And autumn was the time to prepare for winter, to handle it better this time around. Both she and Nick, she thought, had been going through their seasons.

"I only had a big crush on her," he said. "She was very interesting. You know, some people come into a life and change it. She did that. I admit I had a kind of fancy." His next thought he kept to himself: Irina was inexplicable, like fate or even like God. She was beyond both him and Susan in a good way, a way that had decreased his ignorance; he had learned a new kind of sadness and a new kind of joy. "Commitment's the important thing. That's where the heart really is." He kissed Susan. "Right?"

They sat on the couch with reading lights on at both ends. The chirping of crickets drifted in through an open back door. Susan put down her book and snuggled up to Nick.

"I have to tell you something, Nick." She put her warm hand on his wrist, sliding it down to his fingers and tangling them. "I'm pregnant."

"Really!" He threw his arms around Susan and kissed her elatedly on the forehead and cheek, then softly on her thin delicate mouth. Nick laughed ironically. "I'm finally a provider and I don't have a job."

She brushed back his hair.

He said, "Well, as Travis and Anne say, it's better to be poor and alive than rich and dead." He twirled her long brown hair in his fingers.

"Do you want a boy or a girl?" she asked.

"As if you can decide," he chided. He sighed contentedly. "The Marshalls' girl is a few weeks old now."

"Katherine's such a pretty name. I'm so glad Travis didn't chose Nefertiti . . ."

"Susan, he was only joking."

"Thank God."

"Well, if we have a boy, we can name him after my old man."

"If it's a girl . . ." Susan paused, her wide deep eyes looking up into his. "Why not a name from the Bible?"

AUTUMN

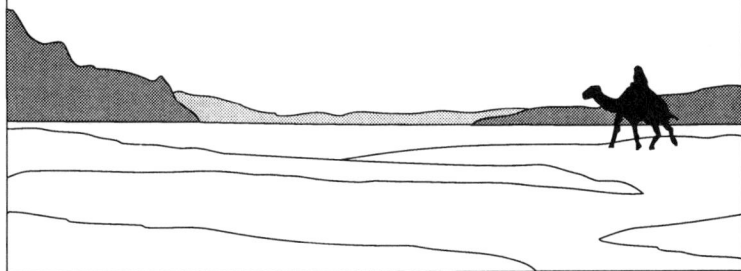

31

The crowds grew denser on the Amman street that passed the Abu Darwish Mosque, fed by foot traffic at day's end. The white and black stone on the mosque's facade was turning shades of pink and deep orange in the low sunlight. The city of seven hills began to summon chilly gusts on fall afternoons like this. The occasional breeze and the human throngs kicked up dust which swirled in patterns defined by the light.

The tall young man from Mazar could see well over the crowd, and his two companions from the Brotherhood, all in heavy robes, stayed at his side and followed his direction.

The short one with the deep wrinkles and large eyes, the veteran of Afghanistan and now Algeria, was at his right. The young militant who often carried his rifle around in south Jordan could not be so conspicuous in the capital city. He carried the Beretta pistol inside his frock.

"The prayers are ending," the tall one said. He could see the flow of people in white turbans and checkered kafiyas exiting the mosque. The crowd fanned out in all directions, but some of it moved into the plaza and waited—for something or someone.

As the tall one had expected, from the mosque came Habib Muhammad. He was becoming known recently for speaking outside a mosque after the prayer. His talk was about cooperation in the Negev, about the Abrahamic faiths.

"Follow me," the tall one said, striding agilely through the crowded street. The two were close on his steps. All of them had escaped the sweep that had taken place after the arrest of militant leaders in Ma'an on drug and weapons charges. "They'll pay for this," the tall one had told the family of one militant who had been arrested, the man who had taught him the ways of Islam.

The crowd changed from a river to a solid mass as Habib starting speaking from atop a stone slab. The traffic continued to flow, pushing against the crowd that swelled on all sides of Habib, creating plenty of distractions and scattered noises. The tall one glanced once more over the heads of the crowd. Habib, who had raised a hand for quiet, was straining to project his voice above the din.

They had planned for this moment. The tall one nodded to his disciples, and slapped one on the back. The three divided up, one darting into the listening crowd. They knew where to meet later. The tall one, feigning clumsiness, knocked over a concession cart, drawing much attention. The young man with the lined face began to chant a protest at the other side of the plaza, a common occurrence for there was always doubt among the locals on whether they could trust the Israelis.

The third man, now a part of the crowd and moving behind the speaker, remembered when Habib Muhammad had asked him why he carried a rifle in Mazar several months earlier. He slipped his hand inside the robe and felt the cool steel.

"Lost a damn good one," G. Henri Bittman grumbled. In the ten months since the Gulf War had begun, he'd also lost some weight and some patience.

Behind him on the wall hung the United Nations emblem, embossed in bronze. Out the window the trees on Vienna's streets and hillsides were turning golden.

"We usually work with scoundrels." Bittman, the veteran drug-fighter, flipped through the report. "He was a saint by comparison."

His associate, Schmidt the idealist, nodded. "He was good."

Commendation had come to the cadre of officers at the International Narcotics Control Board in Vienna from the United Nations Secretariat. The drug trade that filtered from Lebanon and Aqaba had been stemmed, if temporarily. The tide of weapons to radicals had been blocked, if temporarily as well. But short-run accomplishments were in the realm of the possible.

Bittman's face became grimmer as he read the report. News clips from two Jordanian newspapers, a Lebanese news agency and two Israeli newspapers hung from a paper clip. He read the *New York Times* item first.

"They don't understand the implications yet." Bittman flicked the *Times* story with two fingers.

"And we can't tell them, either." Schmidt squinted. "Habib was unique. Though he refused to be our agent, he had all the right instincts on his own. He was totally independent but cooperated when it was in his interest. He wanted to be totally free to speak out on the Negev peace. He urged the Arabs on and one of them didn't like it."

"Shot twice."

"In the back."

"Those dogs!"

"We presume it was radicals, either PLO or the Brotherhood. Can't be Basherbisi. He got the screws a month ago, a settlement with France on the bank fiasco."

"Basherbi . . . oh, yeah. The gunrunner. Another bastard."

Silence hung for a moment in the bright austere office. The ticks of a wall clock echoed off its hard surfaces.

"Why didn't we see it coming?" Bittman's rhetorical question came out angrily. "He was keeping a high profile. Speaking out for the Negev thing. Why didn't the king . . . why didn't we keep an eye on him?"

"Some say he had a death wish."

"A what?"

"Well, more like a fearless, careless approach. Habib was sending out his ideas on audio tapes, just like the ayatollah. He just didn't listen to caution."

"Do any good?"

"Yes, it did give moderates some wherewithal and it got the government off the hook. The regime's scared to death of the radicals."

Bittman read the report a second time. He had served in Amman before and he tried to reconstruct the setting near the Abu Darwish Mosque. The assassin's bullets had hit Habib as he spoke in the plaza, outside the mosque where he had just led prayers. The crowd was dense. Agitation began on the south edge of the square, where threats to Israel were being chanted. The crowd surged for a moment. Witnesses close to the center of the crowd heard shots. When the imam fell, the crowd clashed, then most dispersed. No suspects were reported, though someone in the crowd must have seen the assassin.

"What's the analysis?"

"Says here the killing is widely resented because Habib was a respected moderate, a good man of the people. His backing of the Negev project had nominal support. Many Jordanians fear crossing the PLO or militants, so they didn't come out visibly. But now they may see him as a martyr, build a cause of some kind around his memory." Bittman fell silent and scanned the report for a name. "Here. Says here a young man, name of Kalim Hasan . . . we don't know much about him yet. Well, he's taken up Habib's cause. Quite outspoken."

Schmidt took out a separate report and handed it to his boss. "We do know something about Hasan," he said. "Look at this." He paused a minute. "Do you remember that drug bust in Belgrade? The Bulgarian and the Turk?"

"Yeah, I do," Bittman said.

"Well, Hasan's brother was the Turk, or rather he carried Turkish papers. He was a member of the Brotherhood and somehow got this mission to drive the stuff . . ."

"But he was killed, right? How do you know . . ?"

"It should have been obvious at first, but not everyone's a super-detective out there."

"You're telling me."

"They finally noticed an atlas in the truck cab, one of those . . . I think it was an English-French version. Beautiful maps of the world, names of places, the works. They opened it and inside it said, 'To Jamal Hasan from your brother, Kalim Hasan.' So they traced the names, through Lebanon, Syria, and it checked out in Jordan."

"Says here in the report that Kalim Hasan split with the Brotherhood . . ."

"Split with the radicals, and very likely over how they had treated his brother," Schmidt said.

"So in all, the assassination of Habib has backfired on the radicals?"

"Our sources can't predict. Habib might become a martyr. Or he could become a footnote."

"Useless killings," Bittman said. He had seen another intelligence report and learned that the private conversations of Habib and Rabin with their governments had initiated the Negev peace venture. "In history," Bittman said, "Habib and Rabin won't become footnotes."

"The funeral's going to tell a lot."

"How?"

"That's when we'll see how symbolic he becomes. You know, whether there are big demonstrations, international visitors or what."

Bittman paused, pensive. "We'll wait and see."

Even as the car rumbled, Matthew Cummings heard the exhortation ring in his ears. The roads down to Bethlehem were like old and familiar friends. As Cummings drove, Harlan Stockwood's words were wrapped around his thoughts.

"You tell me right away what it is," the Texas preacher had told his son-in-law over the telephone. "These discoveries are getting out of hand over there. Whatever you get, our Bible college must have a claim on it."

The controversy over the manuscripts Nick Hampton had obtained had shaken Stockwood. His faith never wavered, nor did his confident preaching. But then there were the facts. Old manuscript was fact. Especially manuscripts with sayings by Jesus. Stockwood still yearned for the autographs; might God not deliver them to the truly faithful, to him, before the End Time?

Two days before, Cummings had been contacted in Nazareth by a relative of Pastor Samir Gamal's, whose church stood in Bethlehem. He could remember every detail.

"The Bedouin gave him something and he wants to give it to you," the Arab, an Israeli citizen, had told Cummings.

"What is it?" Cummings had asked.

"He only said you must come. Thursday at two o'clock at his church. He said come alone."

As was his protocol, Cummings had called Stockwood. The flurry over manuscript finds had charged Jerusalem and other parts of the Middle East. The Negev project had added more to the excitement. Stockwood sought the meaning in prophecy. Peace with Arabs? That was not in prophecy, only the gathering and victory of the Jews. Now this.

"Matt, you go down and get whatever it is for our side," Stockwood said. Cummings heard it again and again—"Get whatever it is . . . whatever it is. For our side."

Having been in the Middle East for more than a year, Cummings had changed. Maybe it was the Jerusalem syndrome, whatever it was that caused people to proclaim bizarre things in the streets of the Holy Land. Maybe it was his own soul-searching. Maybe his temperament. That temperament did not allow him to see God's will as a bloody clash. In the hands of chauvinistic and jealous Jews, Christians and Muslims, their religious doctrine could lead to that. Like a volcano deep inside the region, the religious impulse, the longings to find God or to forget God, were more overpowering than anything he'd known in Texas. Yet he could not imagine God wanting the spiritual search extracted in blood. Not now.

The Bible, too. Cummings believed in its power. But could he believe it was inerrant? He recalled what others had said. Too strict an interpretation of the Bible is fragile, for if one argument goes, all the rest go—like dominoes. Cummings' interest in the Bible had grown, but in a spiritual way; its authority moved him, not its literalism.

Over the rise he saw Bethlehem, backed by the autumn haze of the parched Judean wilderness and, farther, the Dead Sea rift. The palms stood as still as the air. Few tourists braved the Holy Land in such heat. The road was quiet. He passed the Israeli checkpoint, with its olive-green jeeps and armed soldiers, and drove down the winding road, curving around the ribs of the mountaintop. Soon he was on the shaded street where Gamal's church was located.

"Please come in," said the pastor's wife, smiling as ever.

The floors creaked and the sanctuary air was cool. He smelled the limestone and the olive oil. From the loft above, Gamal stepped down, greeted Cummings, and beckoned him up. An old rusty fan stirred the warm air, but the walls of stone, nature's best insulation, kept the upstairs bearable.

"Matthew, thank you for coming," Gamal said. "You must be wondering . . . I could not tell you much."

"The man just said be here. So I trusted you."

"Yes, we trust each other. Yes." Gamal directed his wife to bring tea and then concentrated his gaze on the American missionary. "I have nothing to ask of you. But I have been asked to give you something."

"Thank you," Cummings said, waiting to understand.

"You see, well, I don't know. These things the Bedouin find. We are supposed to keep them quiet. The Israelis will come and seize them. Farid tells me this. He is very quiet at his shop. He wanted this but it was given to me because . . . I am to hand it on."

"What is it, Gamal?"

"You know I told you of my relatives, some Bedouin, right?"

Cummings nodded.

"They were paid for this and told to bring it across the desert into Israel and here to give it to the American."

"What American?"

"Well, I just don't know. But you are American."

"What is it?"

Gamal stood and walked to a chest, which was covered with a gray woven rug. He threw it aside and opened the top to remove a dark leather roll. He brought it back to Cummings and sat down.

"It's a map. A map of the desert."

"Which . . ?"

"The Negev." Gamal unrolled the leather, revealing yellowed paper inside. He put his foot on one end and a clay pot on the other to hold it flat. The map was on a large sheet of paper with a thin strip torn diagonally off one edge, a loss that was not crucial. They studied how the contour lines suggested wadis, rivers and canyons. Within those were markings and Arabic numerals.

"What does this say?" Cummings asked, pointing to one citation.

Gamal craned his neck. "Brick wall. Pots. Tablets with writing."

"And here?"

Gamal read the description. Then his eyes caught another. "This says, 'Jesus Scrolls.'"

Goose bumps rose on Cummings' arms. Where, he thought, had the Hampton finds come from? He said to Gamal, "Now, what were you told to do with this?"

"The Bedouin found these," Gamal said. "They traded it to someone in Jordan, who . . ."

"Who in Jordan?"

"I don't know him. They said a man named Hasan. A Muslim."

"And?"

"And he then told the Bedouin to bring it to the West Bank and give it to the American."

Cummings realized the American was not him but Hampton. "Gamal, I don't think they meant me, but I will take it. You can trust me."

"Yes, yes. Perhaps you know who it goes to."

At that moment, Cummings didn't know. It was rightly sent to Hampton. It was expected by Stockwood.

Cummings thanked Gamal and left the cool sanctuary for the street, now beaten by the midday sun. Cars kicked up dust and a gray haze hung on the distant horizon to the southeast. A block away, Cummings slid into his car, its metal and upholstery hot to the touch. And the afternoon became hotter, as if the thermostat measured the rising struggle within himself. He had to make a decision. He released the brake, shifted the gear, and with the pressure of his right foot the car lurched forward, swerving into small empty streets. The leather roll next to him on the car seat rocked back and forth—like his thought process—as he drove back to Jerusalem.

In the stillness of his home, Cummings felt weak from the taxing trip. A tough decision still faced him, but he chose to put it off with a nap. He awoke refreshed. A few hours later, however, he was still uncertain. First he wondered whether to tell Sarah, for she would insist he call her father. She would expect him to do it immediately. He decided to act on his own. He picked up the telephone.

"Yes, operator," Cummings said. "I'd like to place a long-distance call to the United States."

32

The school year was well under way at Northern University, but Hampton rarely visited his office. The administration had given him until mid-October to evacuate. He was saving that job for the eleventh hour. So it was a fluke, he thought, that he had been at his desk two days earlier when the telephone call had come.

His first reaction had been to think, "Oh, no." The man wouldn't say who he was, simply that he had close friends in the Middle East. He wanted to come to Hampton's office. "It's very important," he had said. "I'll explain it to you there." Hampton had been doubtful, but the earnest appeal finally had won his acquiescence.

Today he would learn what he had gotten into. In the foyer, he caught Susan dashing to work and negotiated a long kiss. She struggled to resist but surrendered with a smile, vowing to recover the time on the expressway. Hampton drove to the university early to sort through some office clutter. When the knock came, he called out.

"Come in. It's unlocked."

The door opened slowly and creaked.

"Professor Hampton?" It was the same deep voice he had heard over the phone.

"Come on in."

Hampton walked over and the man offered a handshake, but not his name. He was thin, blond and far younger than his voice had conveyed. On the phone it had almost sounded foreign. A heavy paper bag with handles dangled from his left hand. Hampton pointed to a chair and they both sat down. He was a businessman from Spokane, it turned out, and a deacon in a large Baptist church.

"I'm an old friend of Matt Cummings," the man said. "We went to school together." He explained the phone call from Jerusalem and the problem Cummings faced. "He wanted you to receive this but preferred to, well, not to get too closely associated. He trusts me like a brother. We both have a bit of a rebellious streak, I guess."

The man took a leather scroll from the heavy bag. "He asked me to deliver this personally, Professor Hampton. He doesn't want anyone to know he gave it to you. Is that okay?"

"Fine by me."

They spread it out on the desk. Within the leather was a heavy sheet of yellowed paper. Hampton began to sweat in anticipation and then his eyes popped. Rabin's Negev charts sat only ten feet away in the corner of his office, and now in front of him was the Bedouin map.

"This is a geographic Rosetta Stone." Hampton exulted under his breath. "Two halves of the whole." He was tapping his fingers on the table.

"Pardon me?"

Peering up at his visitor, Hampton silenced his hand and curled a thin smile. Such a loyal friend to Cummings, he thought. He was the intrepid courier who had little clue of his message.

The man grinned. "What is it, a treasure map?"

Jack Winslow was out of retirement quicker than he had gone in. He was heading a funding drive for Negev archaeology. He also wanted to be with young people, so he volunteered to teach a seminar at Princeton.

And there was, of course, the Winslows' social life as organized by Edith. It seemed to have increased since they had returned from vacation in Rome. She was aflutter that day at her afternoon tea party.

"He's so different now," Edith said to her four guests. "He's quit smoking. He says he wants to live longer." She sipped and smiled. "Then he wants to write a book on John the Baptist."

"How interesting," said one woman, a Sunday school teacher at their church. "John the Baptist! Who was that handsome actor who played him in the movie . . . and have you seen the paintings in our picture Bibles?" She sipped her tea. "He was such a great man, wasn't he."

The other women were still trying to recall the actor's name.

Edith said, "Well, Jack has a little different idea about John the Baptist these days."

"Oh, really?" The woman was puzzled.

"When he's done you can read it and find out," Edith said, almost laughing. "He's got this other thing, too." She glanced around, wanting to say it just right. "He goes about the house saying he wants to treat me better, like Jesus would have treated a wife."

"My goodness!" The second woman raised her eyebrows.

"Yes, he says Jesus' *bride*. Can you imagine!"

Their titter sounded like jingling bells.

For these wonders, Edith said, she had given in to her husband one more time. "He's off to the Middle East this week."

"But Edith, didn't he just . . ?"

"Oh, yes." Edith wagged her finger. "But this will be the last time!"

They all nodded and sipped the sweet tea.

In another room, Winslow dialed Hampton at his home. The news about Habib had depressed Winslow for a few days. He had pondered it, prayed about it, and then reviewed his bank account. Nick answered the phone and they exchanged greetings.

"I'm going to attend the funeral, Nick," Winslow said. "You should attend, too. I've got the airfare."

Hampton sighed. "I guess I should." He thought about all that had happened, his need to find a job—and the new excitement of the week. "I guess we owe it to Habib."

Across the living room Susan sat, her shoulders and face cast in the light of a bright lamp. She was looking at Nick. Their eyes glimmered on contact. She smiled and nodded.

"Sure, Jack, let's go."

Hampton counted. The time. Their low financial reserves. Well, Travis Marshall had called and joked that soon he would be able to float "no-interest, long-term loans" to anyone named Hampton. Next summer the baby would arrive. With that thought, Nick's spirits rose. No task seemed too much.

"By the way, Jack. Once we begin matching up Simon Rabin's map and the map that Cummings sent me, it's going to start all over again. The great unknown, Jack. Are you ready?"

The query was not new. Troubled, and less able to contain it in old age, Winslow had already been asking himself, "What if we find more?" He pictured a war, of ideas at least, in Christianity: calls for a married papacy, for women's equality; upheavals in the old concepts of earthly and heavenly salvation—and finally, his entire career admitting to illusions and embracing a revolution in his own beliefs.

In the silence that followed Nick's question, Winslow heard the tea party carrying on in the other room. There was chatter and innocent laughter—as if the world, with its conventions, and people, with their fears and habits and their prosaic religion, would never change.

"Sure, Nick. I'm ready."

EPILOGUE

Tilbury Docks, London: November

Two foghorn blasts wafted up the Thames River to Tilbury Port, where the sounds of cranes, trucks and clanking ships would soon shatter the morning silence.

The unloading of an Israeli freighter, a rare sight at the docks forty miles east of London, had been completed under towering tungsten spotlights the night before. Now the giant cranes slept, except for a few cables that swayed over shipping containers stacked like so many loaves of bread. Two of them, both small twenty-footers, were set aside in a cordoned-off area by a security booth.

Near the street entrance to the mammoth docks, yellow light shone through the windows of a cement-block building. Its sign read, "Her Majesty's Customs and Excise." Four men in dark blue uniforms were shaking off the chill inside when Tim Rawlins, chief customs inspector for the shift, walked in.

"Good morning, mates." Rawlins took a clipboard from the wall and flipped rapidly through the white customs documents. "The day doesn't look too busy."

He wiped condensation off the window to get a view down the battered docks, host to twelve hundred ships each year. In late November the fog lingered through the day, partly because the docks were set inland and lower than the Thames. Rawlins could still read the name on the bow of the black-and-red freighter. "Ben Gurion." A rusty glaze tinged parts of the white lettering.

"We don't get many from Israel, do we?"

"Only a handful each year."

As the men sipped hot tea, Rawlins read the report from the

night before. The Israeli ship had come up the Thames about noon and had been cleared to enter the lock after the Norwegian freighter. The water level of the lock had dropped by 3 P.M. and the Ben Gurion had moved into loading dock No. 12. The ship had carried two "groupage" loads, two containers filled with disparate items.

Rawlins pointed down the dock with his pencil. "Are those the two?"

"Yes, sir."

When the Gulf War had ended nine months earlier, a new customs policy required "preventive" searches of all groupages from the Middle East. More routine than that were "revenue" searches to assess tariffs. Either way it was more work, but Rawlins followed orders. He scribbled his authorization on the front sheet of the documents. "Well, let's get started."

Out on the dock, the driver of the straddle carrier, a platform atop four legs with wheels, revved its engines and moved over the first container so that dangling chains fell at its sides. Dockworkers fastened the hooks. With a grinding sound the chains lifted the container as the carrier drove to the inspection zone at the warehouse entrance. By the time the second container was in place, Rawlins and two customs officers had retrieved the German shepherd and reached the site.

The dockworkers, bundled in padded work overalls, rumbled their shabby encumbered dollies across the cement, into the cool warehouse. They cut bindings on cardboard boxes and used crowbars to pry open crates. As the dog sniffed around, Rawlins checked the manifest against each piece of cargo.

He paused to rub some warmth into his hands as a foghorn, a good distance upriver, sounded twice across the Thames.

The dog's bark came next, so shrill that it prickled the skin on the back of Rawlins' neck. He turned to look at the roughhewn crate, about three feet on each side. "I had a feeling about that one," he said.

The manifest listed the contents as furniture. The port of origin, Haifa, was stamped on the crate and another cluster of black print gave its destination: "London/Tilbury. British Museum."

Rawlins waved over two dock workers. "Open the top."

The crowbars went into action. The smell of straw exuded as they pulled off the lid and swept aside the dried chaff. Rawlins

300

looked in and saw a peaked surface painted with tiny gray rectangles, like shingles on a roof.

"Open two sides."

The wood separated quickly, barely creaking under the rough and skillful hands of Her Majesty's stevedores. They pulled some straw aside. The dog sat, quiet but alert.

"My God, what do we have here?" Rawlins chuckled. "Clean it out a bit." He leaned down to look into the miniature structure, with its several rooms, doors and windows. It was painted in bright blues and greens and the trim was white.

"Who would ship an old doll house from the Middle East?"

All its interiors were exposed and with the packing straw gone there was no place for anything to be hidden.

Rawlins looked at the dog. "Why did you bark fella?" he asked, exhaling a breath of steam. "I hope he's not losing his scent." He turned his attention to the toy, charmed by its craftsmanship and detail, and chuckled again. His young daughter would love it. "So this is what the British Museum is collecting these days." He reached inside and his long fingers evened up the tattered curtains on the windows.

Rawlins saw a folded paper, like a note, tacked on the doll house floor and removed it. It was scrawled by hand in large letters.

"Dear Travis Marshall. I am sorry that it took so long to retrieve this from the south. Thank you for the money. When my late father built this for Simon Rabin's daughter, I remember it was a labor of love. I hope your daughter enjoys it."

The signature was illegible.

Rawlins put the letter back inside, stood, and waved a hand. "It's okay. Close it up."